TSUBASA

CLAMP

TRANSLATED AND ADAPTED BY

William Flanagan

LETTERED BY

Dana Hayward

BALLANTINE BOOKS · NEW YORK

Tsubasa crosses over with *xxxHOLiC*. Although it isn't necessary to read *xxxHOLiC* to understand the events in *Tsubasa*, you'll get to see the same events from different perspectives if you read both!

A Del Rey® Book
Published by The Random House Publishing Group
Copyright © 2004 CLAMP. All rights reserved.

This publication — rights arranged through Kodansha Ltd.

All rights reserved under International and Pan-American Copyright Conventions. Published in the United States by Del Rey Books, an imprint of The Random House Publishing Group, a division of Random House, Inc., New York, and simultaneously in Canada by Random House of Canada Limited, Toronto. First published in Japan in serialization and subsequently published in book form by Kodansha, Ltd. Tokyo in 2003.

Del Rey is a registered trademark and the Del Rey colophon is a trademark of Random House, Inc.

www.delreymanga.com

Library of Congress Control Number is available from the publisher upon request.

ISBN 0-345-47183-0

Manufactured in the United States of America

9 8 7 6 5 4 3 2

First Edition: November 2004

Text design by Dana Hayward

Contents

Honorifics

Throughout the Del Rey Manga books, you will find Japanese honorifics left intact in the translations. For those not familiar with how the Japanese use honorifics, and more important, how they differ from American honorifics, we present this brief overview.

Politeness has always been a critical facet of Japanese culture. Ever since the feudal era, when Japan was a highly stratified society, use of honorifics — which can be defined as polite speech that indicates relationship or status — has played an essential role in the Japanese language. When addressing someone in Japanese, an honorific usually takes the form of a suffix attached to one's name (example: "Asuna-san"), or as a title at the end of one's name or in place of the name itself (example: "Negi-sensei," or simply "Sensei!").

Honorifics can be expressions of respect or endearment. In the context of manga and anime, honorifics give insight into the nature of the relationship between characters. Many translations into English leave out these important honorifics, and therefore distort the "feel" of the original Japanese. Because Japanese honorifics contain nuances that English honorifics lack, it is our policy at Del Rey not to translate them. Here, instead, is a guide to some of the honorifics you may encounter in Del Rey Manga.

-san: This is the most common honorific, and is equivalent to Mr., Miss, Ms., Mrs., etc. It is the all-purpose honorific and can be used in any situation where politeness is required.

-sama: This is one level higher than "-san." It is used to confer great respect.

-dono: This comes from the word "tono," which means "lord." It is an even higher level than "-sama," and confers utmost respect.

-kun: This suffix is used at the end of boys' names to express familiarity or endearment. It is also sometimes used by men among friends, or when addressing someone younger or of a lower station.

-chan: This is used to express endearment, mostly toward girls. It is also used for little boys, pets, and even among lovers. It gives a sense of childish cuteness.

Bozu: This is an informal way to refer to a boy, similar to the English term "kid" or "squirt."

Sempai: This title suggests that the addressee is one's "senior" in a group or organization. It is most often used in a school setting, where underclassmen refer to their upperclassmen as "sempai." It can also be used in the workplace, such as when a newer employee addresses an employee who has seniority in the company.

Kohai: This is the opposite of "sempai," and is used toward underclassmen in school or newcomers in the workplace. It connotes that the addressee is of lower station.

Sensei: Literally meaning "one who has come before," this title is used for teachers, doctors, or masters of any profession or art.

-[blank]: Usually forgotten in these lists, but perhaps the most significant difference between Japanese and English. The lack of honorific means that the speaker has permission to address the person in a very intimate way. Usually, only family, spouses, or very close friends have this kind of permission. Known as *yobisute*, it can be gratifying when someone who has earned the intimacy starts to call one by one's name without an honorific. But when that intimacy hasn't been earned, it can also be very insulting.

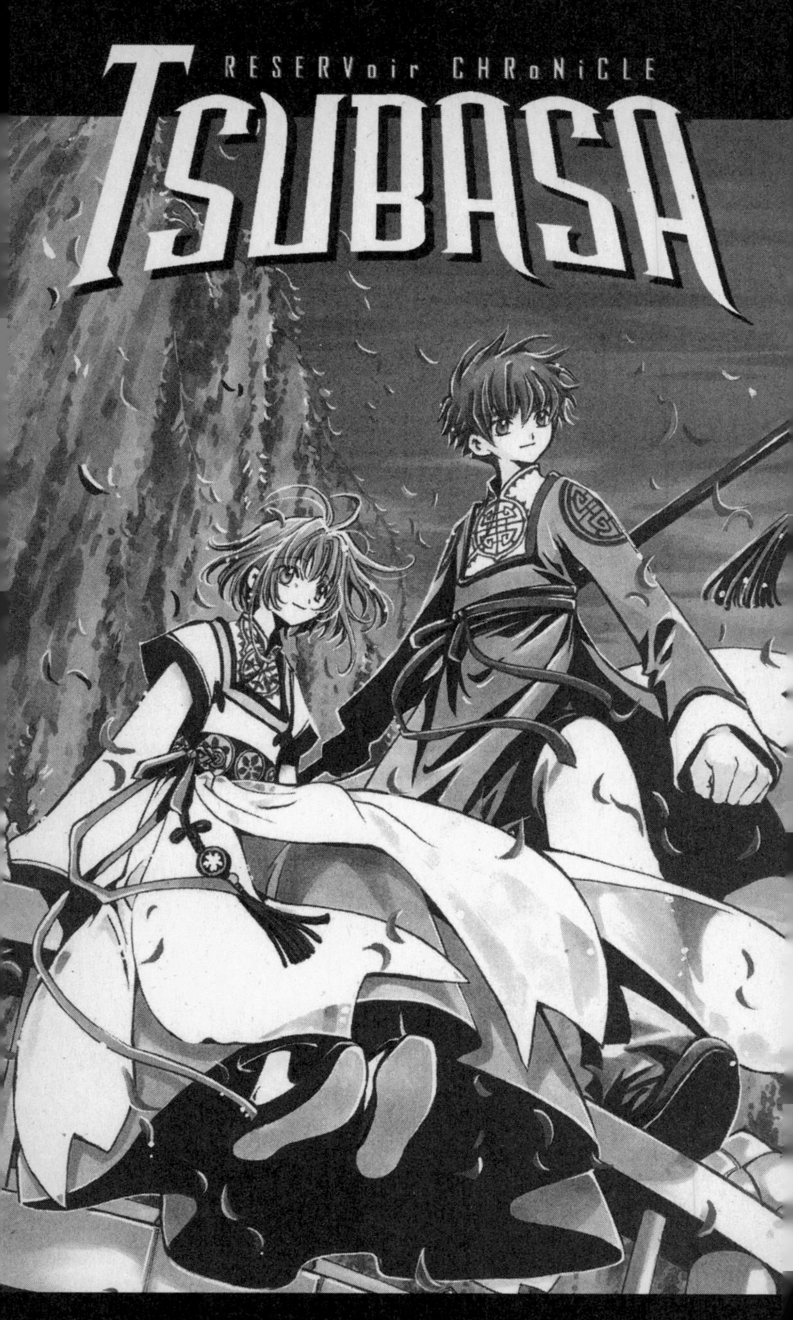
RESERVoir CHRoNiCLE
TSUBASA

ツバサ

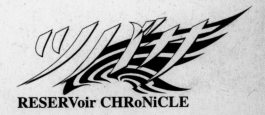

RESERVoir CHRoNiCLE

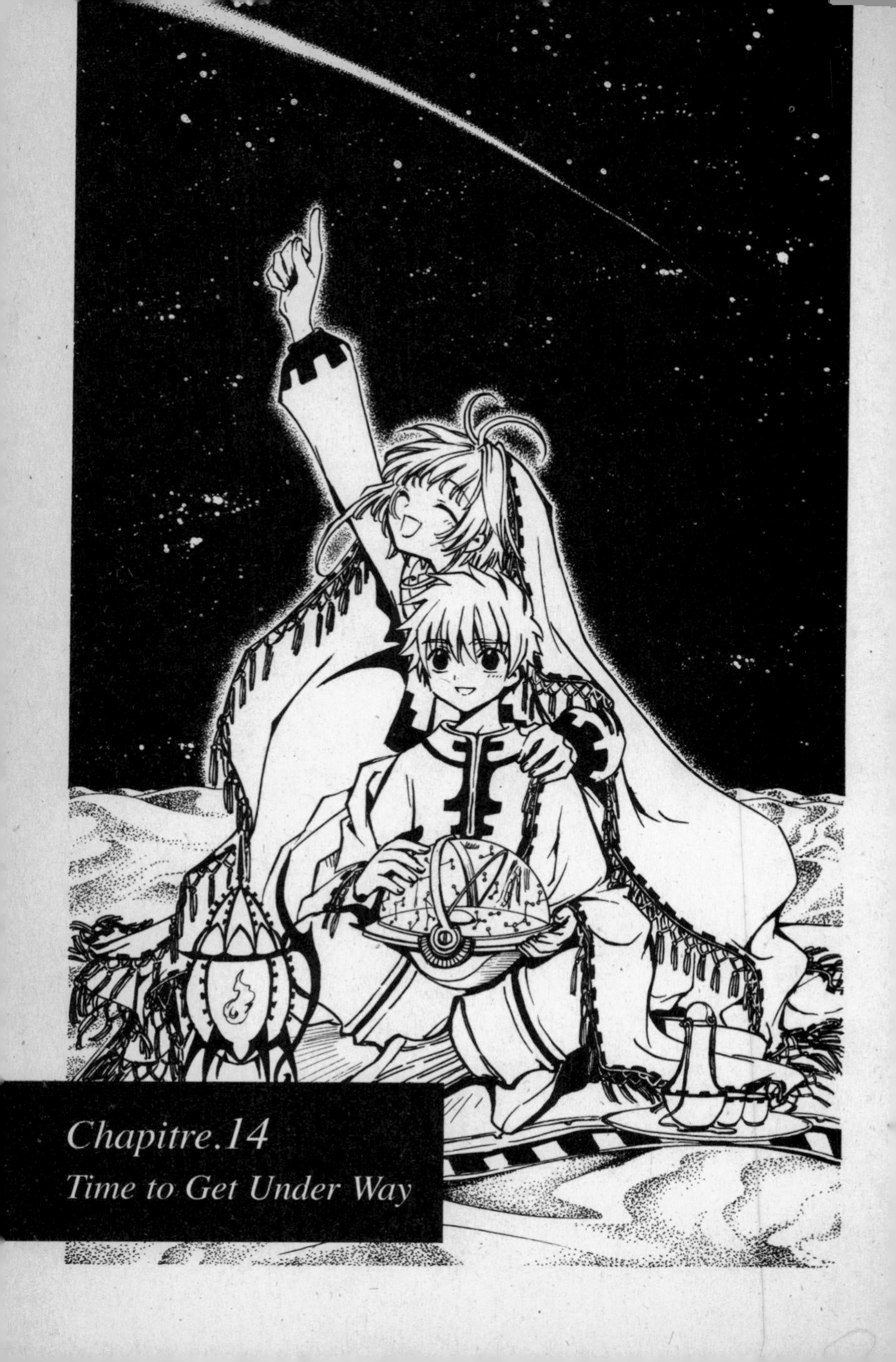

Chapitre.14
Time to Get Under Way

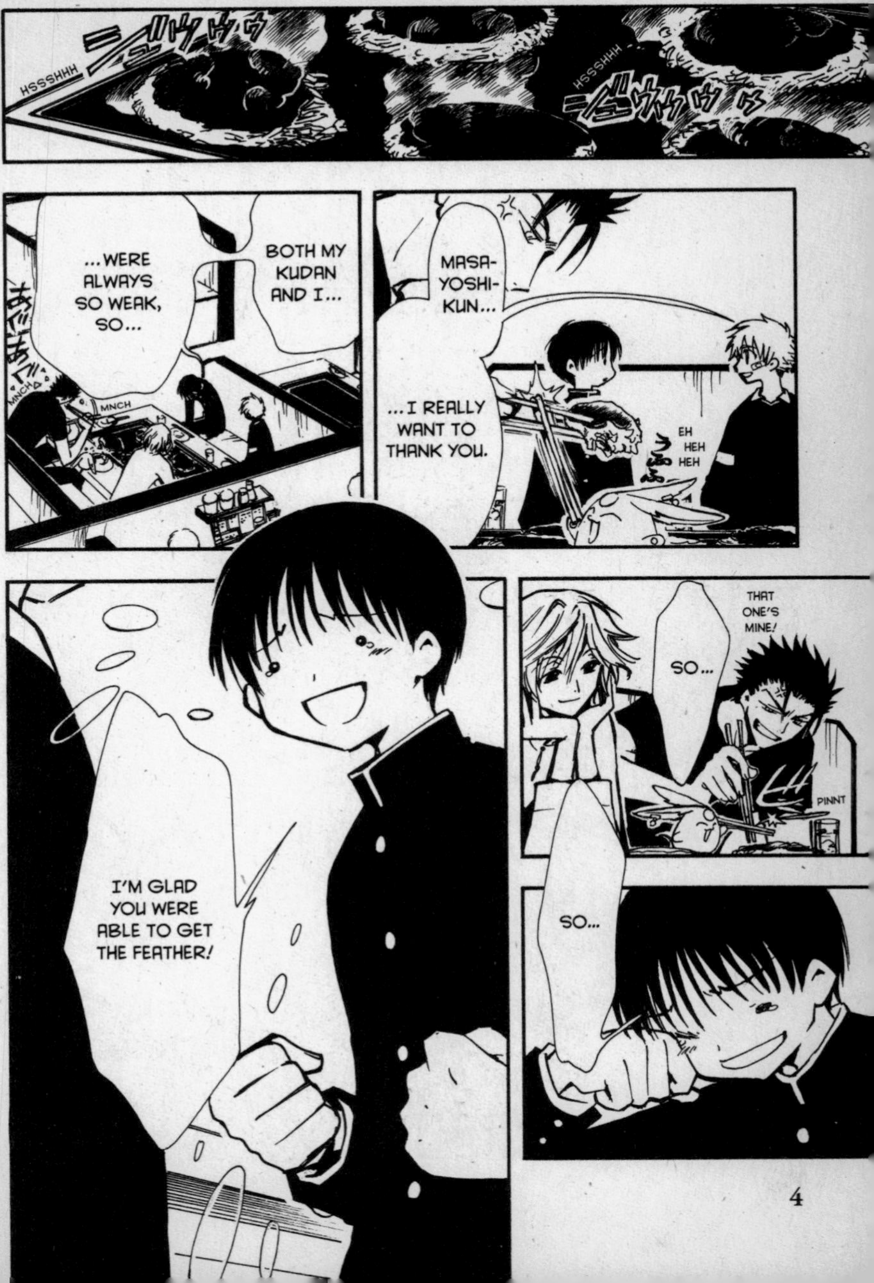
HSSSHHH
HSSSHHH
MASA-YOSHI-KUN...
...I REALLY WANT TO THANK YOU.
EH HEH HEH
BOTH MY KUDAN AND I...
...WERE ALWAYS SO WEAK, SO...
MNCH
MNCH
THAT ONE'S MINE!
SO...
PINNT
SO...
I'M GLAD YOU WERE ABLE TO GET THE FEATHER!

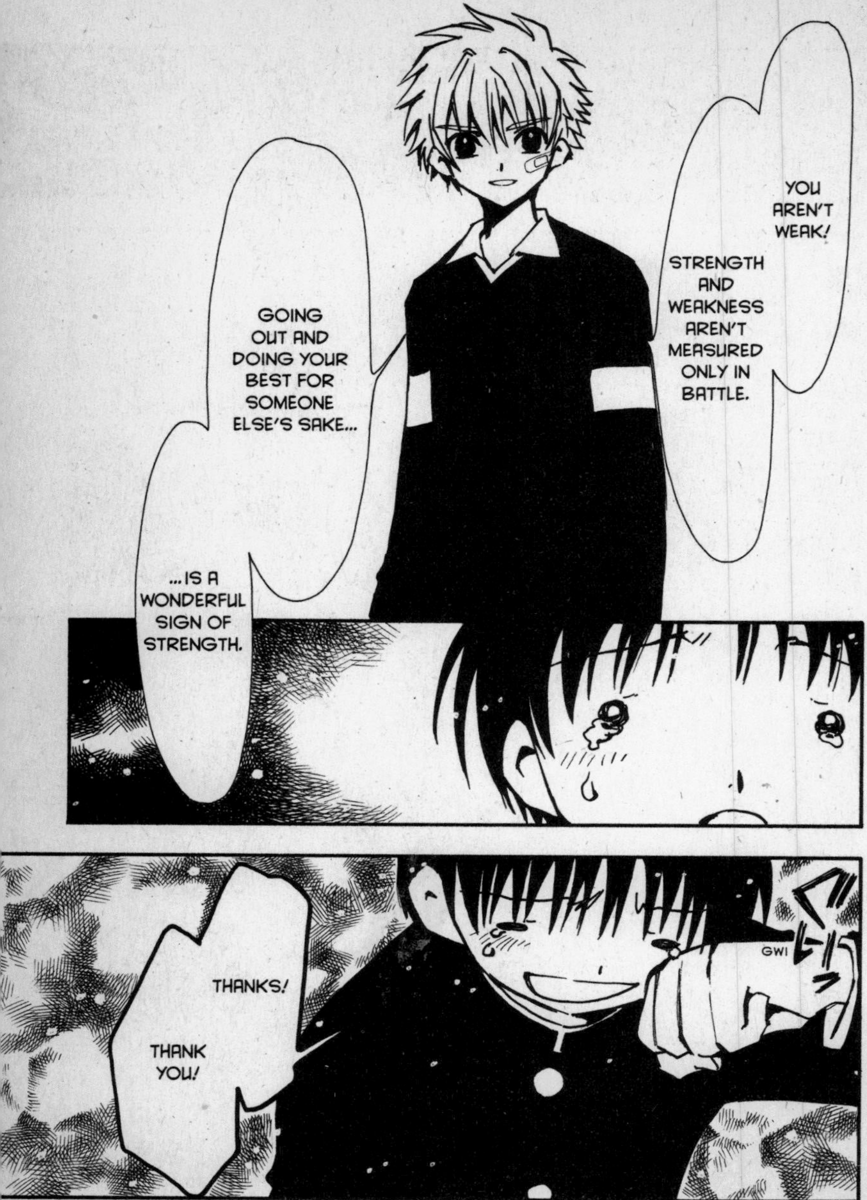
YOU AREN'T WEAK!
STRENGTH AND WEAKNESS AREN'T MEASURED ONLY IN BATTLE.
GOING OUT AND DOING YOUR BEST FOR SOMEONE ELSE'S SAKE...
...IS A WONDERFUL SIGN OF STRENGTH.
GWI
THANKS!
THANK YOU!

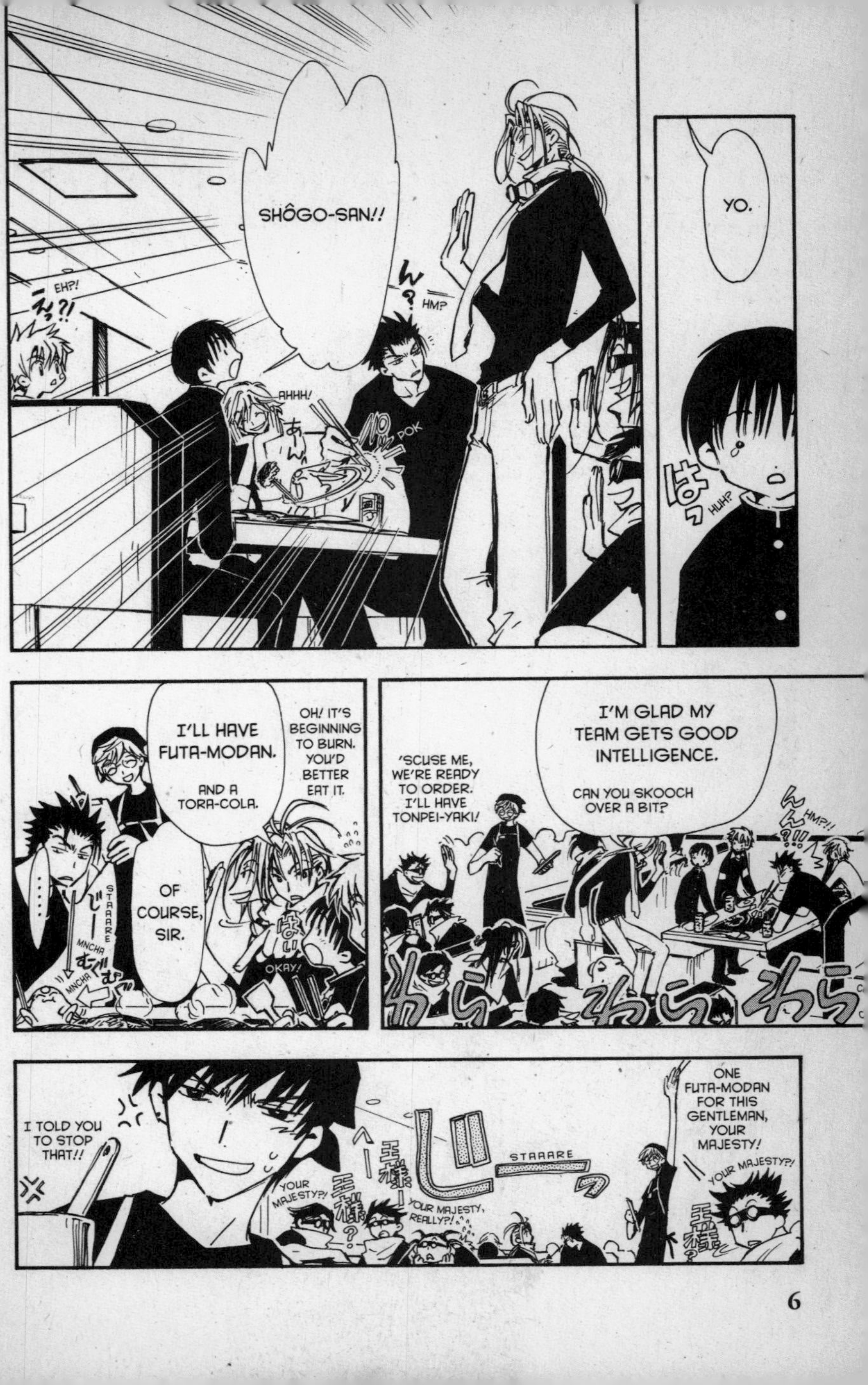

YO.
HUH?
SHÔGO-SAN!!
HM?
EH?!
AHHH!
POK
I'M GLAD MY TEAM GETS GOOD INTELLIGENCE.
CAN YOU SKOOCH OVER A BIT?
HM?!!
'SCUSE ME, WE'RE READY TO ORDER. I'LL HAVE TONPEI-YAKI!
OH! IT'S BEGINNING TO BURN. YOU'D BETTER EAT IT.
I'LL HAVE FUTA-MODAN.
AND A TORA-COLA.
OF COURSE, SIR.
OKAY!
STAAARE
MNCHA
MNCHA
ONE FUTA-MODAN FOR THIS GENTLEMAN, YOUR MAJESTY!
YOUR MAJESTY?!
STAAARE
YOUR MAJESTY, REALLY?!
YOUR MAJESTY?!
I TOLD YOU TO STOP THAT!!

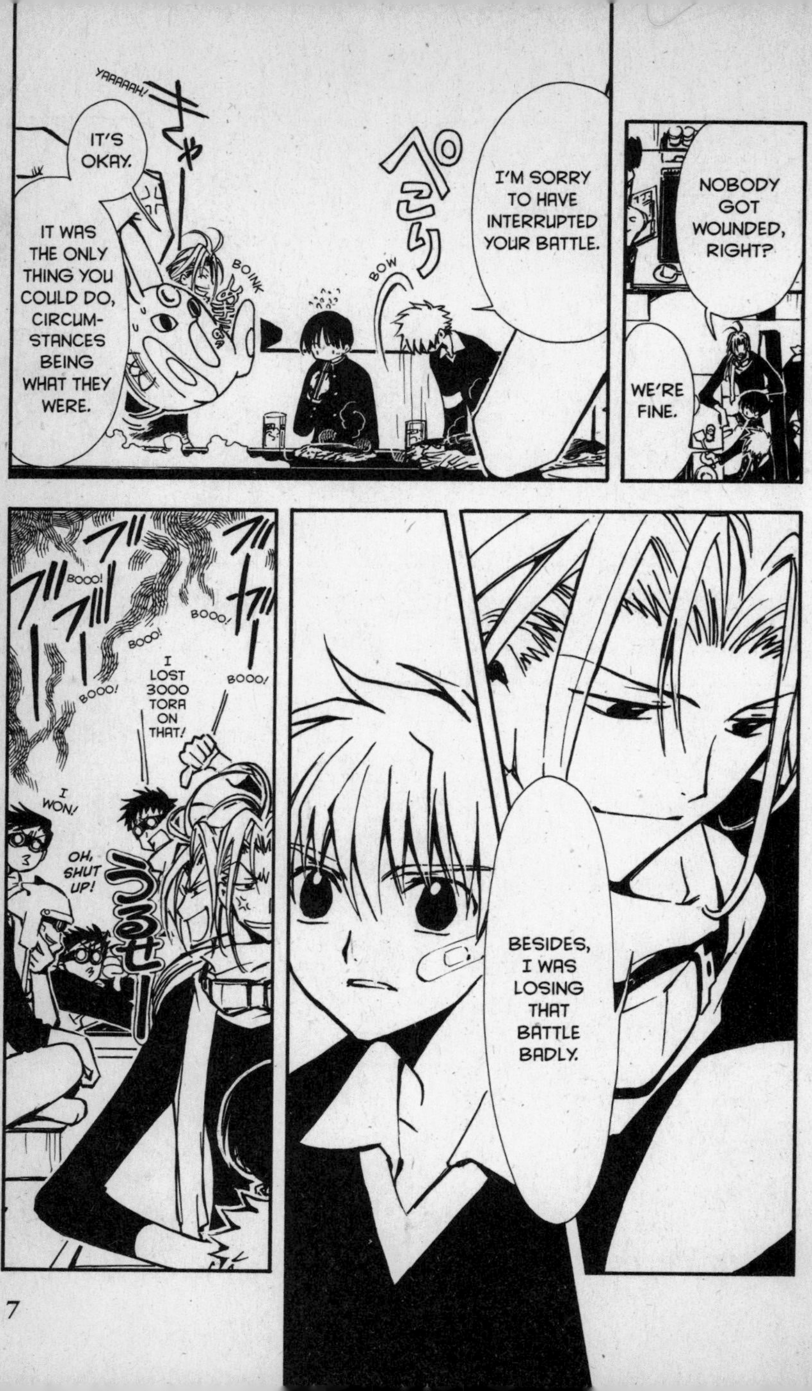
NOBODY GOT WOUNDED, RIGHT?
WE'RE FINE.
I'M SORRY TO HAVE INTERRUPTED YOUR BATTLE.
BOW
YAAAAAH!
BOINK
IT'S OKAY.
IT WAS THE ONLY THING YOU COULD DO, CIRCUMSTANCES BEING WHAT THEY WERE.
BESIDES, I WAS LOSING THAT BATTLE BADLY.
BOOO!
BOOO!
BOOO!
BOOO!
BOOO!
I LOST 3000 TORA ON THAT!
I WON!
OH, SHUT UP!

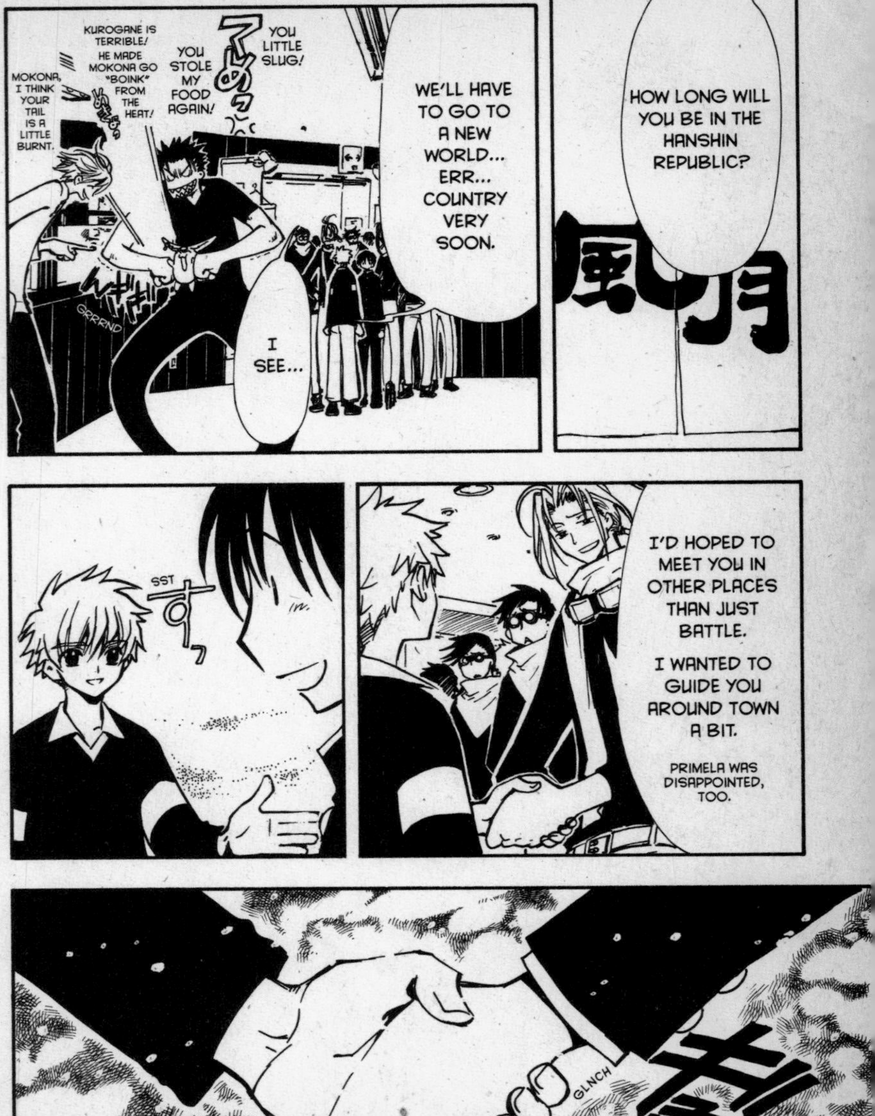
HOW LONG WILL YOU BE IN THE HANSHIN REPUBLIC?
WE'LL HAVE TO GO TO A NEW WORLD... ERR... COUNTRY VERY SOON.
I SEE...
YOU LITTLE SLUG!
YOU STOLE MY FOOD AGAIN!
KUROGANE IS TERRIBLE! HE MADE MOKONA GO "BOINK" FROM THE HEAT!
MOKONA, I THINK YOUR TAIL IS A LITTLE BURNT.
GRRRND
I'D HOPED TO MEET YOU IN OTHER PLACES THAN JUST BATTLE.
I WANTED TO GUIDE YOU AROUND TOWN A BIT.
PRIMELA WAS DISAPPOINTED, TOO.
SST
GLNCH

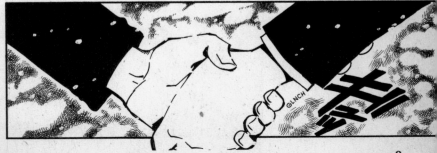

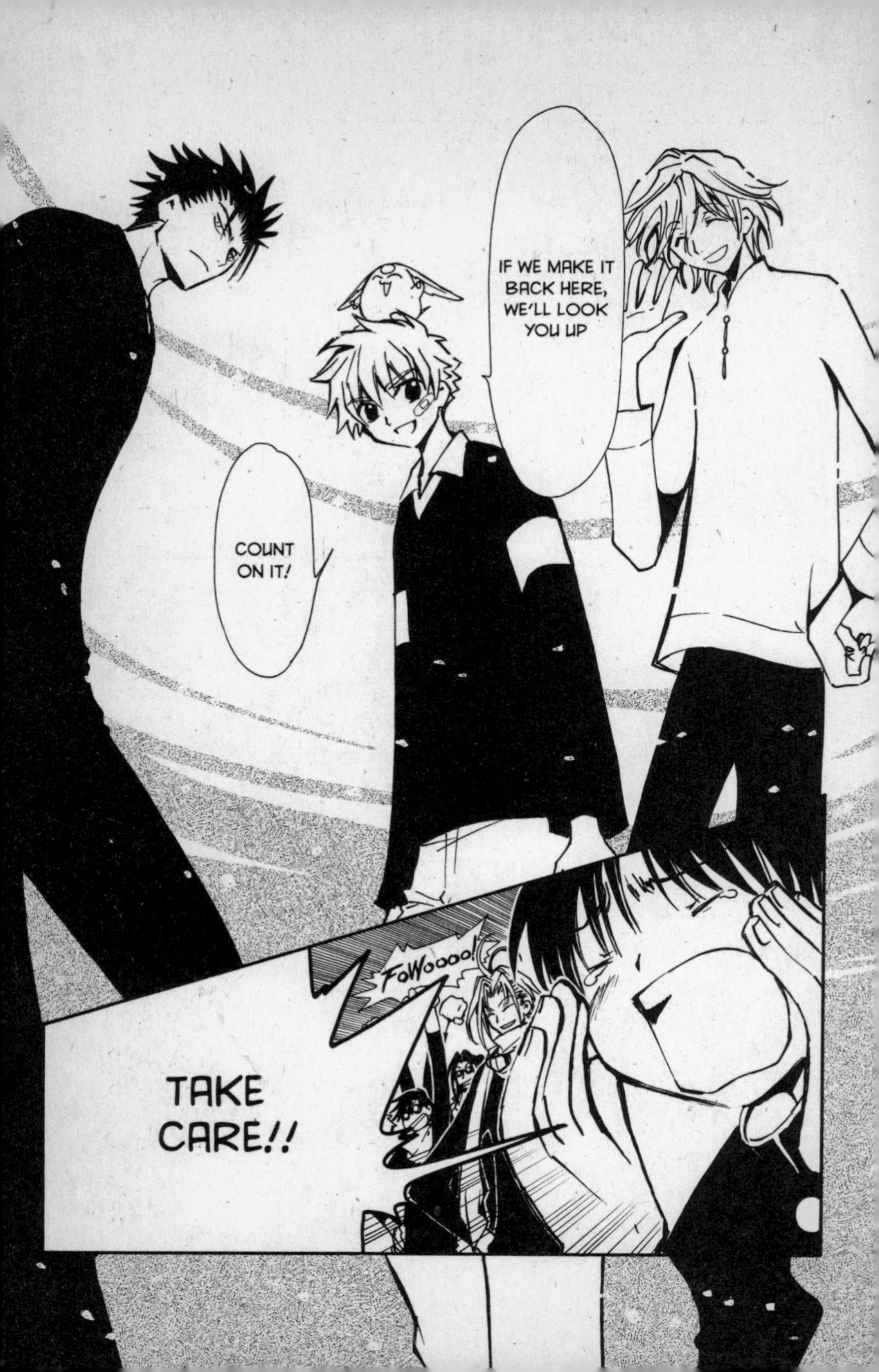
IF WE MAKE IT BACK HERE, WE'LL LOOK YOU UP
COUNT ON IT!
FoWoooo!
TAKE CARE!!

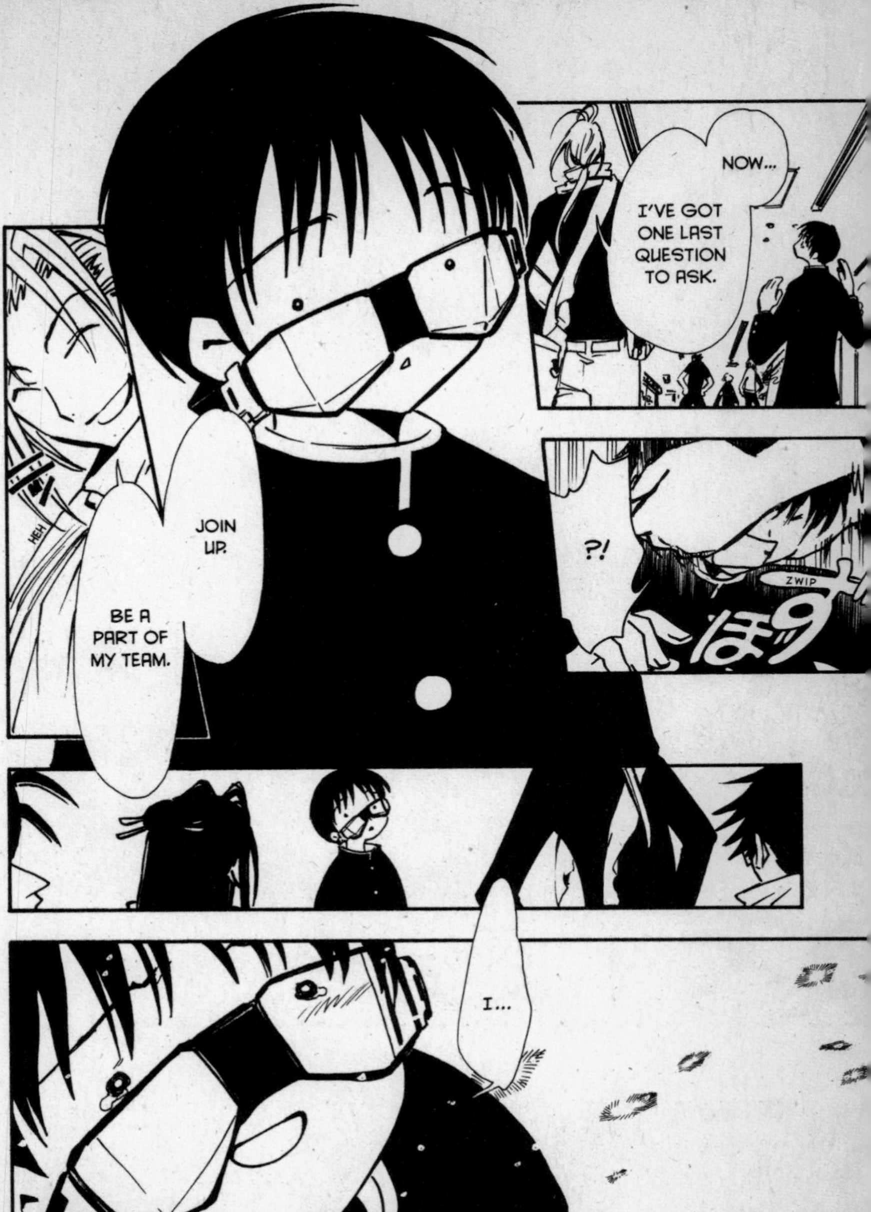
NOW...
I'VE GOT ONE LAST QUESTION TO ASK.
?!
ZWIP
JOIN UP.
BE A PART OF MY TEAM.
HEH
I...

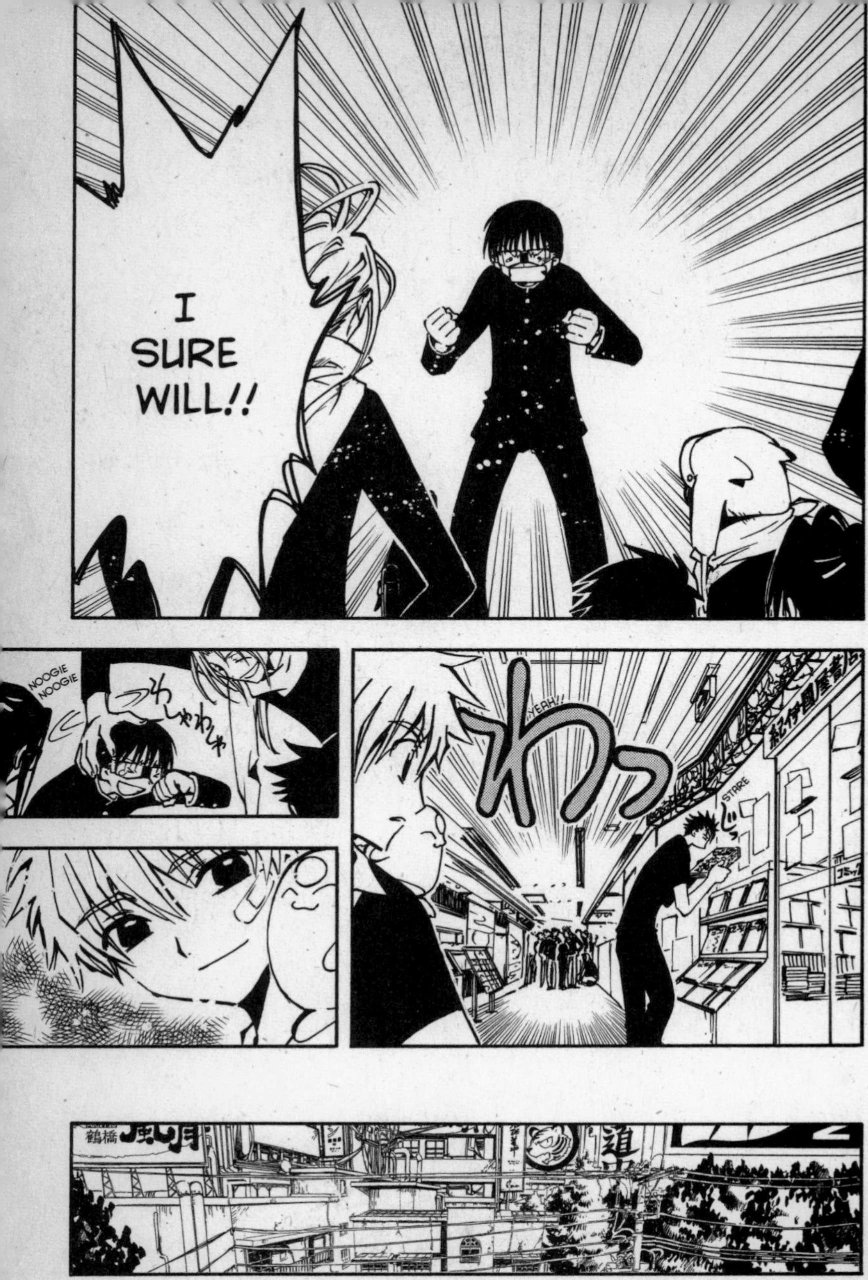

I SURE WILL!!
わっ
YEAH!!
STARE
じっ
NOOGIE NOOGIE
わしゃわしゃ
鶴橋

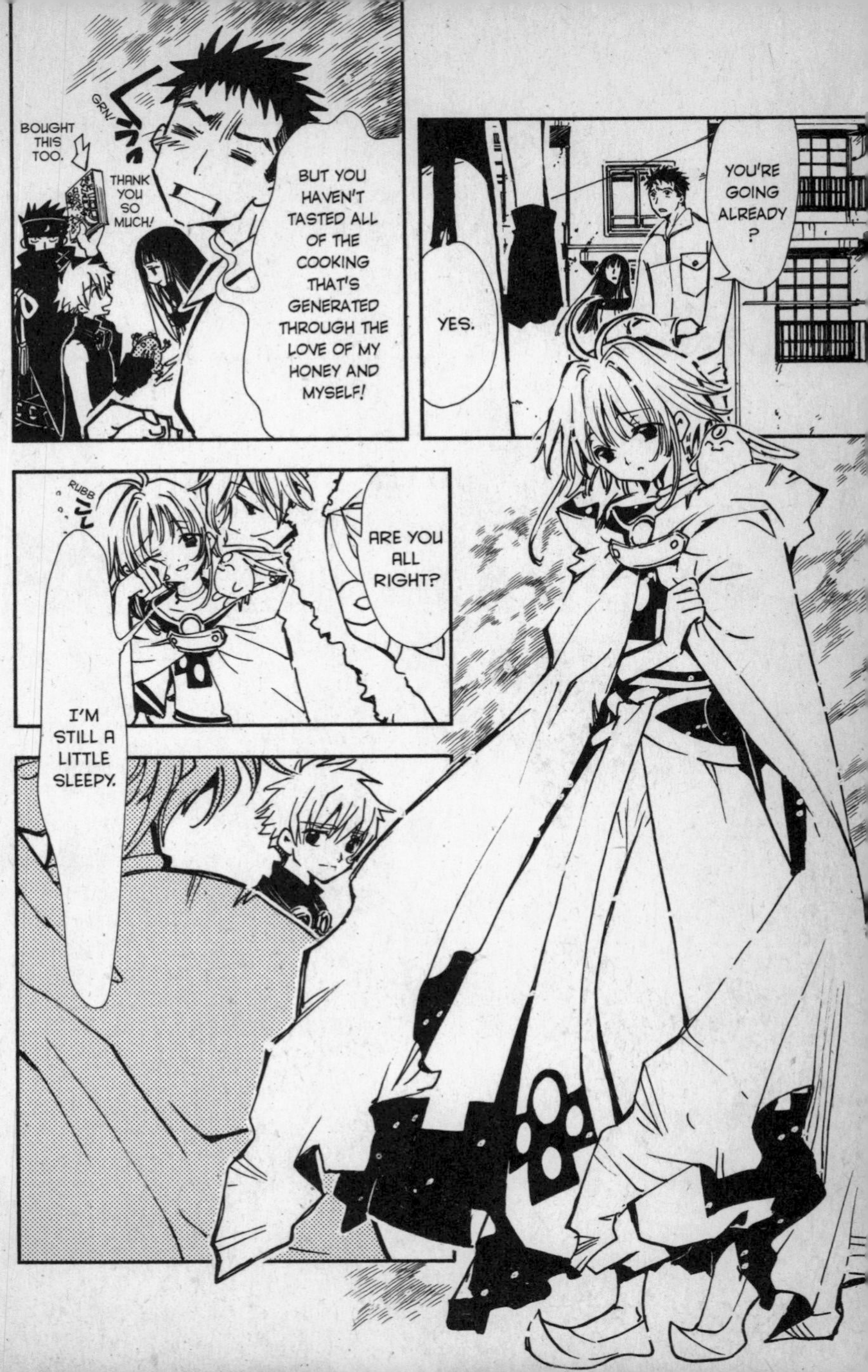
YOU'RE GOING ALREADY?
YES.
BUT YOU HAVEN'T TASTED ALL OF THE COOKING THAT'S GENERATED THROUGH THE LOVE OF MY HONEY AND MYSELF!
GRN!
THANK YOU SO MUCH!
BOUGHT THIS TOO.
ARE YOU ALL RIGHT?
RUBB
I'M STILL A LITTLE SLEEPY.

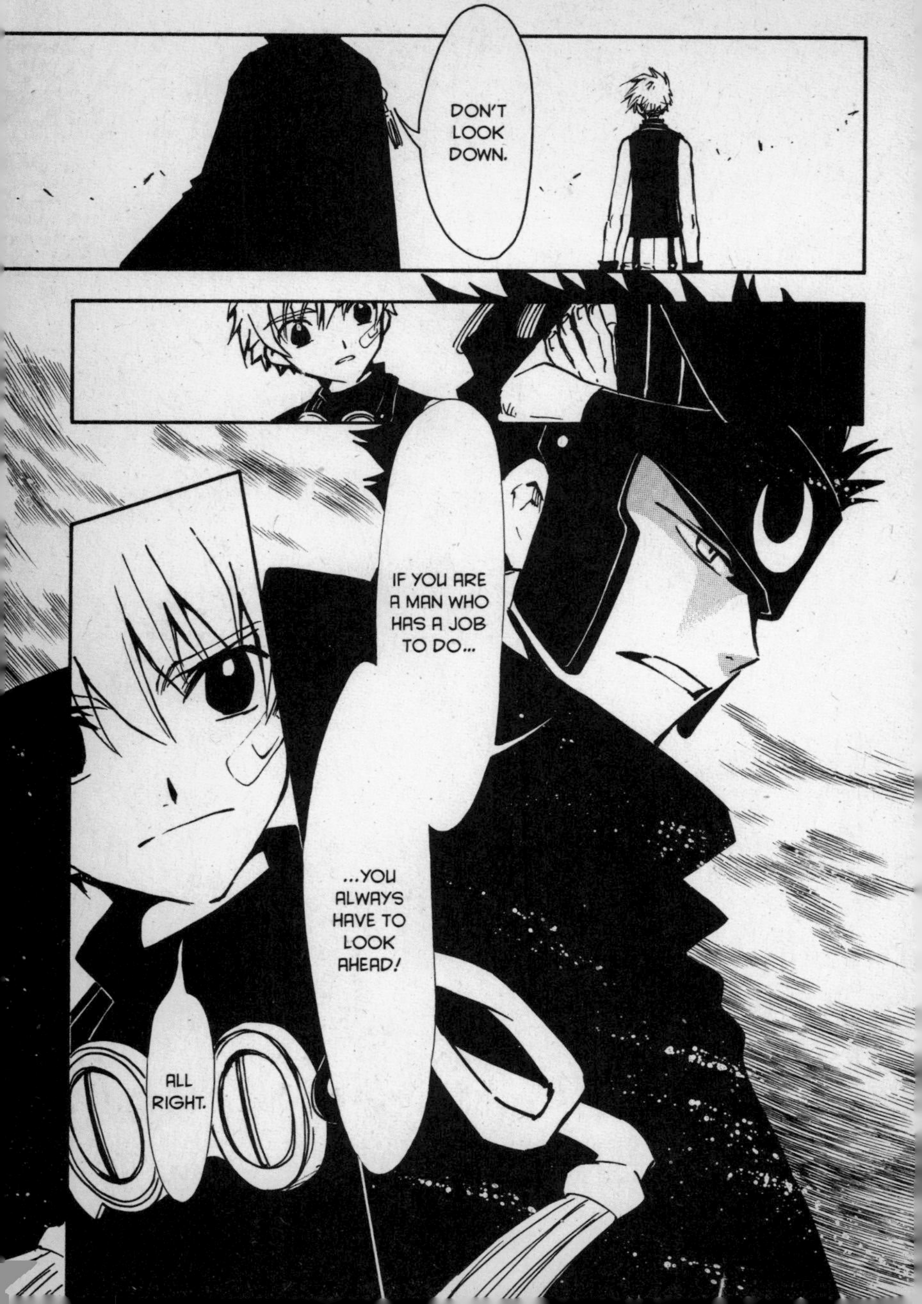
DON'T LOOK DOWN.
IF YOU ARE A MAN WHO HAS A JOB TO DO...
...YOU ALWAYS HAVE TO LOOK AHEAD!
ALL RIGHT.

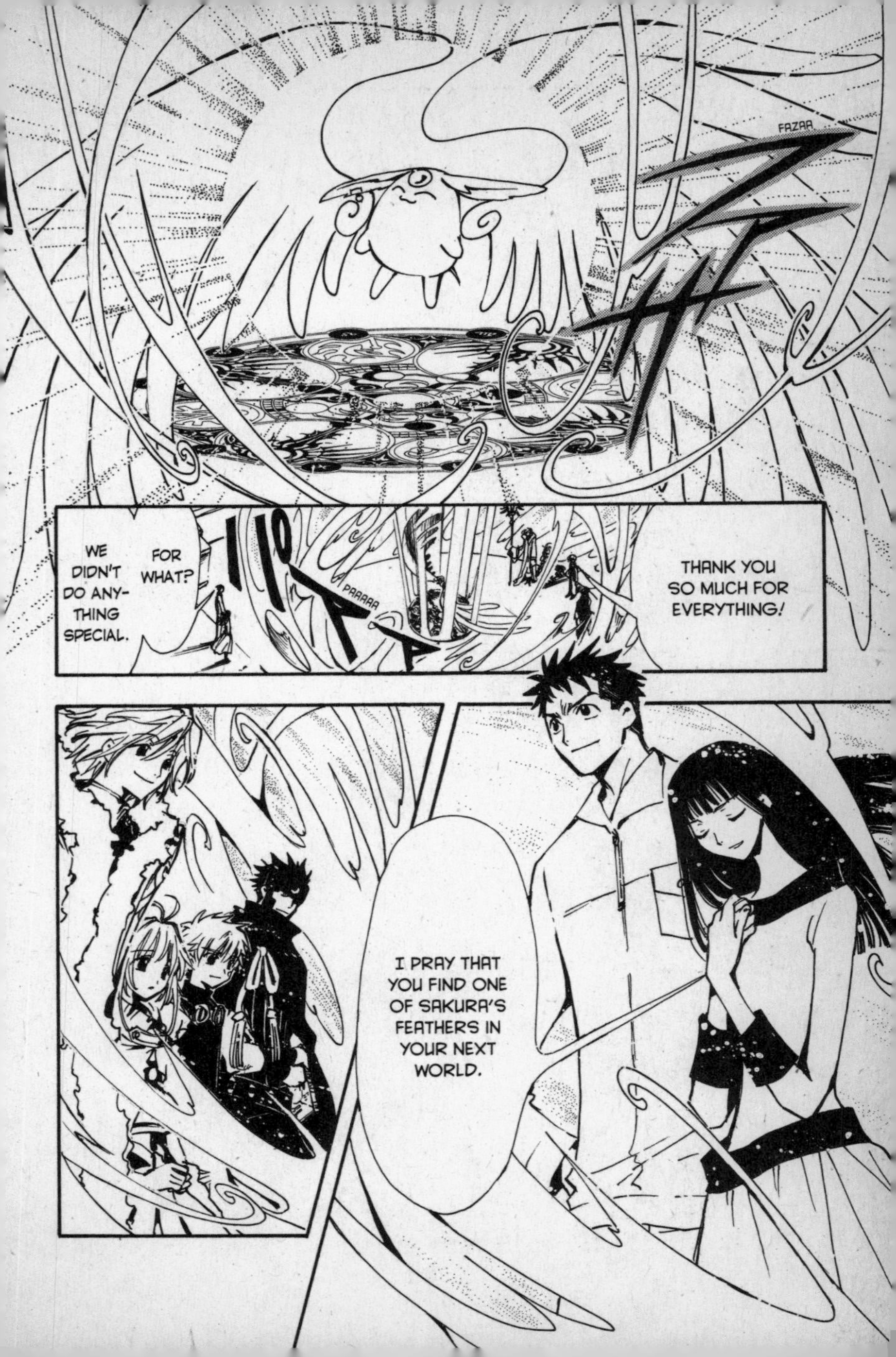
FAZAA
THANK YOU SO MUCH FOR EVERYTHING!
PAAAAA
FOR WHAT?
WE DIDN'T DO ANY-THING SPECIAL.
I PRAY THAT YOU FIND ONE OF SAKURA'S FEATHERS IN YOUR NEXT WORLD.

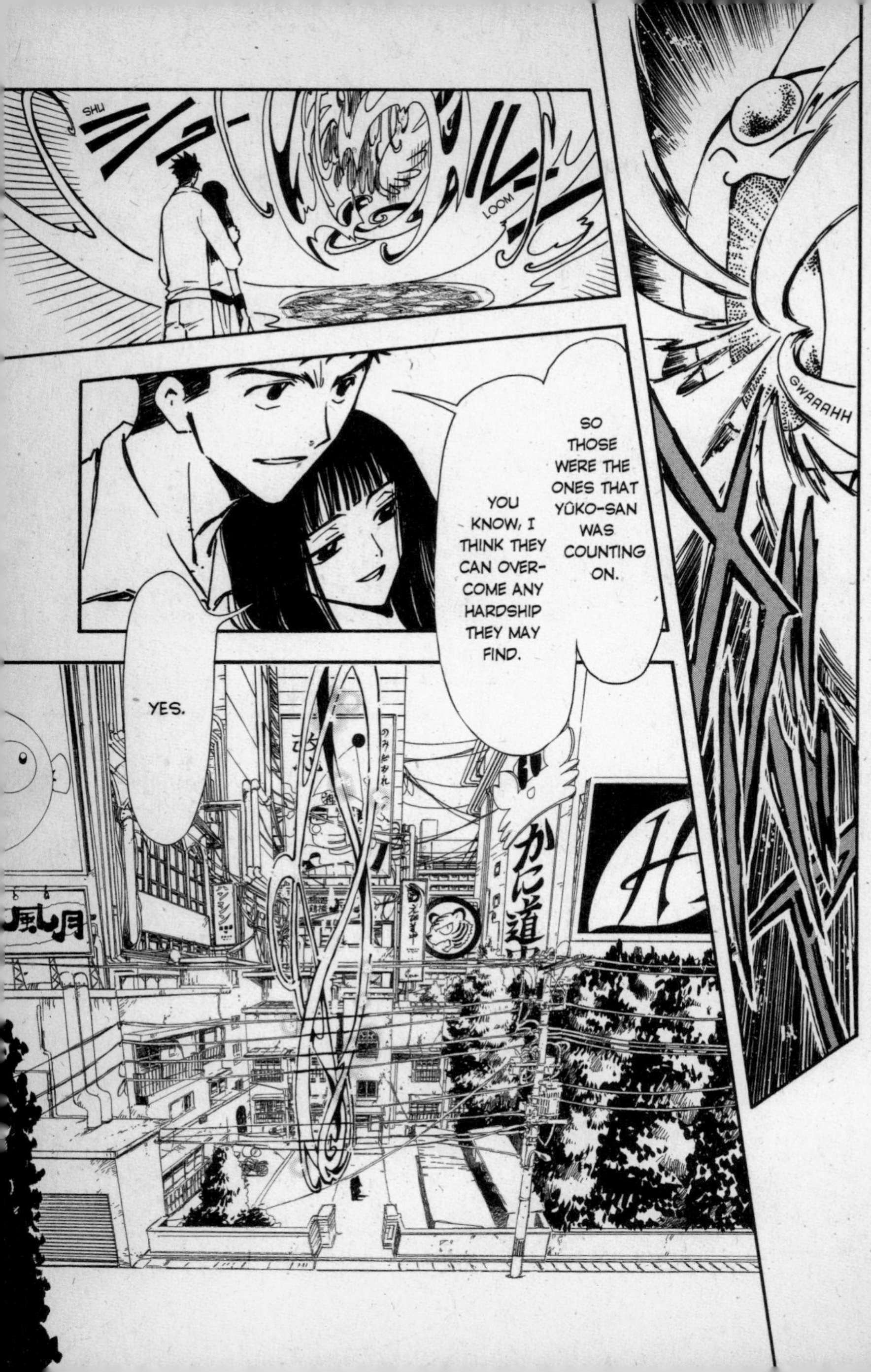
GWAAAHH
SHU
LOOM
SO THOSE WERE THE ONES THAT YŪKO-SAN WAS COUNTING ON.
YOU KNOW, I THINK THEY CAN OVERCOME ANY HARDSHIP THEY MAY FIND.
YES.

GOWARRRRR

THANK
YOU!

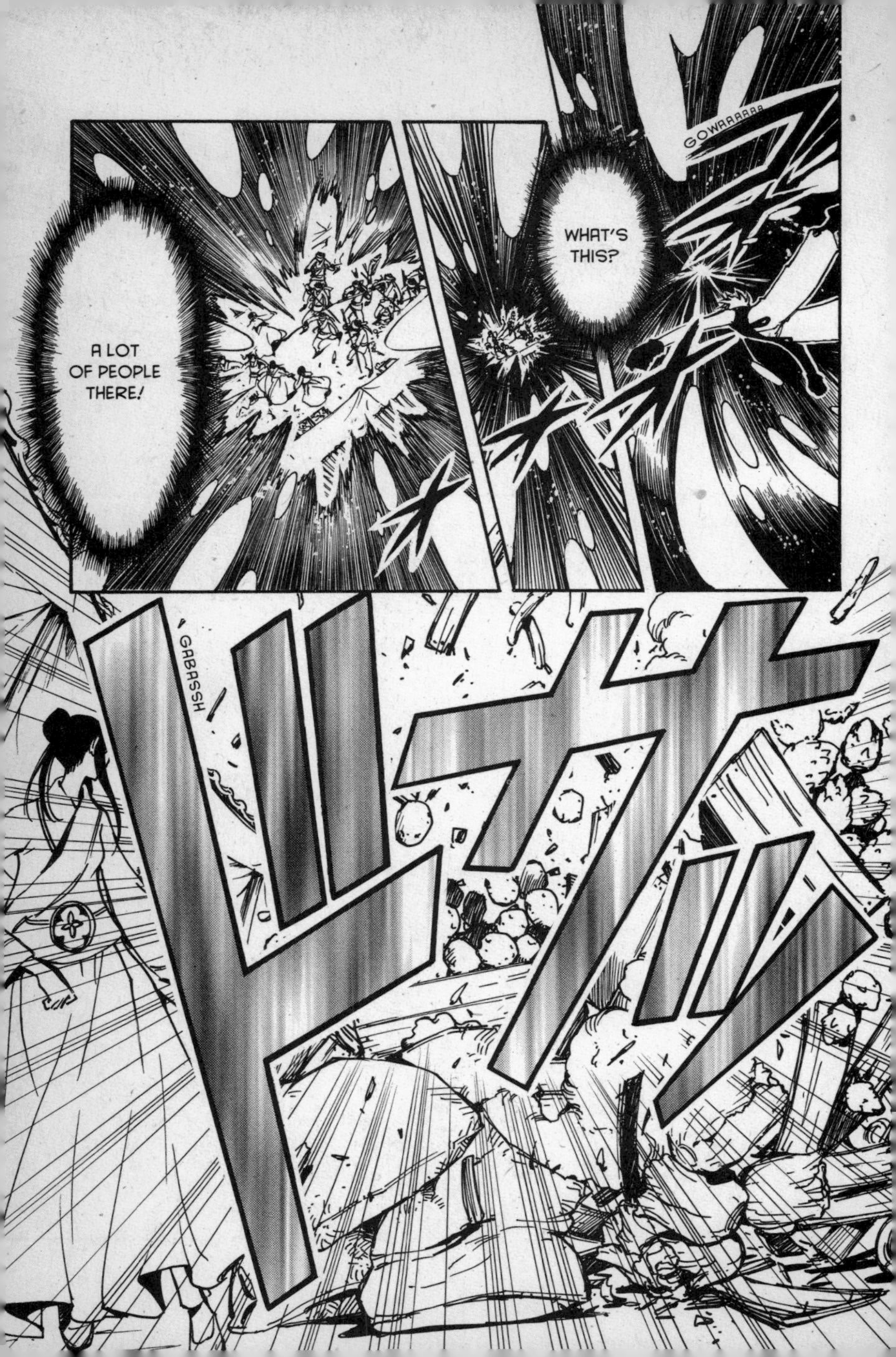
GOWAAAAAAA
WHAT'S THIS?
A LOT OF PEOPLE THERE!
GABASSH

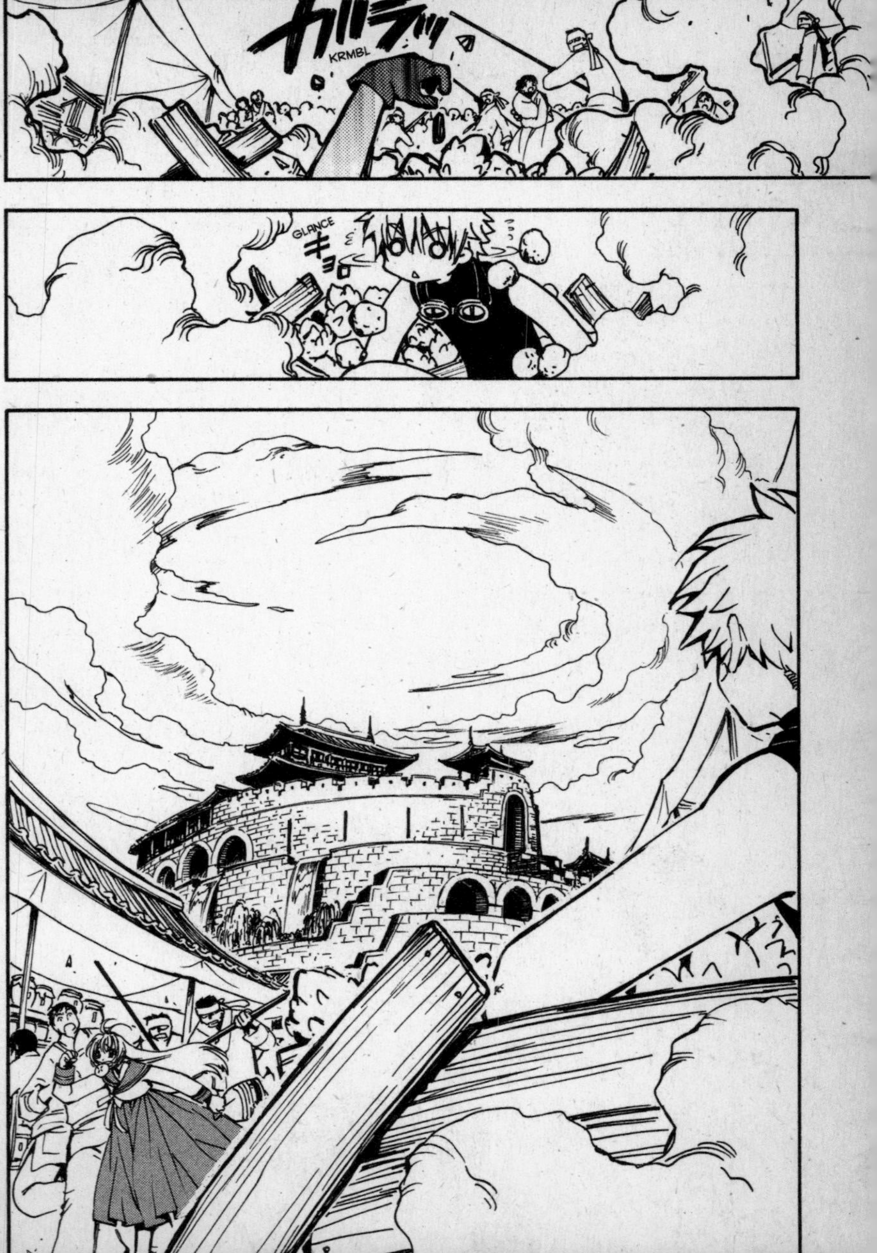
カルラッ
KRMBL
キョロ
GLANCE

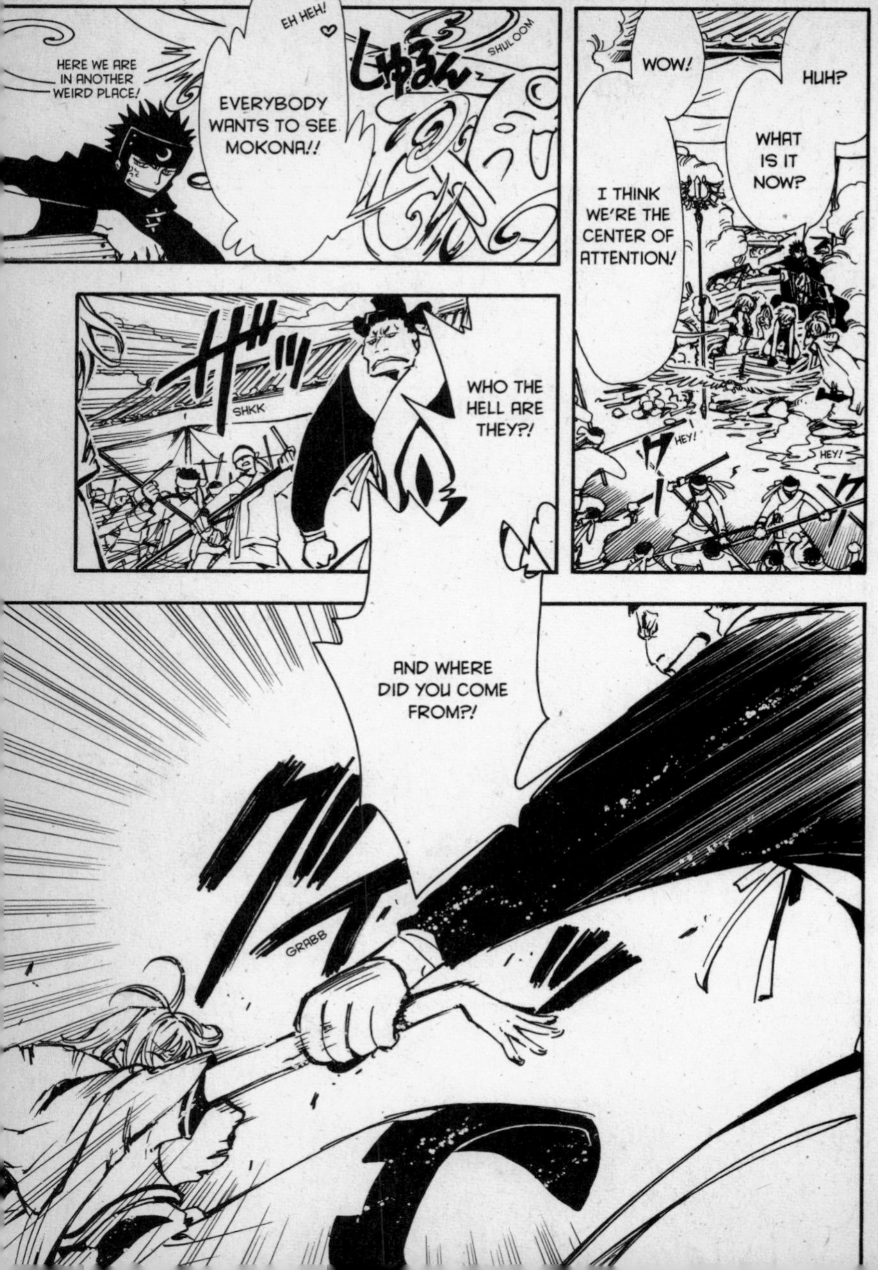
HUH?
WHAT IS IT NOW?
WOW!
I THINK WE'RE THE CENTER OF ATTENTION!
HEY!
HEY!
しゅるん
SHULOOM
EH HEH! ♡
EVERYBODY WANTS TO SEE MOKONA!!
HERE WE ARE IN ANOTHER WEIRD PLACE!
WHO THE HELL ARE THEY?!
ザッ
SHKK
AND WHERE DID YOU COME FROM?!
GRABB

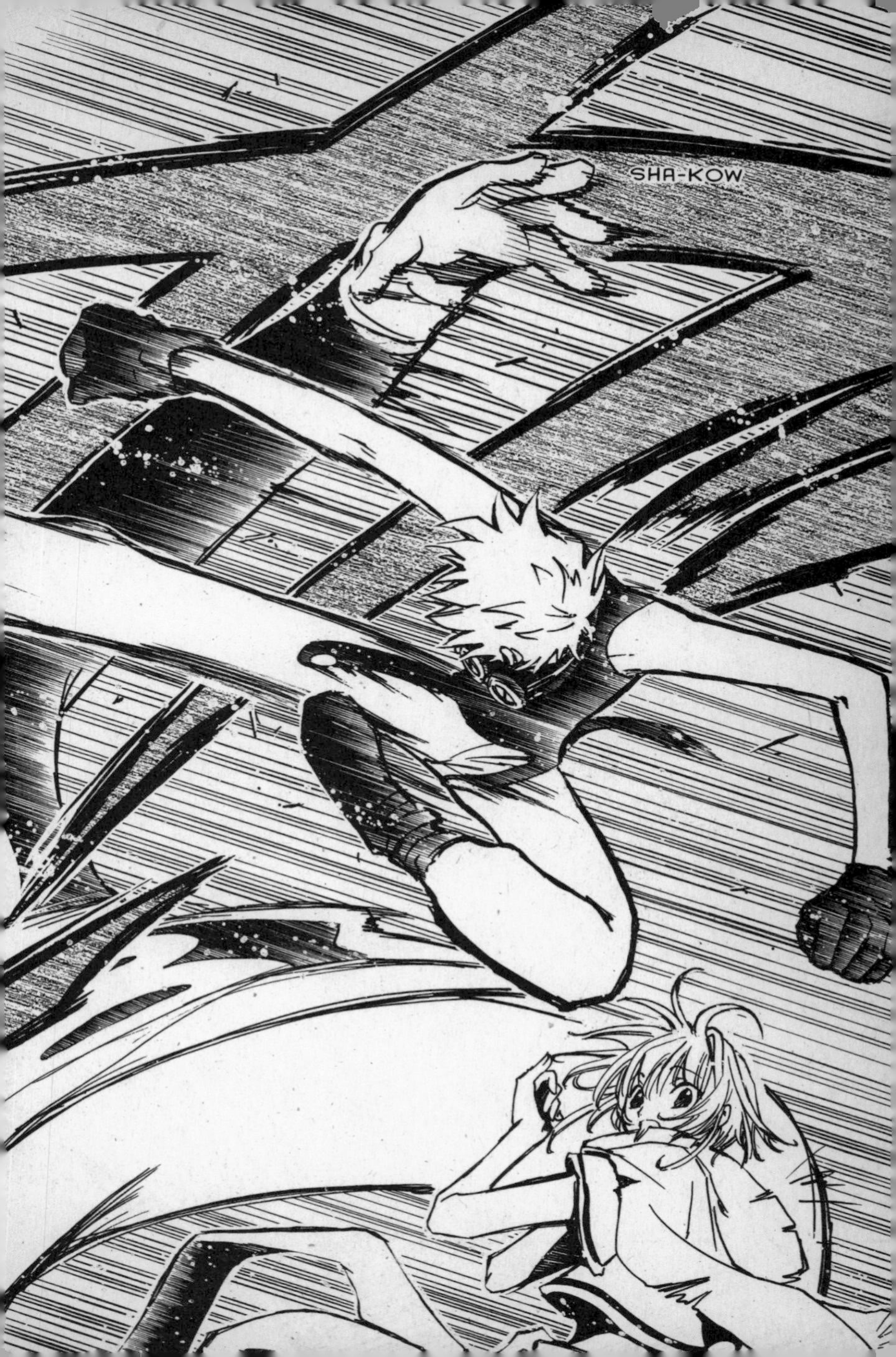
SHA-KOW

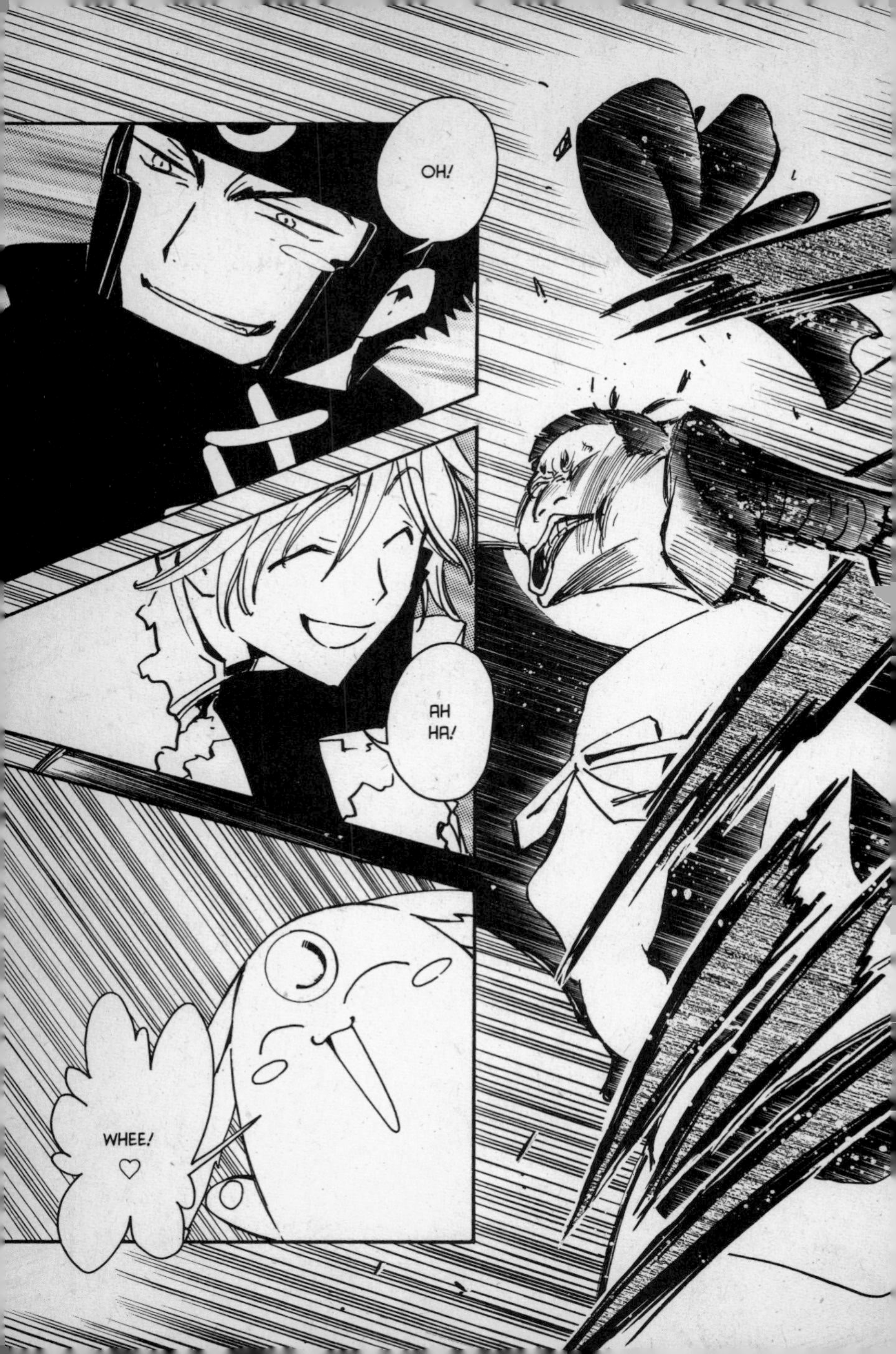
OH!
AH HA!
WHEE! ♡

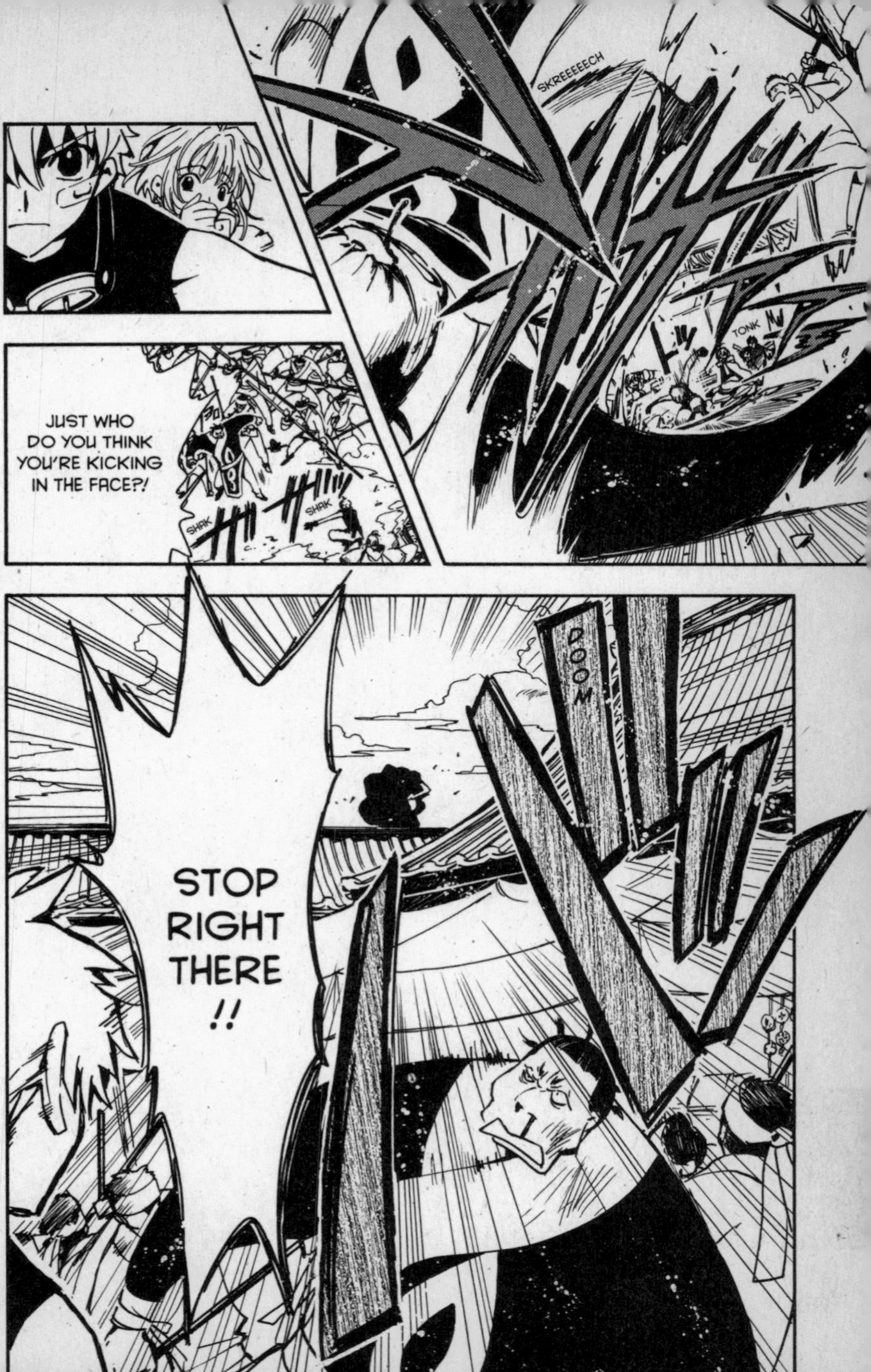
SKREEEEECH
TONK
JUST WHO DO YOU THINK YOU'RE KICKING IN THE FACE?!
SHAK
SHAK
DOOM
STOP RIGHT THERE!!

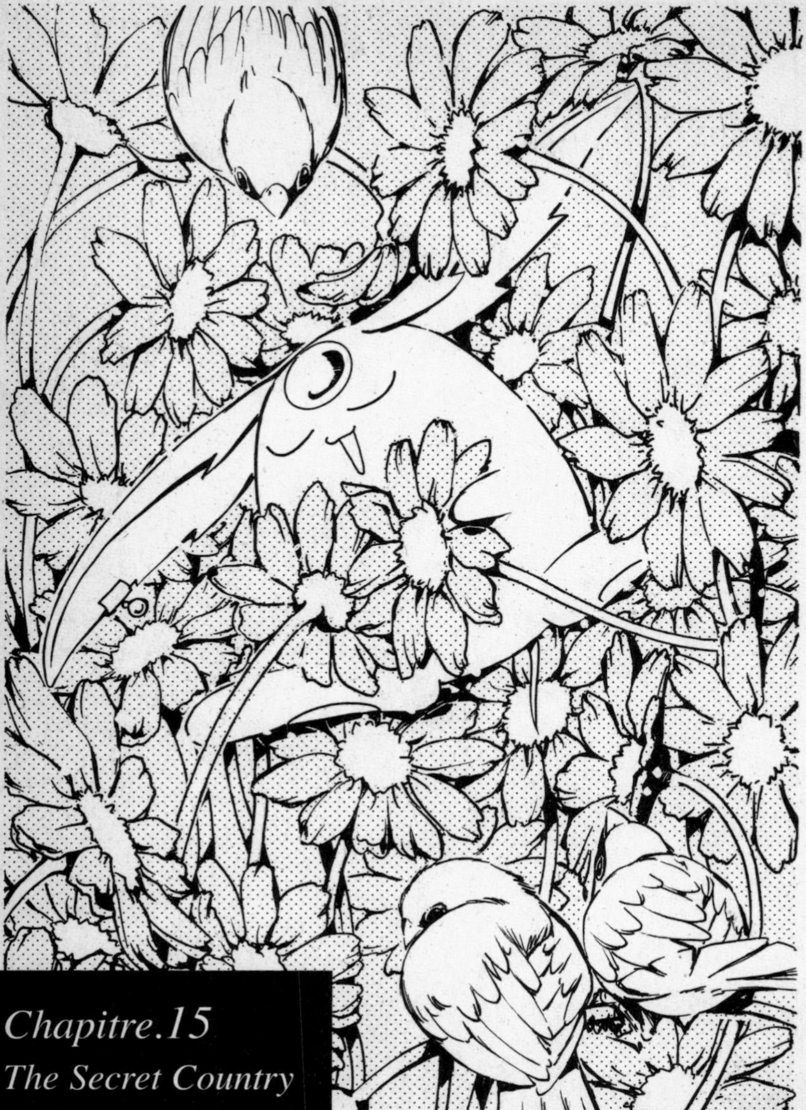

Chapitre.15
The Secret Country

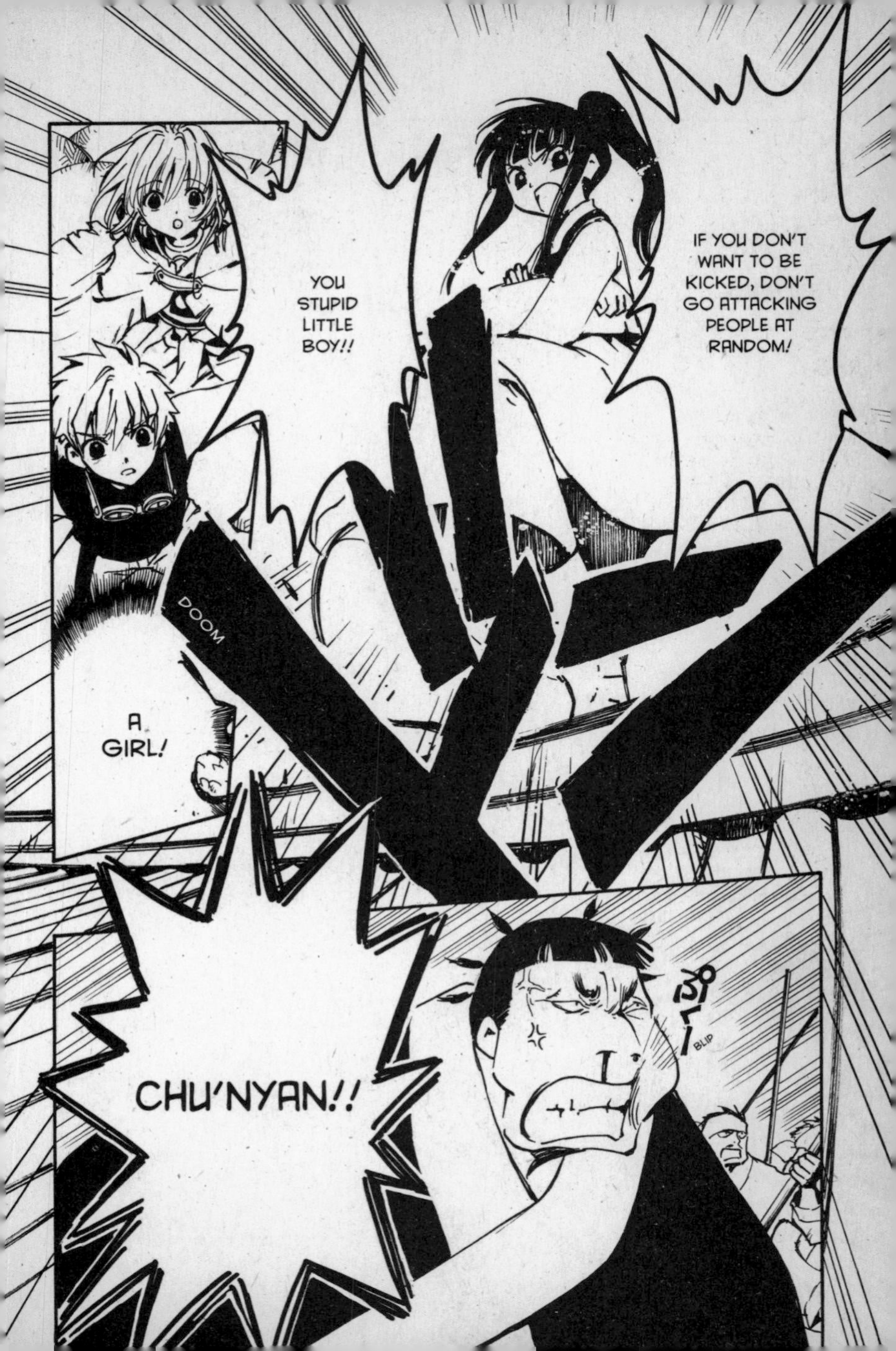
IF YOU DON'T WANT TO BE KICKED, DON'T GO ATTACKING PEOPLE AT RANDOM!
YOU STUPID LITTLE BOY!!
DOOM
A GIRL!
BLIP
CHU'NYAN!!

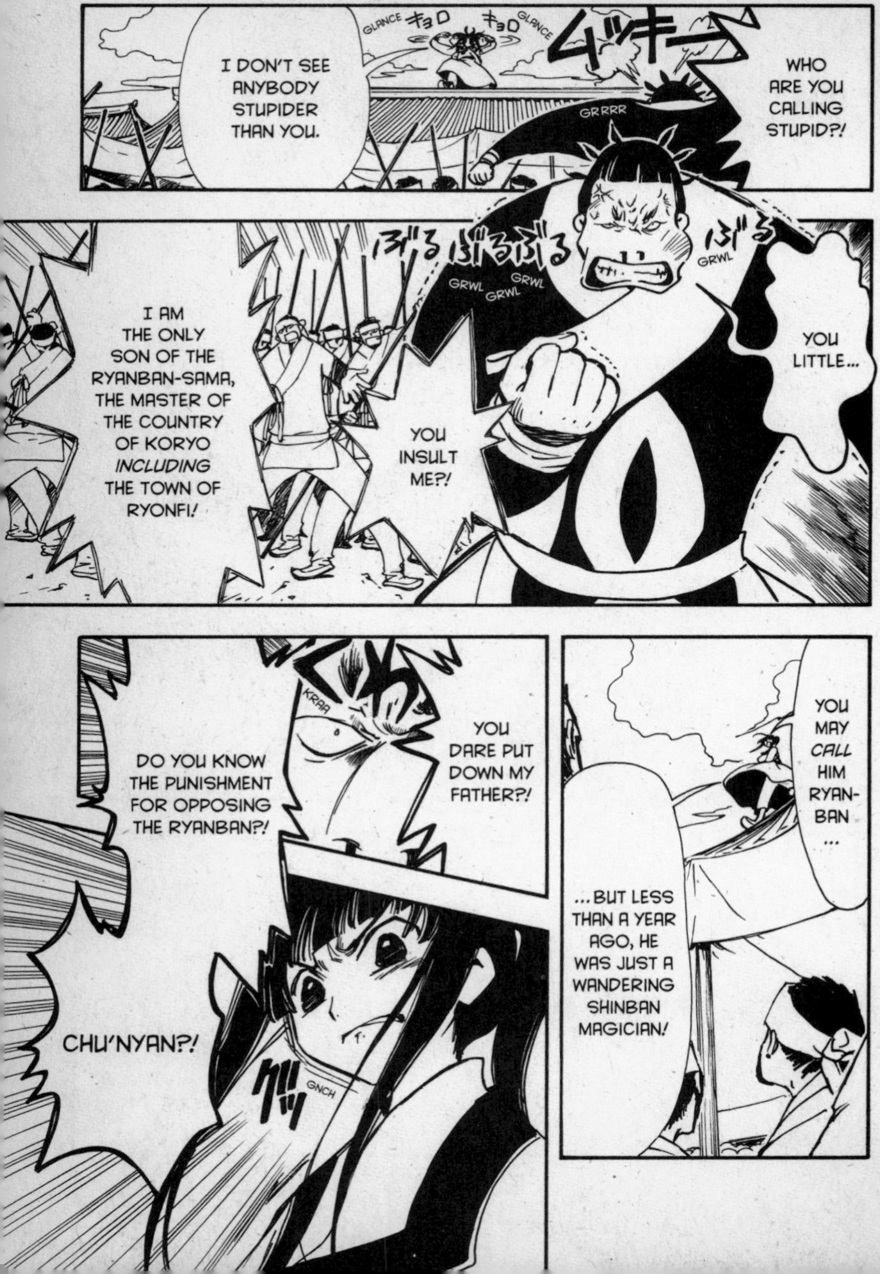
WHO ARE YOU CALLING STUPID?!
ムッキーッ
GRRRR
GLANCE キョロ
キョロ GLANCE
I DON'T SEE ANYBODY STUPIDER THAN YOU.
YOU LITTLE...
ぶる GRWL
ぶるぶるぶる GRWL GRWL GRWL
YOU INSULT ME?!
I AM THE ONLY SON OF THE RYANBAN-SAMA, THE MASTER OF THE COUNTRY OF KORYO *INCLUDING* THE TOWN OF RYONFI!
YOU MAY *CALL* HIM RYAN-BAN...
...BUT LESS THAN A YEAR AGO, HE WAS JUST A WANDERING SHINBAN MAGICIAN!
KRAA
YOU DARE PUT DOWN MY FATHER?!
DO YOU KNOW THE PUNISHMENT FOR OPPOSING THE RYANBAN?!
CHU'NYAN?!
GNCH

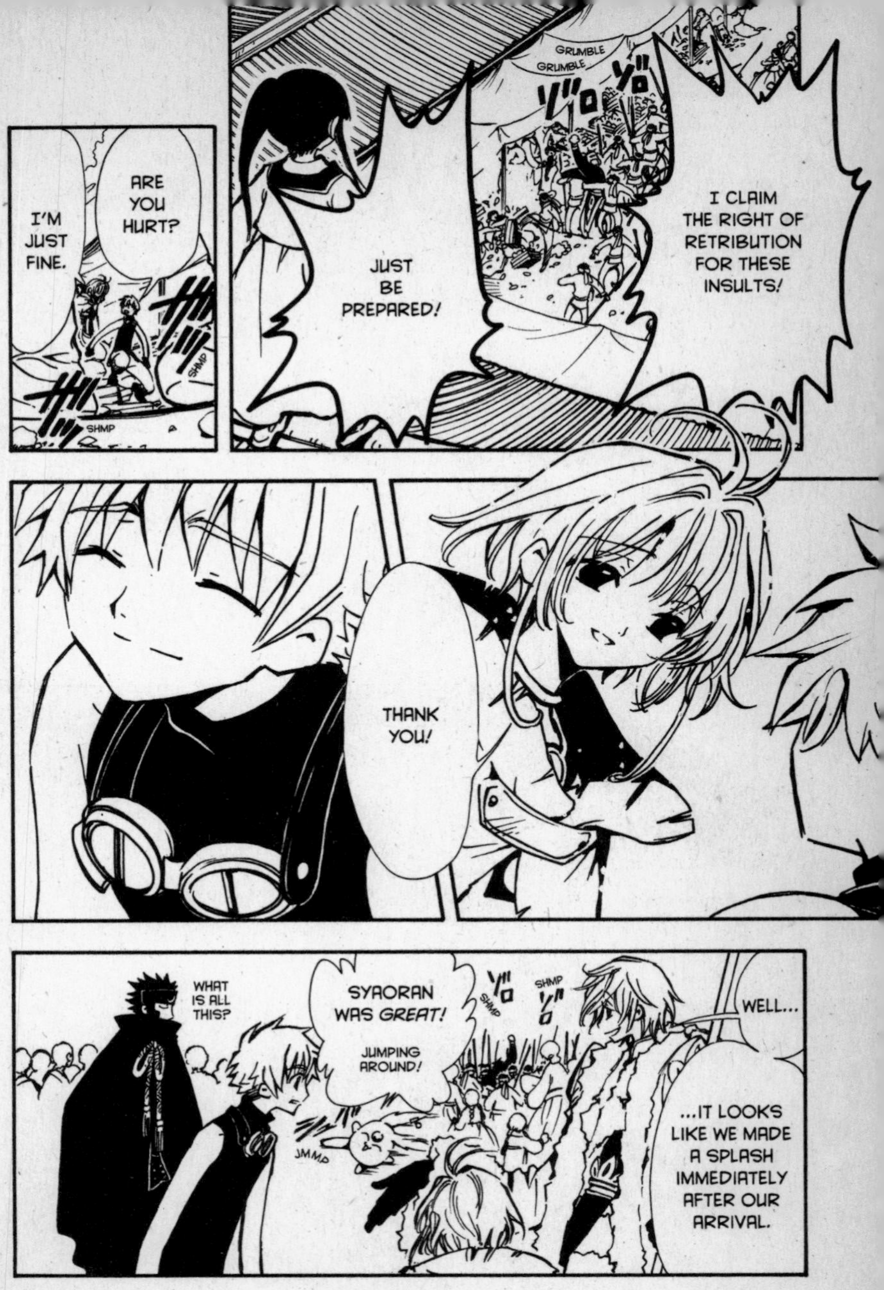
GRUMBLE
GRUMBLE
ゾロ
ゾロ
I CLAIM THE RIGHT OF RETRIBUTION FOR THESE INSULTS!
JUST BE PREPARED!
ARE YOU HURT?
I'M JUST FINE.
SHMP
SHMP
THANK YOU!
WELL...
...IT LOOKS LIKE WE MADE A SPLASH IMMEDIATELY AFTER OUR ARRIVAL.
SHMP
ゾロ
SHMP
ゾロ
SYAORAN WAS GREAT!
JUMPING AROUND!
JMMP
WHAT IS ALL THIS?

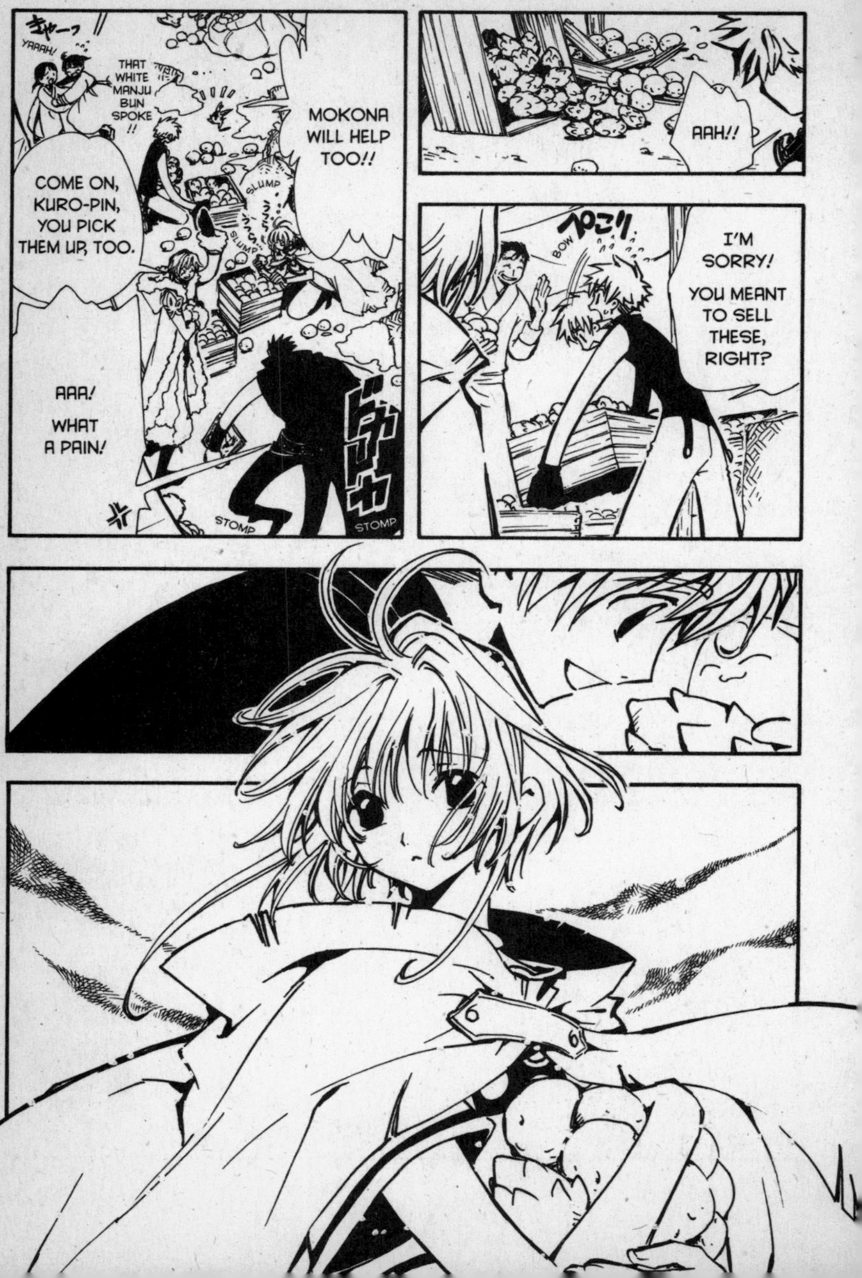
AAH!!
BOW
I'M SORRY!
YOU MEANT TO SELL THESE, RIGHT?
MOKONA WILL HELP TOO!!
THAT WHITE MANJU BUN SPOKE!!
YAAAH!
SLUMP
SLUMP
COME ON, KURO-PIN, YOU PICK THEM UP, TOO.
AAA! WHAT A PAIN!
STOMP
STOMP

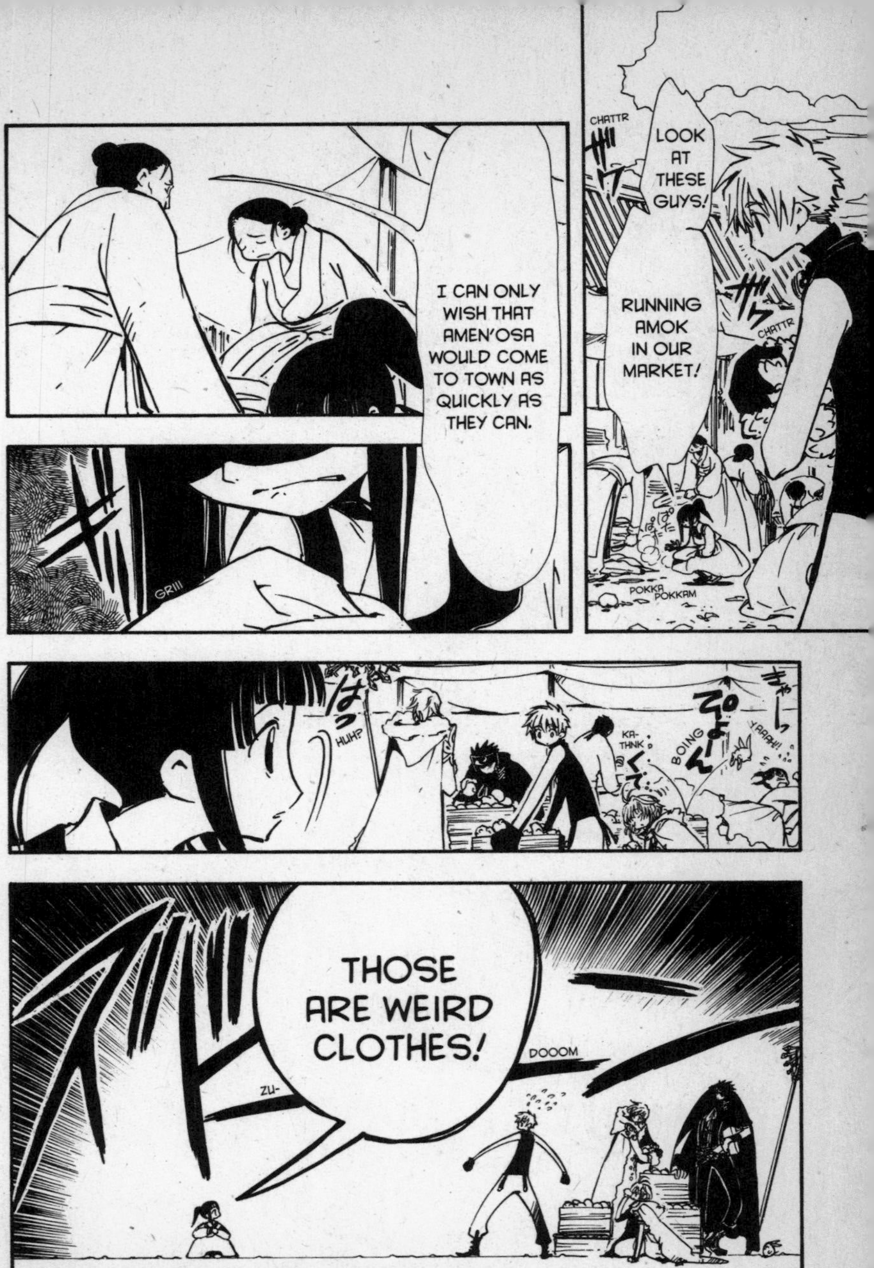
CHATTR
LOOK AT THESE GUYS!
RUNNING AMOK IN OUR MARKET!
CHATTR
POKKA POKKAM
I CAN ONLY WISH THAT AMEN'OSA WOULD COME TO TOWN AS QUICKLY AS THEY CAN.
GRIII
YAAAH!!
BOING
KA-THNK
HUH?
THOSE ARE WEIRD CLOTHES!
DOOOM
ZU-

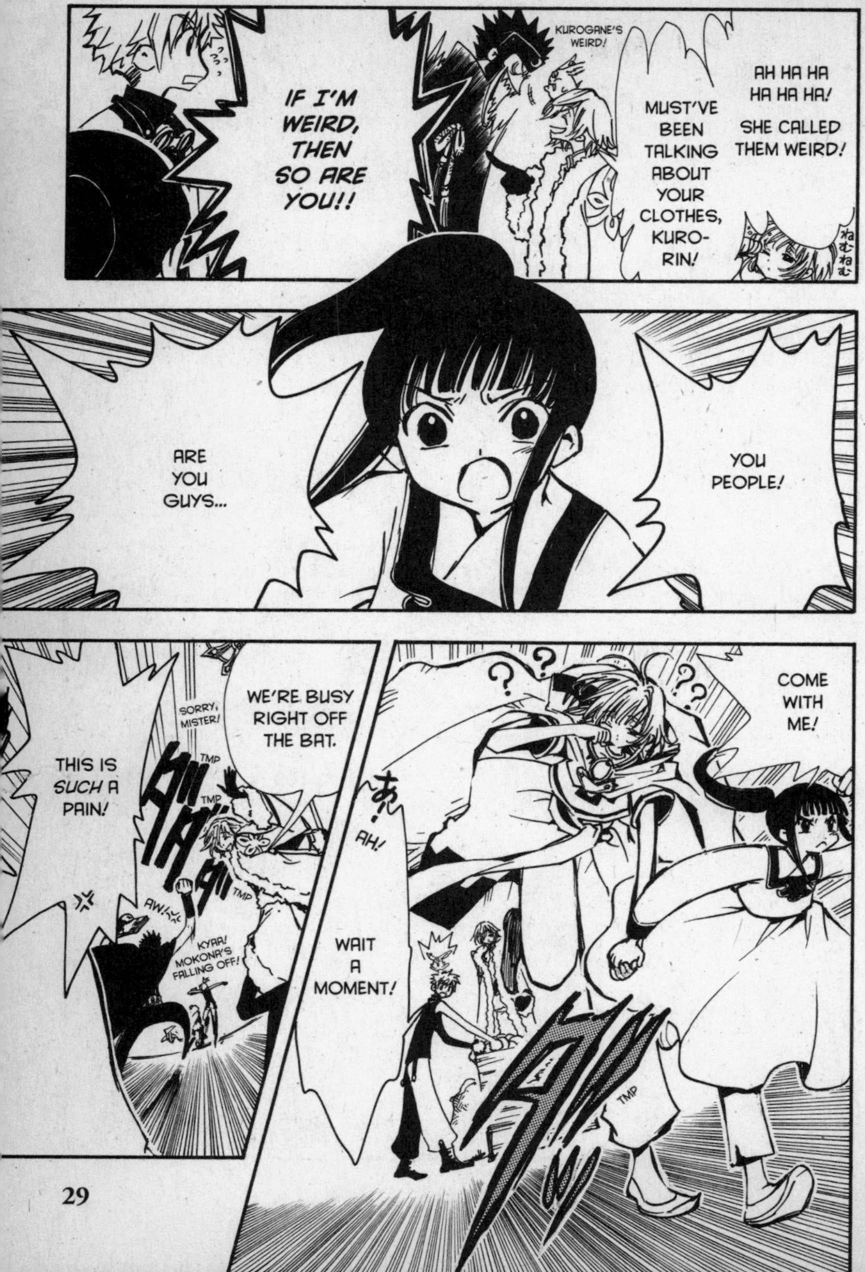
KUROGANE'S WEIRD!
AH HA HA HA HA HA!
SHE CALLED THEM WEIRD!
MUST'VE BEEN TALKING ABOUT YOUR CLOTHES, KURO-RIN!
ねむねむ
IF I'M WEIRD, THEN SO ARE YOU!!
YOU PEOPLE!
ARE YOU GUYS...
COME WITH ME!
あ!
AH!
WAIT A MOMENT!
TMP
WE'RE BUSY RIGHT OFF THE BAT.
SORRY, MISTER!
TMP
TMP
THIS IS SUCH A PAIN!
AW!
KYAA! MOKONA'S FALLING OFF!
TMP

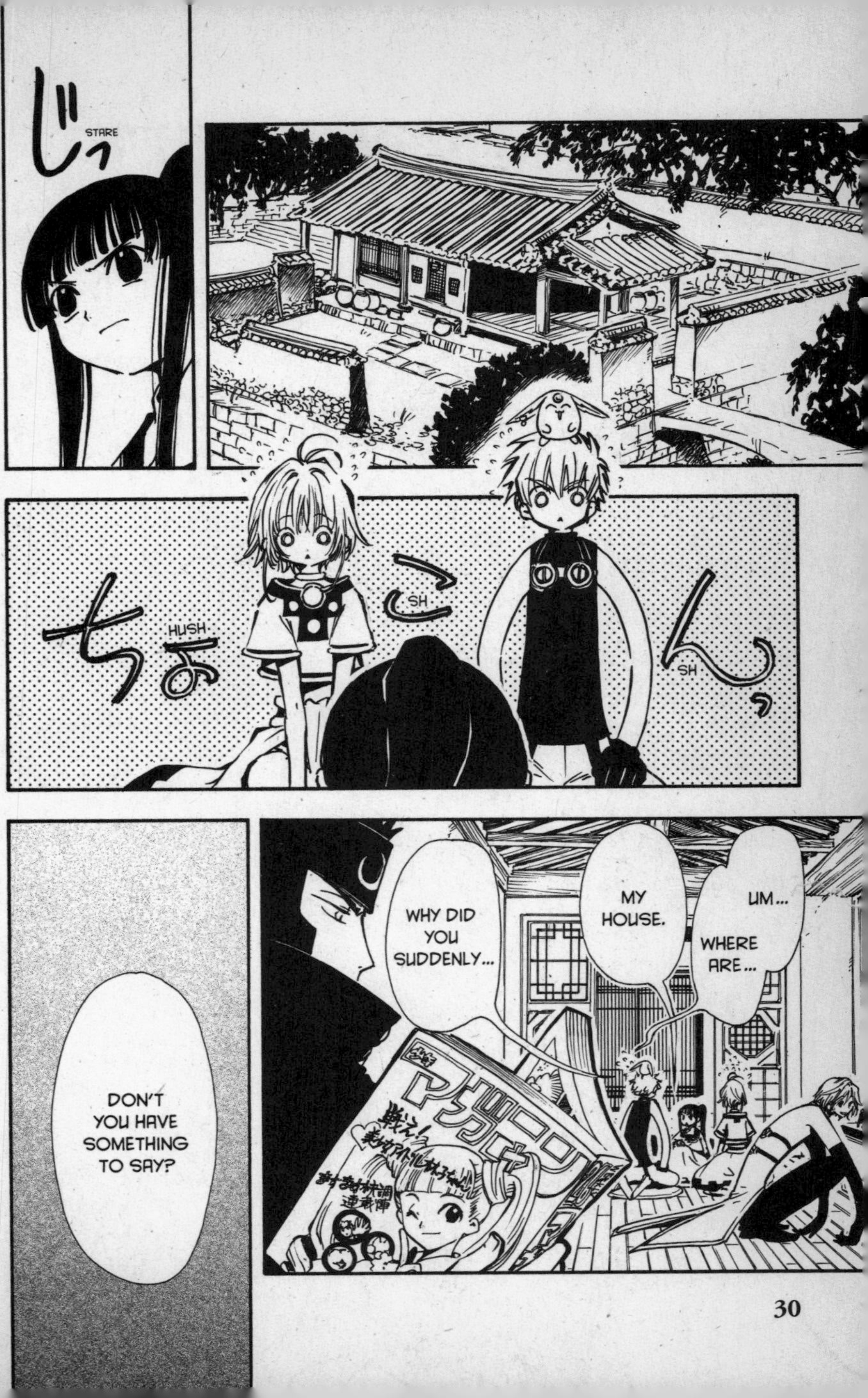
じっ
STARE
ちょこん
HUSH
SH
SH
UM...
WHERE ARE...
MY HOUSE.
WHY DID YOU SUDDENLY...
DON'T YOU HAVE SOMETHING TO SAY?

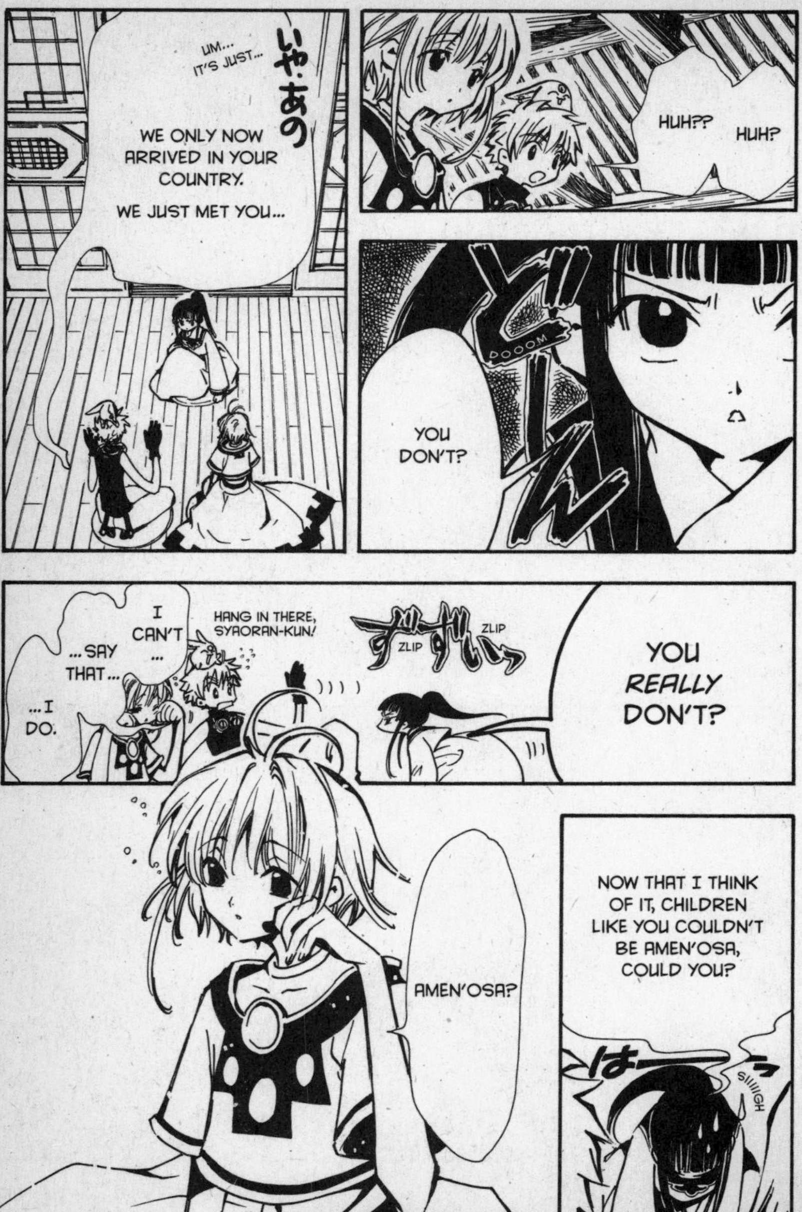
HUH??
HUH?
DOOOM
YOU DON'T?
いや・あの
UM... IT'S JUST...
WE ONLY NOW ARRIVED IN YOUR COUNTRY.
WE JUST MET YOU...
YOU REALLY DON'T?
ZLIP
ZLIP
HANG IN THERE, SYAORAN-KUN!
I CAN'T ...
...SAY THAT...
...I DO.
NOW THAT I THINK OF IT, CHILDREN LIKE YOU COULDN'T BE AMEN'OSA, COULD YOU?
SIIIIGH
AMEN'OSA?

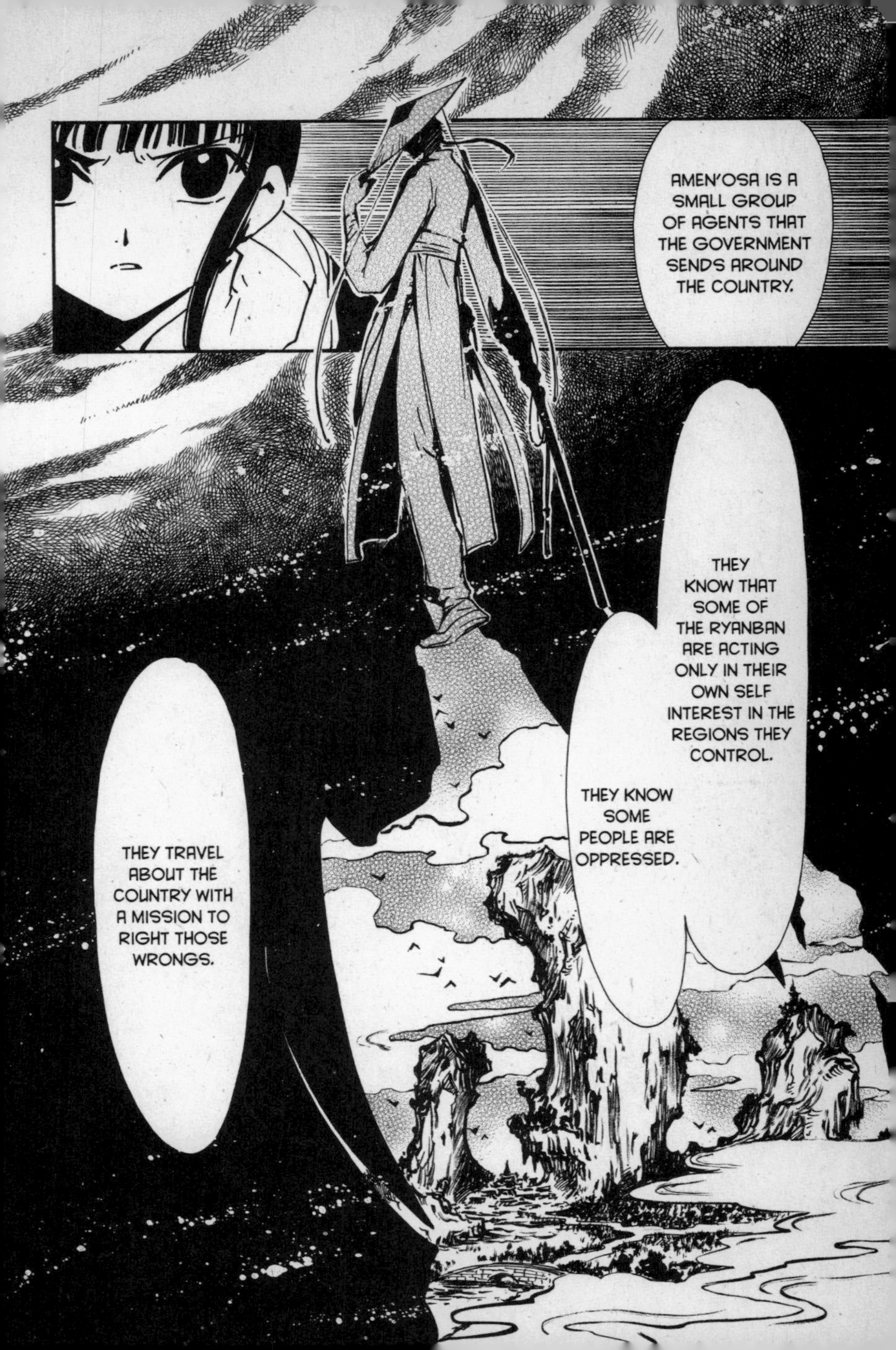
AMEN'OSA IS A SMALL GROUP OF AGENTS THAT THE GOVERNMENT SENDS AROUND THE COUNTRY.
THEY KNOW THAT SOME OF THE RYANBAN ARE ACTING ONLY IN THEIR OWN SELF INTEREST IN THE REGIONS THEY CONTROL.
THEY KNOW SOME PEOPLE ARE OPPRESSED.
THEY TRAVEL ABOUT THE COUNTRY WITH A MISSION TO RIGHT THOSE WRONGS.

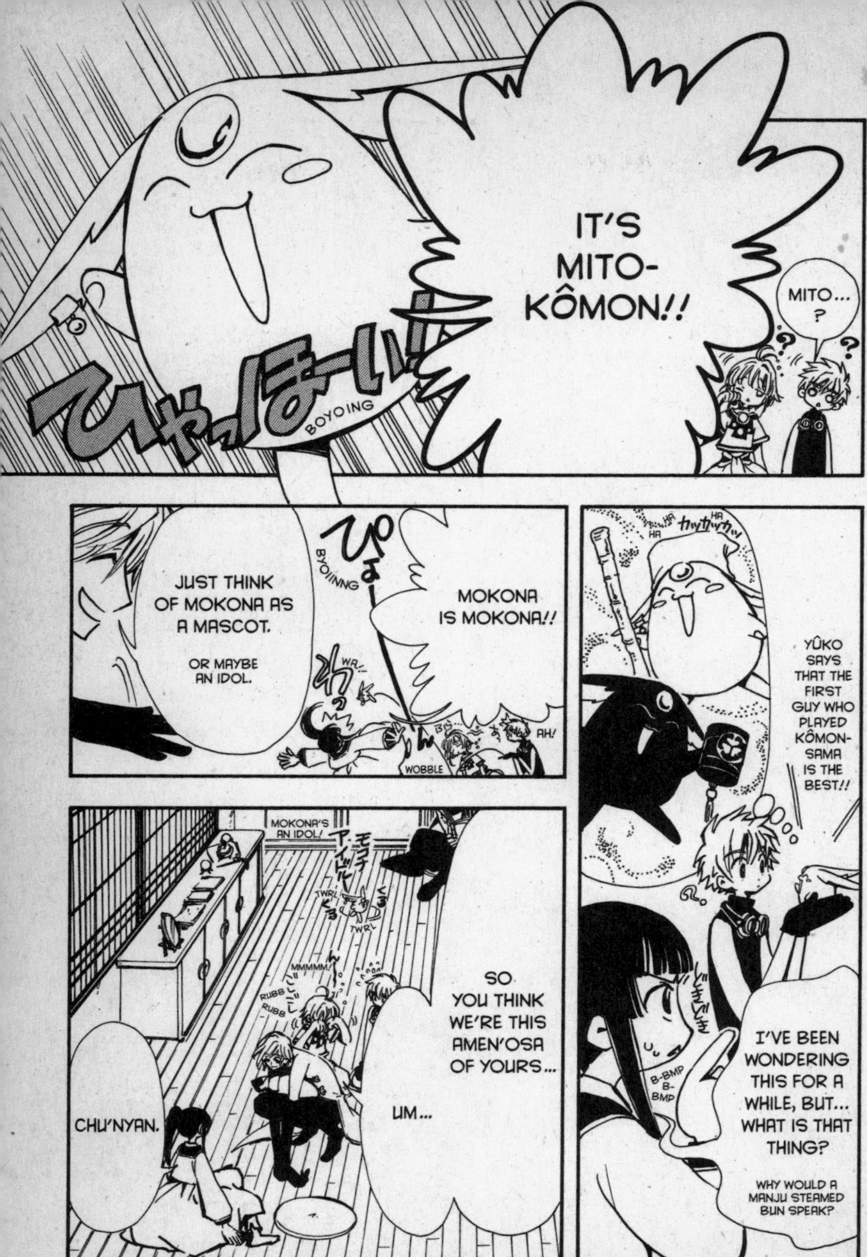
IT'S MITO-KÔMON!!
MITO... ?
ひゃっほーい!!
BOYOING
HA HA
カッカッカッ
HA
YÛKO SAYS THAT THE FIRST GUY WHO PLAYED KÔMON-SAMA IS THE BEST!!
B-BMP B-BMP
I'VE BEEN WONDERING THIS FOR A WHILE, BUT... WHAT IS THAT THING?
WHY WOULD A MANJU STEAMED BUN SPEAK?
ぴょ
BYOIINNG
MOKONA IS MOKONA!!
JUST THINK OF MOKONA AS A MASCOT.
OR MAYBE AN IDOL.
WA!!
AH!
WOBBLE
MOKONA'S AN IDOL!
TWRL
TWRL
SO YOU THINK WE'RE THIS AMEN'OSA OF YOURS...
UM...
MMMMM!
RUBB RUBB
CHU'NYAN.

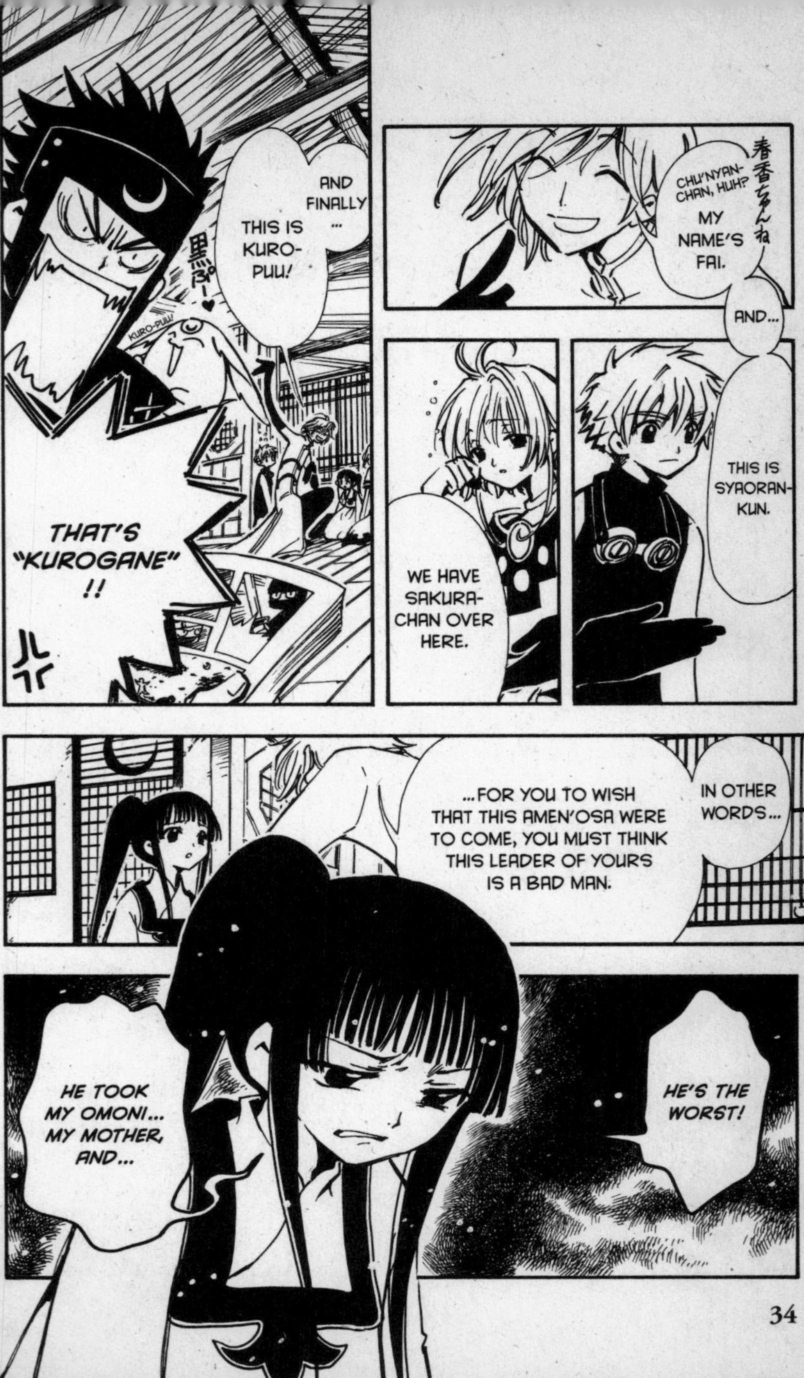

CHU'NYAN-CHAN, HUH?
春香ちゃんね
MY NAME'S FAI.
AND...
THIS IS SYAORAN-KUN.
WE HAVE SAKURA-CHAN OVER HERE.
AND FINALLY ...
THIS IS KURO-PUU!
黒ぷー♥
KURO-PUU!
THAT'S "KUROGANE" !!
IN OTHER WORDS...
...FOR YOU TO WISH THAT THIS AMEN'OSA WERE TO COME, YOU MUST THINK THIS LEADER OF YOURS IS A BAD MAN.
HE'S THE WORST!
HE TOOK MY OMONI... MY MOTHER, AND...

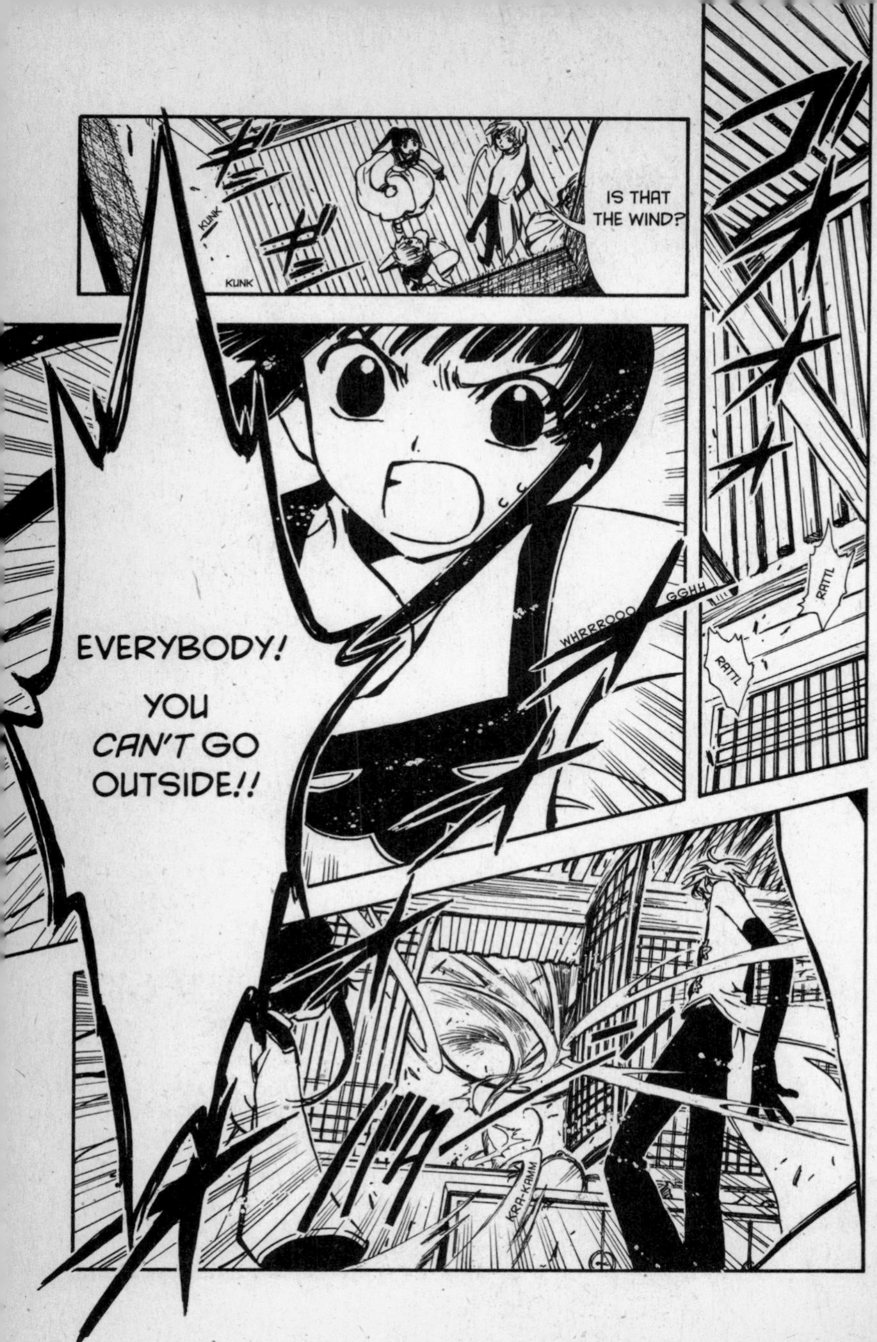
RATTL
RATTL
IS THAT THE WIND?
KUNK
KUNK
WHRRROOO GGHH
EVERYBODY!
YOU CAN'T GO OUTSIDE!!
KRA-KAMM

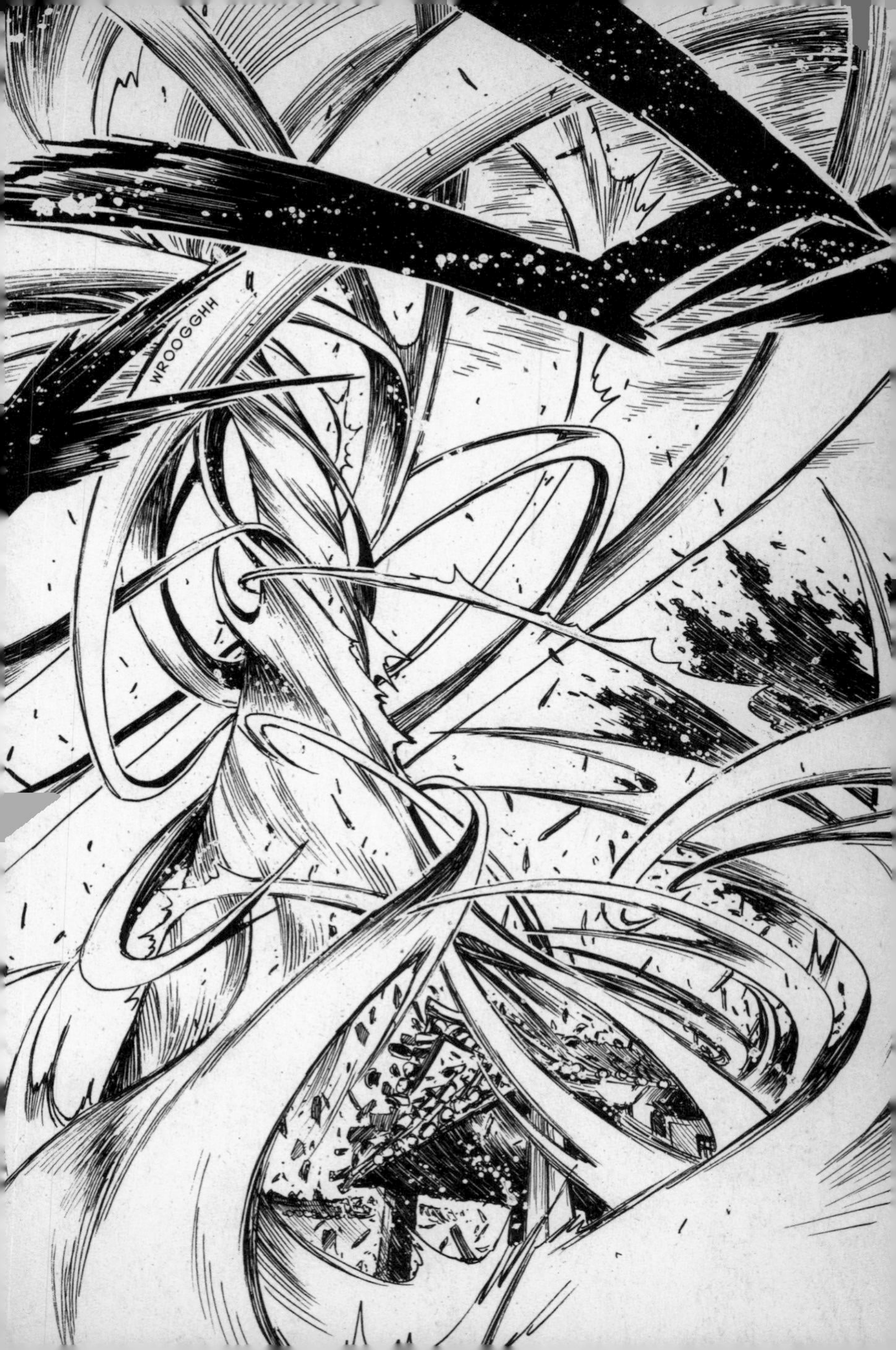
WROOGGHH

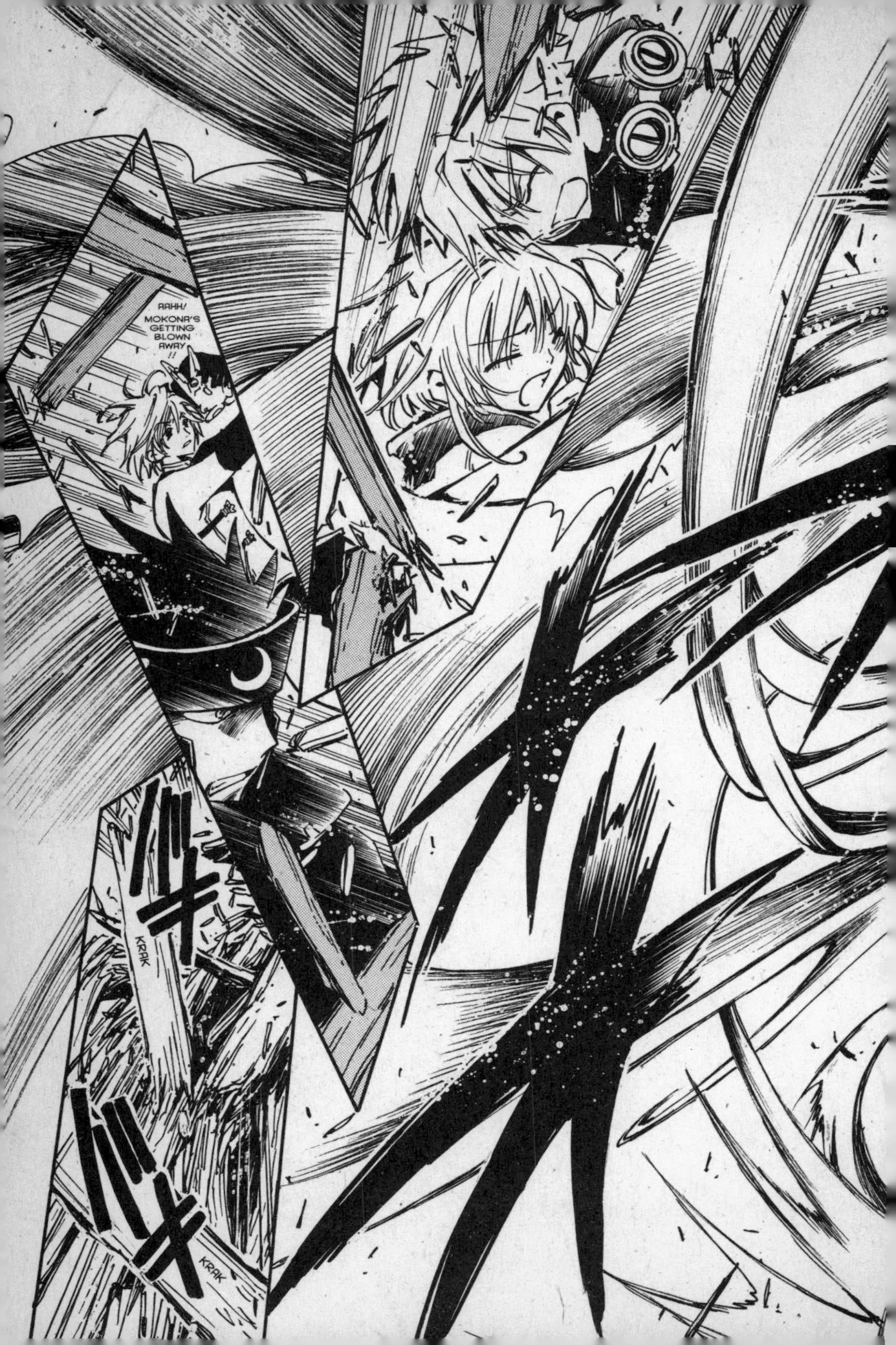
AAHH! MOKONA'S GETTING BLOWN AWAY !!
KRAK
KRAK

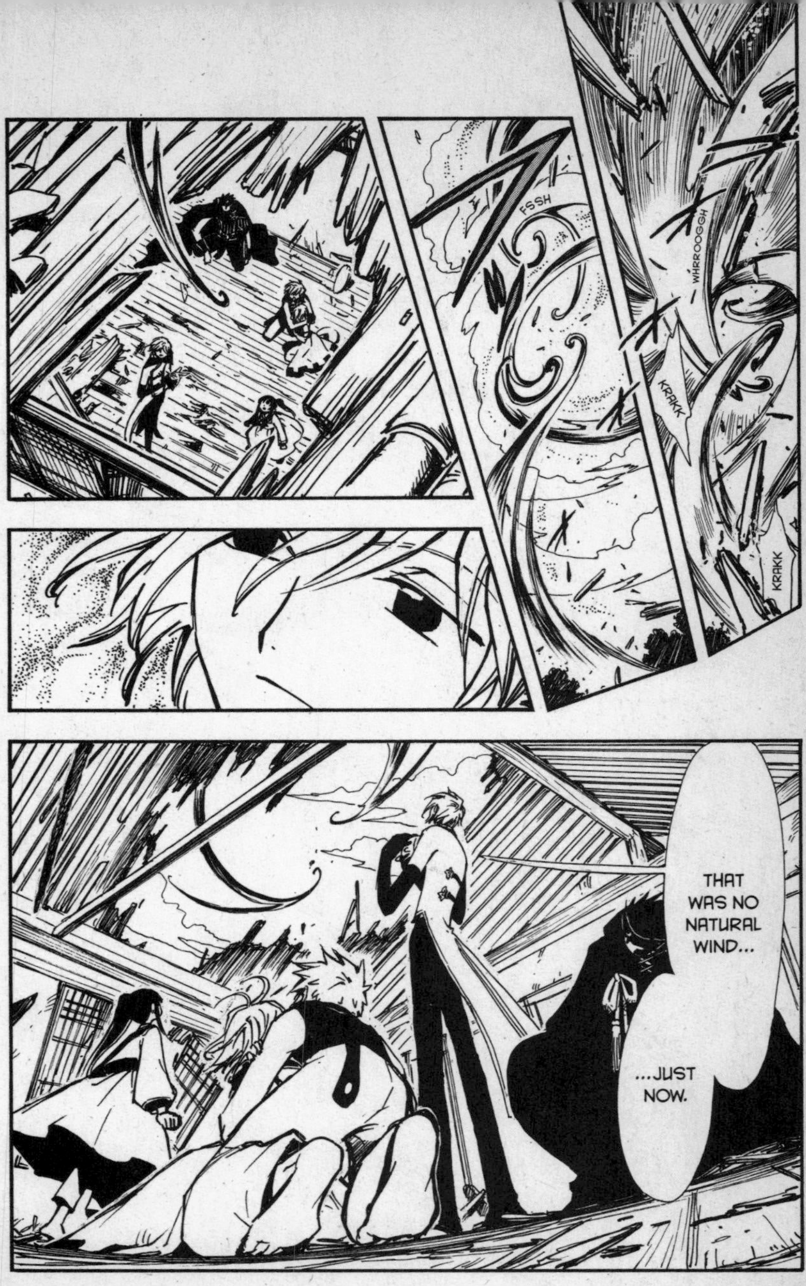
WHRROOGGH
KRAKK
KRAKK
FSSH
THAT WAS NO NATURAL WIND...
...JUST NOW.

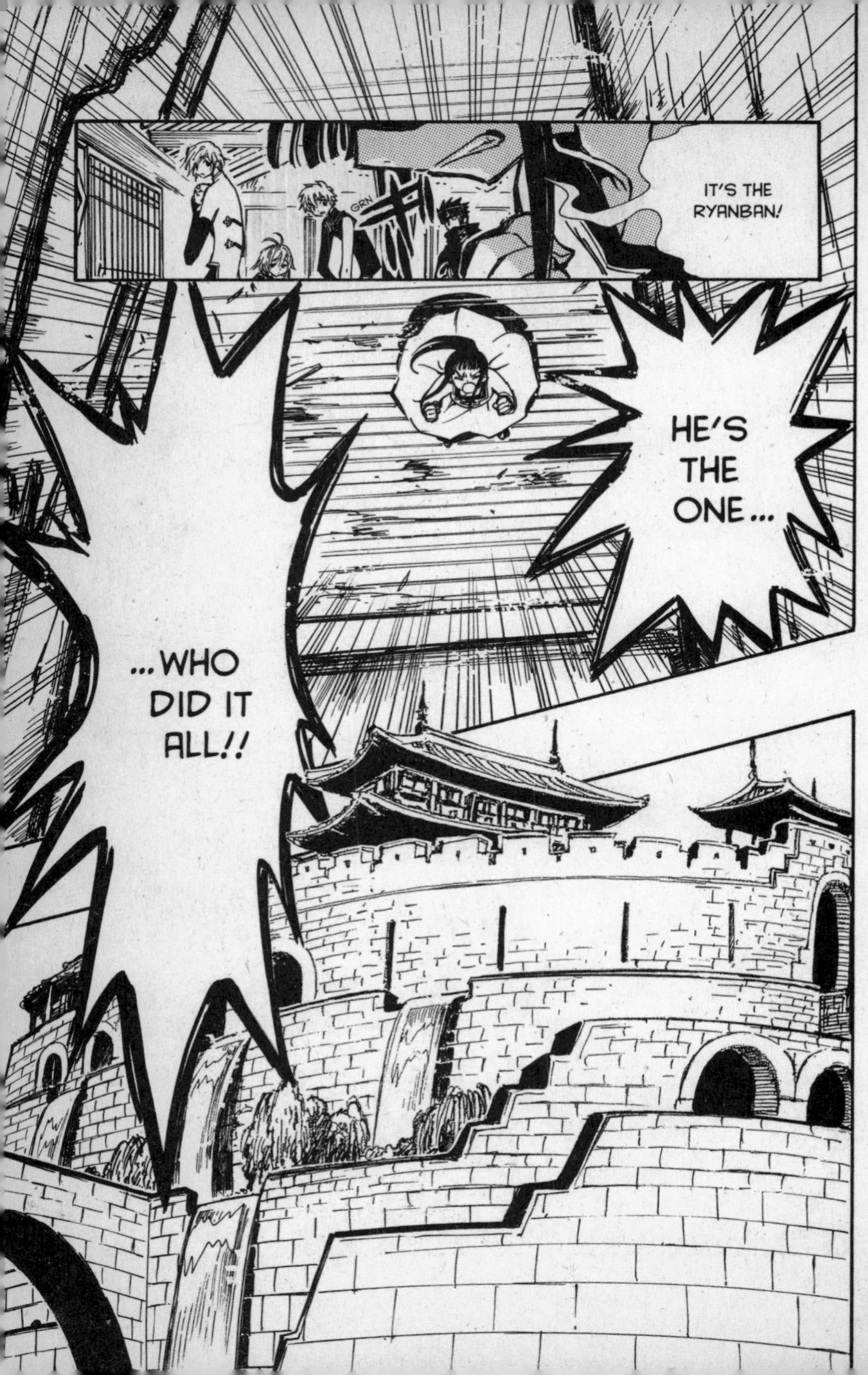
IT'S THE RYANBAN!
GRN
HE'S THE ONE...
...WHO DID IT ALL!!

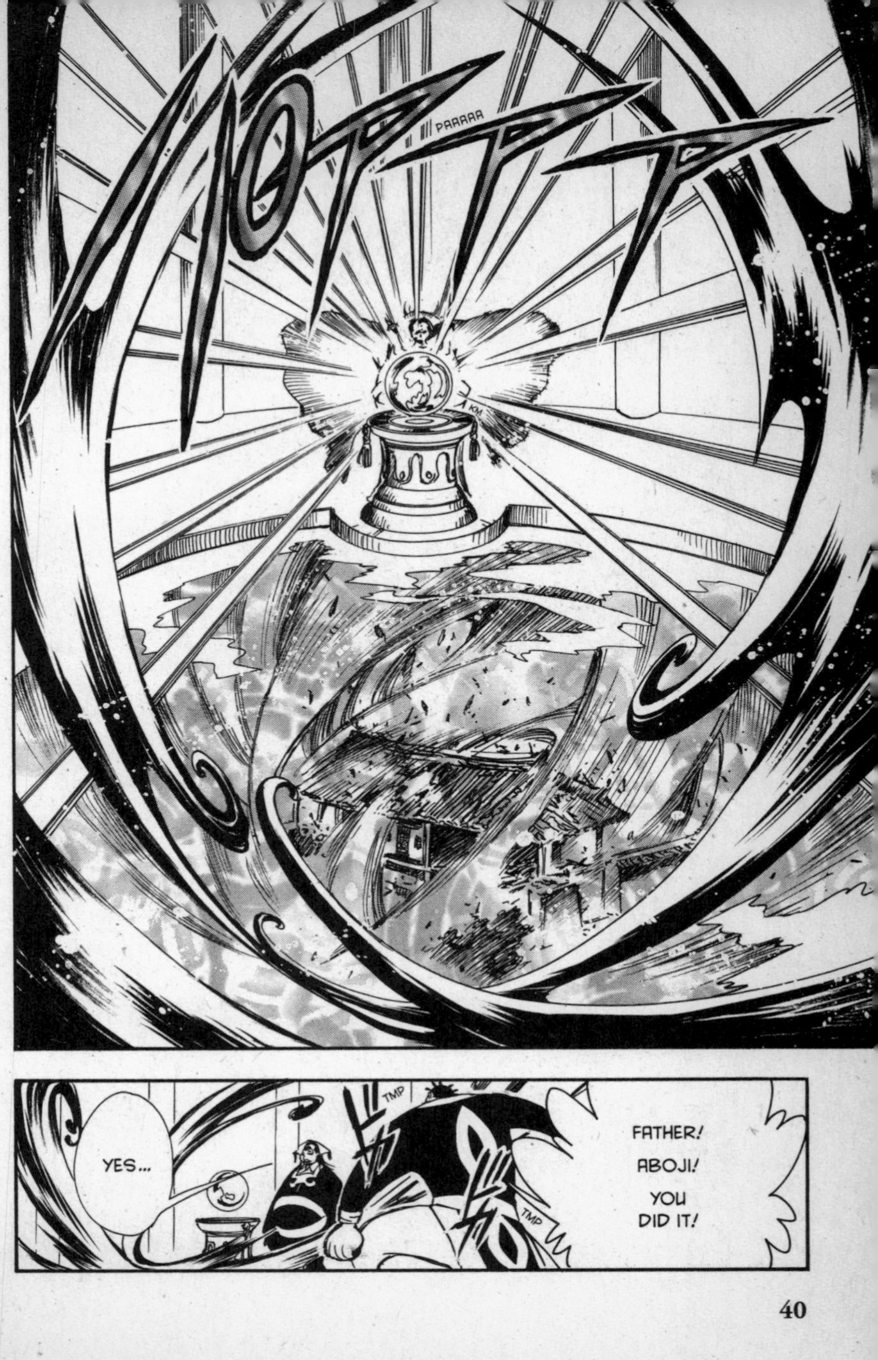
PARRRRR
KM
FATHER!
ABOJI!
YOU DID IT!
TMP
TMP
YES...

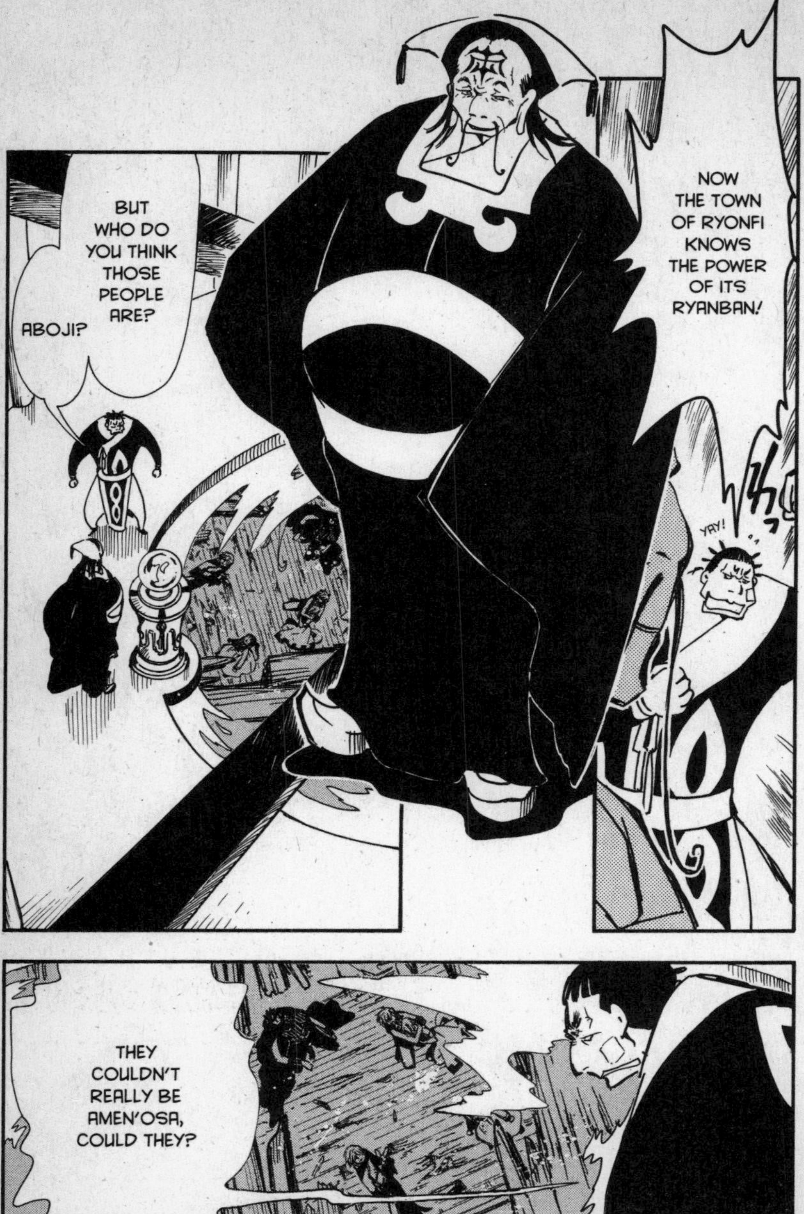
NOW THE TOWN OF RYONFI KNOWS THE POWER OF ITS RYANBAN!
YAY!
BUT WHO DO YOU THINK THOSE PEOPLE ARE?
ABOJI?
THEY COULDN'T REALLY BE AMEN'OSA, COULD THEY?

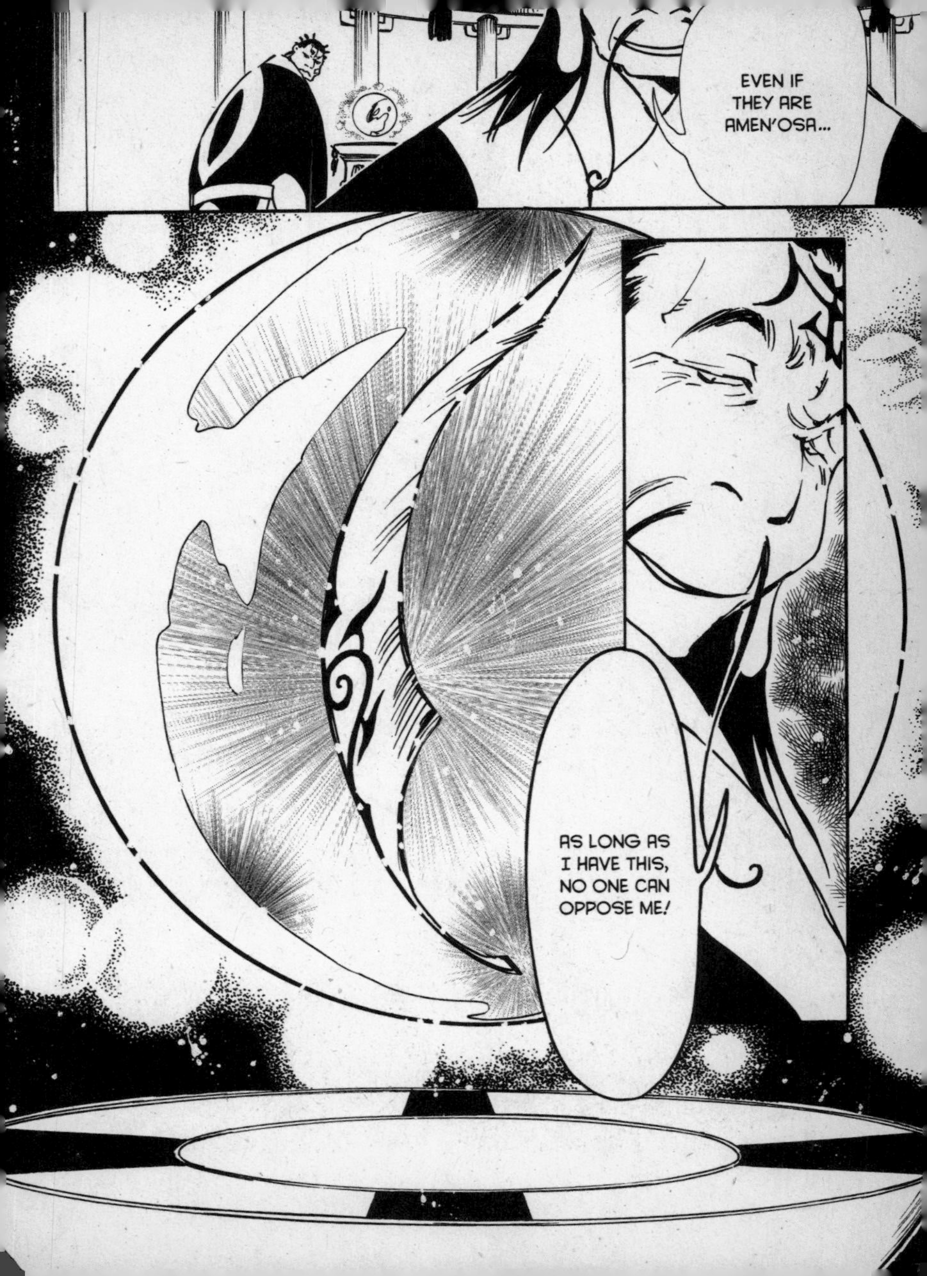
EVEN IF THEY ARE AMEN'OSA...
AS LONG AS I HAVE THIS, NO ONE CAN OPPOSE ME!

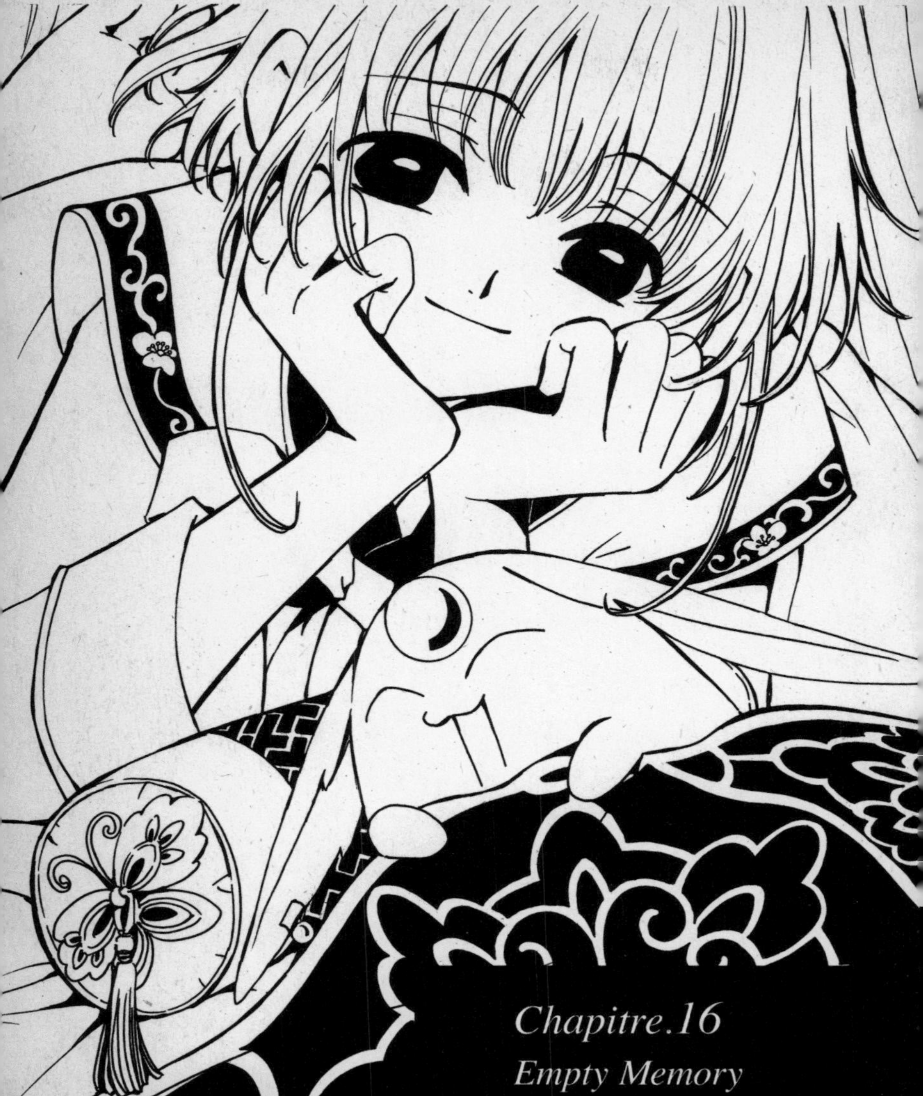
Chapitre.16
Empty Memory

ツバサ
RESERVoir CHRoNiCLE

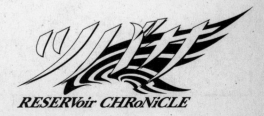

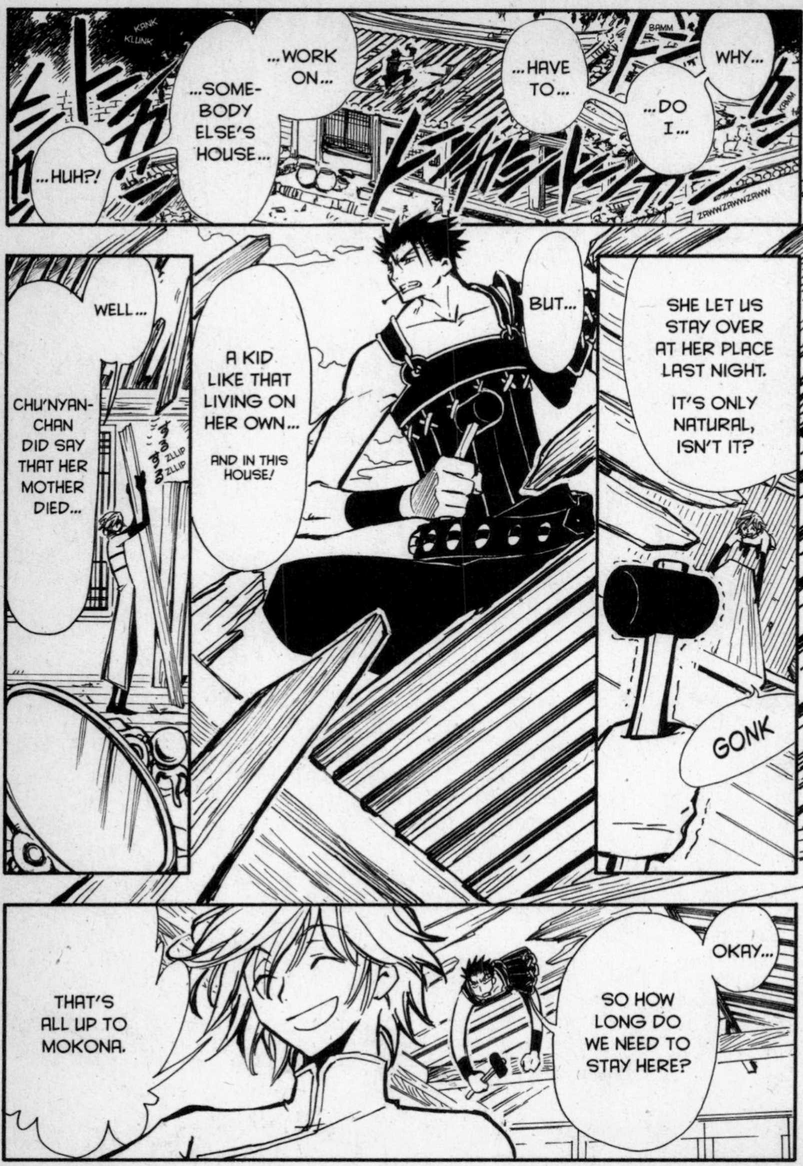
WHY...
BAMM
...DO I...
KRAMM
ZAWWZAWWZAWW
...HAVE TO...
...WORK ON...
...SOMEBODY ELSE'S HOUSE...
KANK KLUNK
...HUH?!
SHE LET US STAY OVER AT HER PLACE LAST NIGHT.
IT'S ONLY NATURAL, ISN'T IT?
GONK
BUT...
A KID LIKE THAT LIVING ON HER OWN...
AND IN THIS HOUSE!
WELL...
CHU'NYAN-CHAN DID SAY THAT HER MOTHER DIED...
するする
ZLLIP ZLLIP
OKAY...
SO HOW LONG DO WE NEED TO STAY HERE?
THAT'S ALL UP TO MOKONA.

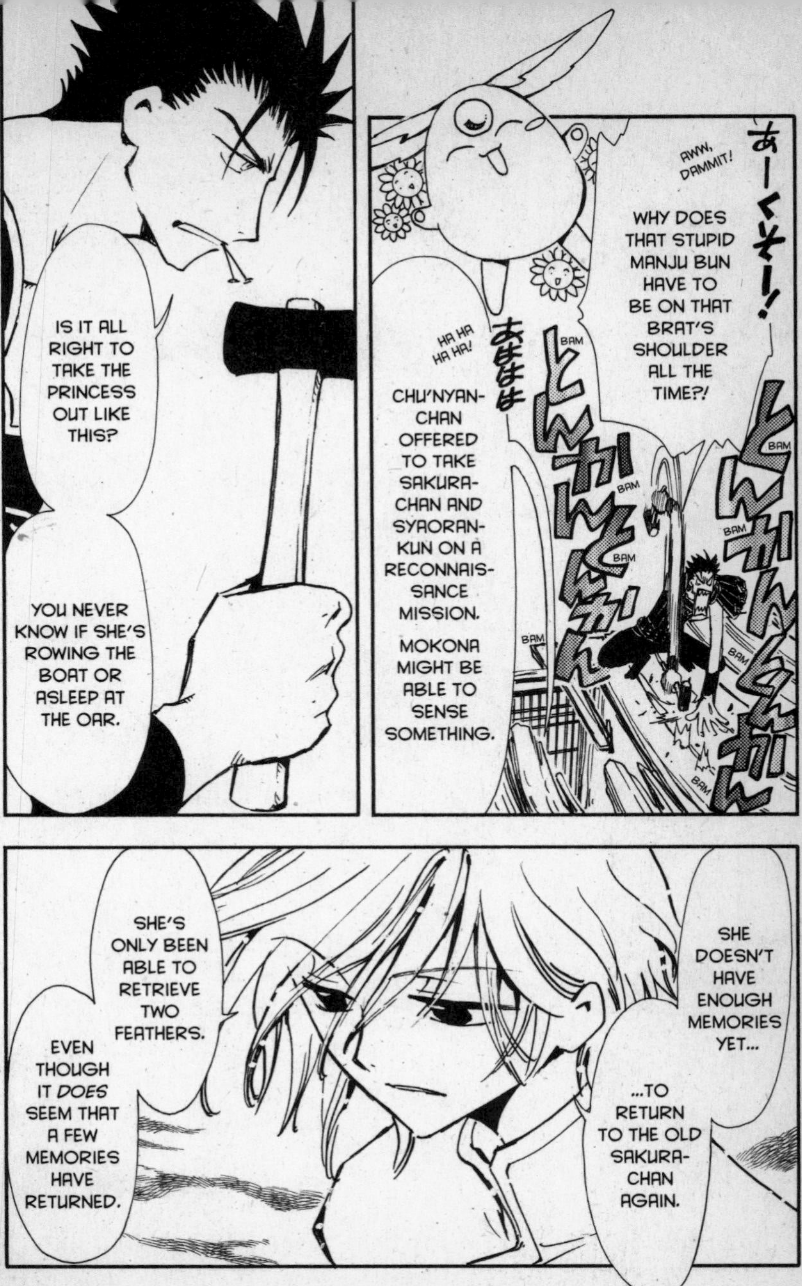

あーくそー!
AWW, DAMMIT!
WHY DOES THAT STUPID MANJU BUN HAVE TO BE ON THAT BRAT'S SHOULDER ALL THE TIME?!
とんがんとんがん
BAM BAM BAM BAM
とんがんとんがん
BAM BAM BAM BAM
あははは
HA HA HA HA!
CHU'NYAN-CHAN OFFERED TO TAKE SAKURA-CHAN AND SYAORAN-KUN ON A RECONNAIS-SANCE MISSION.
MOKONA MIGHT BE ABLE TO SENSE SOMETHING.
IS IT ALL RIGHT TO TAKE THE PRINCESS OUT LIKE THIS?
YOU NEVER KNOW IF SHE'S ROWING THE BOAT OR ASLEEP AT THE OAR.
SHE DOESN'T HAVE ENOUGH MEMORIES YET...
...TO RETURN TO THE OLD SAKURA-CHAN AGAIN.
SHE'S ONLY BEEN ABLE TO RETRIEVE TWO FEATHERS.
EVEN THOUGH IT *DOES* SEEM THAT A FEW MEMORIES HAVE RETURNED.

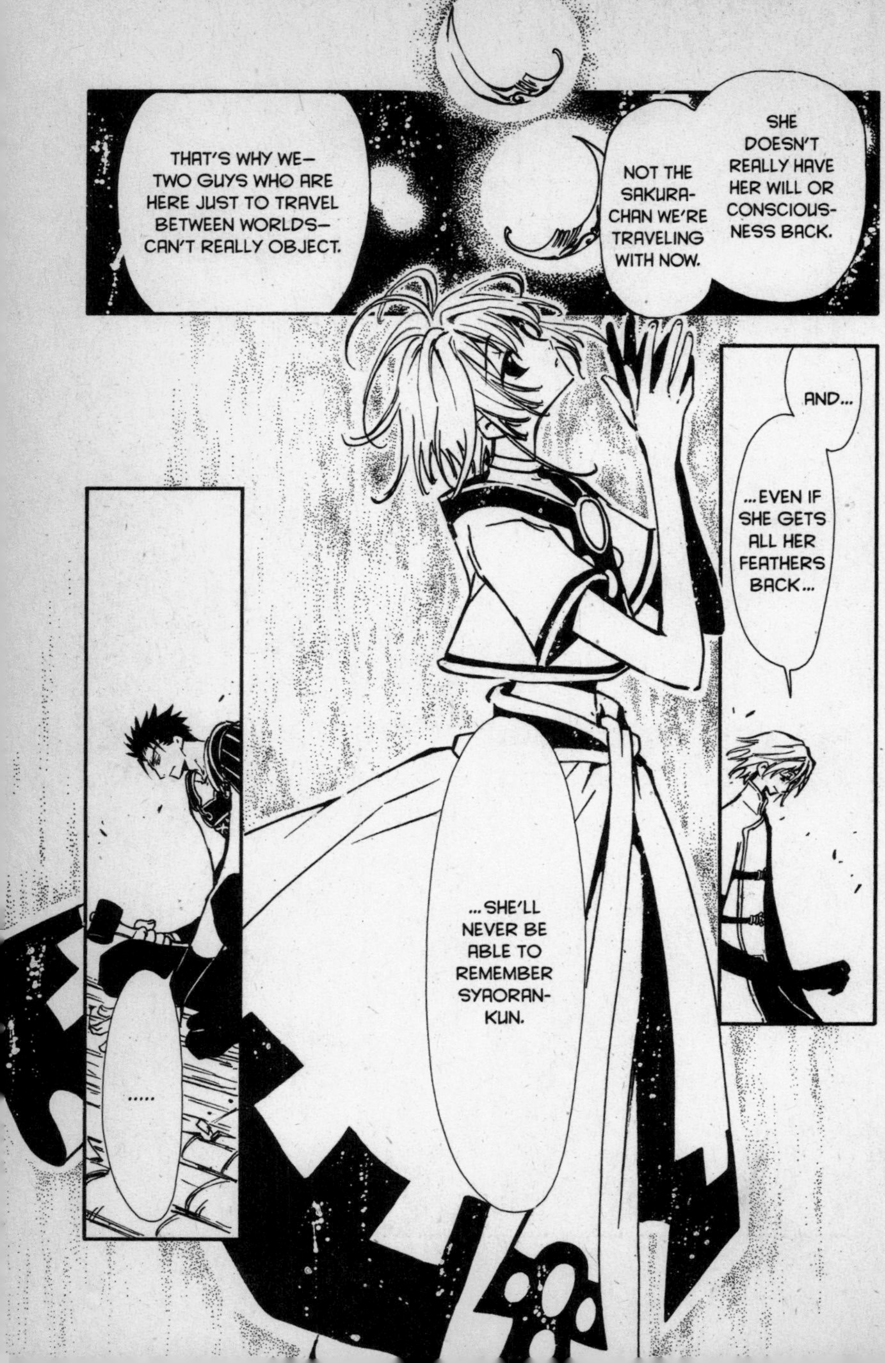
SHE DOESN'T REALLY HAVE HER WILL OR CONSCIOUS-NESS BACK.
NOT THE SAKURA-CHAN WE'RE TRAVELING WITH NOW.
THAT'S WHY WE— TWO GUYS WHO ARE HERE JUST TO TRAVEL BETWEEN WORLDS— CAN'T REALLY OBJECT.
AND...
...EVEN IF SHE GETS ALL HER FEATHERS BACK...
...SHE'LL NEVER BE ABLE TO REMEMBER SYAORAN-KUN.
.....

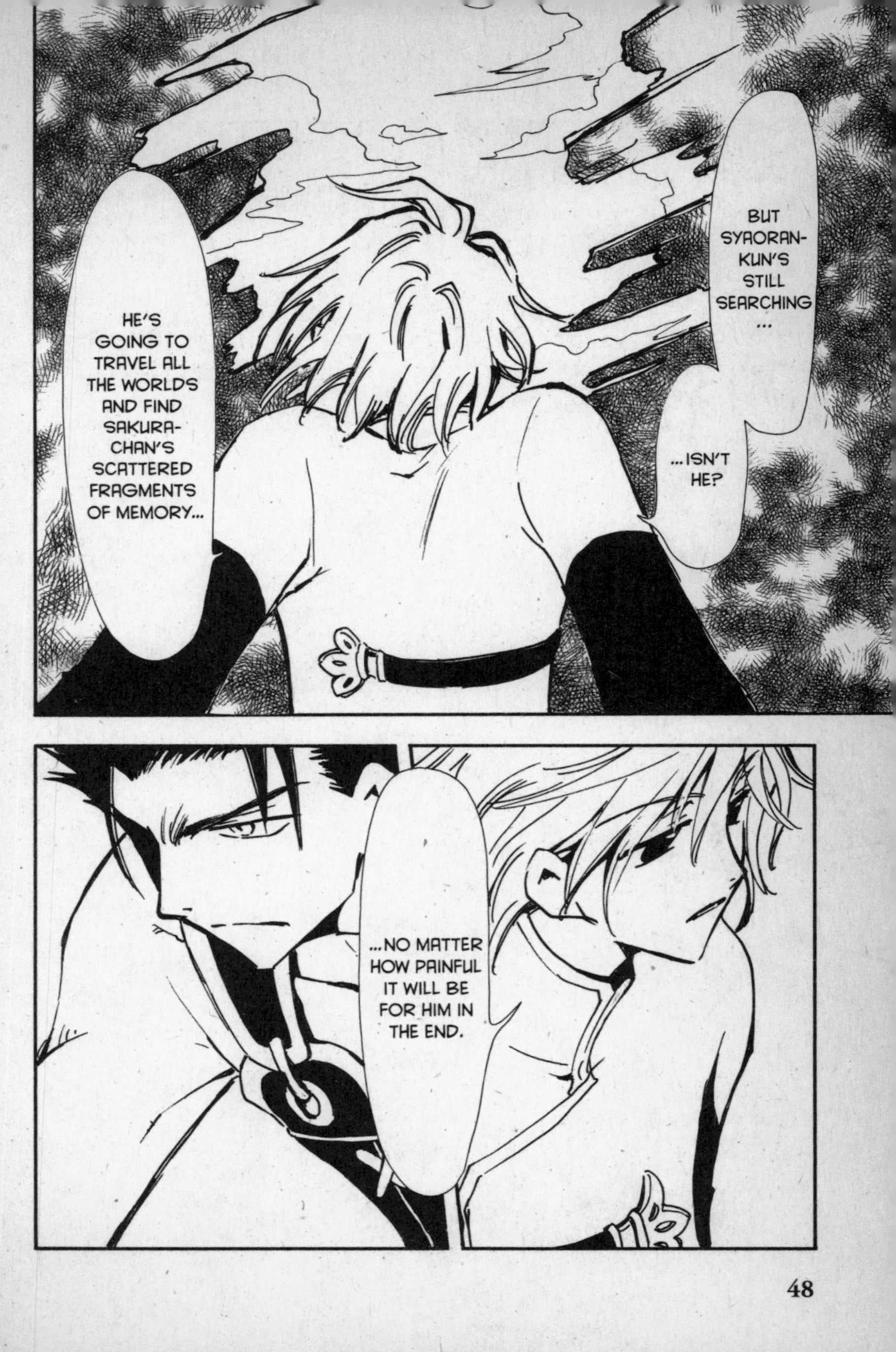
BUT SYAORAN-KUN'S STILL SEARCHING ...
...ISN'T HE?
HE'S GOING TO TRAVEL ALL THE WORLDS AND FIND SAKURA-CHAN'S SCATTERED FRAGMENTS OF MEMORY...
...NO MATTER HOW PAINFUL IT WILL BE FOR HIM IN THE END.

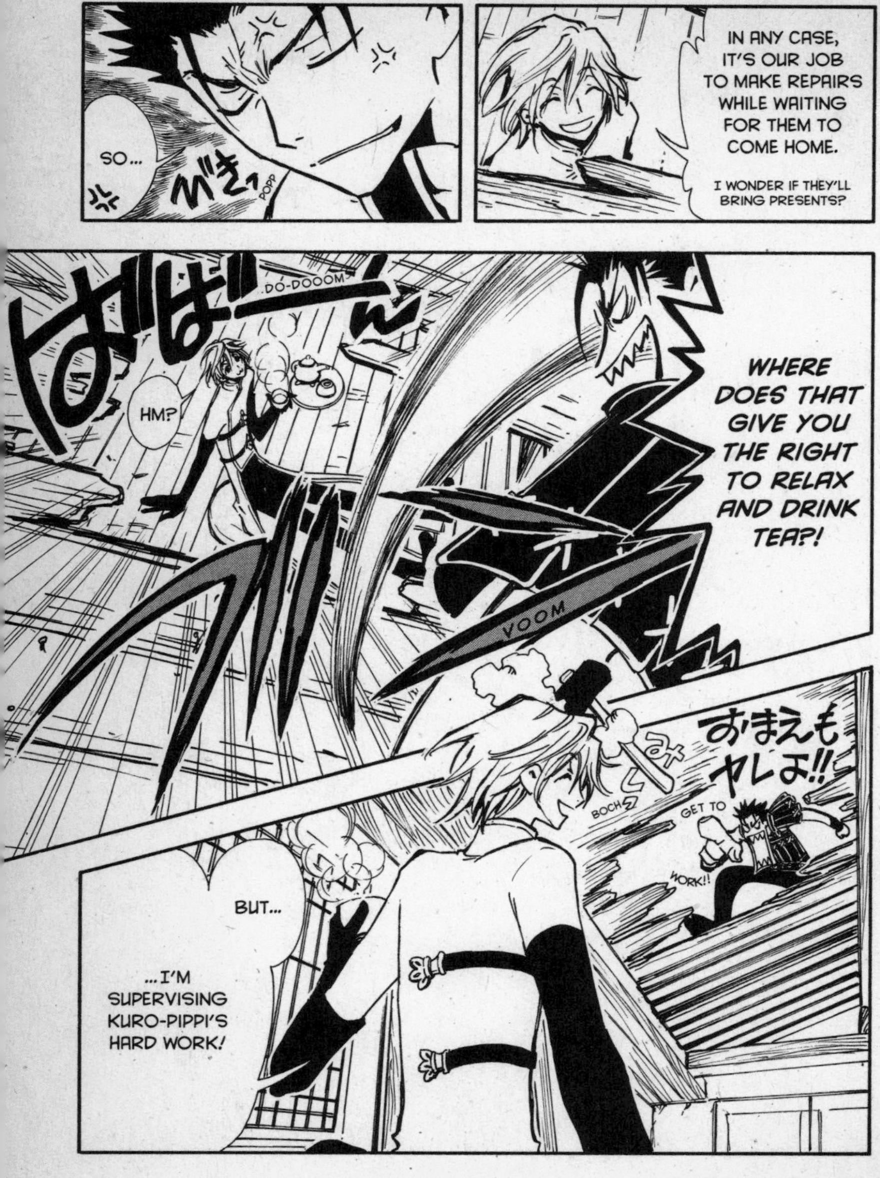
IN ANY CASE, IT'S OUR JOB TO MAKE REPAIRS WHILE WAITING FOR THEM TO COME HOME.
I WONDER IF THEY'LL BRING PRESENTS?
SO...
POPP
WHERE DOES THAT GIVE YOU THE RIGHT TO RELAX AND DRINK TEA?!
DO-DOOOM
HM?
VOOM
おまえもヤレよ!!
GET TO WORK!!
BOCH
BUT...
...I'M SUPERVISING KURO-PIPPI'S HARD WORK!

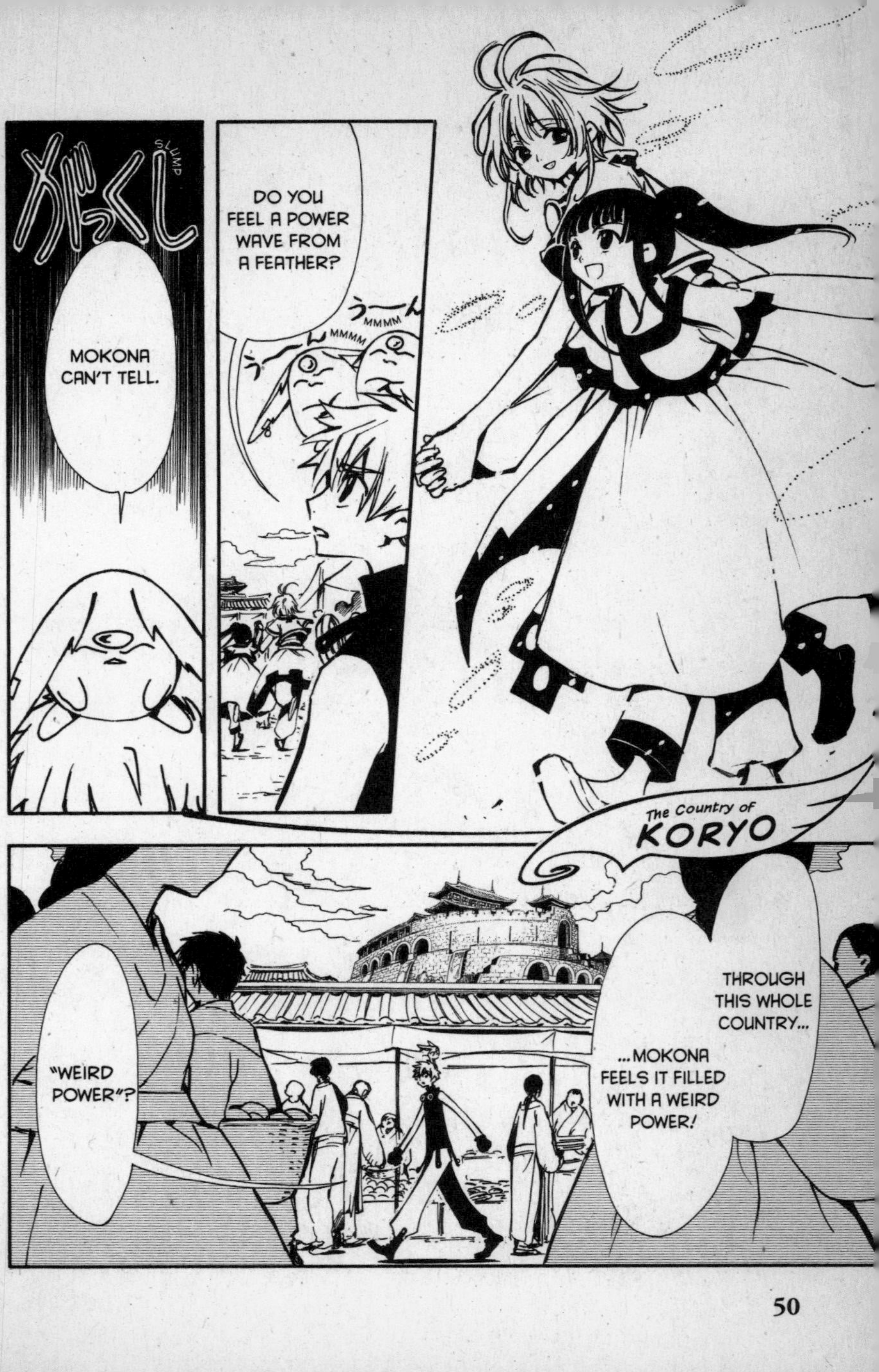
DO YOU FEEL A POWER WAVE FROM A FEATHER?
うーん MMMM
うーん MMMM
がっくし SLUMP
MOKONA CAN'T TELL.
The Country of KORYO
THROUGH THIS WHOLE COUNTRY...
...MOKONA FEELS IT FILLED WITH A WEIRD POWER!
"WEIRD POWER"?

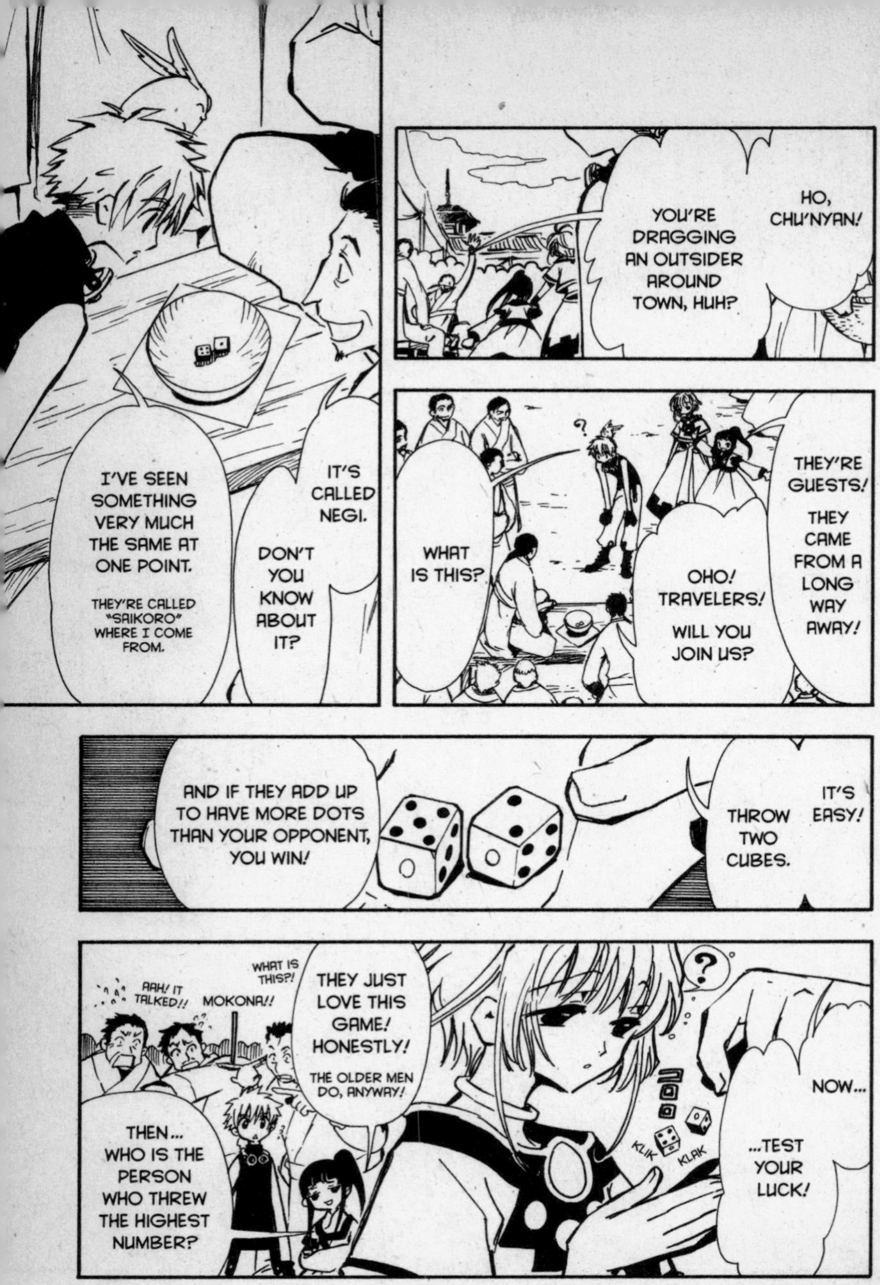
HO, CHU'NYAN!
YOU'RE DRAGGING AN OUTSIDER AROUND TOWN, HUH?
THEY'RE GUESTS!
THEY CAME FROM A LONG WAY AWAY!
OHO! TRAVELERS!
WILL YOU JOIN US?
WHAT IS THIS?
IT'S CALLED NEGI.
DON'T YOU KNOW ABOUT IT?
I'VE SEEN SOMETHING VERY MUCH THE SAME AT ONE POINT.
THEY'RE CALLED "SAIKORO" WHERE I COME FROM.
IT'S EASY!
THROW TWO CUBES.
AND IF THEY ADD UP TO HAVE MORE DOTS THAN YOUR OPPONENT, YOU WIN!
NOW...
...TEST YOUR LUCK!
KLIK
KLAK
THEY JUST LOVE THIS GAME! HONESTLY!
THE OLDER MEN DO, ANYWAY!
WHAT IS THIS?!
MOKONA!!
AAH! IT TALKED!!
THEN... WHO IS THE PERSON WHO THREW THE HIGHEST NUMBER?

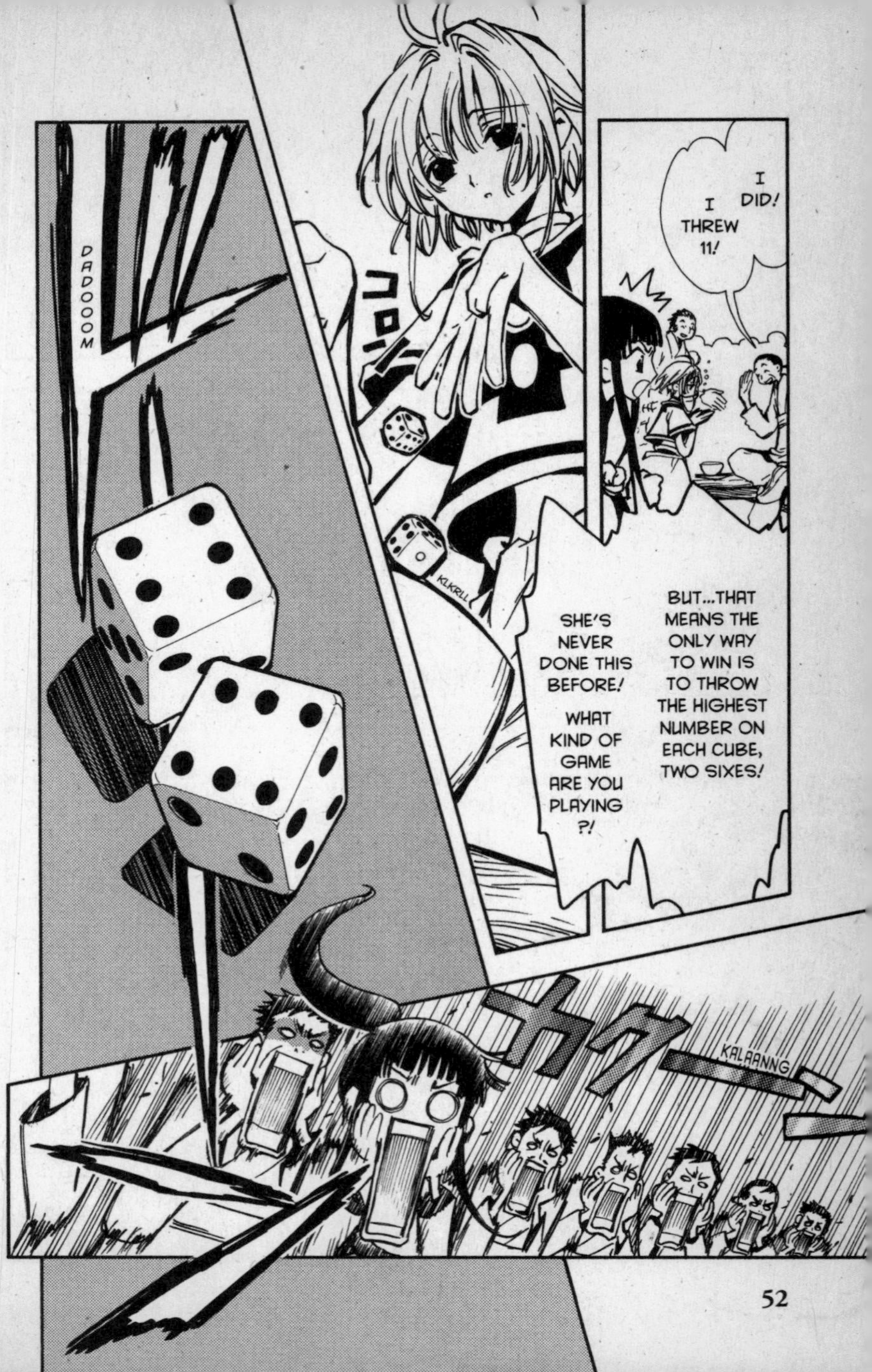
I DID!
I THREW 11!
コロン
KLKRLL
BUT...THAT MEANS THE ONLY WAY TO WIN IS TO THROW THE HIGHEST NUMBER ON EACH CUBE, TWO SIXES!
SHE'S NEVER DONE THIS BEFORE!
WHAT KIND OF GAME ARE YOU PLAYING ?!
DADOOOM
KALAANNG

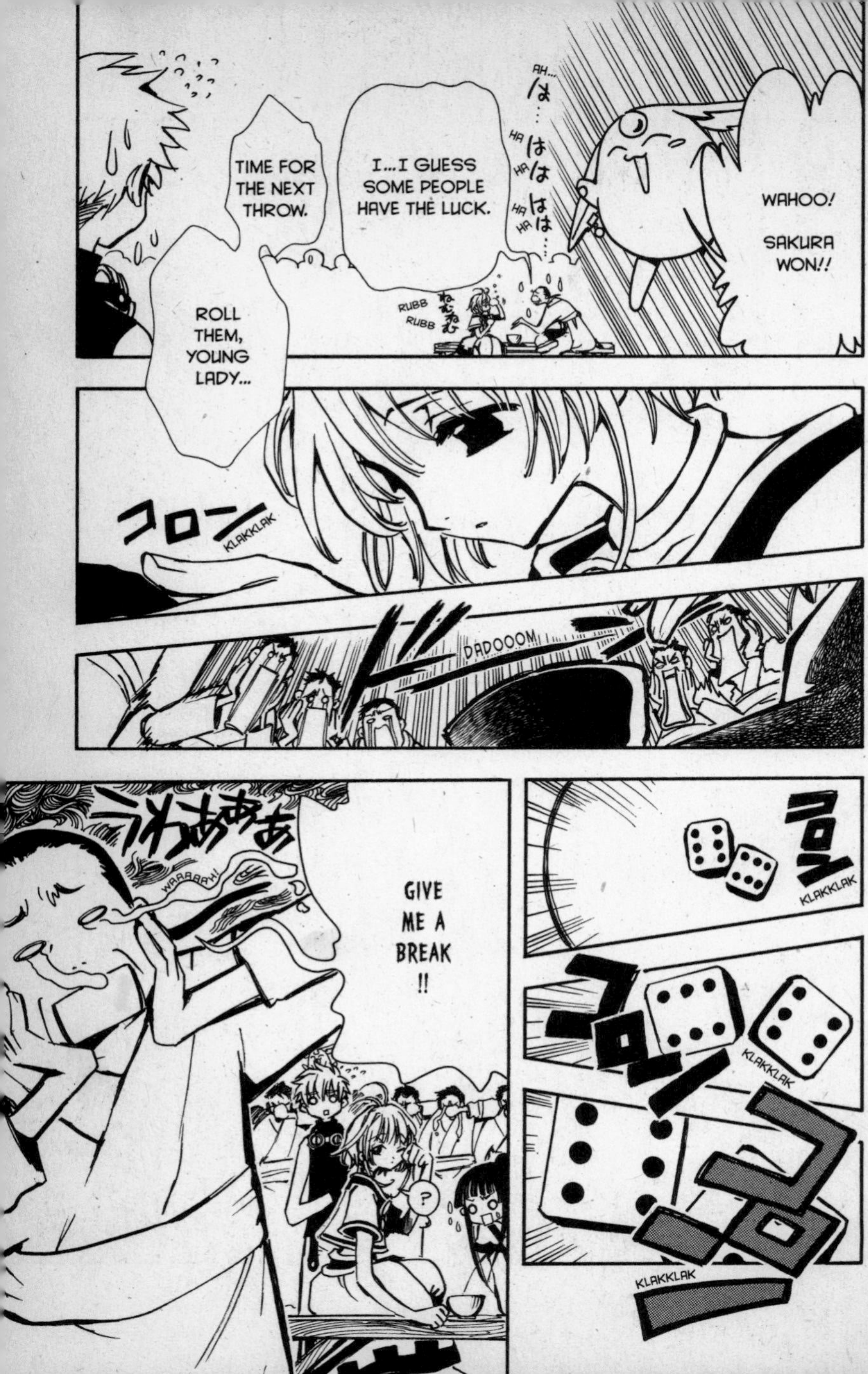
WAHOO!
SAKURA WON!!
AH...
は...
HA HA HA HA
ははは...
I...I GUESS SOME PEOPLE HAVE THE LUCK.
TIME FOR THE NEXT THROW.
RUBB RUBB
ROLL THEM, YOUNG LADY...
コロン
KLAKKLAK
DADOOOM
KLAKKLAK
KLAKKLAK
KLAKKLAK
WAAAAAH!
GIVE ME A BREAK!!

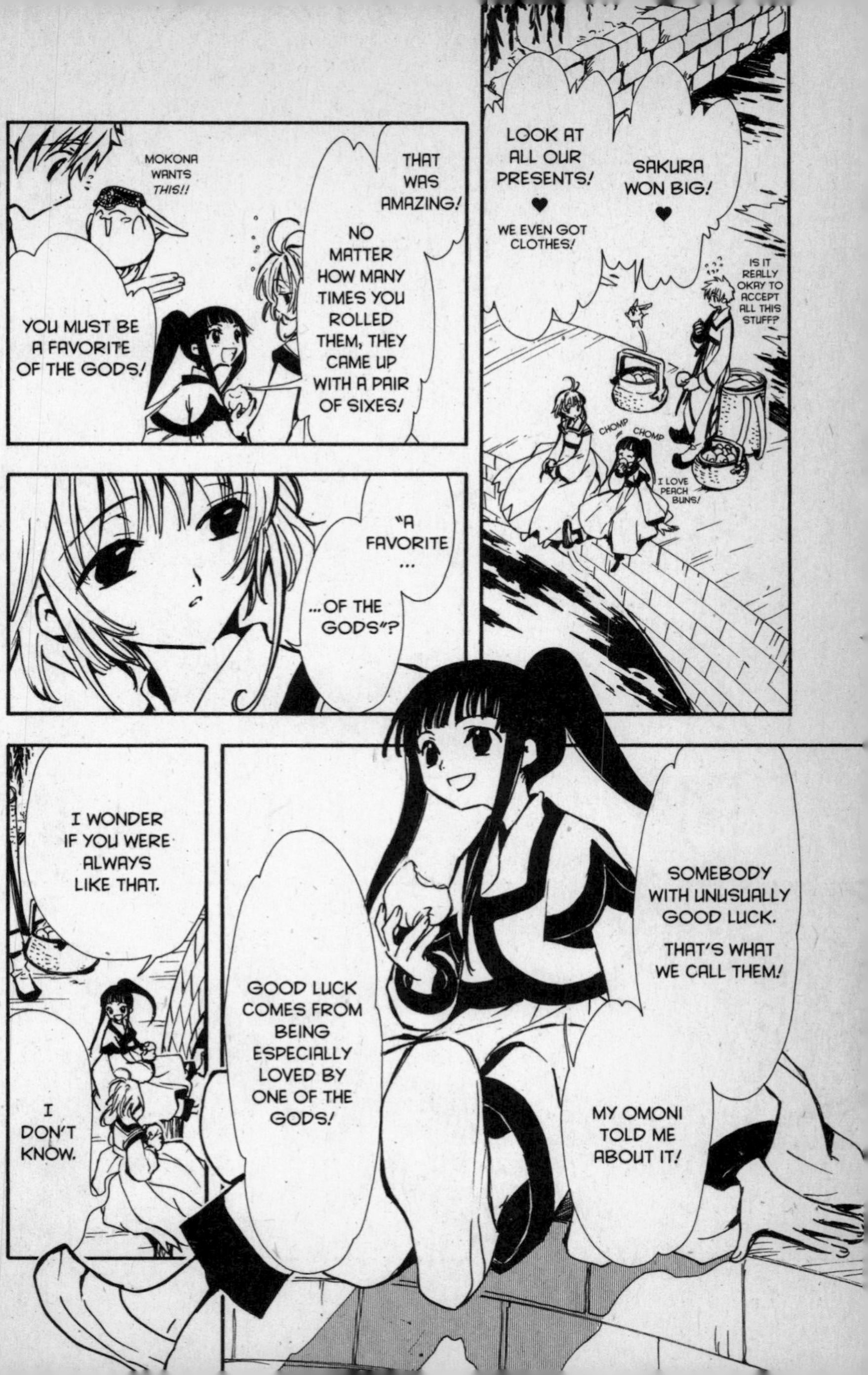
SAKURA WON BIG! ♥
LOOK AT ALL OUR PRESENTS! ♥
WE EVEN GOT CLOTHES!
IS IT REALLY OKAY TO ACCEPT ALL THIS STUFF?
CHOMP CHOMP
I LOVE PEACH BUNS!
THAT WAS AMAZING!
NO MATTER HOW MANY TIMES YOU ROLLED THEM, THEY CAME UP WITH A PAIR OF SIXES!
MOKONA WANTS *THIS!!*
YOU MUST BE A FAVORITE OF THE GODS!
"A FAVORITE...
...OF THE GODS"?
SOMEBODY WITH UNUSUALLY GOOD LUCK.
THAT'S WHAT WE CALL THEM!
MY OMONI TOLD ME ABOUT IT!
GOOD LUCK COMES FROM BEING ESPECIALLY LOVED BY ONE OF THE GODS!
I WONDER IF YOU WERE ALWAYS LIKE THAT.
I DON'T KNOW.

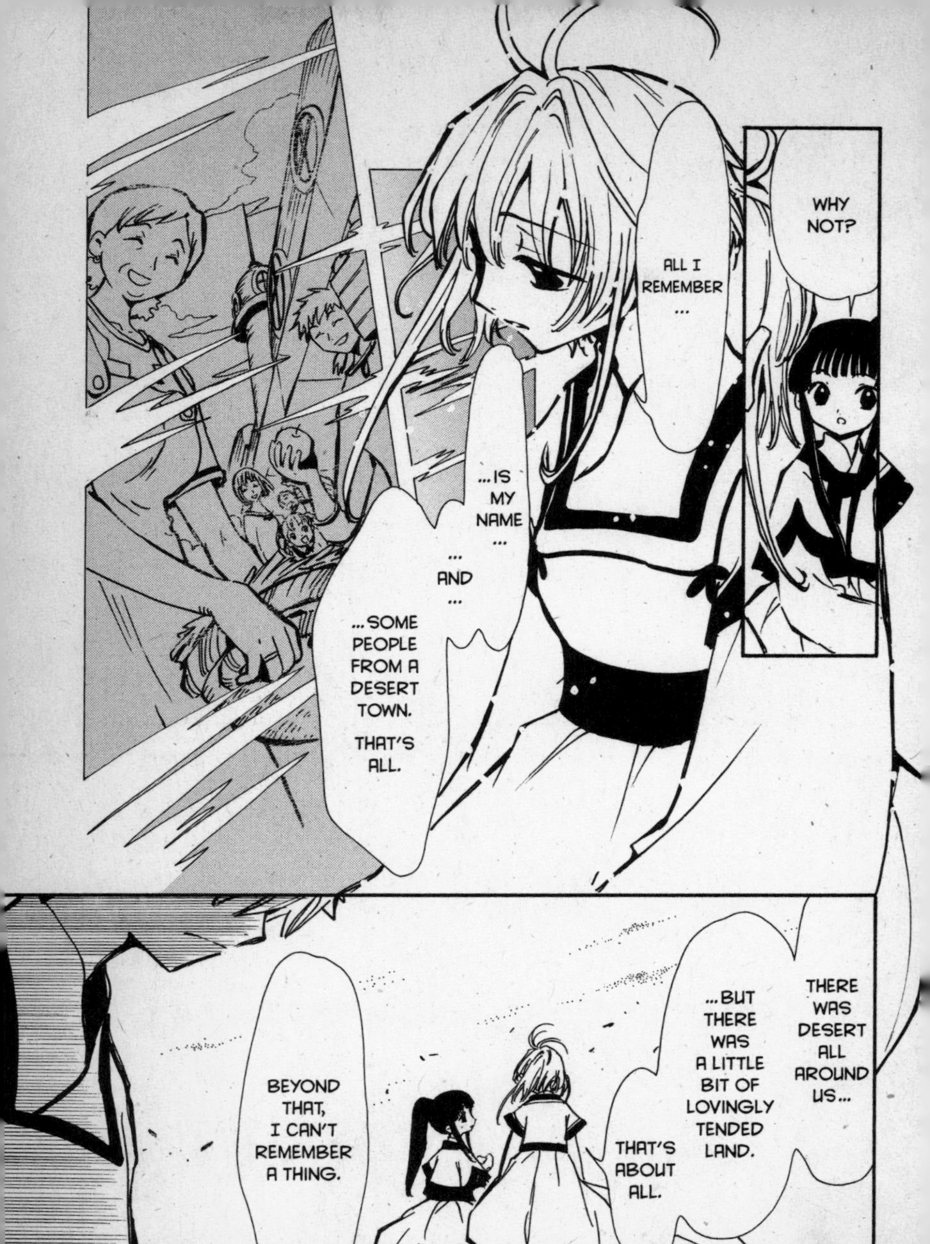
WHY NOT?
ALL I REMEMBER ...
...IS MY NAME ...
... AND ...
...SOME PEOPLE FROM A DESERT TOWN.
THAT'S ALL.
THERE WAS DESERT ALL AROUND US...
...BUT THERE WAS A LITTLE BIT OF LOVINGLY TENDED LAND.
THAT'S ABOUT ALL.
BEYOND THAT, I CAN'T REMEMBER A THING.

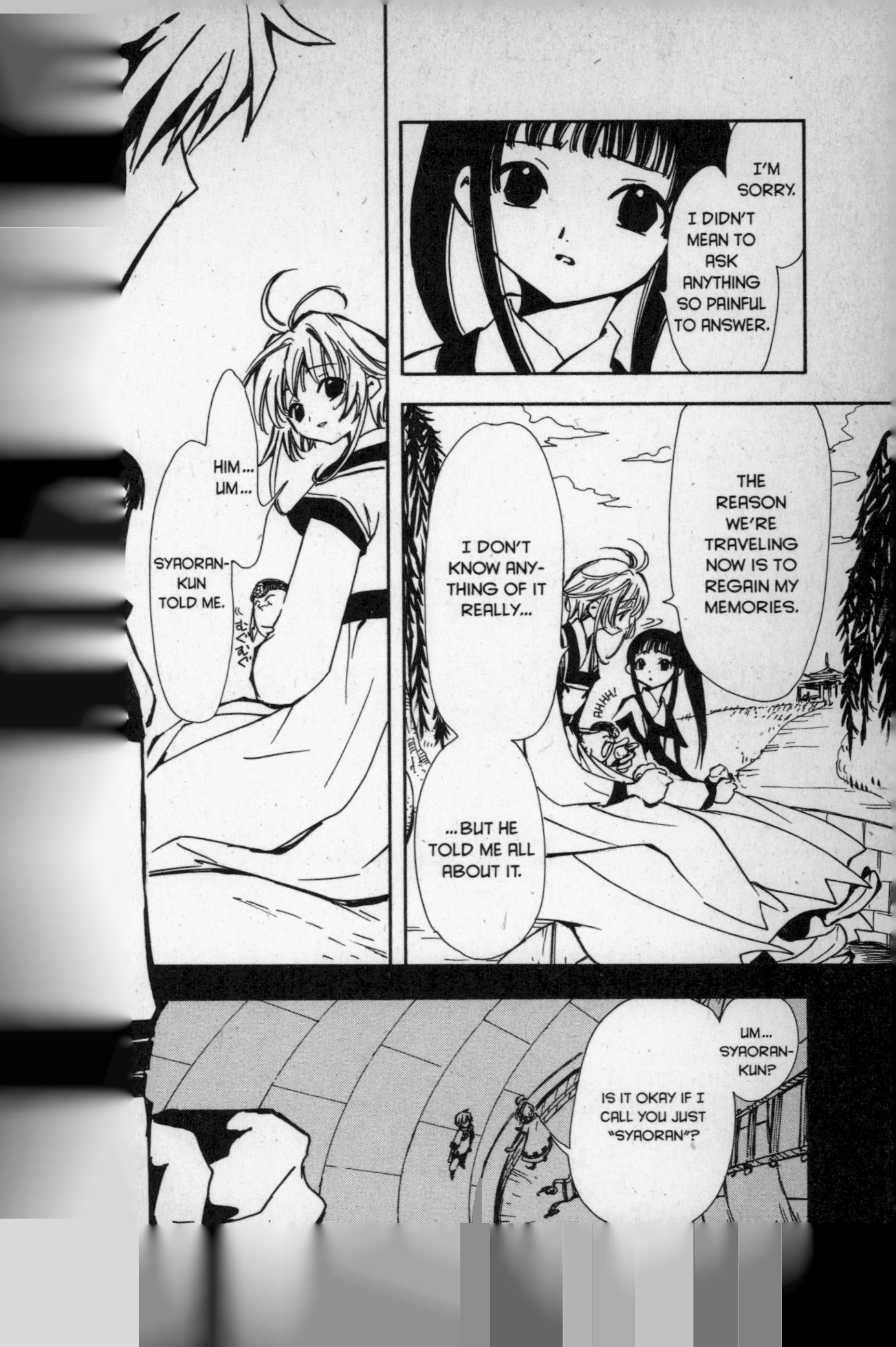
I'M SORRY.
I DIDN'T MEAN TO ASK ANYTHING SO PAINFUL TO ANSWER.
THE REASON WE'RE TRAVELING NOW IS TO REGAIN MY MEMORIES.
I DON'T KNOW ANY-THING OF IT REALLY...
...BUT HE TOLD ME ALL ABOUT IT.
HIM... UM...
SYAORAN-KUN TOLD ME.
UM... SYAORAN-KUN?
IS IT OKAY IF I CALL YOU JUST "SYAORAN"?

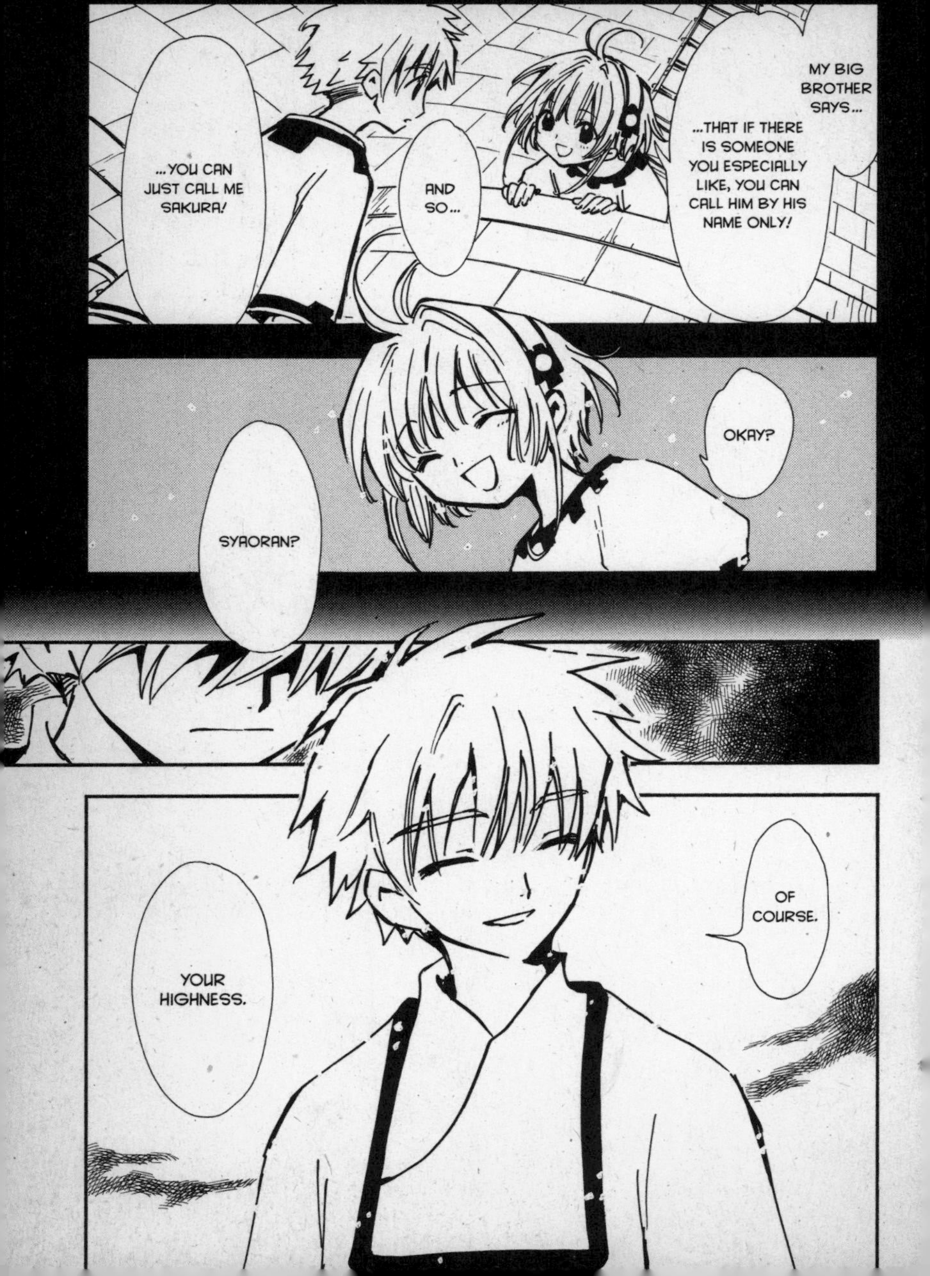
MY BIG BROTHER SAYS...
...THAT IF THERE IS SOMEONE YOU ESPECIALLY LIKE, YOU CAN CALL HIM BY HIS NAME ONLY!
AND SO...
...YOU CAN JUST CALL ME SAKURA!
OKAY?
SYAORAN?
OF COURSE.
YOUR HIGHNESS.

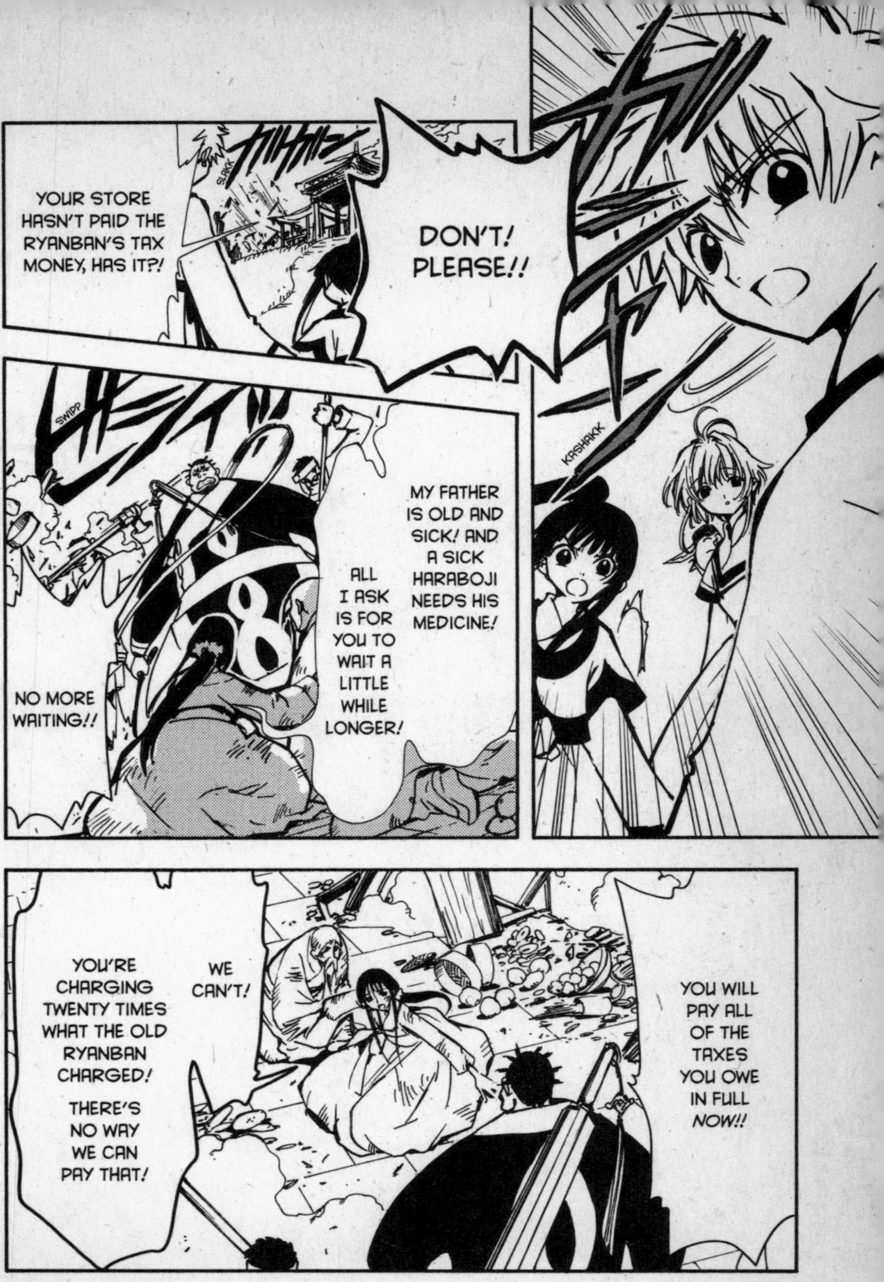
SLAKK
YOUR STORE HASN'T PAID THE RYANBAN'S TAX MONEY, HAS IT?!
DON'T! PLEASE!!
KASHAKK
SWIPP
MY FATHER IS OLD AND SICK! AND A SICK HARABOJI NEEDS HIS MEDICINE!
ALL I ASK IS FOR YOU TO WAIT A LITTLE WHILE LONGER!
NO MORE WAITING!!
YOU WILL PAY ALL OF THE TAXES YOU OWE IN FULL *NOW!!*
WE CAN'T!
YOU'RE CHARGING TWENTY TIMES WHAT THE OLD RYANBAN CHARGED!
THERE'S NO WAY WE CAN PAY THAT!

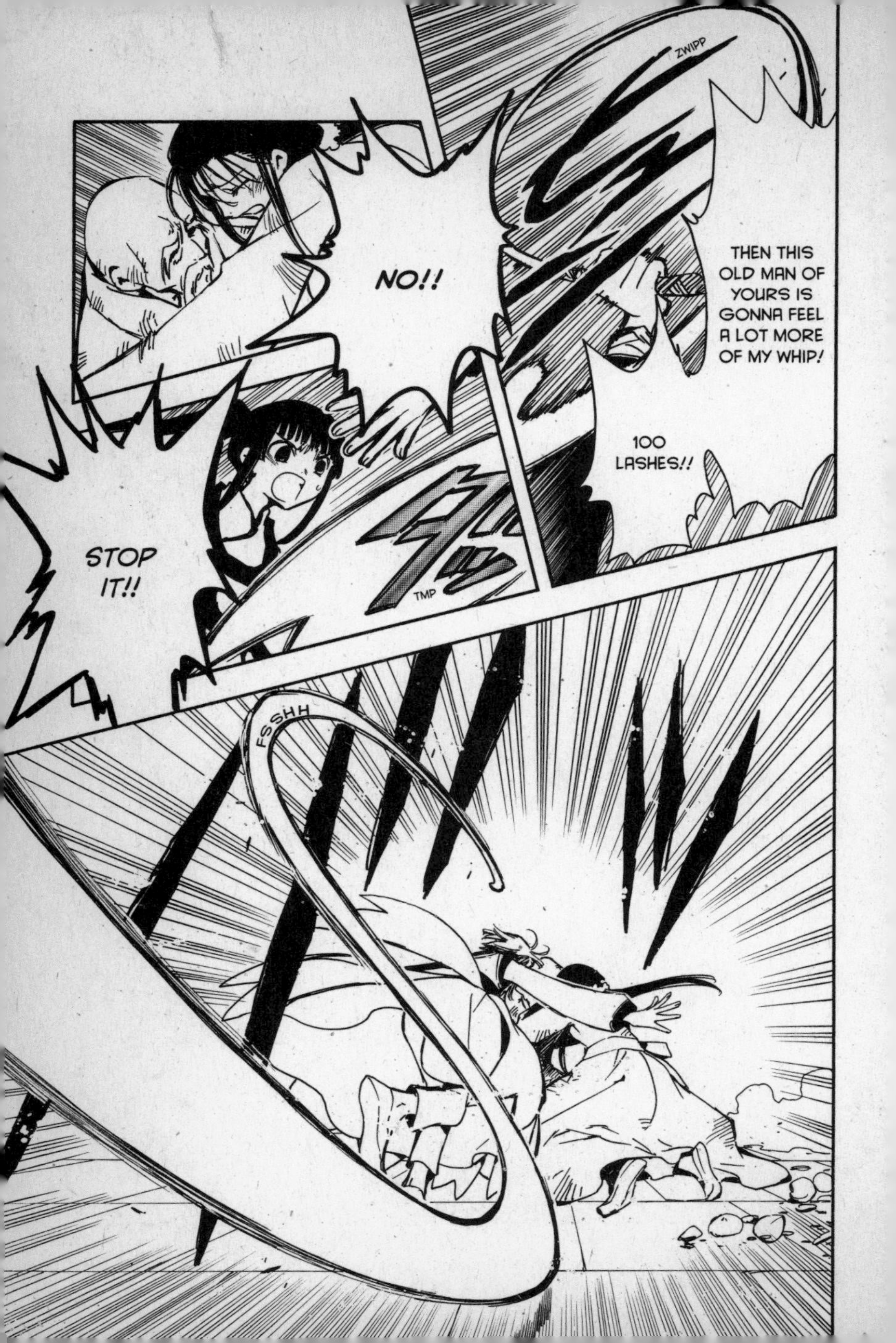
ZWIPP
THEN THIS OLD MAN OF YOURS IS GONNA FEEL A LOT MORE OF MY WHIP!
100 LASHES!!
NO!!
STOP IT!!
TMP
FSSHH

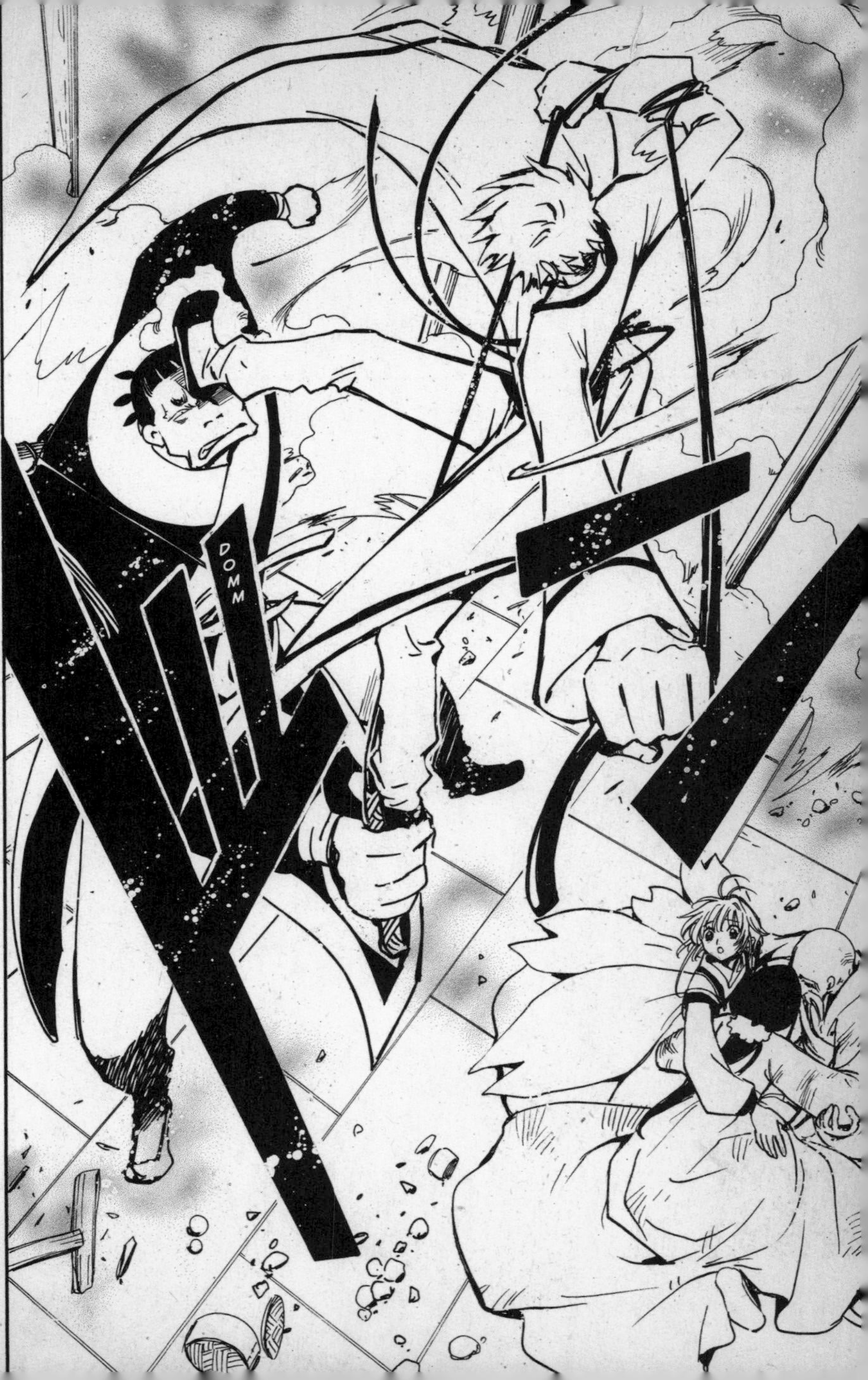
DOMM

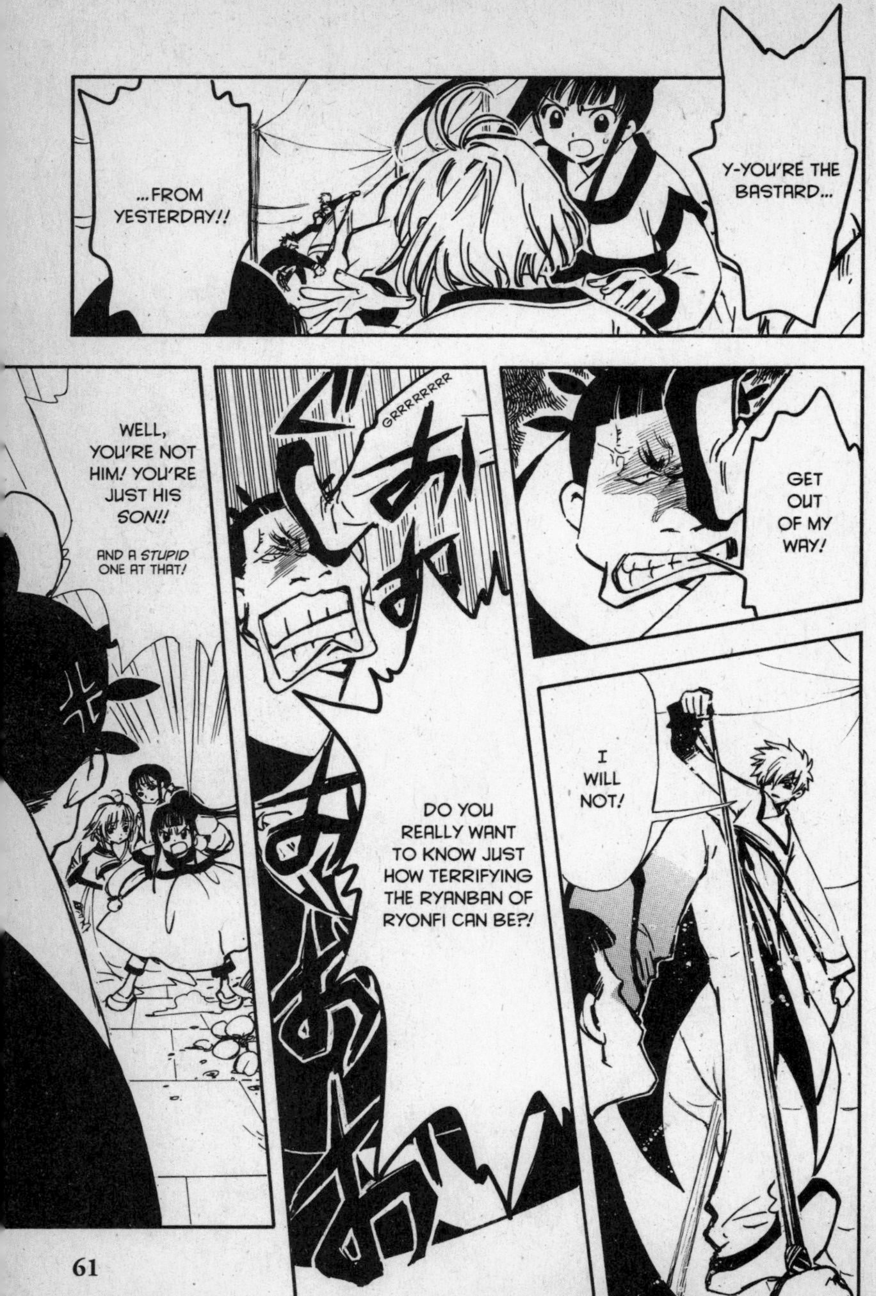
Y-YOU'RE THE BASTARD...
...FROM YESTERDAY!!
GET OUT OF MY WAY!
I WILL NOT!
GRRRRRRR
DO YOU REALLY WANT TO KNOW JUST HOW TERRIFYING THE RYANBAN OF RYONFI CAN BE?!
WELL, YOU'RE NOT HIM! YOU'RE JUST HIS *SON*!!
AND A *STUPID* ONE AT THAT!

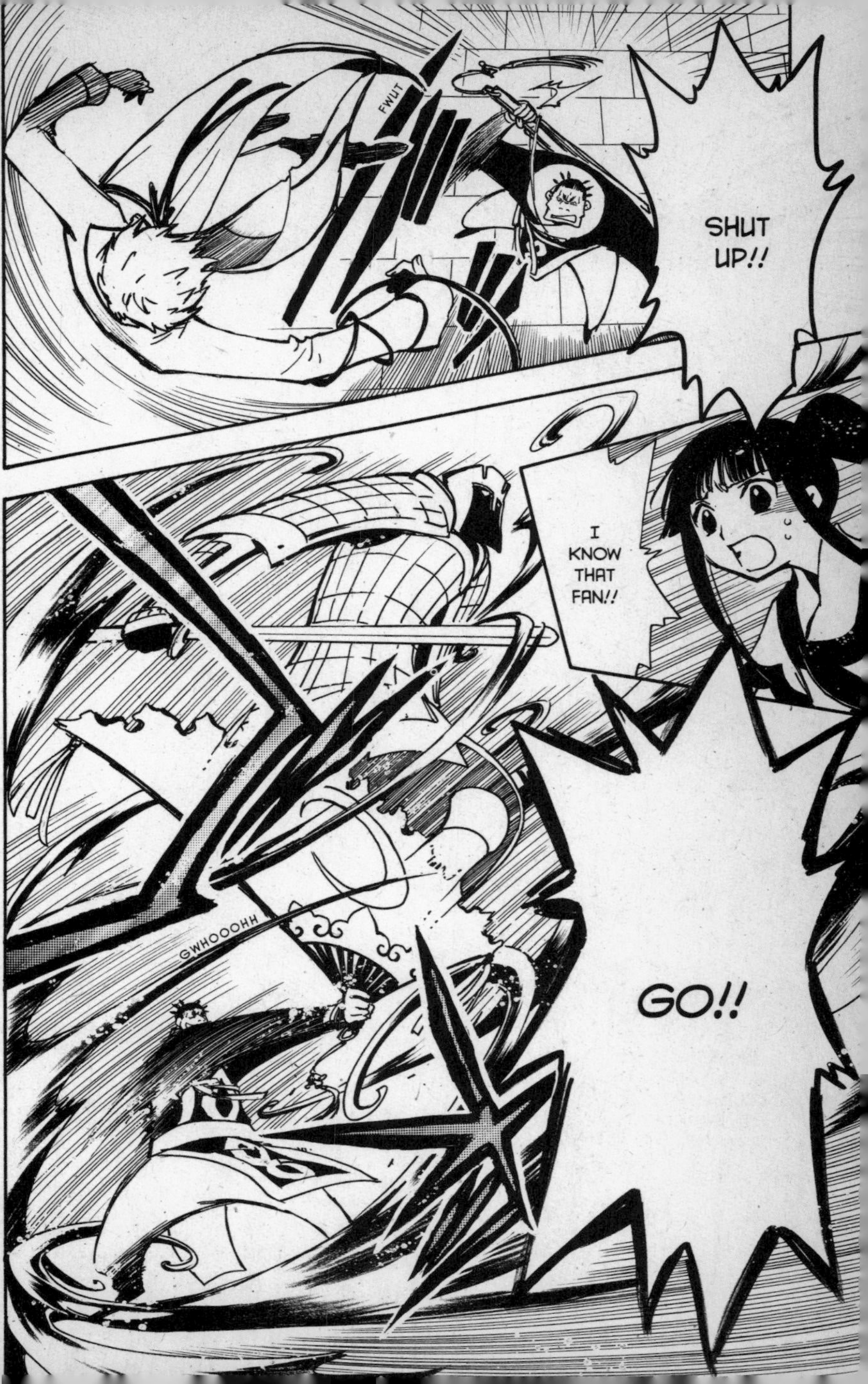
SHUT UP!!
FWUT
I KNOW THAT FAN!!
GO!!
GWHOOOHH

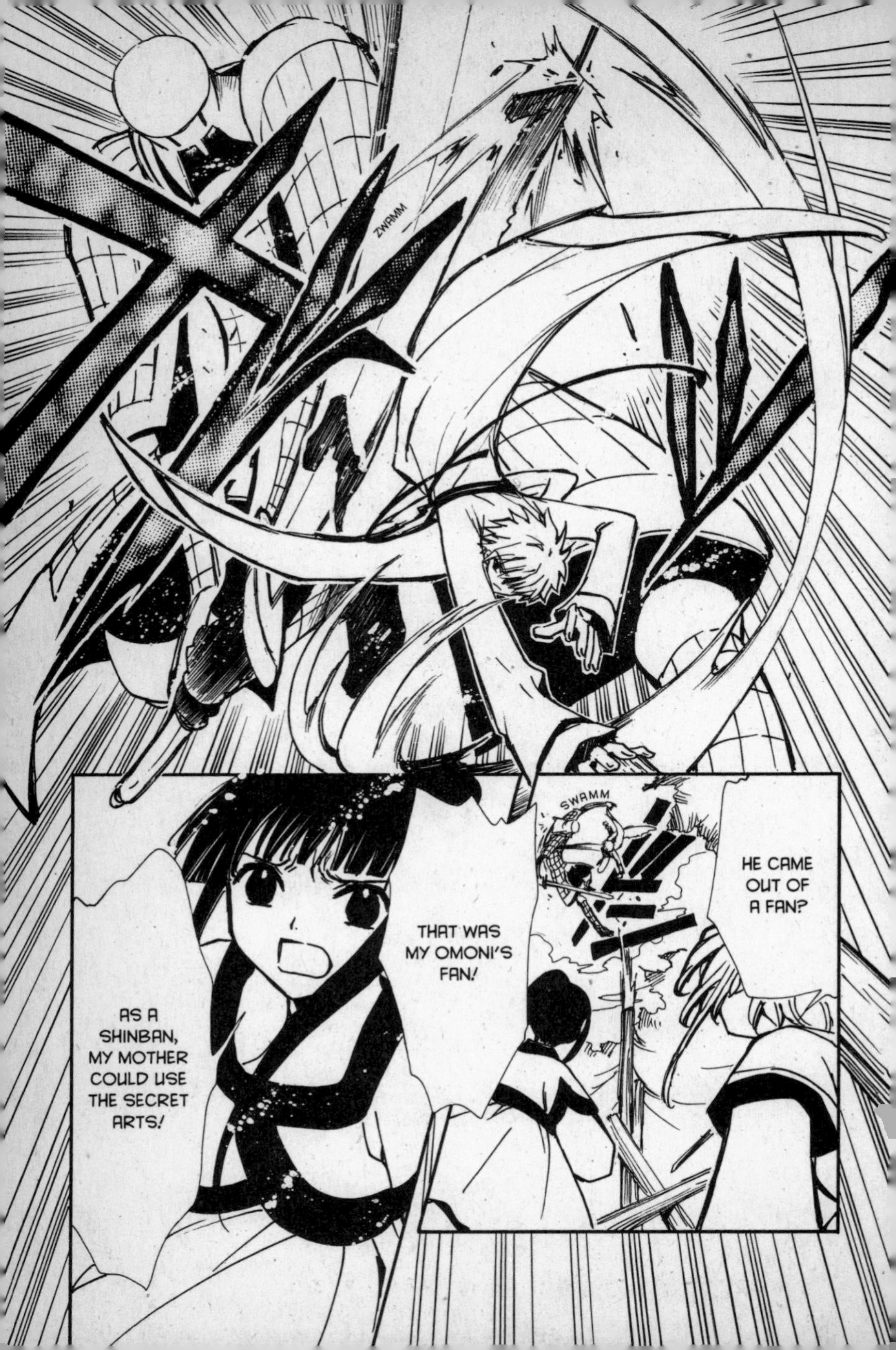
ZWAMM
SWAMM
HE CAME OUT OF A FAN?
THAT WAS MY OMONI'S FAN!
AS A SHINBAN, MY MOTHER COULD USE THE SECRET ARTS!

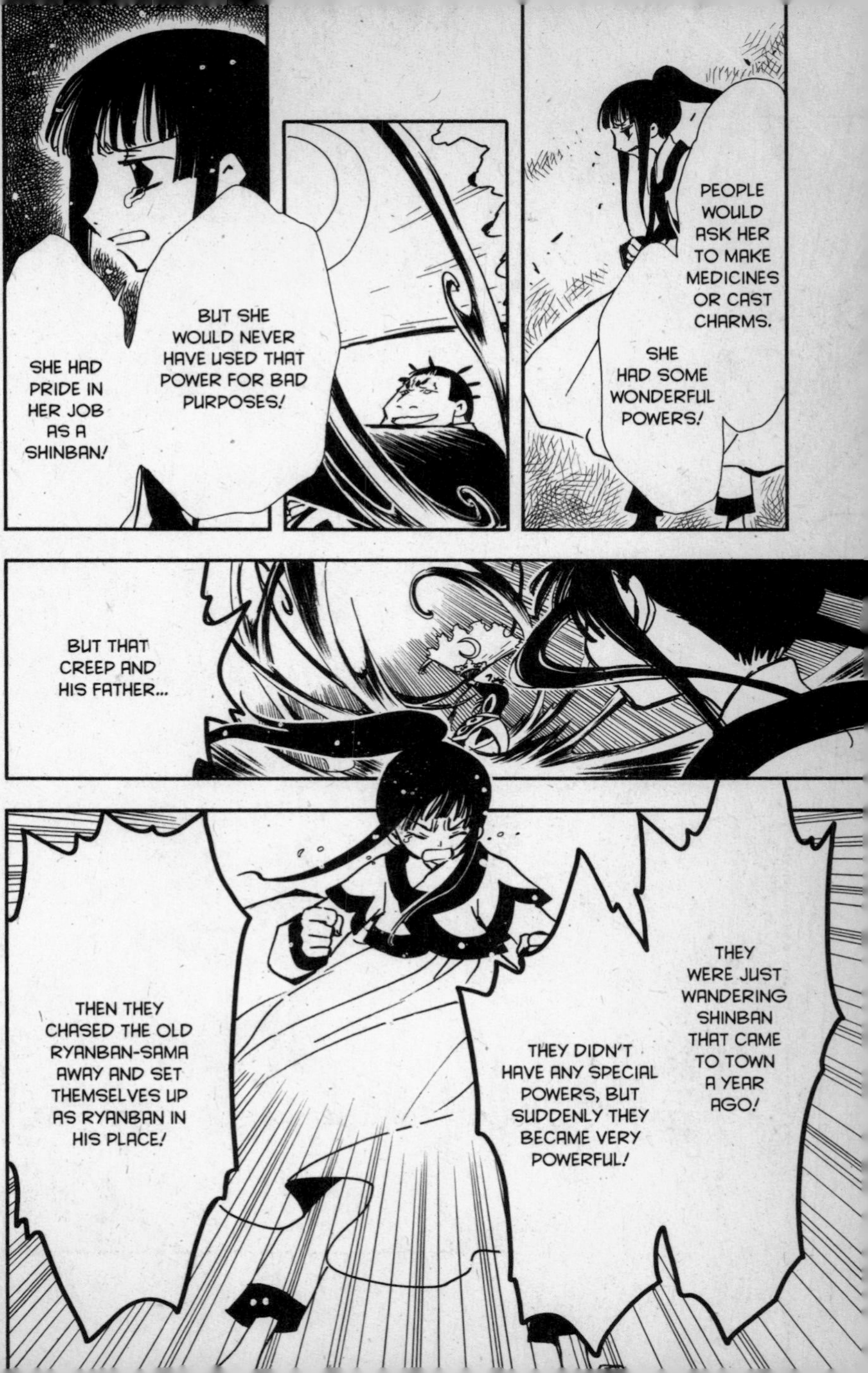
PEOPLE WOULD ASK HER TO MAKE MEDICINES OR CAST CHARMS.
SHE HAD SOME WONDERFUL POWERS!
BUT SHE WOULD NEVER HAVE USED THAT POWER FOR BAD PURPOSES!
SHE HAD PRIDE IN HER JOB AS A SHINBAN!
BUT THAT CREEP AND HIS FATHER...
THEY WERE JUST WANDERING SHINBAN THAT CAME TO TOWN A YEAR AGO!
THEY DIDN'T HAVE ANY SPECIAL POWERS, BUT SUDDENLY THEY BECAME VERY POWERFUL!
THEN THEY CHASED THE OLD RYANBAN-SAMA AWAY AND SET THEMSELVES UP AS RYANBAN IN HIS PLACE!

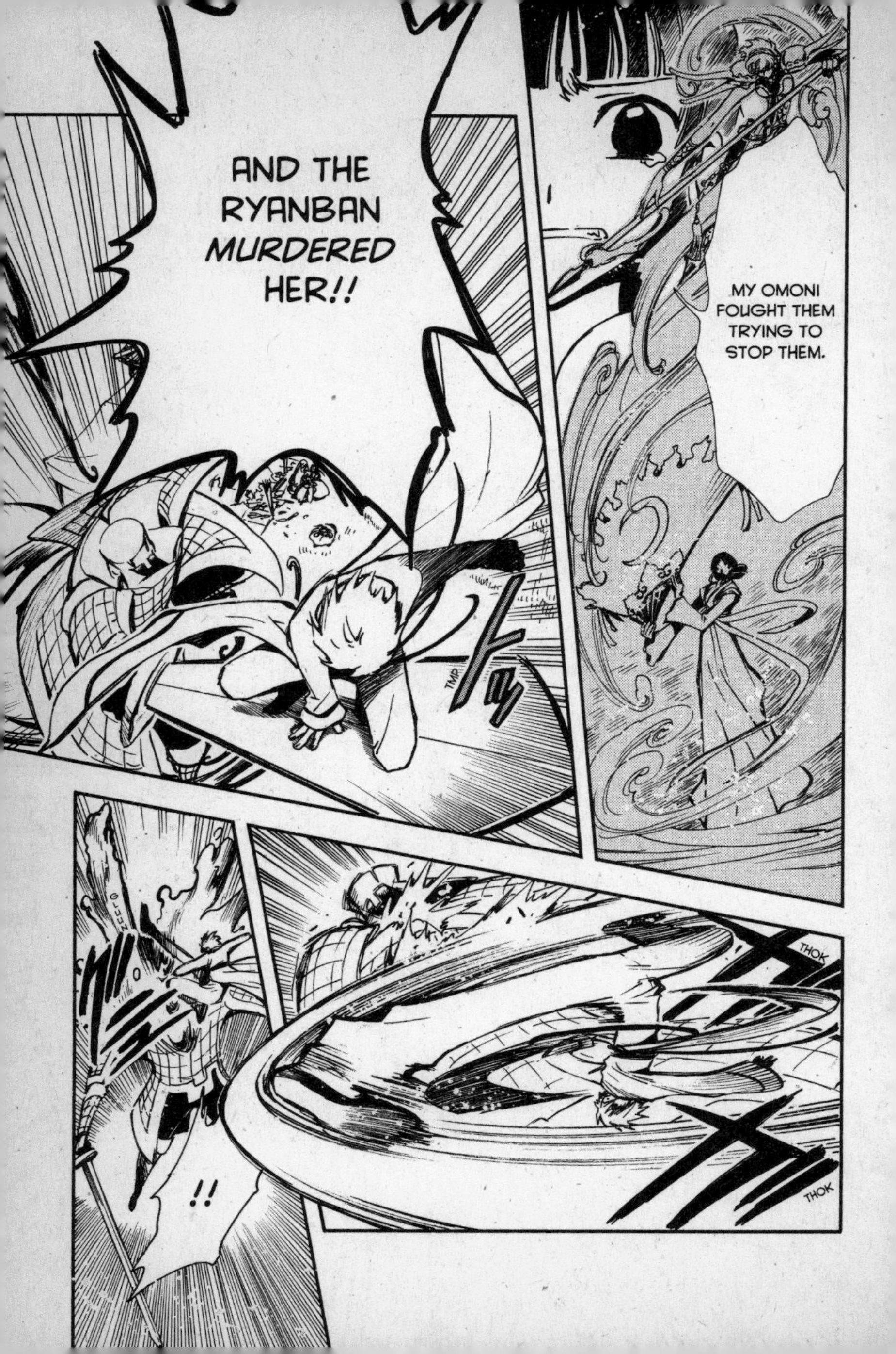
MY OMONI FOUGHT THEM TRYING TO STOP THEM.
AND THE RYANBAN *MURDERED* HER!!
TMP
THOK
THOK
!!

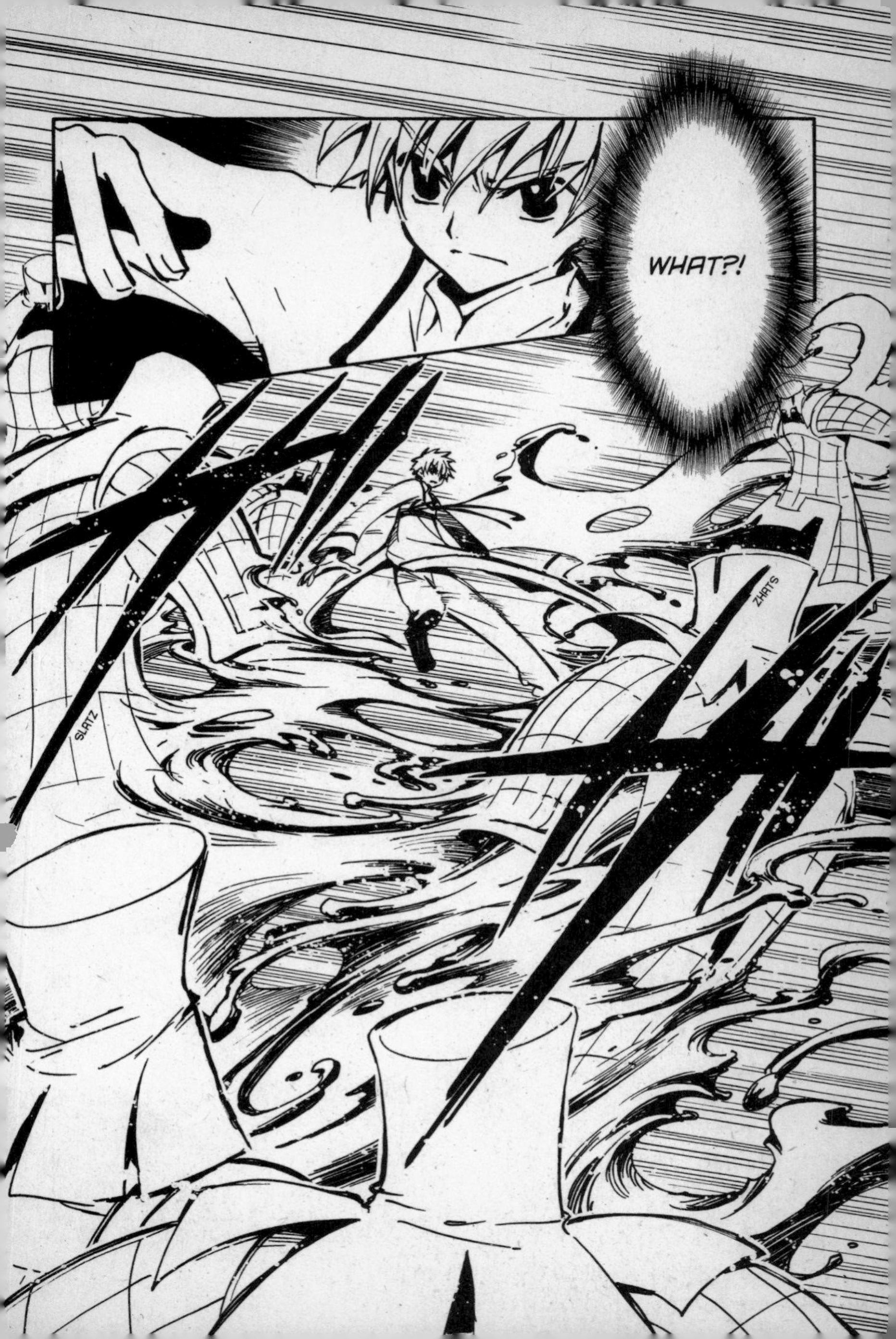
WHAT?!
ZHAT'S
SLATZ

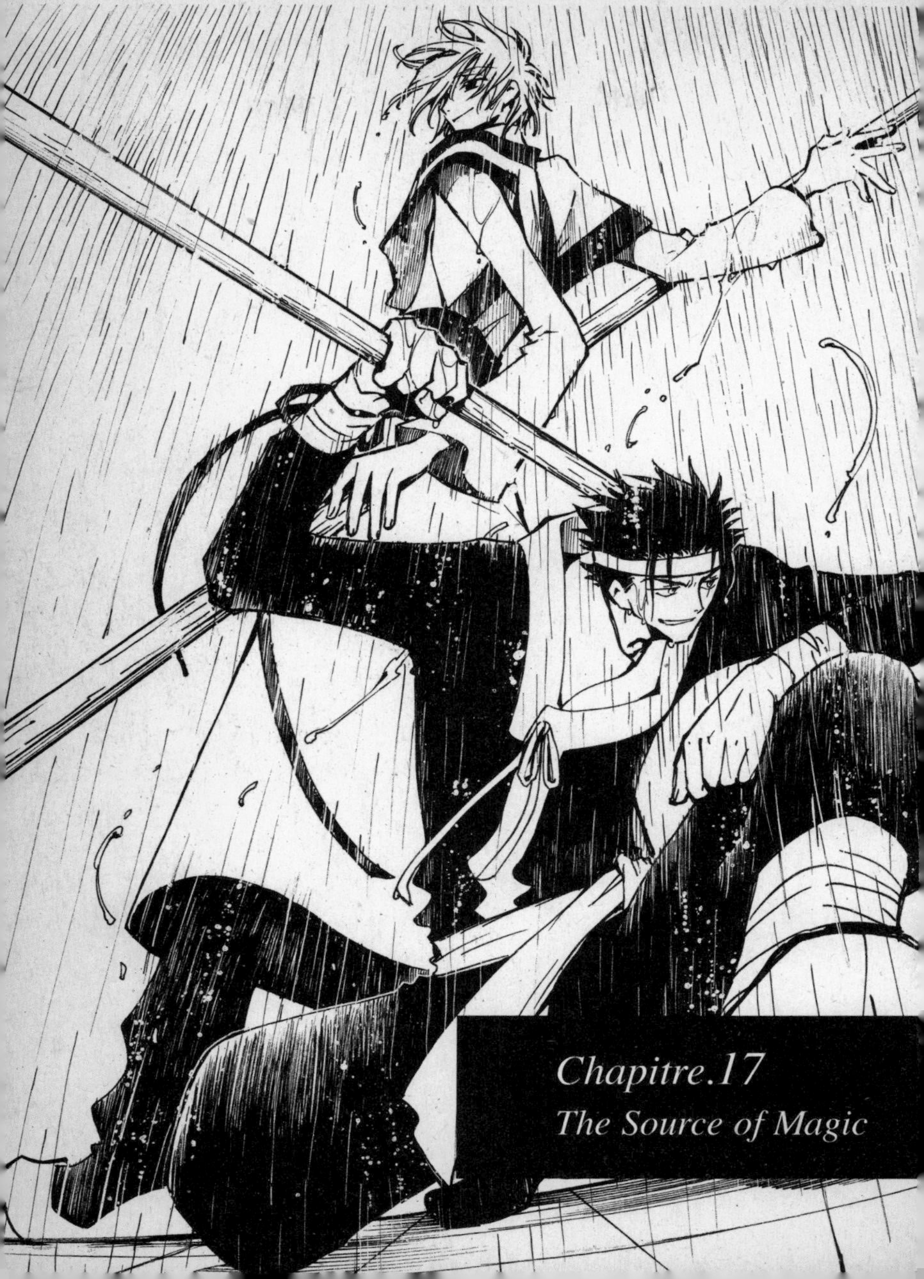

Chapitre.17
The Source of Magic

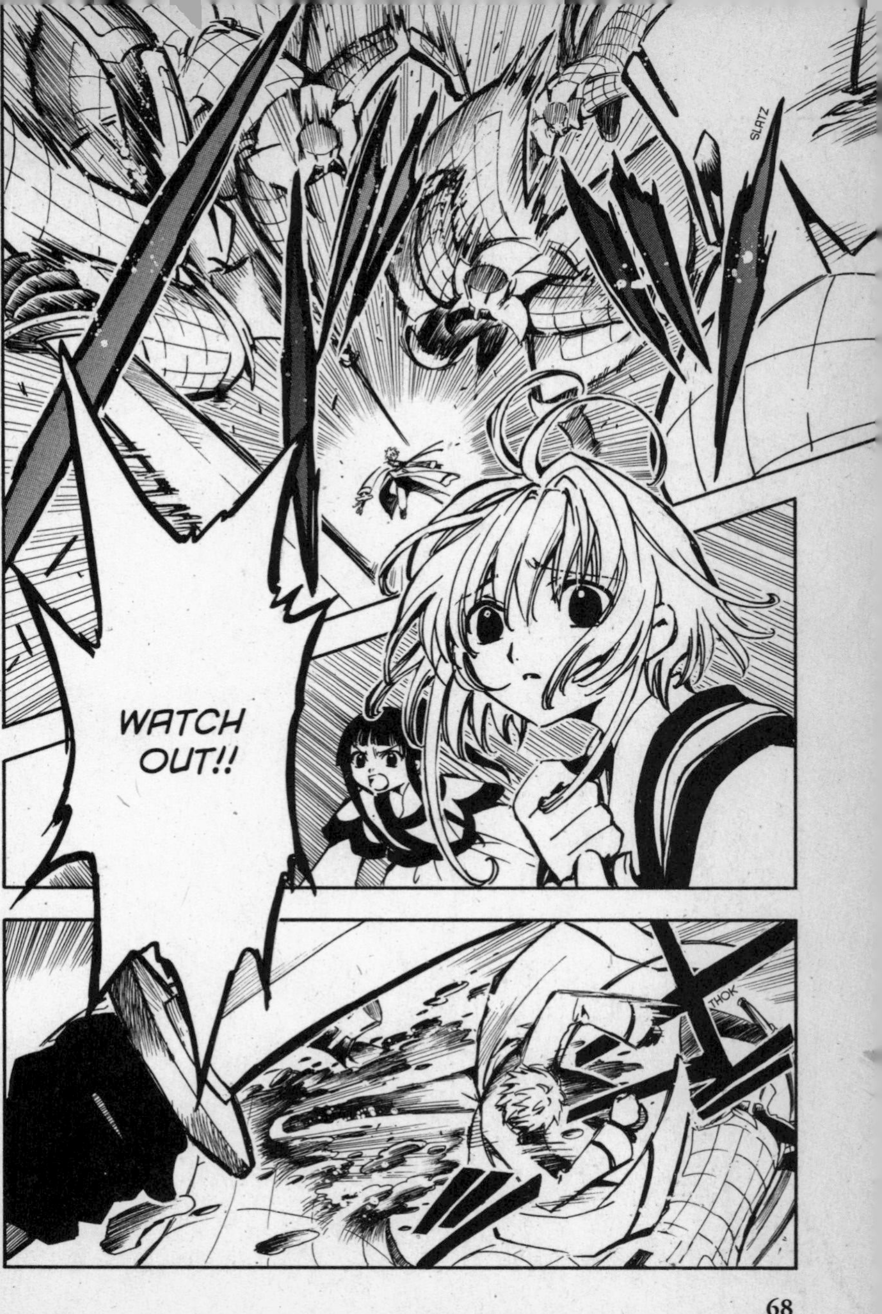
SLATZ
WATCH OUT!!
THOK

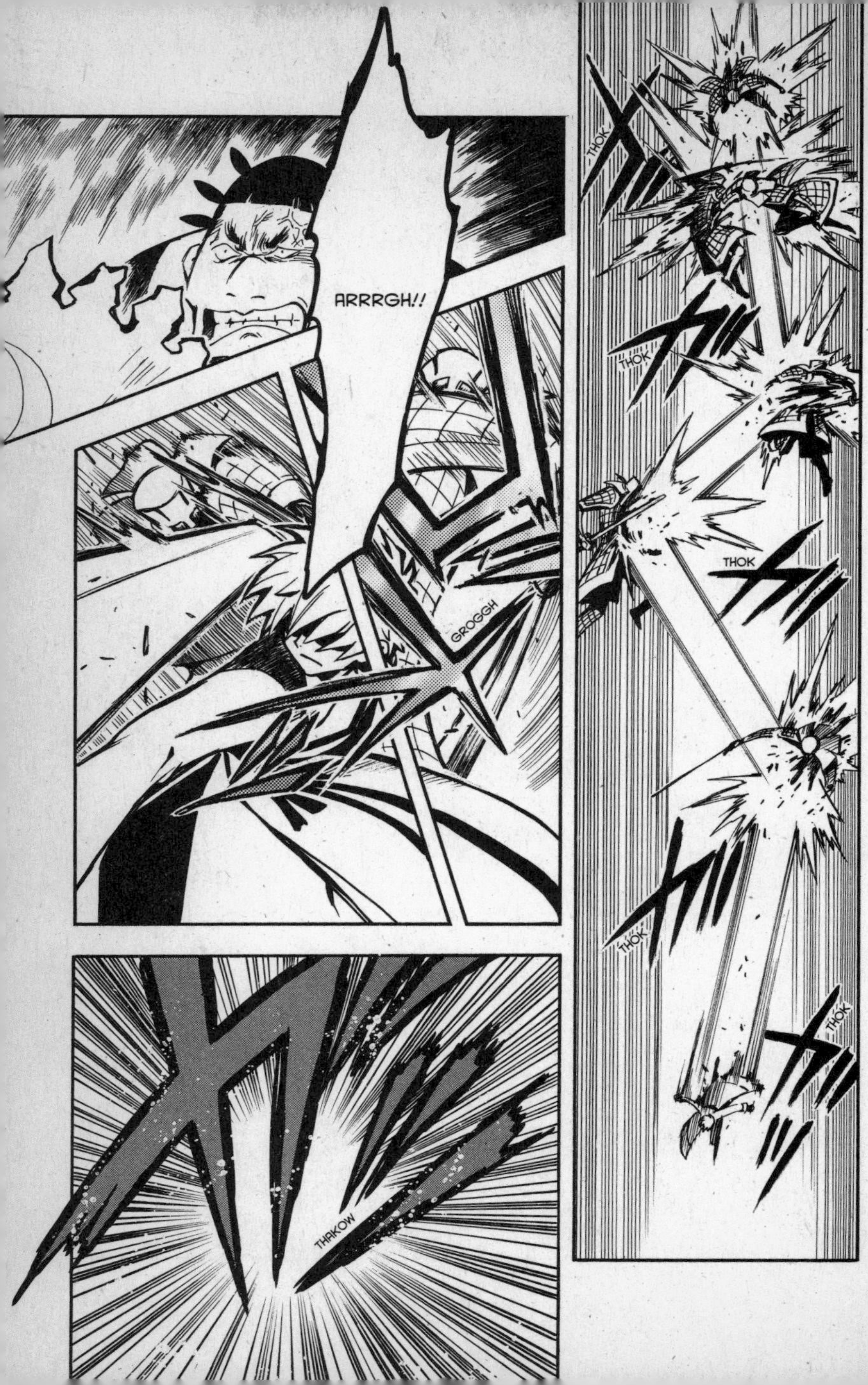
THOK
THOK
THOK
THOK
THOK
ARRRGH!!
GROGGH
THAKOW

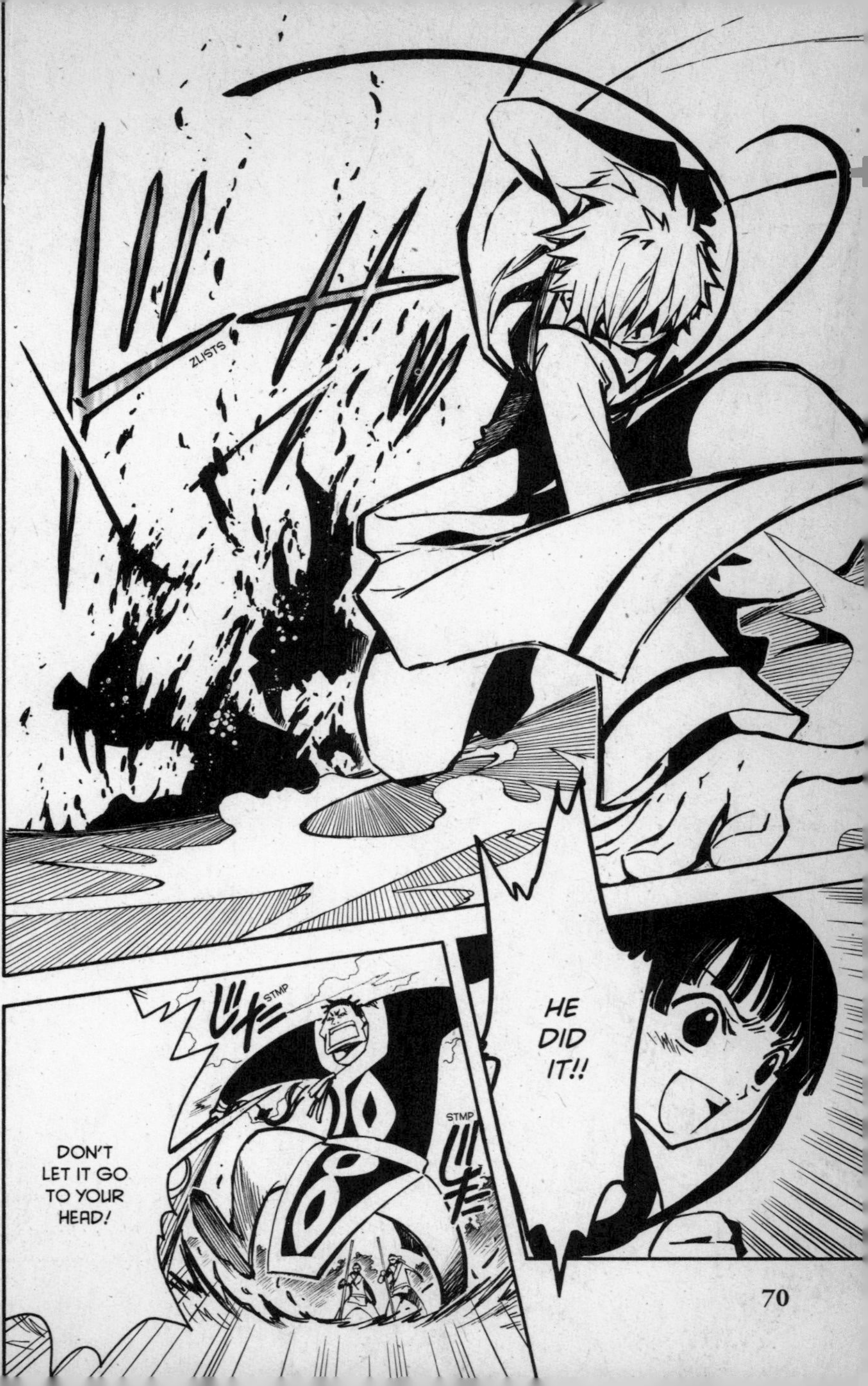
ZLISTS
HE DID IT!!
STMP
STMP
DON'T LET IT GO TO YOUR HEAD!

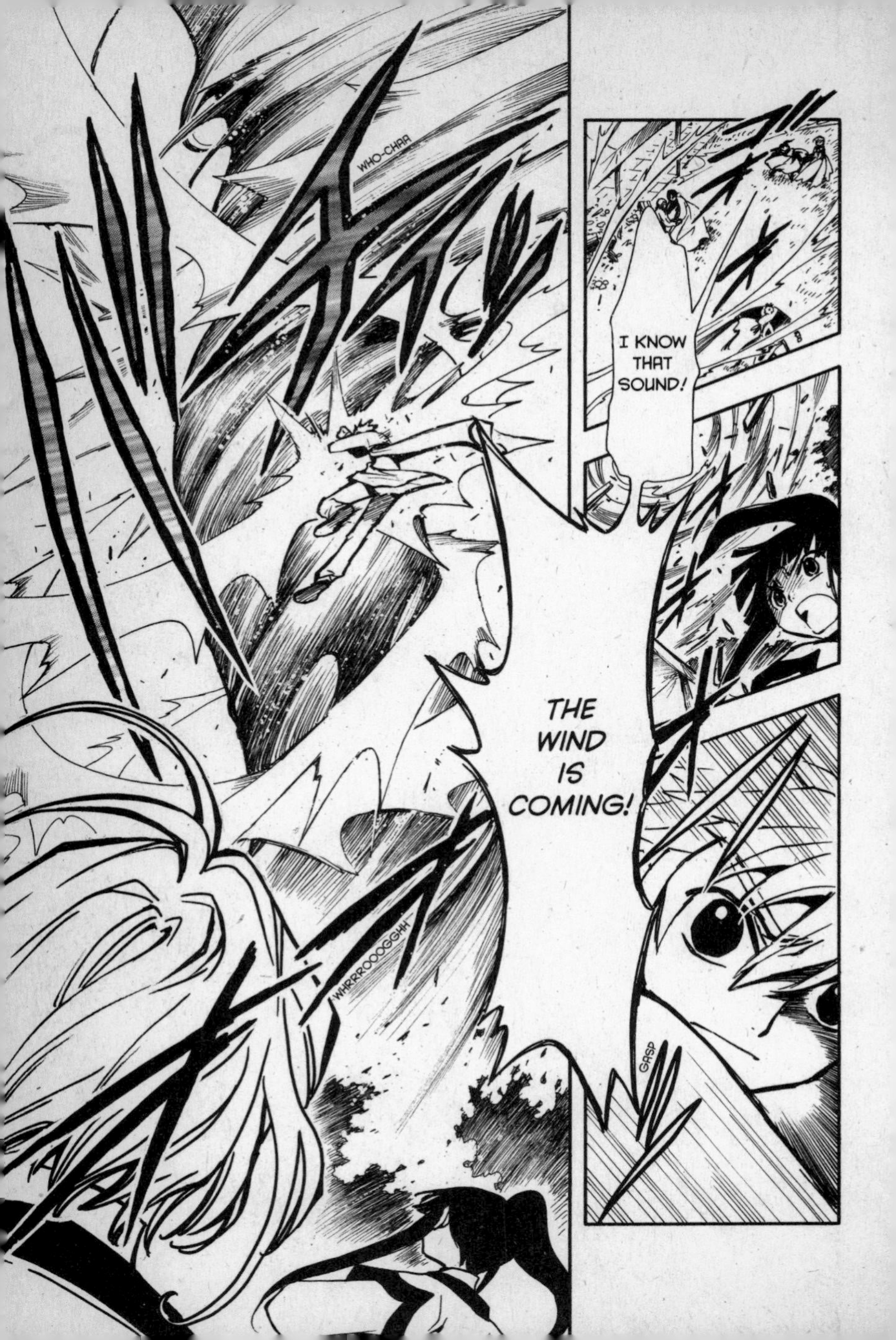
I KNOW THAT SOUND!
THE WIND IS COMING!
GASP
WHO-CHAA
WHRRROOOGGHH

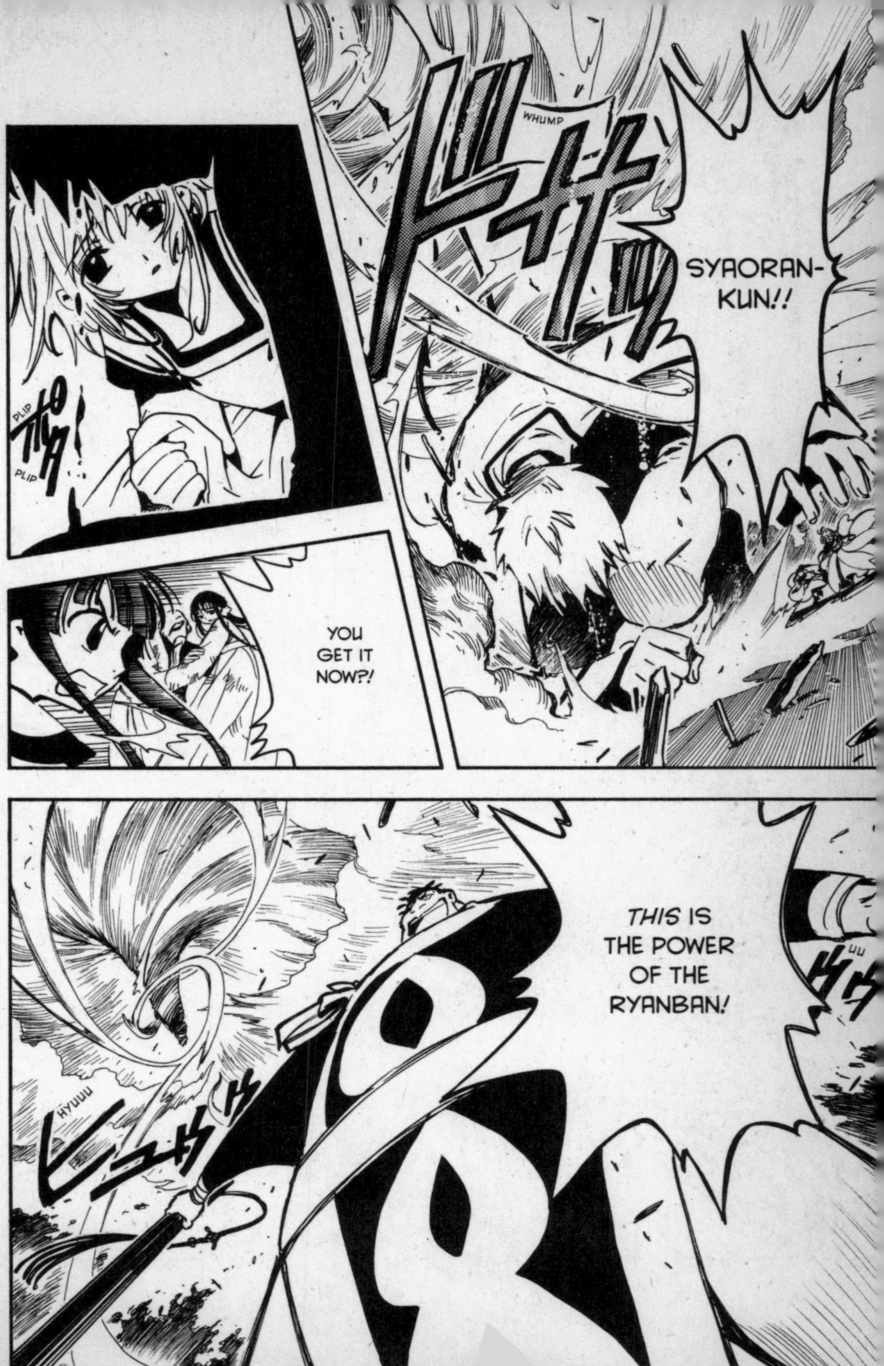
WHUMP
SYAORAN-KUN!!
PLIP PLIP
YOU GET IT NOW?!
THIS IS THE POWER OF THE RYANBAN!
HYUUU

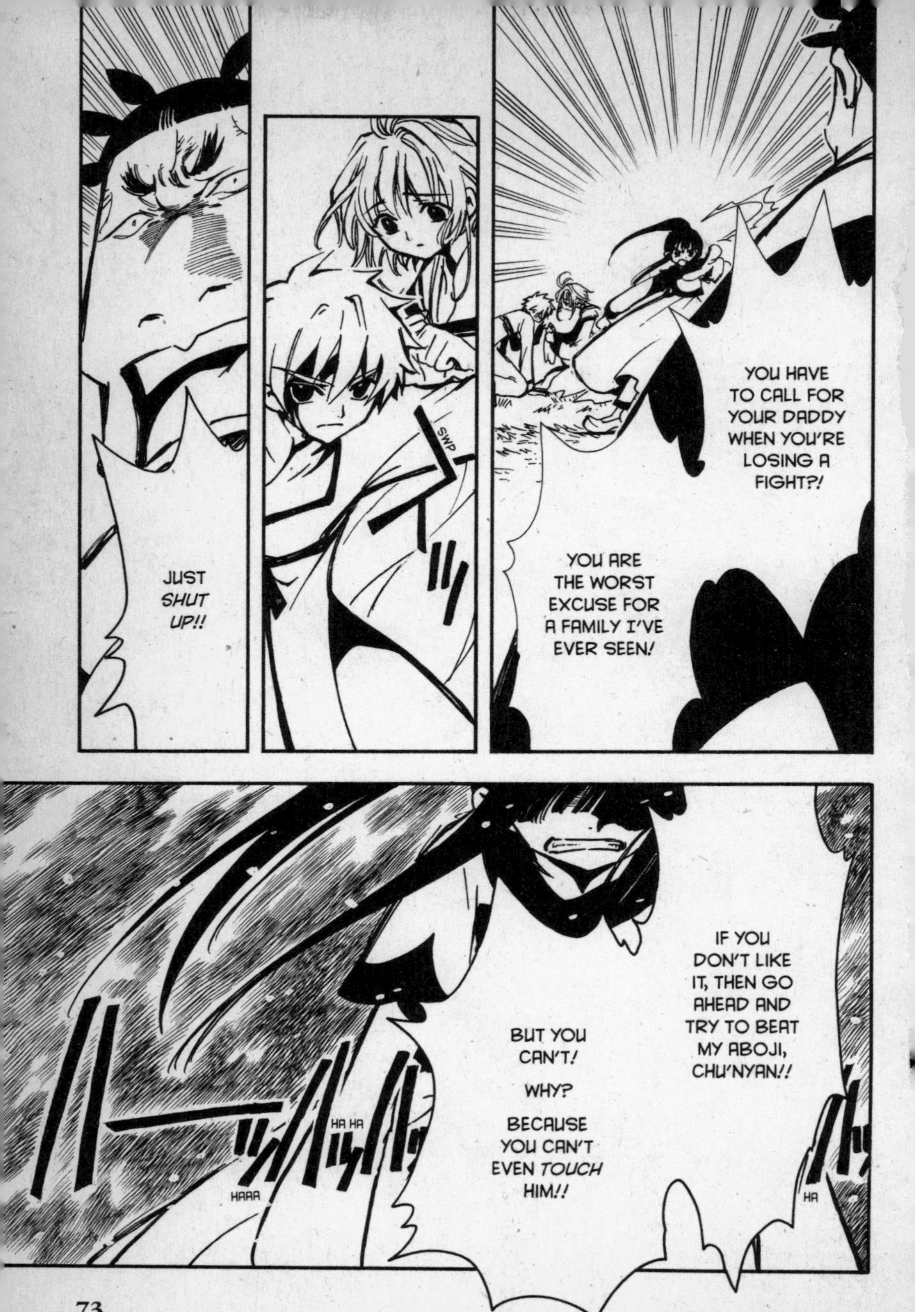
YOU HAVE TO CALL FOR YOUR DADDY WHEN YOU'RE LOSING A FIGHT?!
YOU ARE THE WORST EXCUSE FOR A FAMILY I'VE EVER SEEN!
SWP
JUST SHUT UP!!
IF YOU DON'T LIKE IT, THEN GO AHEAD AND TRY TO BEAT MY ABOJI, CHU'NYAN!!
BUT YOU CAN'T!
WHY?
BECAUSE YOU CAN'T EVEN TOUCH HIM!!
HA
HA HA
HAAA

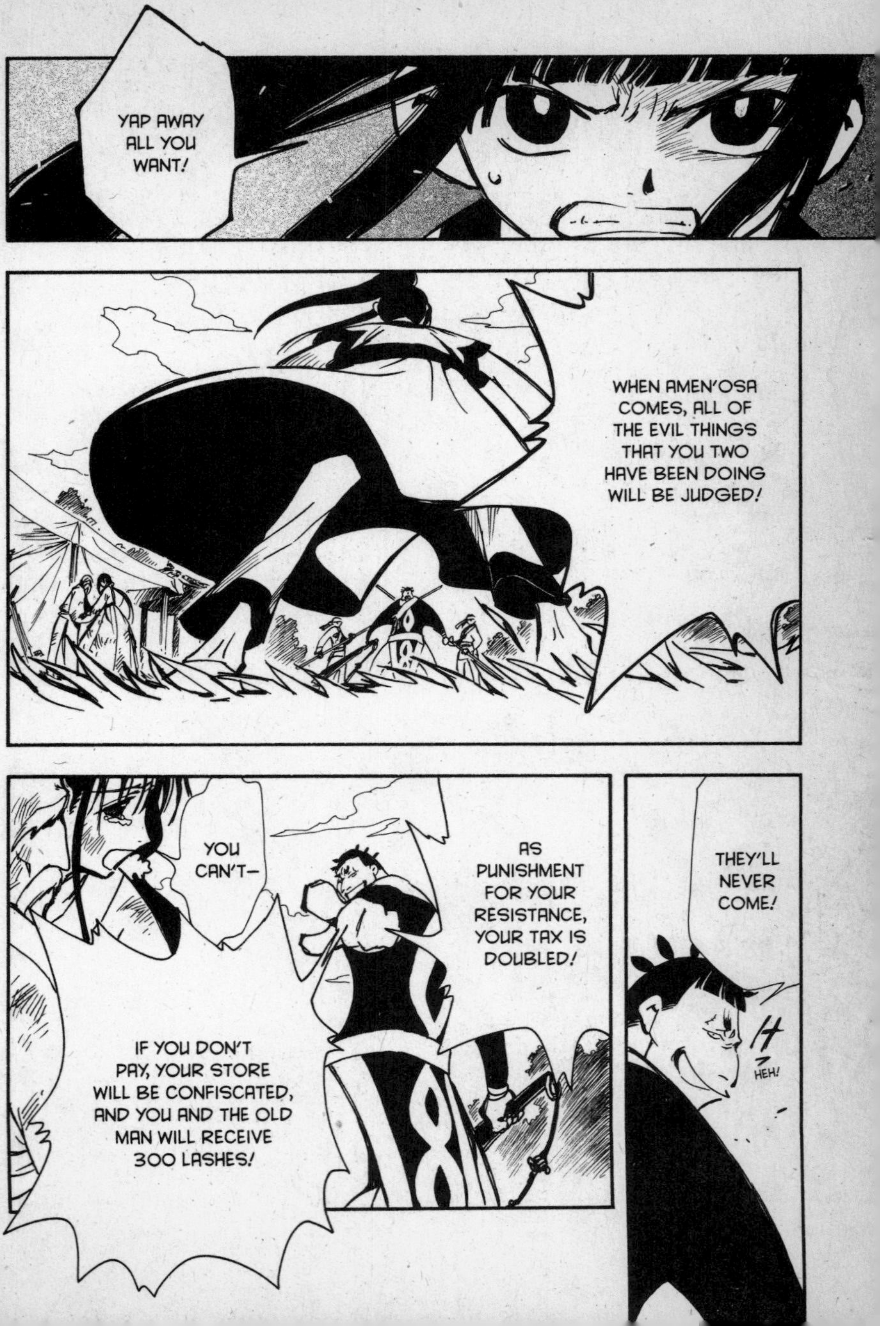
YAP AWAY ALL YOU WANT!
WHEN AMEN'OSA COMES, ALL OF THE EVIL THINGS THAT YOU TWO HAVE BEEN DOING WILL BE JUDGED!
THEY'LL NEVER COME!
HEH!
AS PUNISHMENT FOR YOUR RESISTANCE, YOUR TAX IS DOUBLED!
YOU CAN'T—
IF YOU DON'T PAY, YOUR STORE WILL BE CONFISCATED, AND YOU AND THE OLD MAN WILL RECEIVE 300 LASHES!

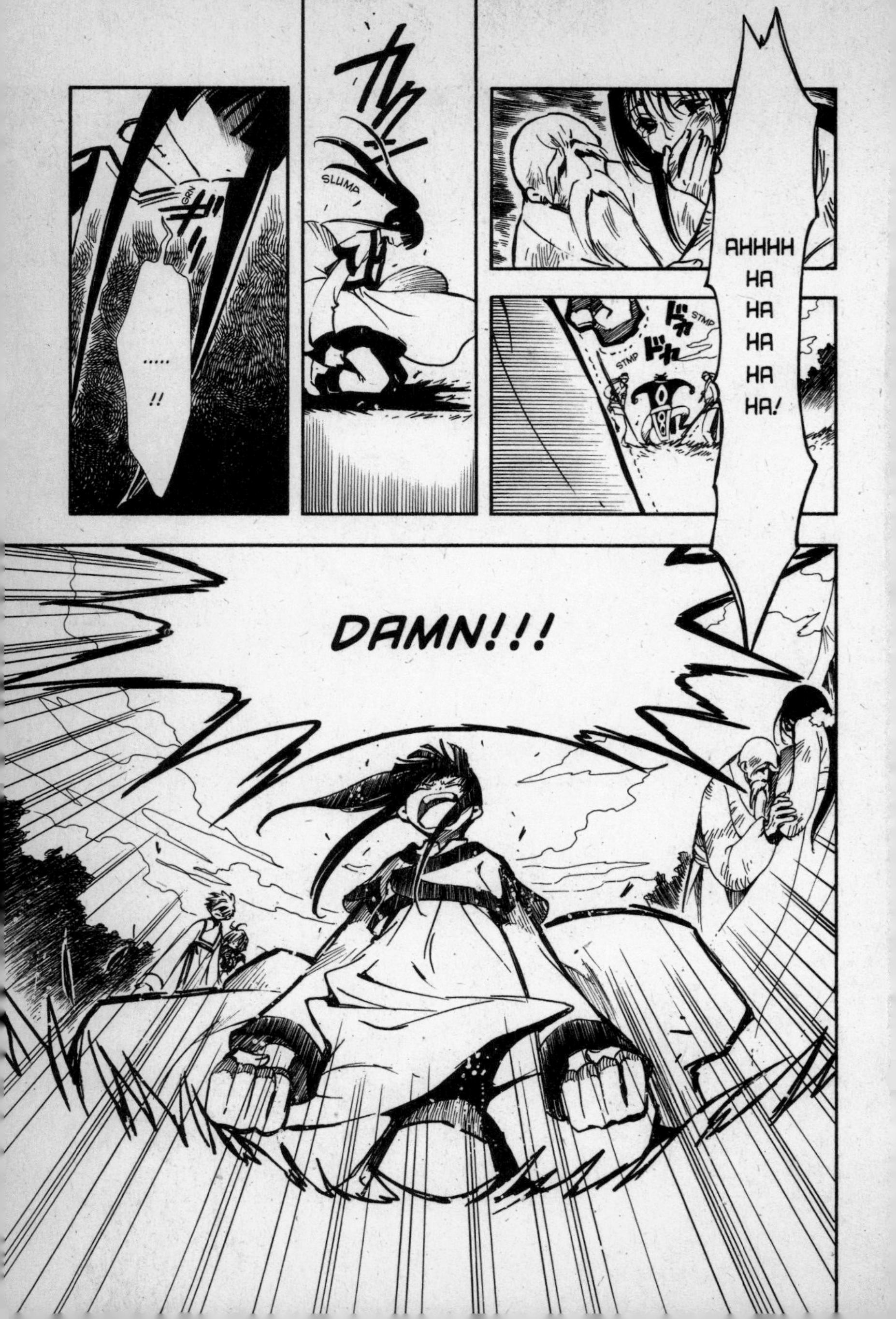

AHHHH HA HA HA HA HA!
ドカ
STMP
ドカ
STMP
カク
SLUMP
ギリ
GRN
.....
!!
DAMN!!!

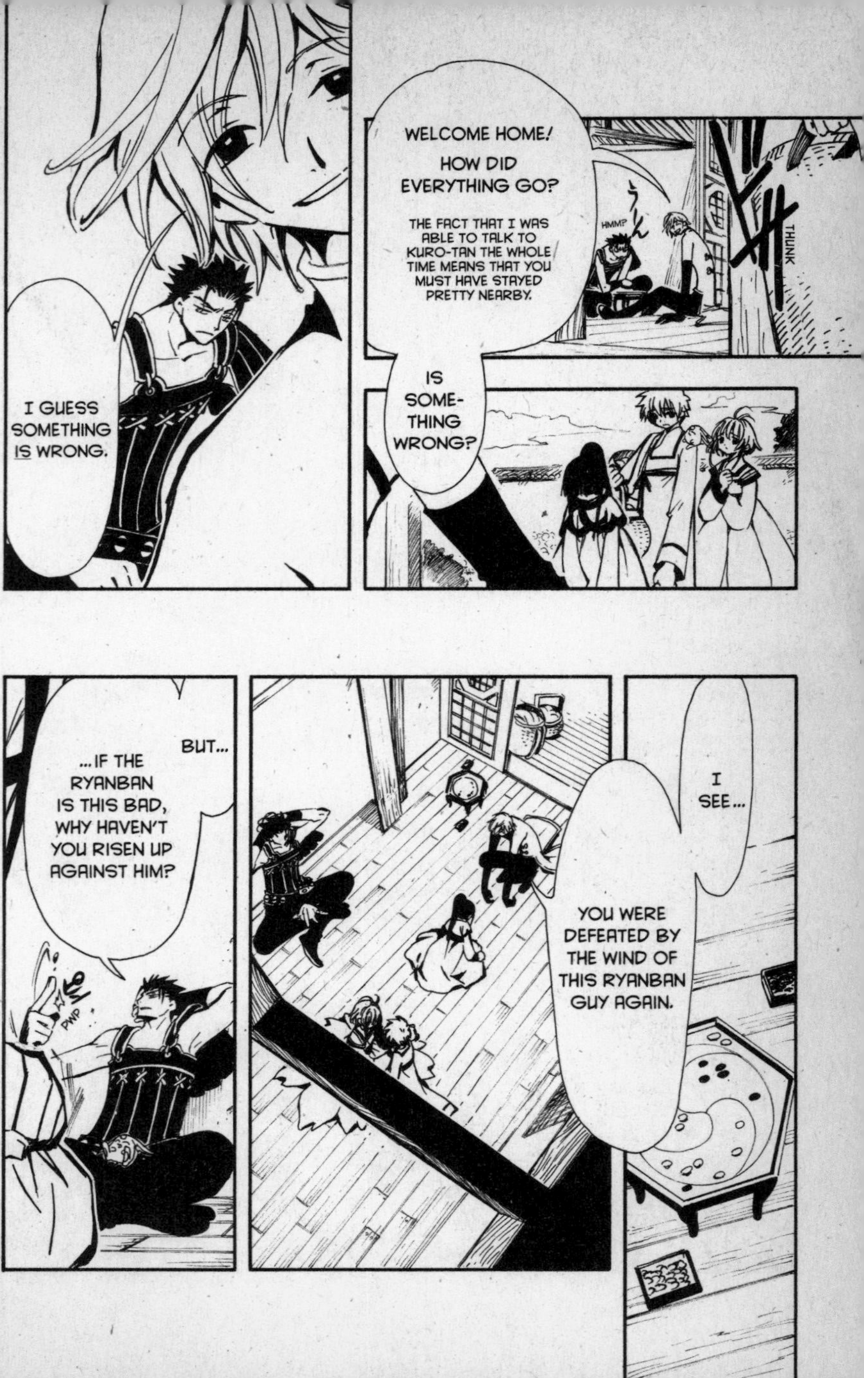
WELCOME HOME!
HOW DID EVERYTHING GO?
THE FACT THAT I WAS ABLE TO TALK TO KURO-TAN THE WHOLE TIME MEANS THAT YOU MUST HAVE STAYED PRETTY NEARBY.
HMM?
THUNK
IS SOME-THING WRONG?
I GUESS SOMETHING IS WRONG.
I SEE...
YOU WERE DEFEATED BY THE WIND OF THIS RYANBAN GUY AGAIN.
BUT...
...IF THE RYANBAN IS THIS BAD, WHY HAVEN'T YOU RISEN UP AGAINST HIM?
PWP

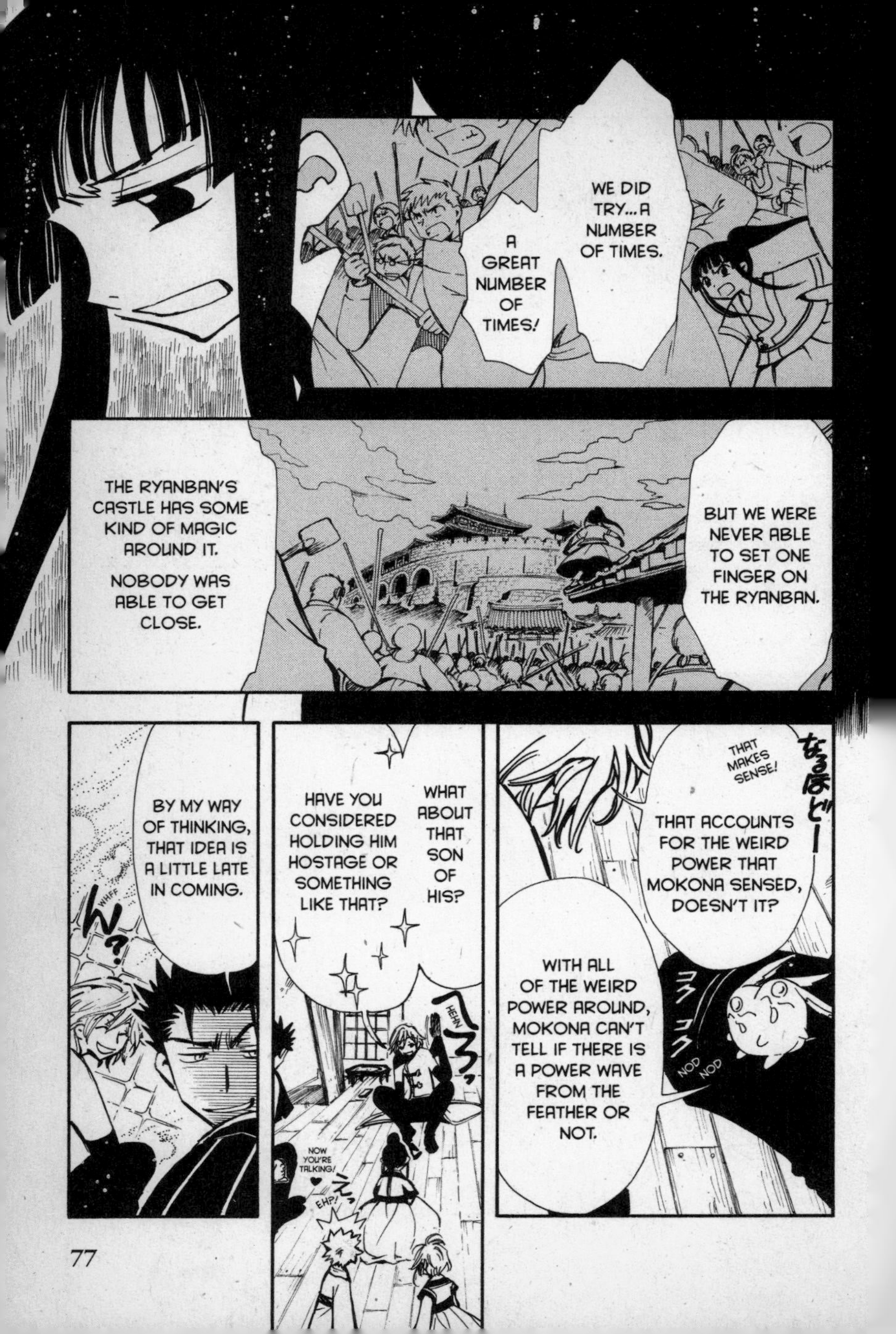
WE DID TRY... A NUMBER OF TIMES.
A GREAT NUMBER OF TIMES!
BUT WE WERE NEVER ABLE TO SET ONE FINGER ON THE RYANBAN.
THE RYANBAN'S CASTLE HAS SOME KIND OF MAGIC AROUND IT.
NOBODY WAS ABLE TO GET CLOSE.
なるほどー
THAT MAKES SENSE!
THAT ACCOUNTS FOR THE WEIRD POWER THAT MOKONA SENSED, DOESN'T IT?
WITH ALL OF THE WEIRD POWER AROUND, MOKONA CAN'T TELL IF THERE IS A POWER WAVE FROM THE FEATHER OR NOT.
コクコク
NOD NOD
WHAT ABOUT THAT SON OF HIS?
HAVE YOU CONSIDERED HOLDING HIM HOSTAGE OR SOMETHING LIKE THAT?
HEHN
NOW YOU'RE TALKING!
EHP?!
BY MY WAY OF THINKING, THAT IDEA IS A LITTLE LATE IN COMING.
WHFF

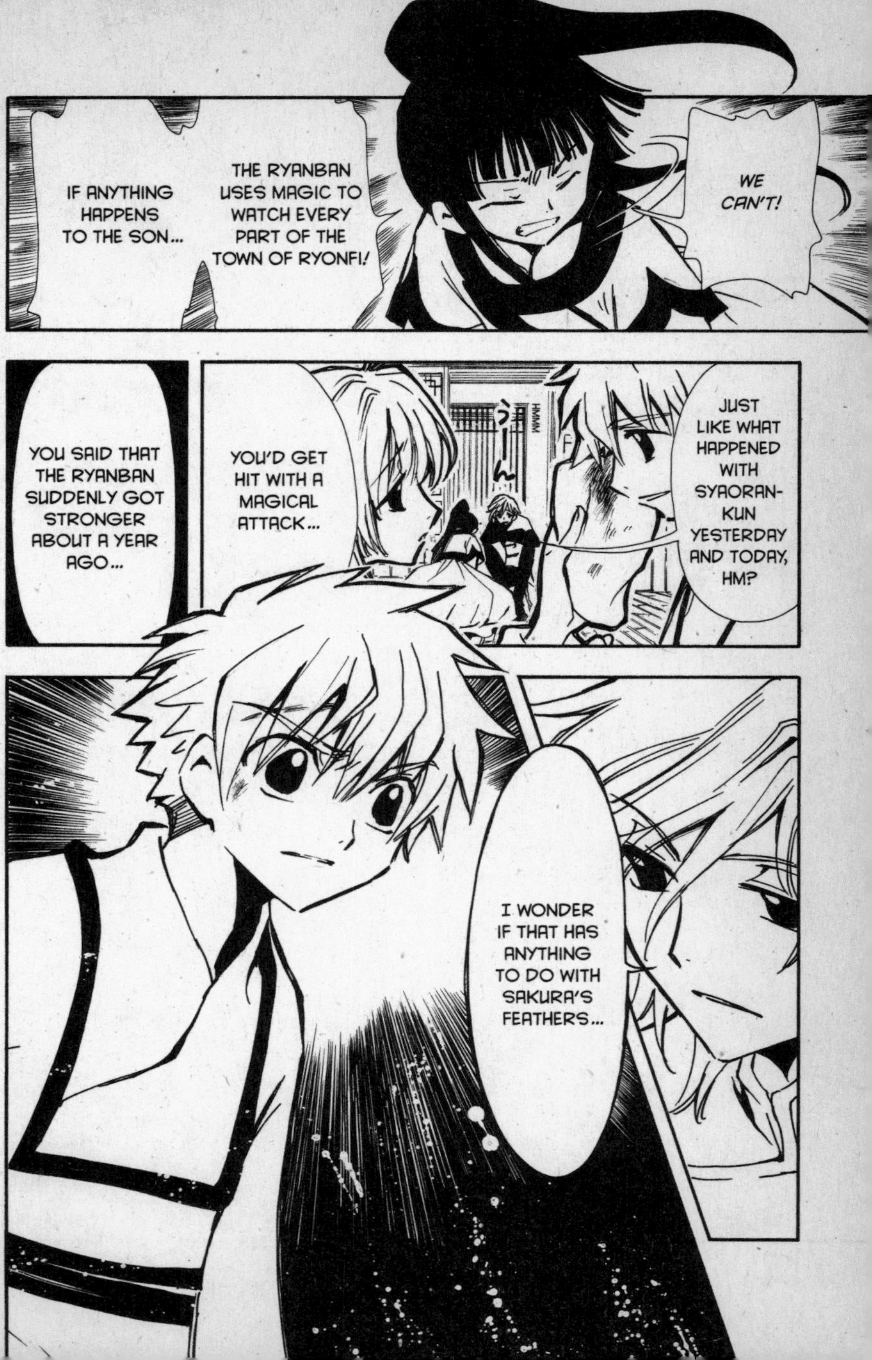
WE CAN'T!
THE RYANBAN USES MAGIC TO WATCH EVERY PART OF THE TOWN OF RYONFI!
IF ANYTHING HAPPENS TO THE SON...
JUST LIKE WHAT HAPPENED WITH SYAORAN-KUN YESTERDAY AND TODAY, HM?
うーん
HMMM
YOU'D GET HIT WITH A MAGICAL ATTACK...
YOU SAID THAT THE RYANBAN SUDDENLY GOT STRONGER ABOUT A YEAR AGO...
I WONDER IF THAT HAS ANYTHING TO DO WITH SAKURA'S FEATHERS...

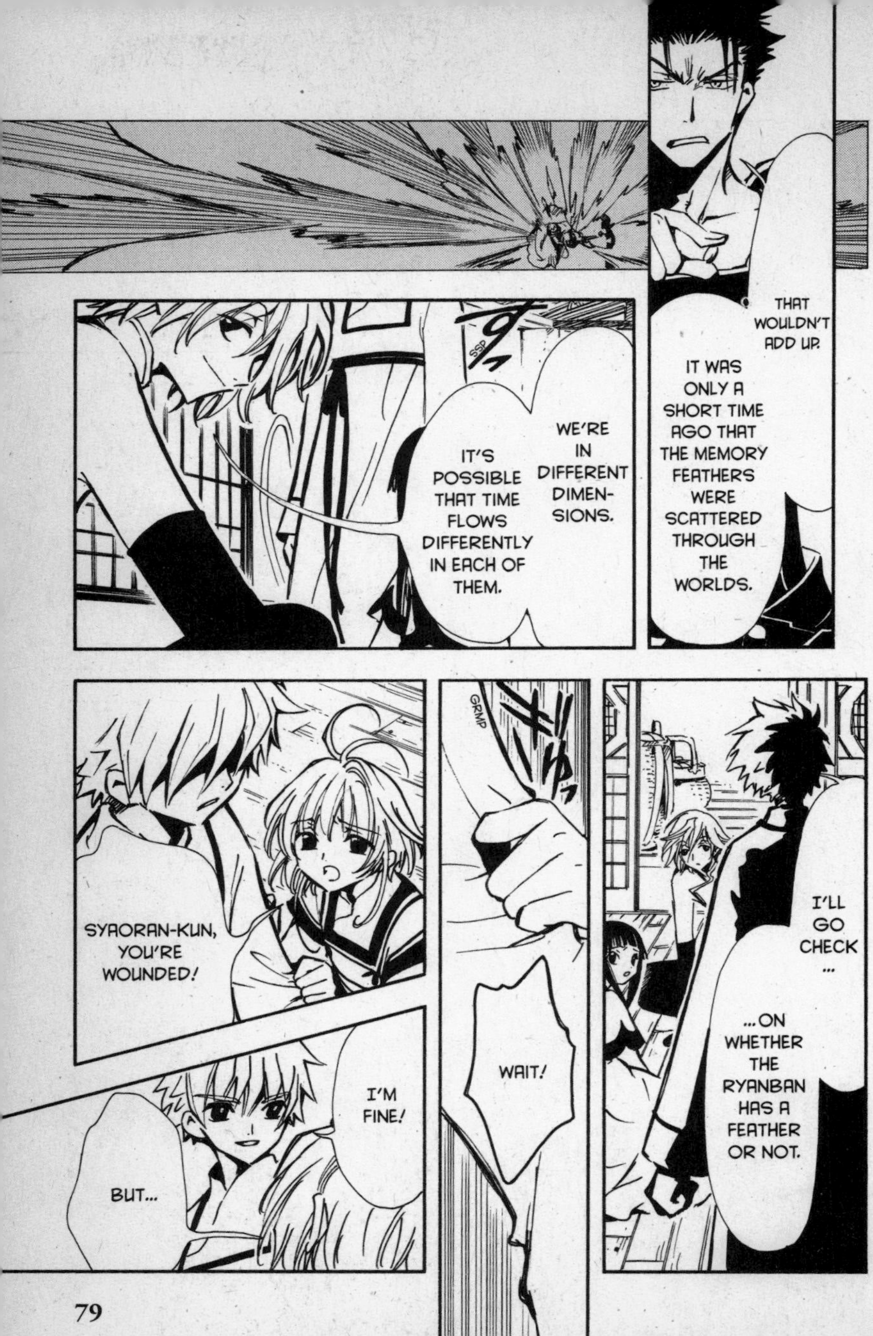
THAT WOULDN'T ADD UP.
IT WAS ONLY A SHORT TIME AGO THAT THE MEMORY FEATHERS WERE SCATTERED THROUGH THE WORLDS.
SSP
WE'RE IN DIFFERENT DIMEN-SIONS.
IT'S POSSIBLE THAT TIME FLOWS DIFFERENTLY IN EACH OF THEM.
I'LL GO CHECK...
...ON WHETHER THE RYANBAN HAS A FEATHER OR NOT.
GRMP
WAIT!
SYAORAN-KUN, YOU'RE WOUNDED!
I'M FINE!
BUT...

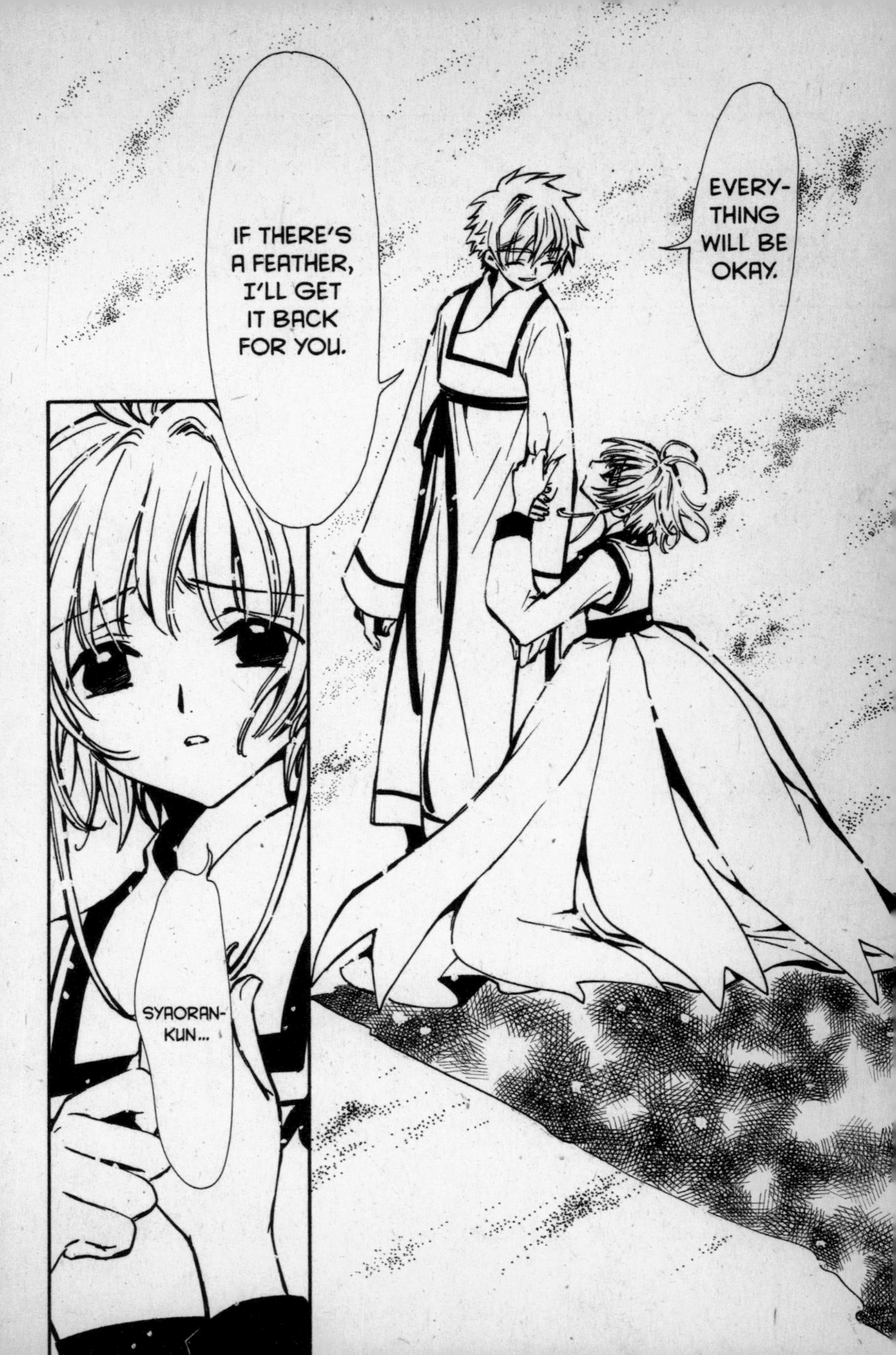
EVERY-THING WILL BE OKAY.
IF THERE'S A FEATHER, I'LL GET IT BACK FOR YOU.
SYAORAN-KUN...

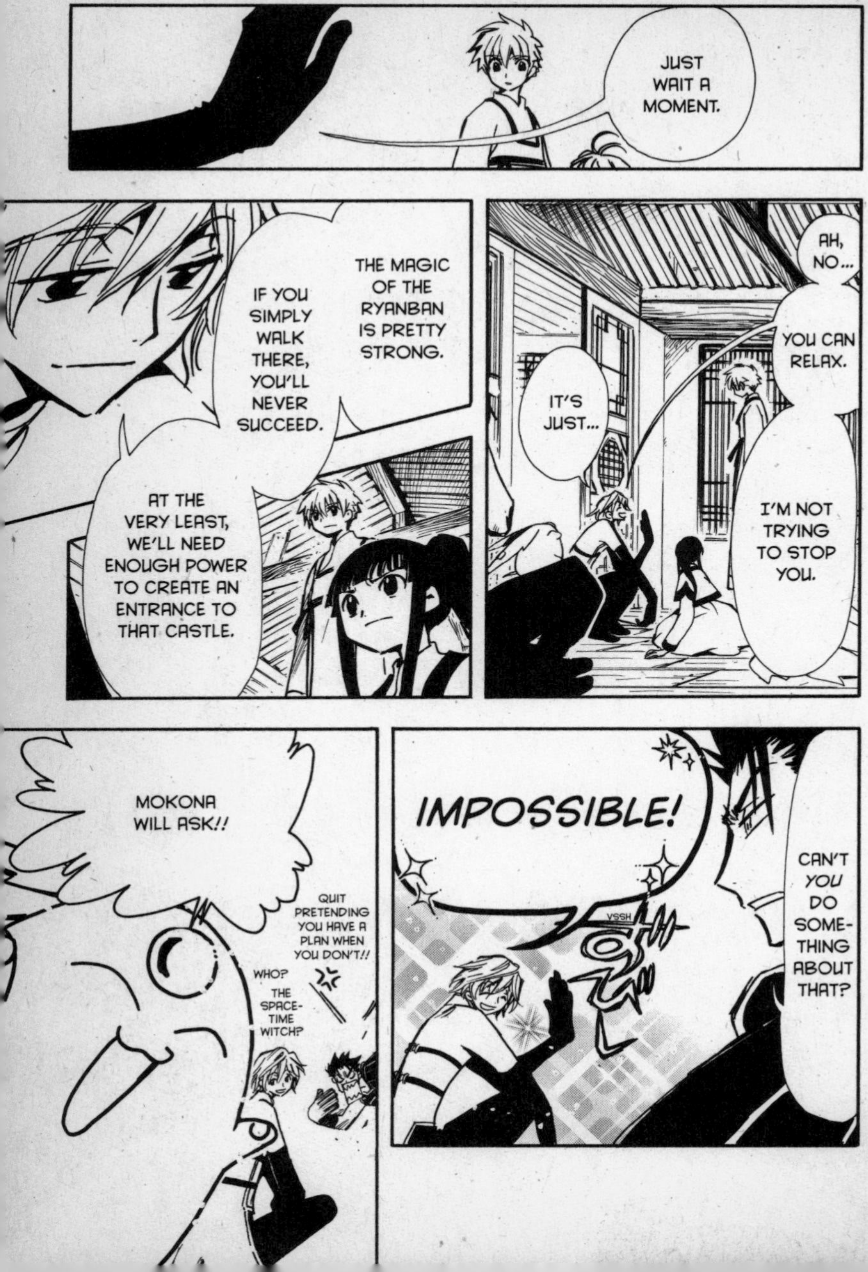
JUST WAIT A MOMENT.
AH, NO...
YOU CAN RELAX.
I'M NOT TRYING TO STOP YOU.
IT'S JUST...
THE MAGIC OF THE RYANBAN IS PRETTY STRONG.
IF YOU SIMPLY WALK THERE, YOU'LL NEVER SUCCEED.
AT THE VERY LEAST, WE'LL NEED ENOUGH POWER TO CREATE AN ENTRANCE TO THAT CASTLE.
CAN'T *YOU* DO SOME-THING ABOUT THAT?
IMPOSSIBLE!
VSSH
MOKONA WILL ASK!!
WHO? THE SPACE-TIME WITCH?
QUIT PRETENDING YOU HAVE A PLAN WHEN YOU DON'T!!

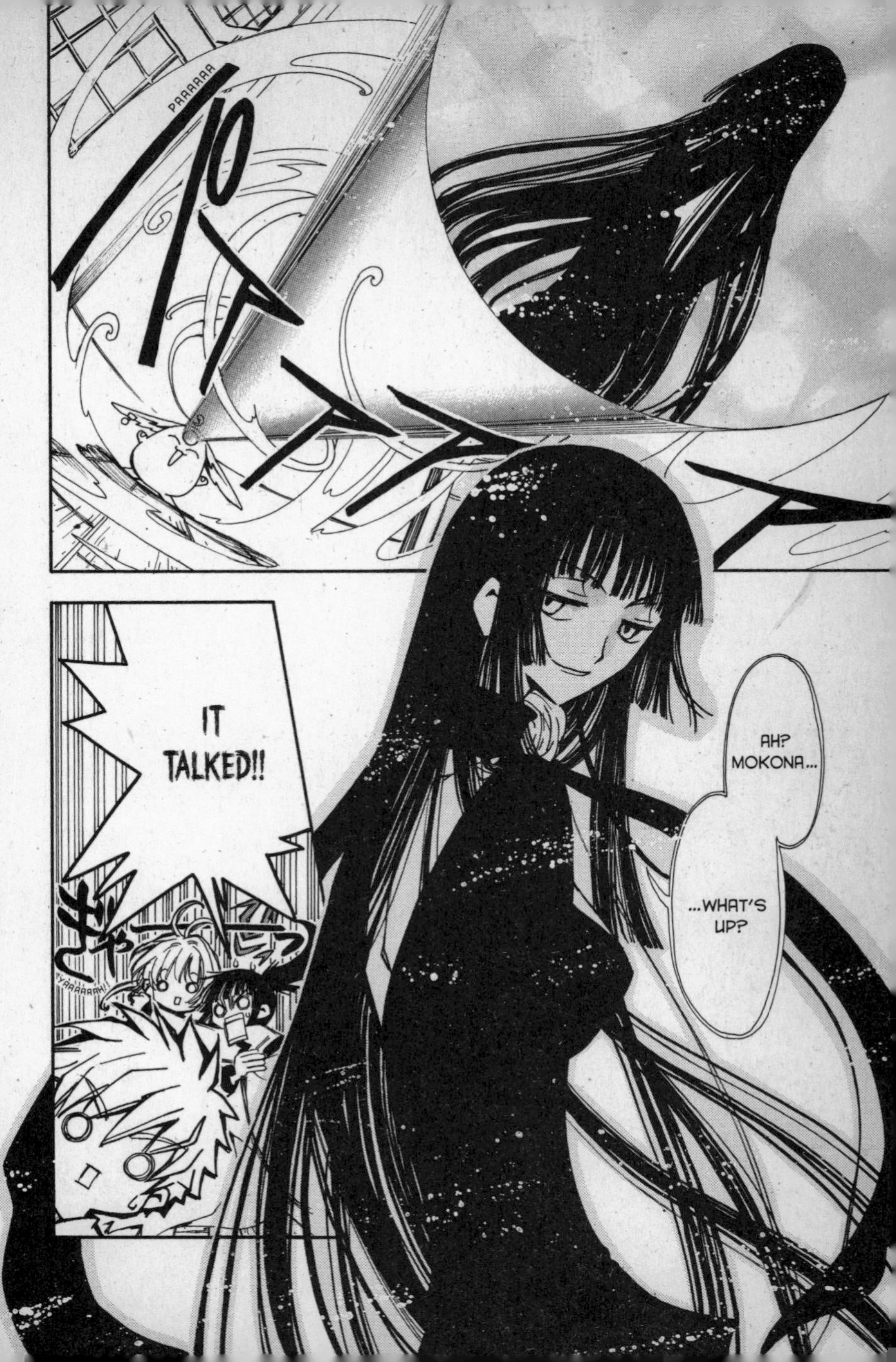
PAAAAAA
AH? MOKONA...
...WHAT'S UP?
IT TALKED!!
きゃ
YAAAAAAH!!

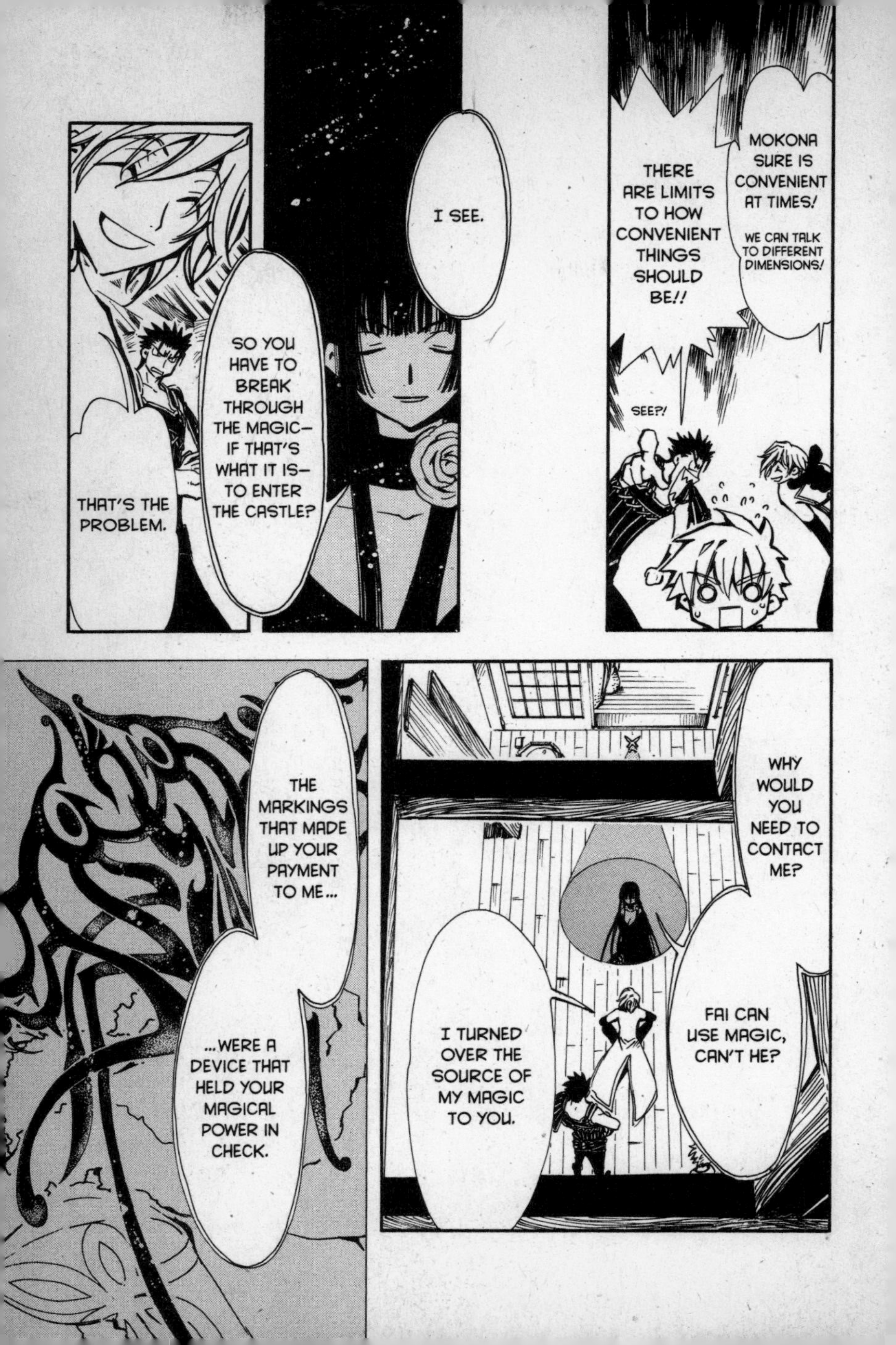

MOKONA SURE IS CONVENIENT AT TIMES!
WE CAN TALK TO DIFFERENT DIMENSIONS!
THERE ARE LIMITS TO HOW CONVENIENT THINGS SHOULD BE!!
SEE?!
I SEE.
SO YOU HAVE TO BREAK THROUGH THE MAGIC—IF THAT'S WHAT IT IS—TO ENTER THE CASTLE?
THAT'S THE PROBLEM.
WHY WOULD YOU NEED TO CONTACT ME?
FAI CAN USE MAGIC, CAN'T HE?
I TURNED OVER THE SOURCE OF MY MAGIC TO YOU.
THE MARKINGS THAT MADE UP YOUR PAYMENT TO ME...
...WERE A DEVICE THAT HELD YOUR MAGICAL POWER IN CHECK.

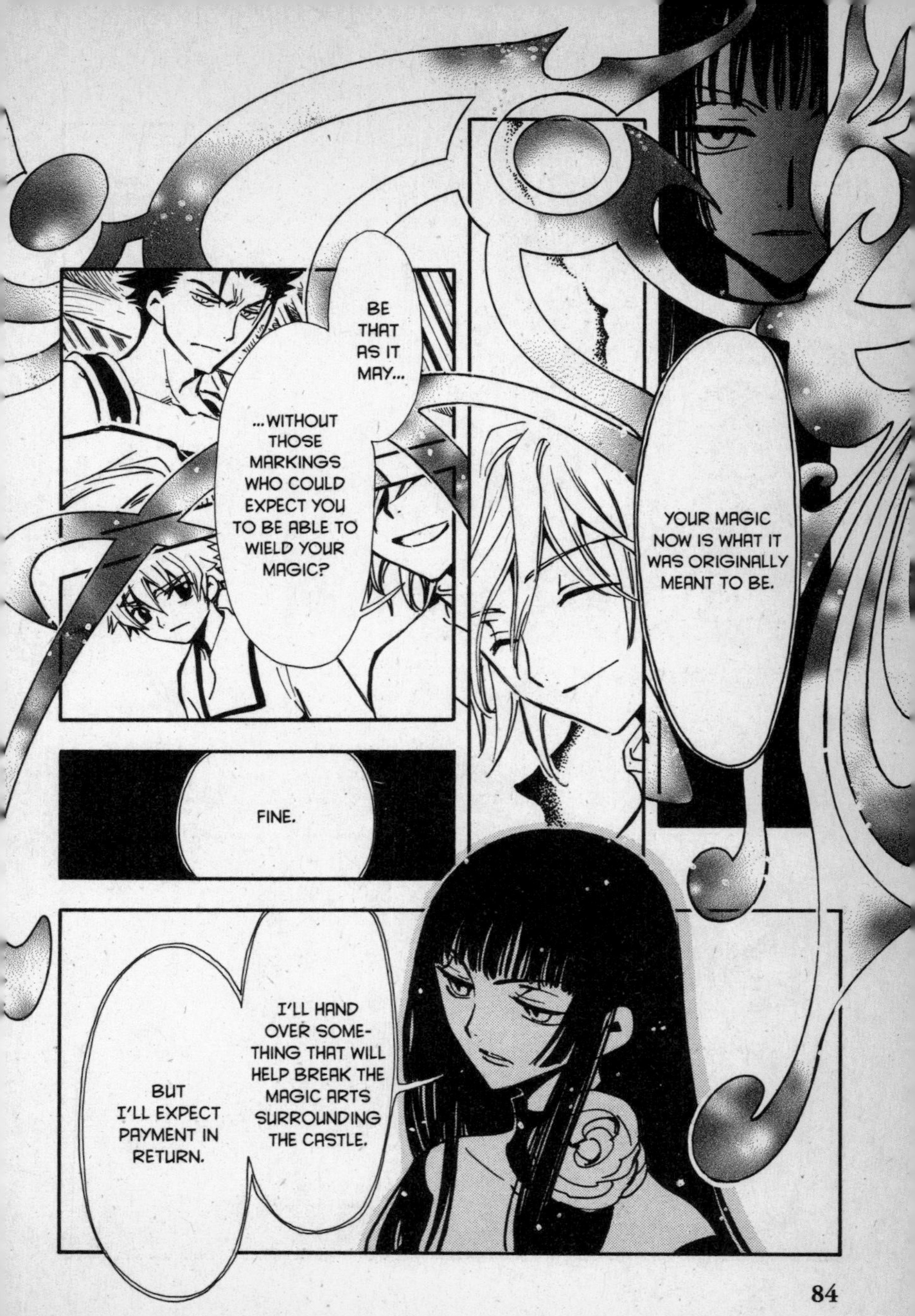
YOUR MAGIC NOW IS WHAT IT WAS ORIGINALLY MEANT TO BE.
BE THAT AS IT MAY...
...WITHOUT THOSE MARKINGS WHO COULD EXPECT YOU TO BE ABLE TO WIELD YOUR MAGIC?
FINE.
I'LL HAND OVER SOME-THING THAT WILL HELP BREAK THE MAGIC ARTS SURROUNDING THE CASTLE.
BUT I'LL EXPECT PAYMENT IN RETURN.

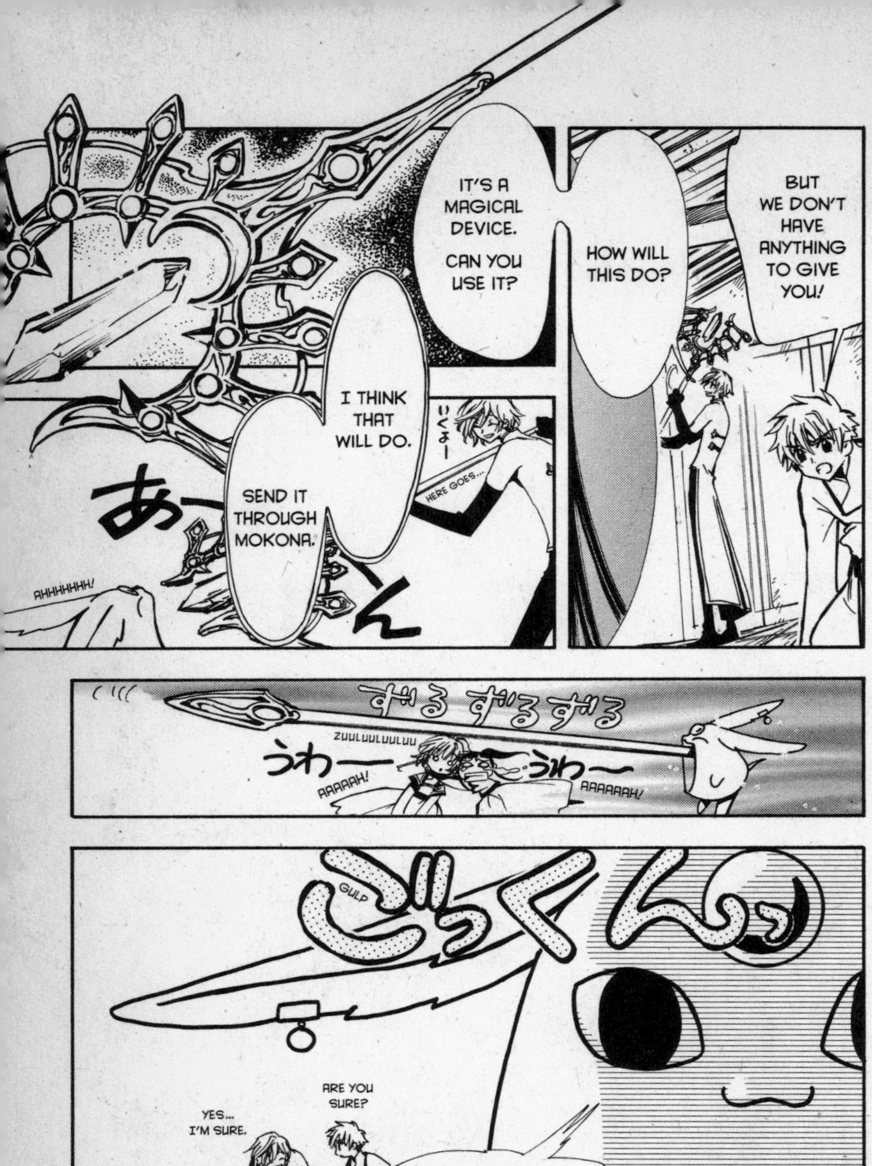

BUT WE DON'T HAVE ANYTHING TO GIVE YOU!
HOW WILL THIS DO?
IT'S A MAGICAL DEVICE.
CAN YOU USE IT?
I THINK THAT WILL DO.
いくよー
HERE GOES...
SEND IT THROUGH MOKONA.
あーん
AHHHHHHH!
ずるずるずる
ZUULUULUULUU
うわー
AAAAAAH!
うわ〜
AAAAAAH!
ごっくんっ
GULP
ARE YOU SURE?
YES... I'M SURE.
BOINK

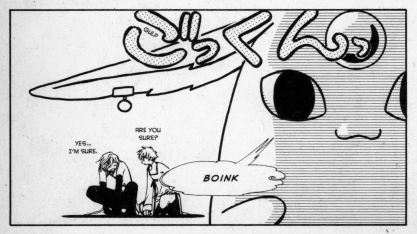

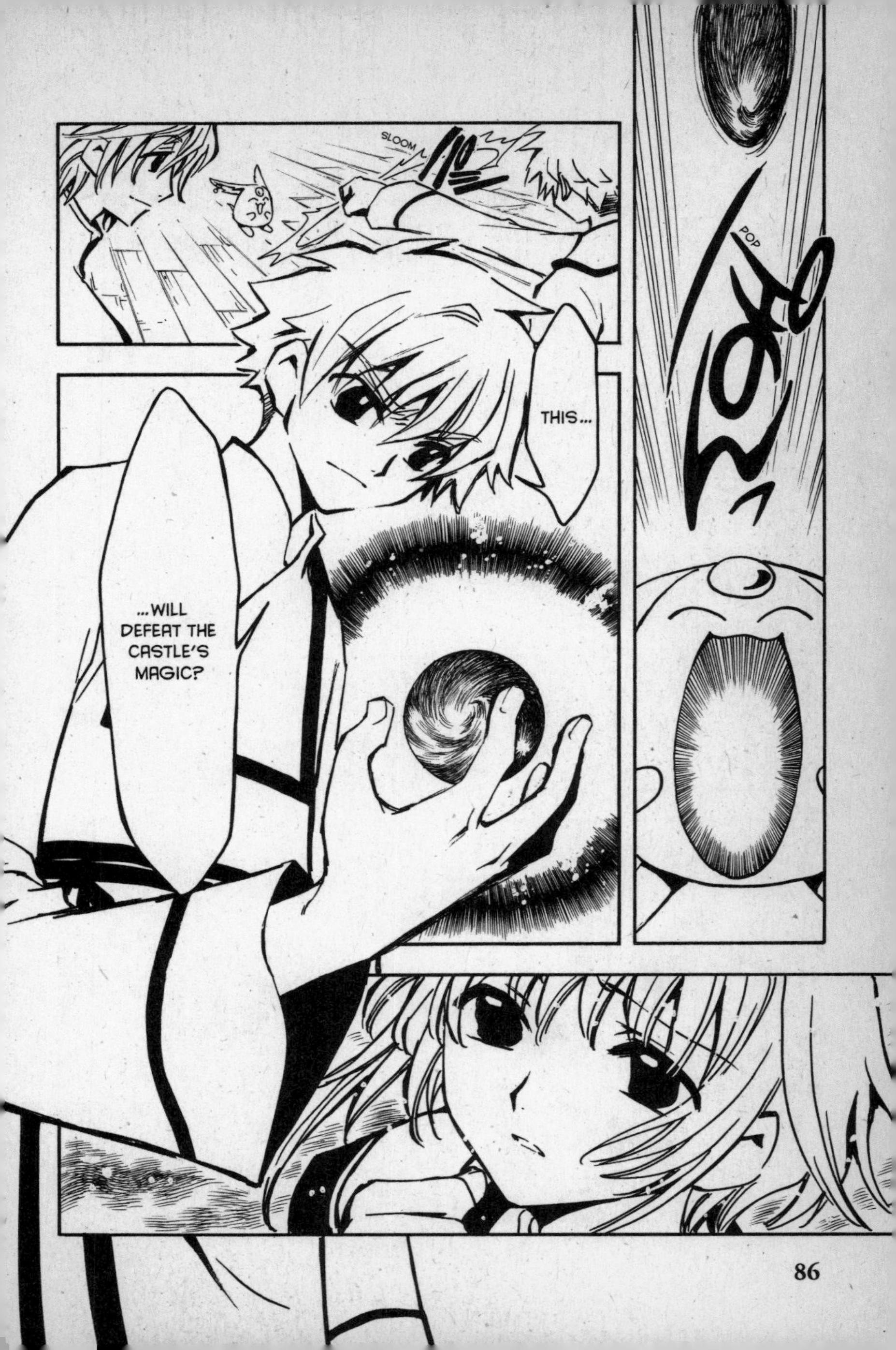
POP
SLOOM
THIS...
...WILL DEFEAT THE CASTLE'S MAGIC?

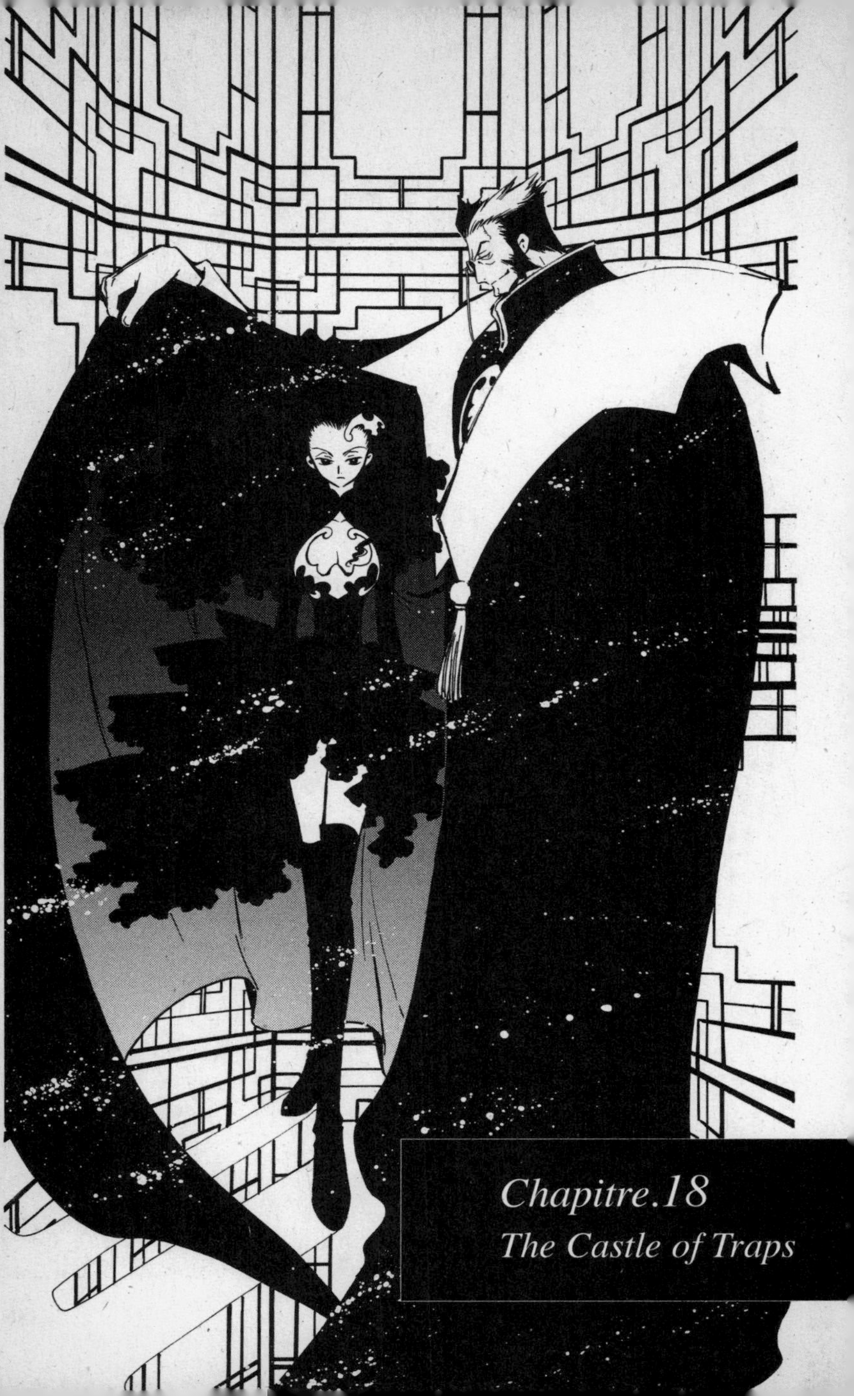

Chapitre.18
The Castle of Traps

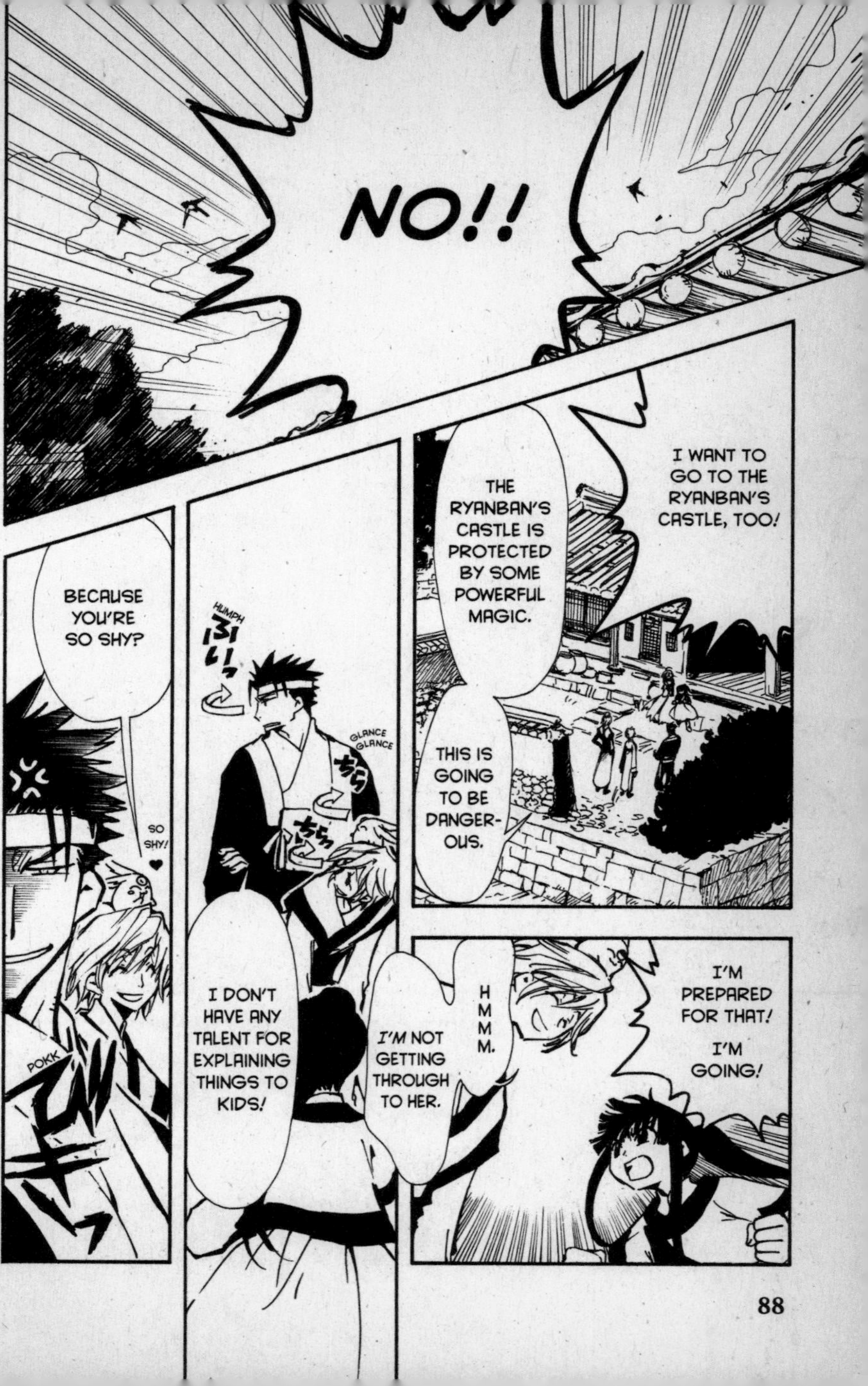
NO!!
I WANT TO GO TO THE RYANBAN'S CASTLE, TOO!
THE RYANBAN'S CASTLE IS PROTECTED BY SOME POWERFUL MAGIC.
THIS IS GOING TO BE DANGER-OUS.
I'M PREPARED FOR THAT!
I'M GOING!
HMMM.
I'M NOT GETTING THROUGH TO HER.
HUMPH
ふいっ
GLANCE GLANCE
ちら
ちら
I DON'T HAVE ANY TALENT FOR EXPLAINING THINGS TO KIDS!
BECAUSE YOU'RE SO SHY?
SO SHY! ♥
POKK

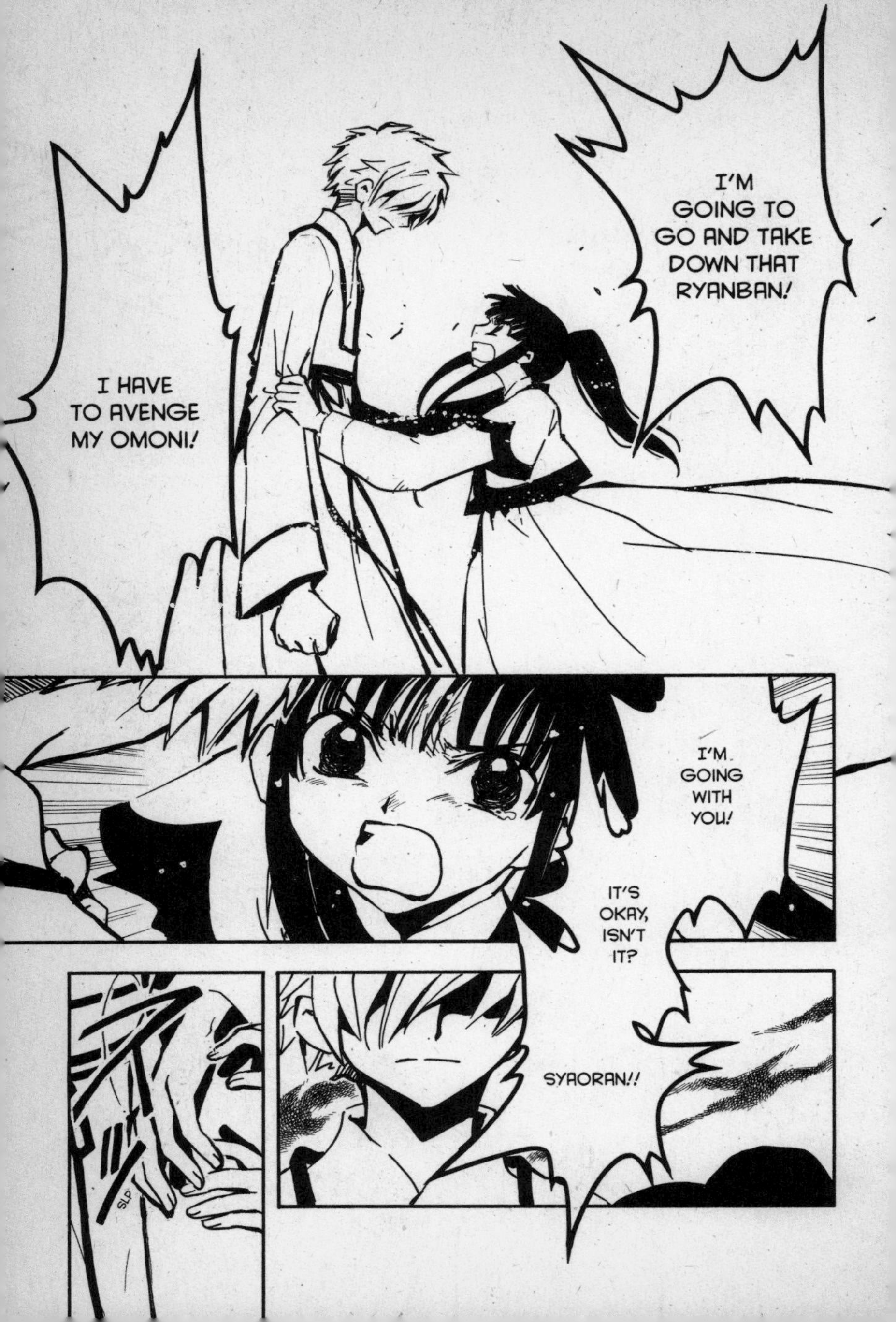
I'M GOING TO GO AND TAKE DOWN THAT RYANBAN!
I HAVE TO AVENGE MY OMONI!
I'M GOING WITH YOU!
IT'S OKAY, ISN'T IT?
SYAORAN!!
SLP

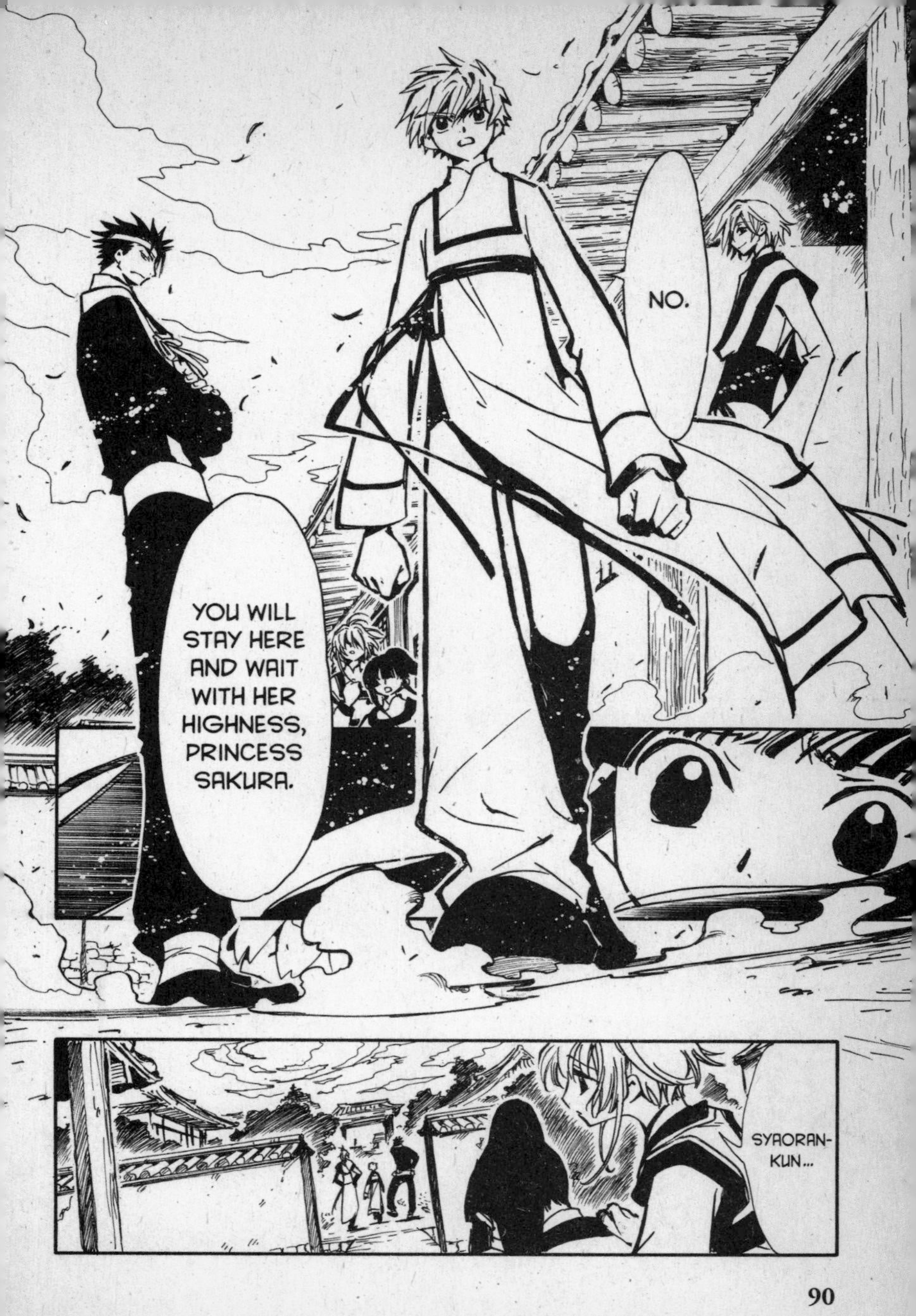
NO.
YOU WILL STAY HERE AND WAIT WITH HER HIGHNESS, PRINCESS SAKURA.
SYAORAN-KUN...

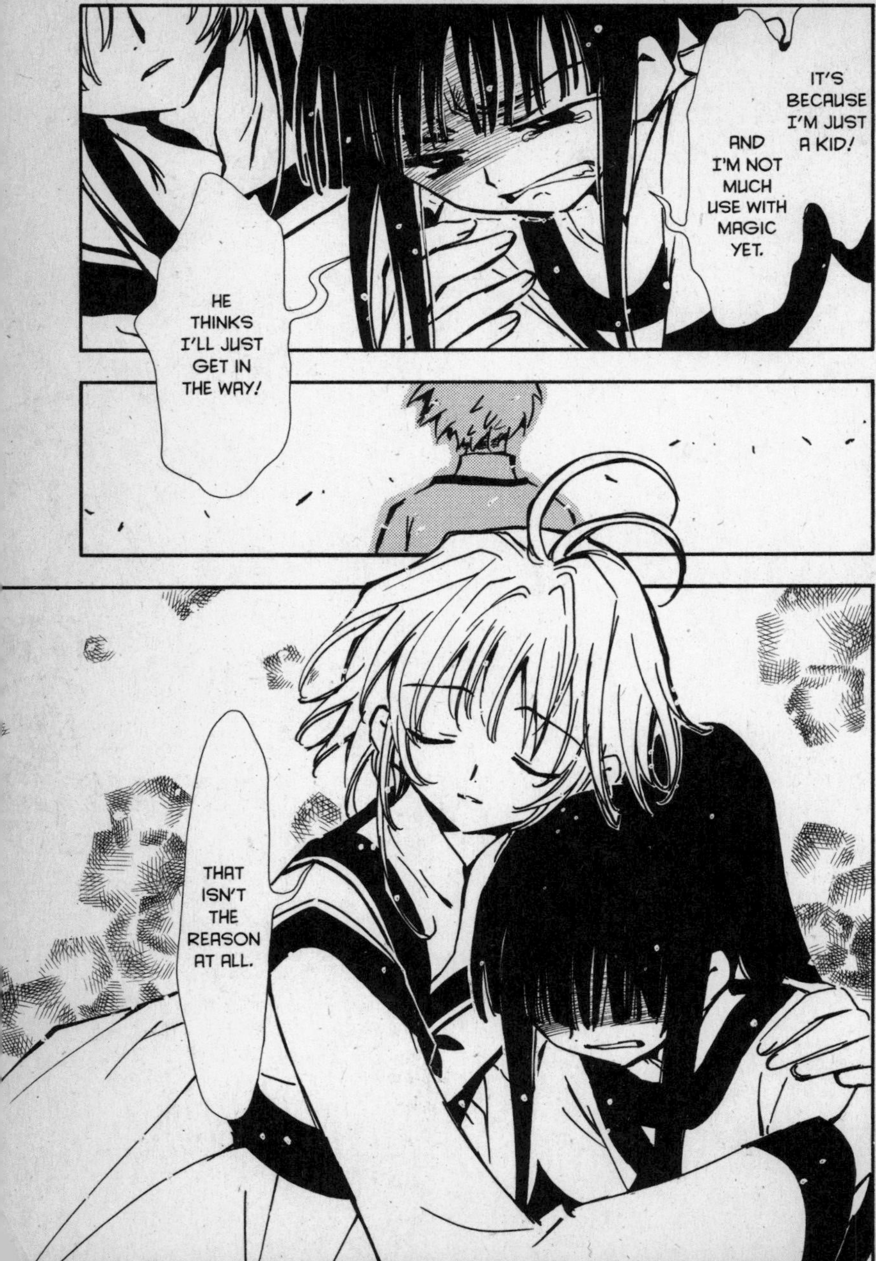
IT'S BECAUSE I'M JUST A KID!
AND I'M NOT MUCH USE WITH MAGIC YET.
HE THINKS I'LL JUST GET IN THE WAY!
THAT ISN'T THE REASON AT ALL.

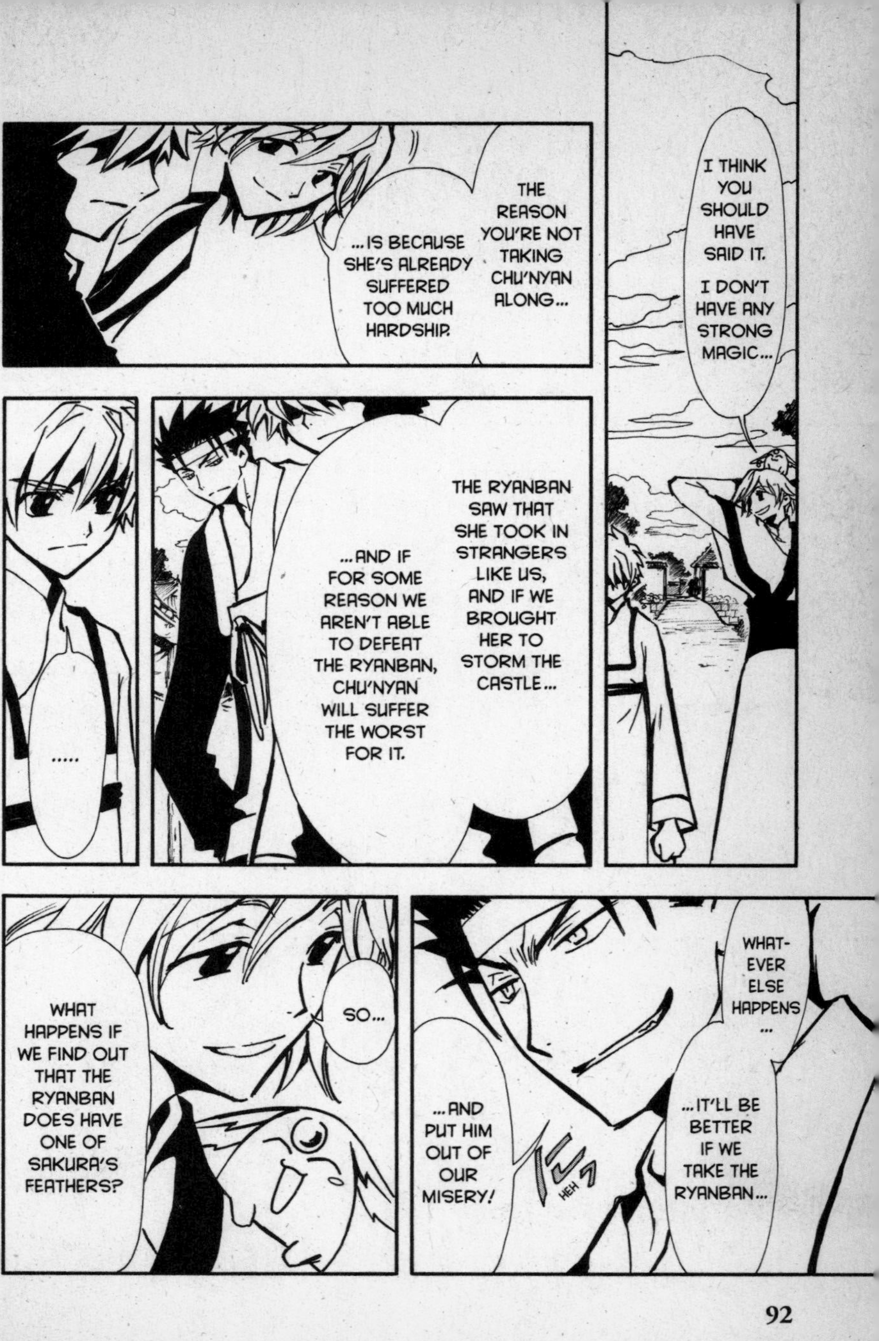
I THINK YOU SHOULD HAVE SAID IT.
I DON'T HAVE ANY STRONG MAGIC...
THE REASON YOU'RE NOT TAKING CHU'NYAN ALONG...
...IS BECAUSE SHE'S ALREADY SUFFERED TOO MUCH HARDSHIP.
THE RYANBAN SAW THAT SHE TOOK IN STRANGERS LIKE US, AND IF WE BROUGHT HER TO STORM THE CASTLE...
...AND IF FOR SOME REASON WE AREN'T ABLE TO DEFEAT THE RYANBAN, CHU'NYAN WILL SUFFER THE WORST FOR IT.
.....
WHAT-EVER ELSE HAPPENS...
...IT'LL BE BETTER IF WE TAKE THE RYANBAN...
...AND PUT HIM OUT OF OUR MISERY!
HEH
SO...
WHAT HAPPENS IF WE FIND OUT THAT THE RYANBAN DOES HAVE ONE OF SAKURA'S FEATHERS?

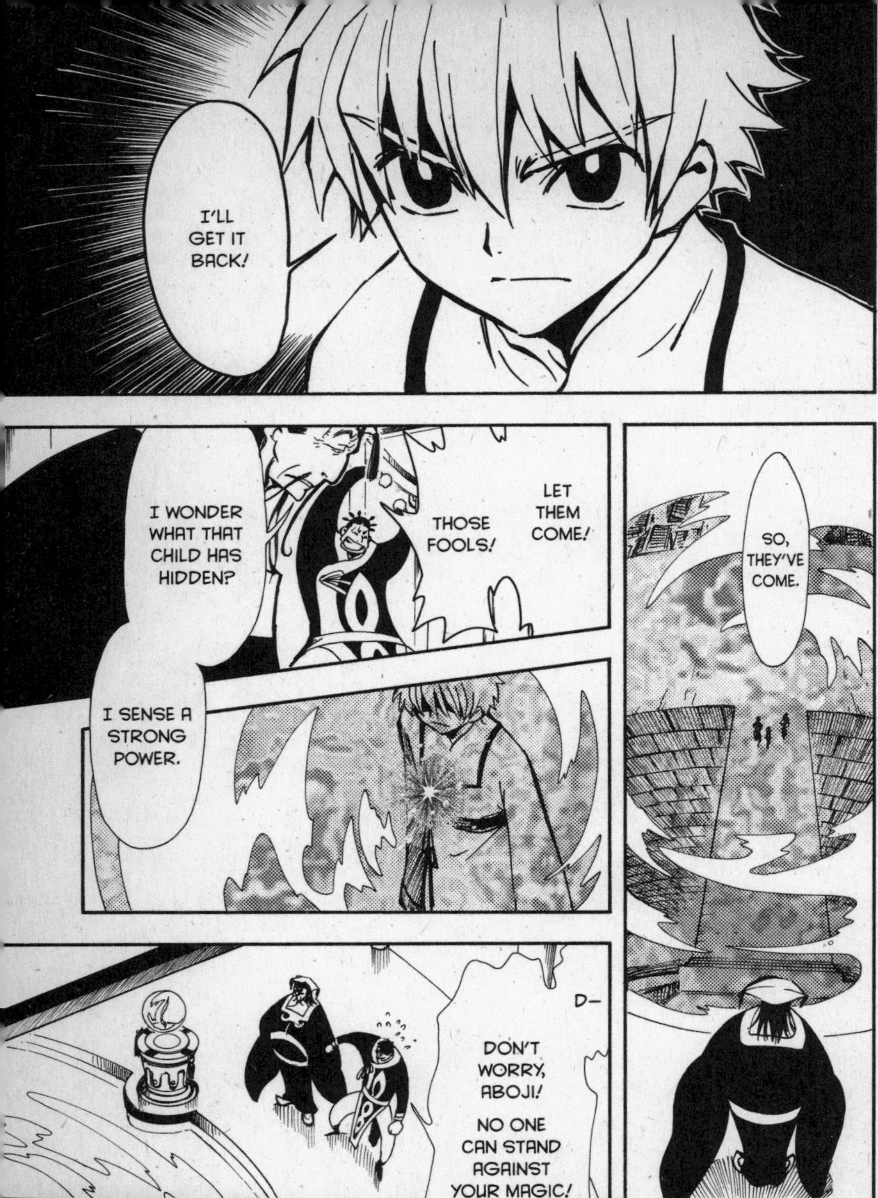
I'LL GET IT BACK!
SO, THEY'VE COME.
LET THEM COME!
THOSE FOOLS!
I WONDER WHAT THAT CHILD HAS HIDDEN?
I SENSE A STRONG POWER.
D—
DON'T WORRY, ABOJI!
NO ONE CAN STAND AGAINST YOUR MAGIC!

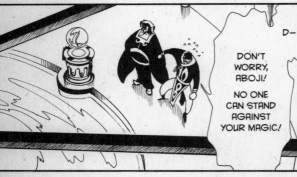

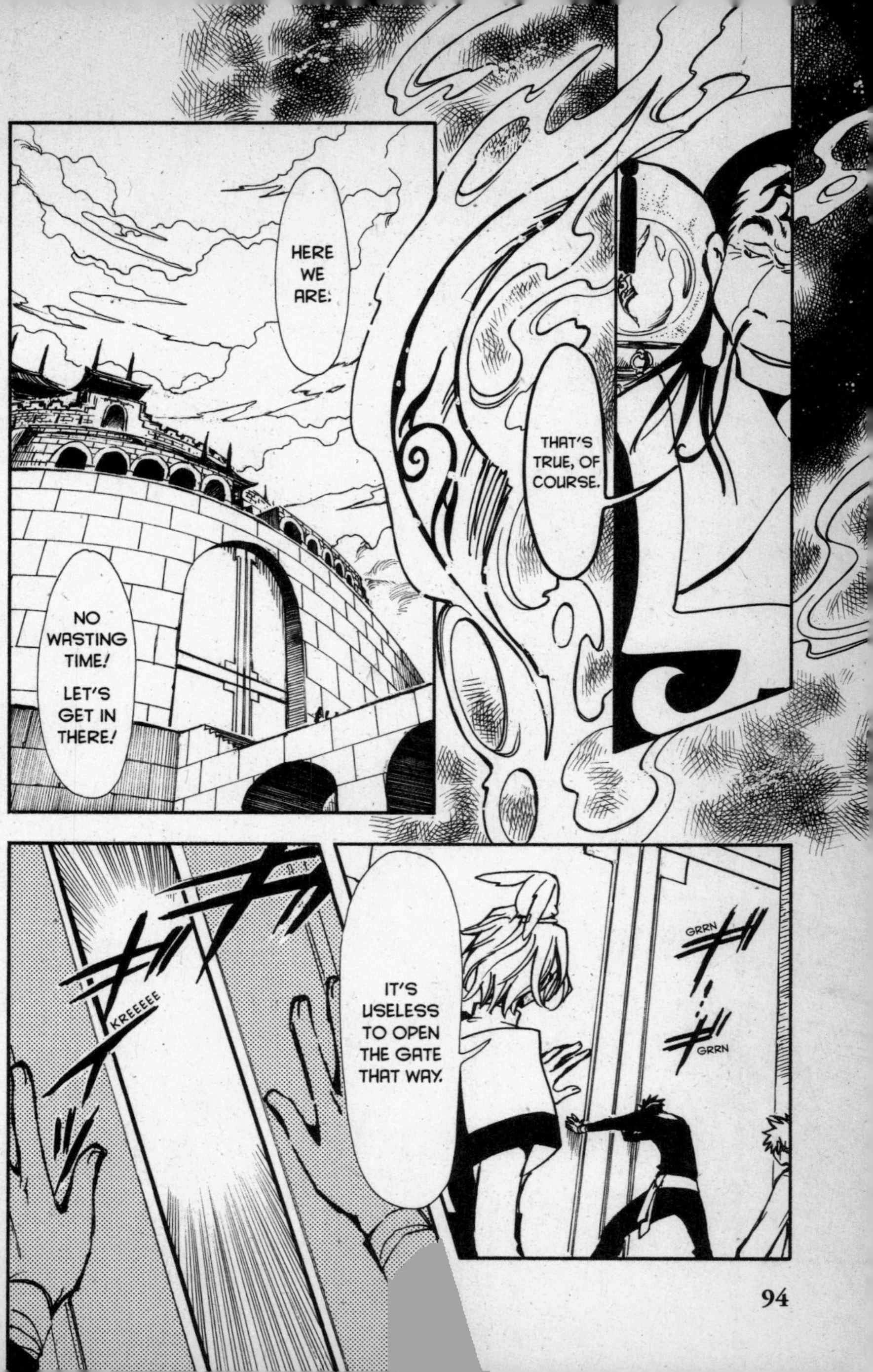

THAT'S TRUE, OF COURSE.
HERE WE ARE:
NO WASTING TIME!
LET'S GET IN THERE!
GRRN
GRRN
IT'S USELESS TO OPEN THE GATE THAT WAY.
KREEEEE

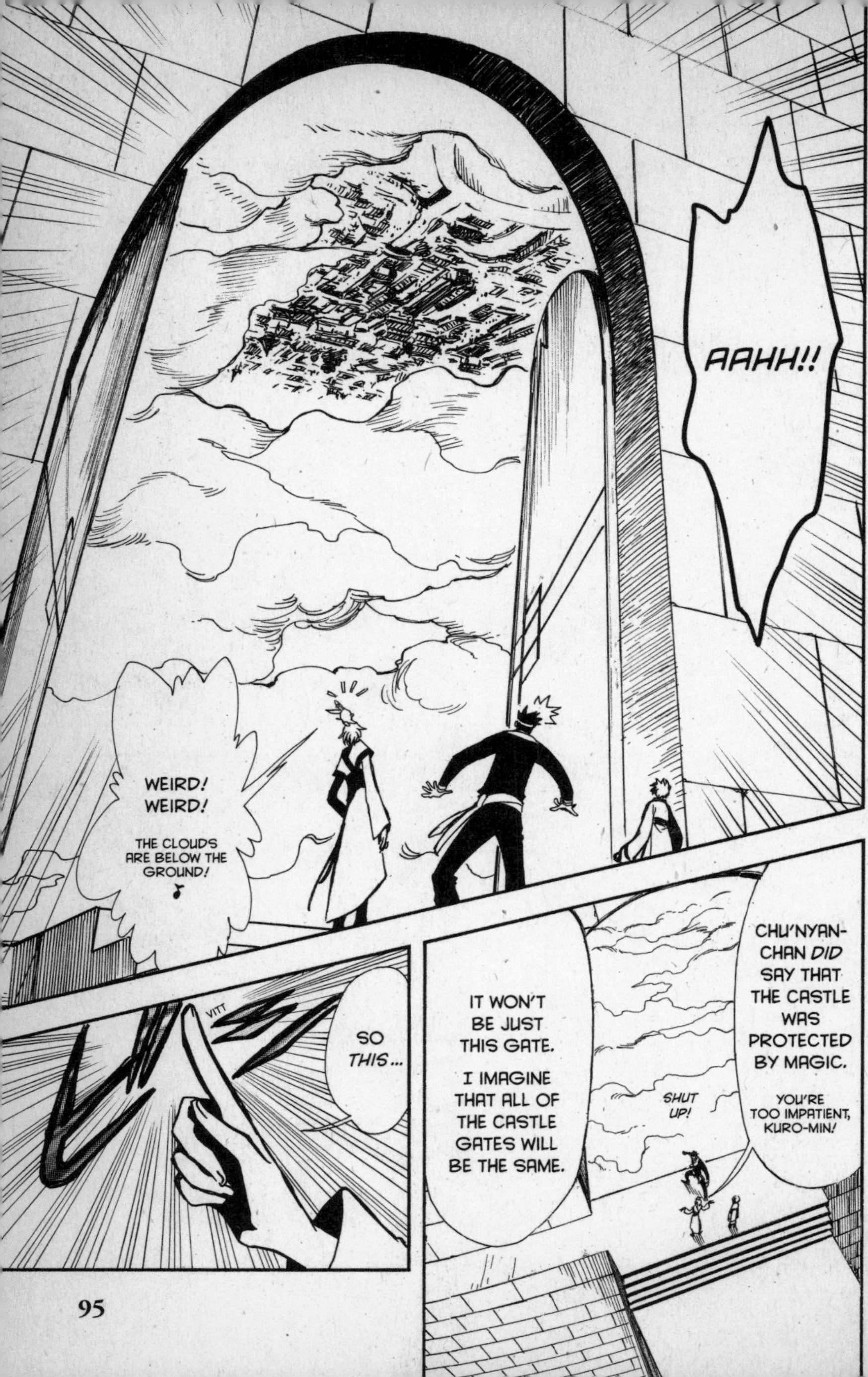
AAHH!!
WEIRD! WEIRD!
THE CLOUDS ARE BELOW THE GROUND!
CHU'NYAN-CHAN *DID* SAY THAT THE CASTLE WAS PROTECTED BY MAGIC.
YOU'RE TOO IMPATIENT, KURO-MIN!
SHUT UP!
IT WON'T BE JUST THIS GATE.
I IMAGINE THAT ALL OF THE CASTLE GATES WILL BE THE SAME.
VITT
SO *THIS*...

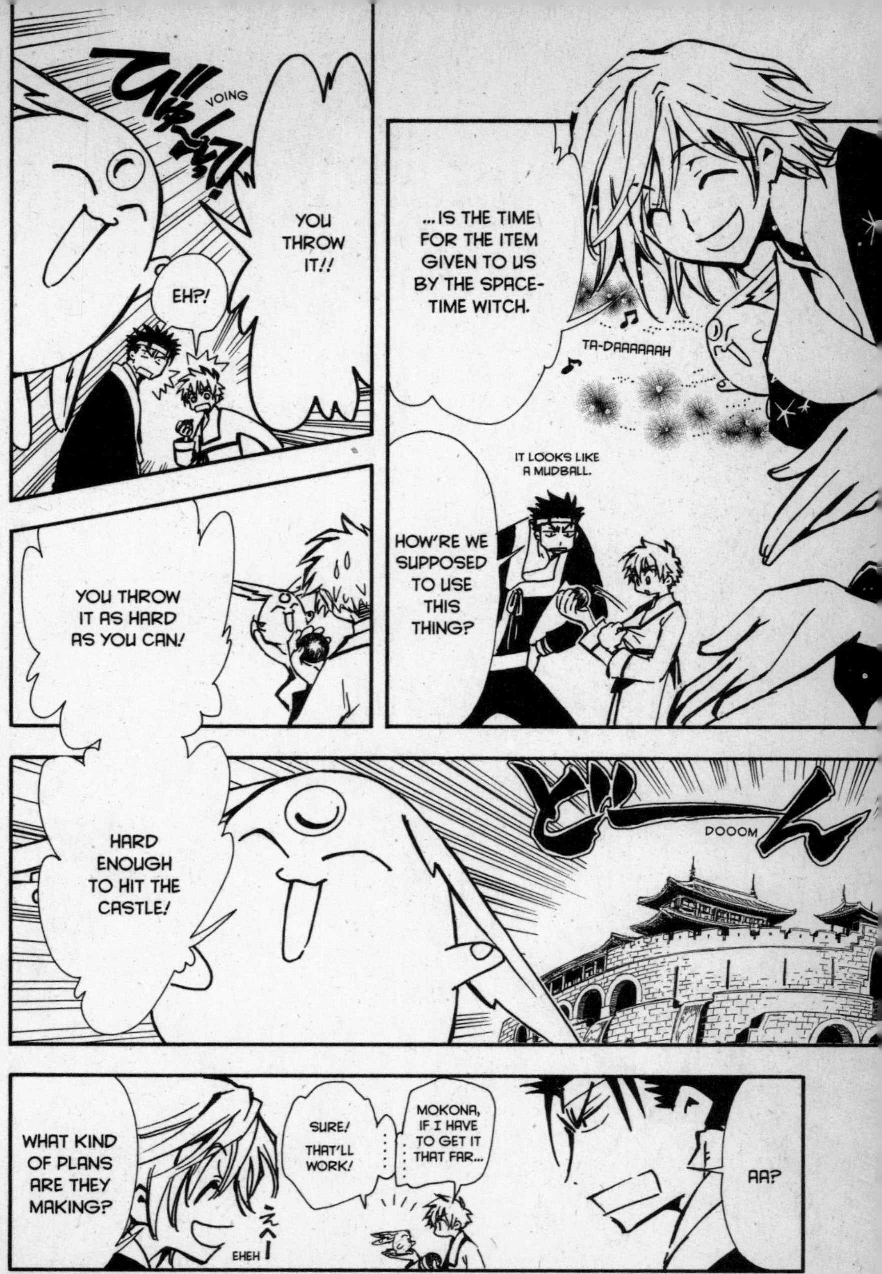
...IS THE TIME FOR THE ITEM GIVEN TO US BY THE SPACE-TIME WITCH.
TA-DAAAAAAH
IT LOOKS LIKE A MUDBALL.
HOW'RE WE SUPPOSED TO USE THIS THING?
YOU THROW IT!!
VOING
EH?!
YOU THROW IT AS HARD AS YOU CAN!
DOOOM
HARD ENOUGH TO HIT THE CASTLE!
AA?
MOKONA, IF I HAVE TO GET IT THAT FAR...
......
SURE! THAT'LL WORK!
WHAT KIND OF PLANS ARE THEY MAKING?
EHEH

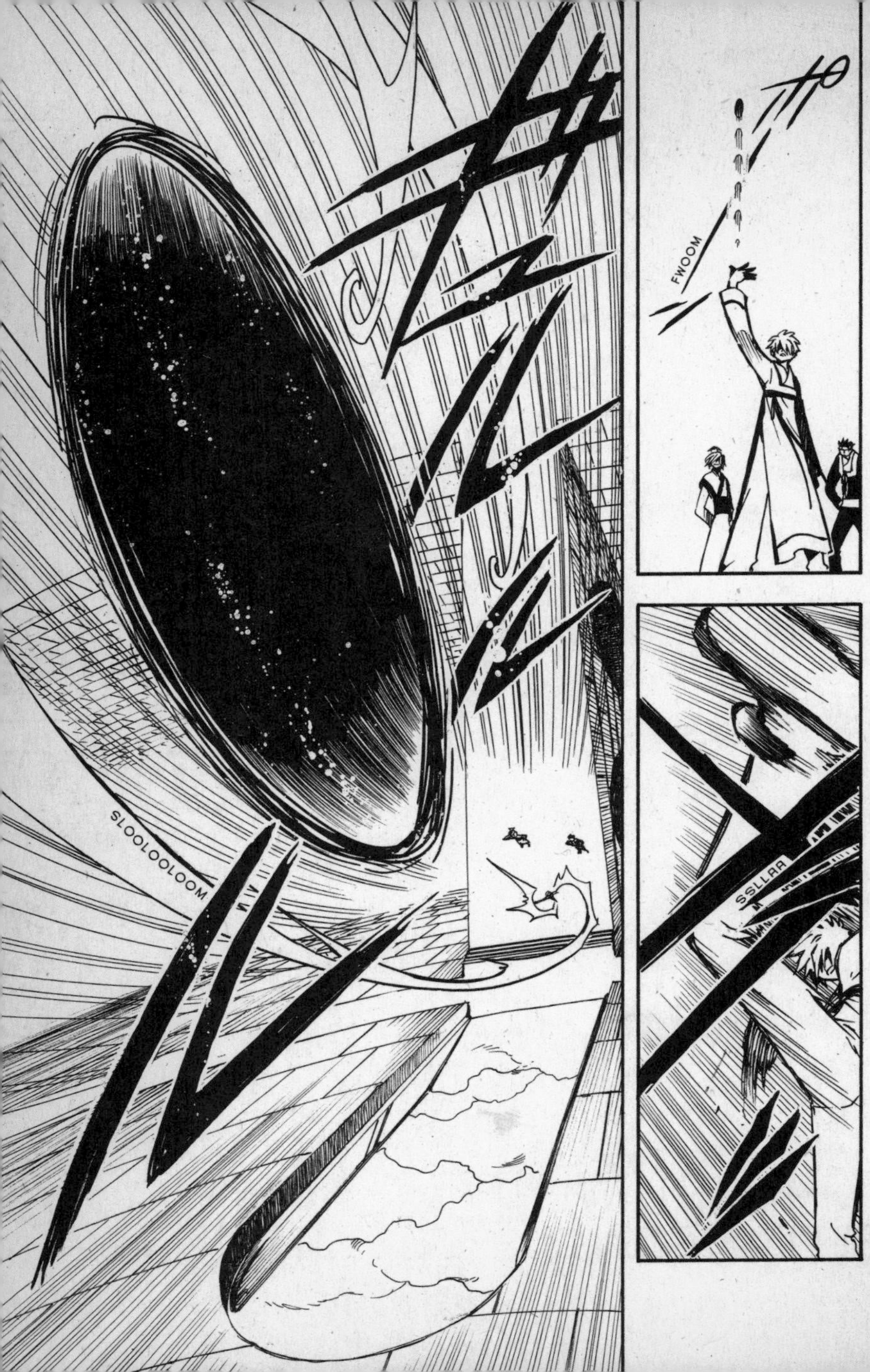
FWOOM
SSLLAA
SLOOLOOLOOM

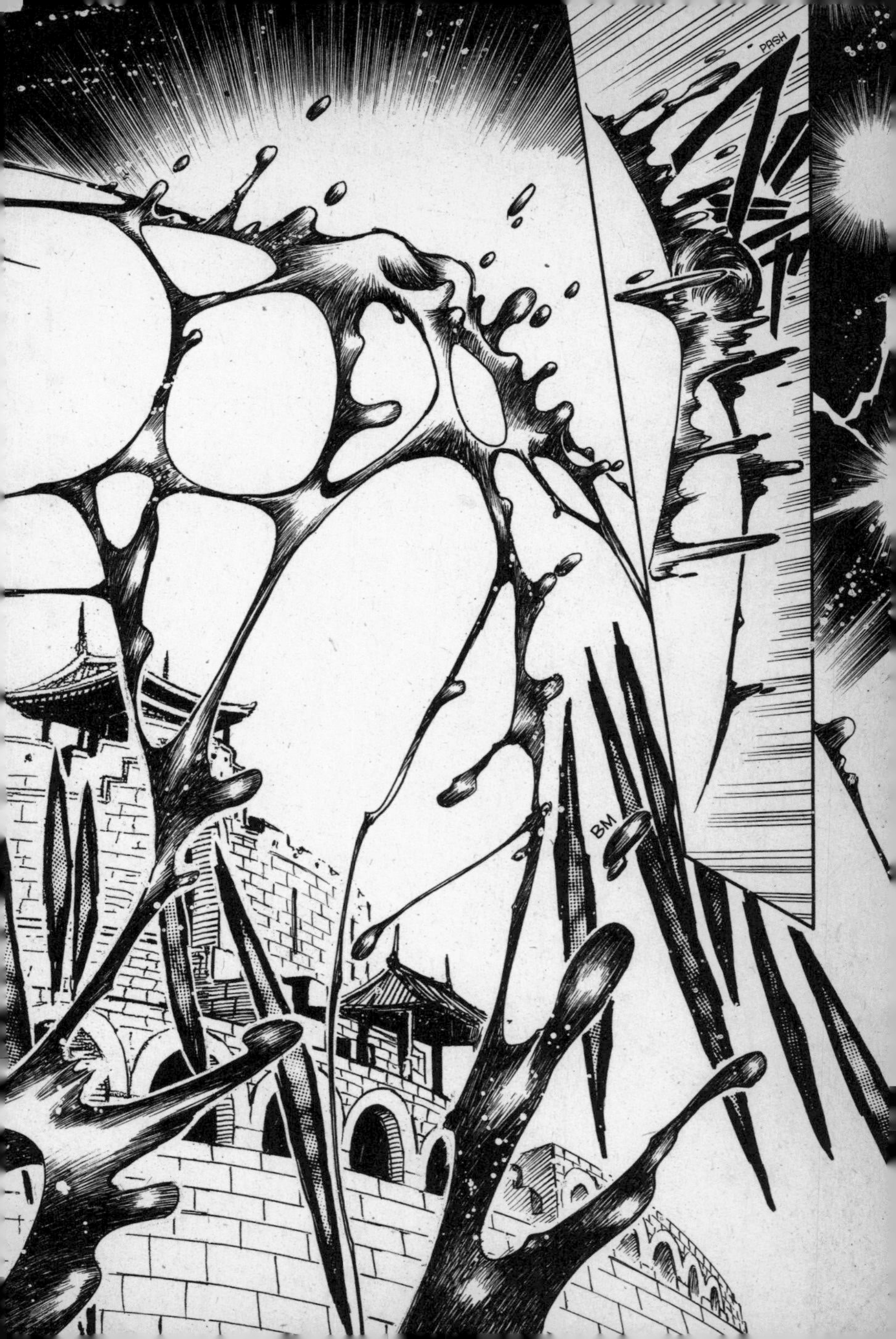
PASH
BM

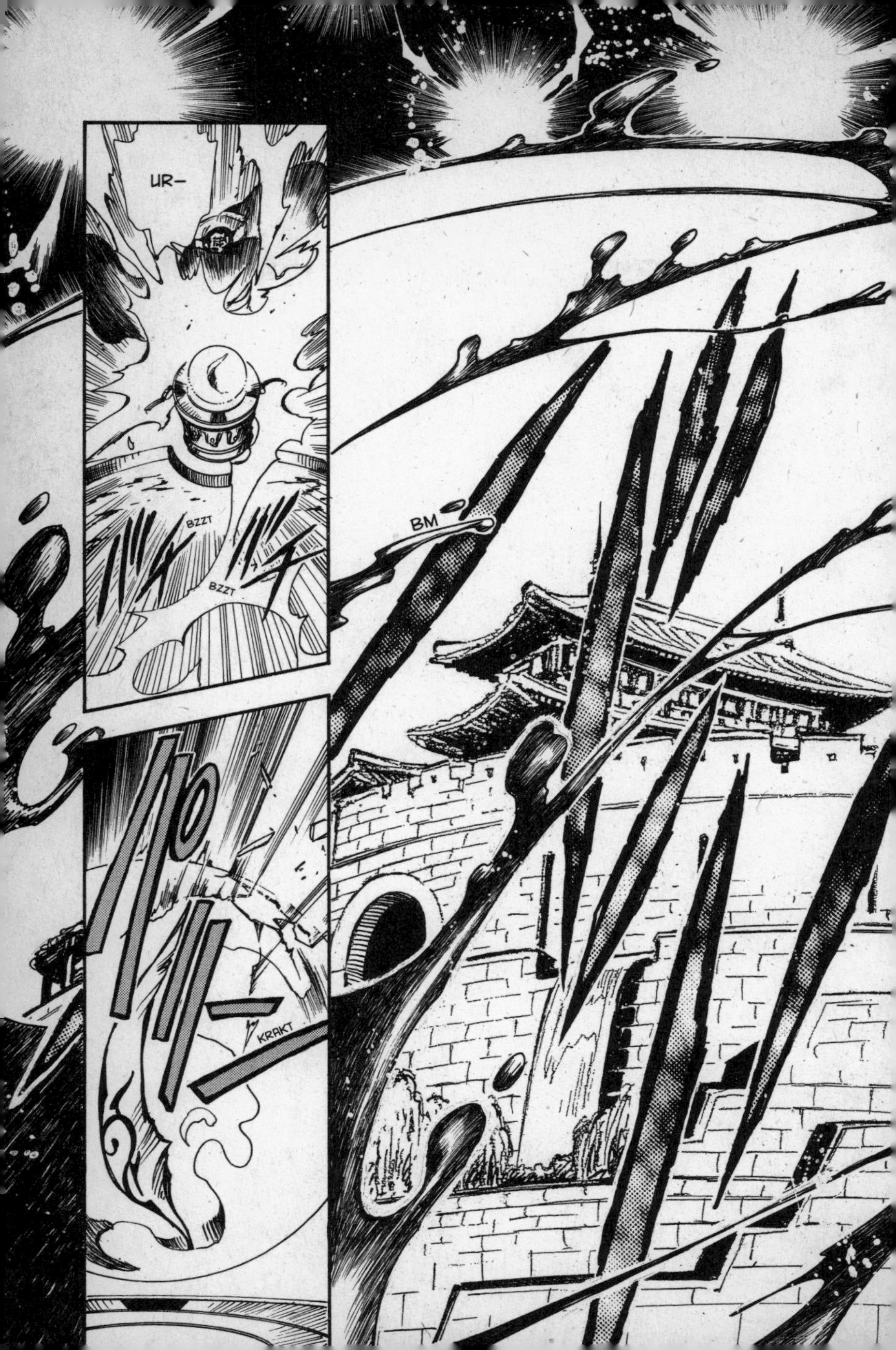
BM
UR–
BZZT
BZZT
KRAKT

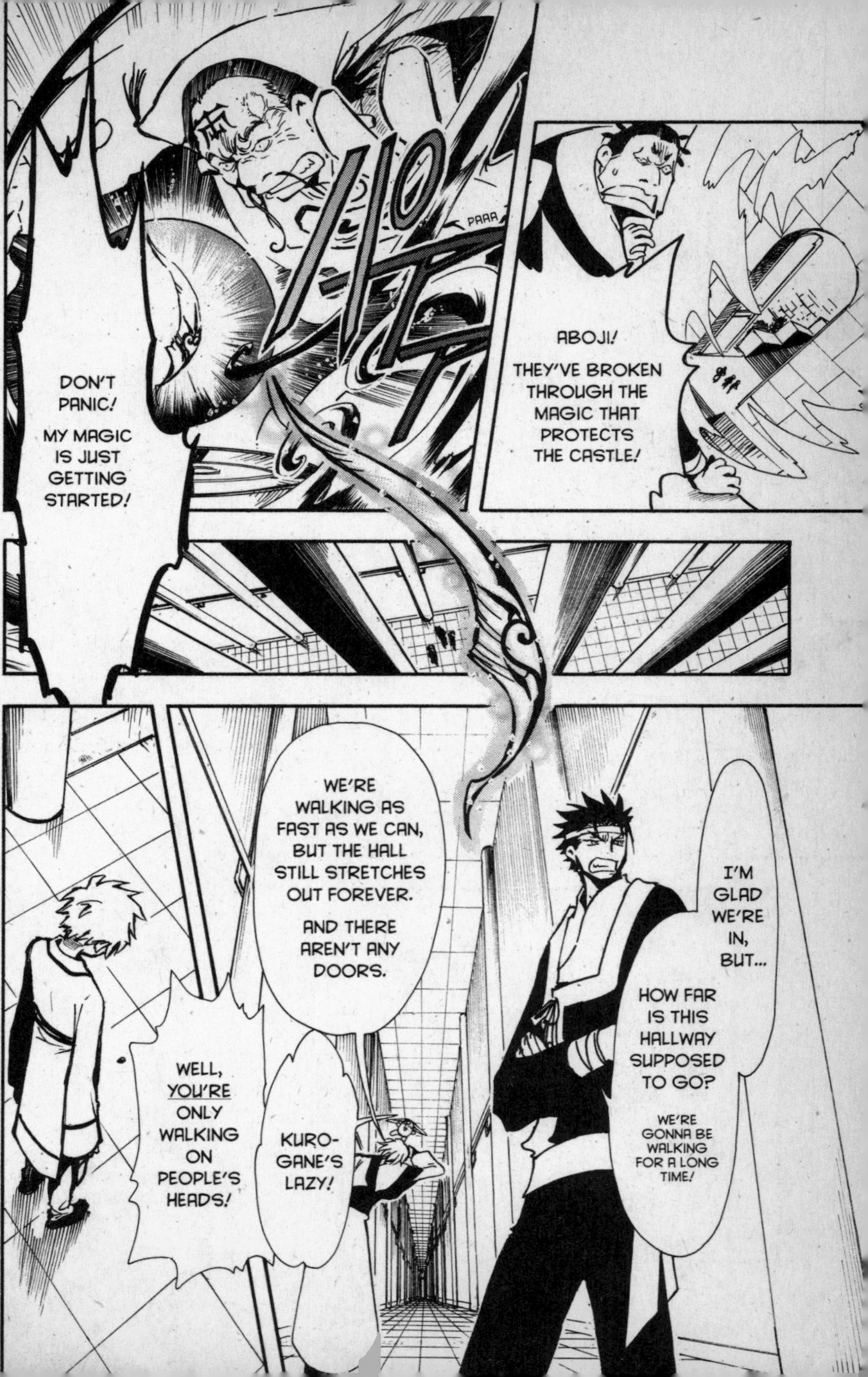
ABOJI!
THEY'VE BROKEN THROUGH THE MAGIC THAT PROTECTS THE CASTLE!
PAAA
DON'T PANIC!
MY MAGIC IS JUST GETTING STARTED!
I'M GLAD WE'RE IN, BUT...
HOW FAR IS THIS HALLWAY SUPPOSED TO GO?
WE'RE GONNA BE WALKING FOR A LONG TIME!
WE'RE WALKING AS FAST AS WE CAN, BUT THE HALL STILL STRETCHES OUT FOREVER.
AND THERE AREN'T ANY DOORS.
KURO-GANE'S LAZY!
WELL, YOU'RE ONLY WALKING ON PEOPLE'S HEADS!

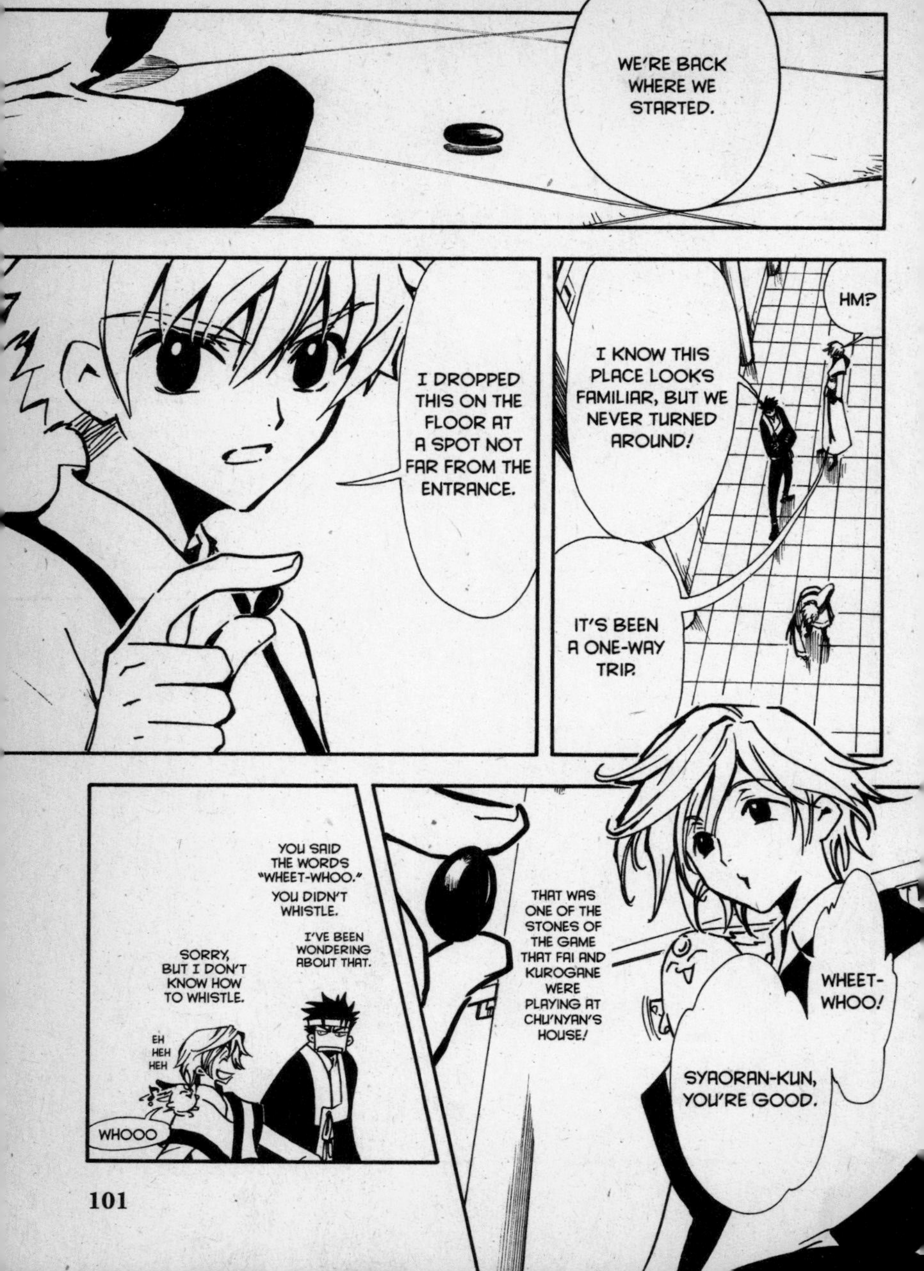
WE'RE BACK WHERE WE STARTED.
HM?
I KNOW THIS PLACE LOOKS FAMILIAR, BUT WE NEVER TURNED AROUND!
IT'S BEEN A ONE-WAY TRIP.
I DROPPED THIS ON THE FLOOR AT A SPOT NOT FAR FROM THE ENTRANCE.
WHEET-WHOO!
SYAORAN-KUN, YOU'RE GOOD.
THAT WAS ONE OF THE STONES OF THE GAME THAT FAI AND KUROGANE WERE PLAYING AT CHU'NYAN'S HOUSE!
YOU SAID THE WORDS "WHEET-WHOO." YOU DIDN'T WHISTLE.
I'VE BEEN WONDERING ABOUT THAT.
SORRY, BUT I DON'T KNOW HOW TO WHISTLE.
EH HEH HEH
WHOOO

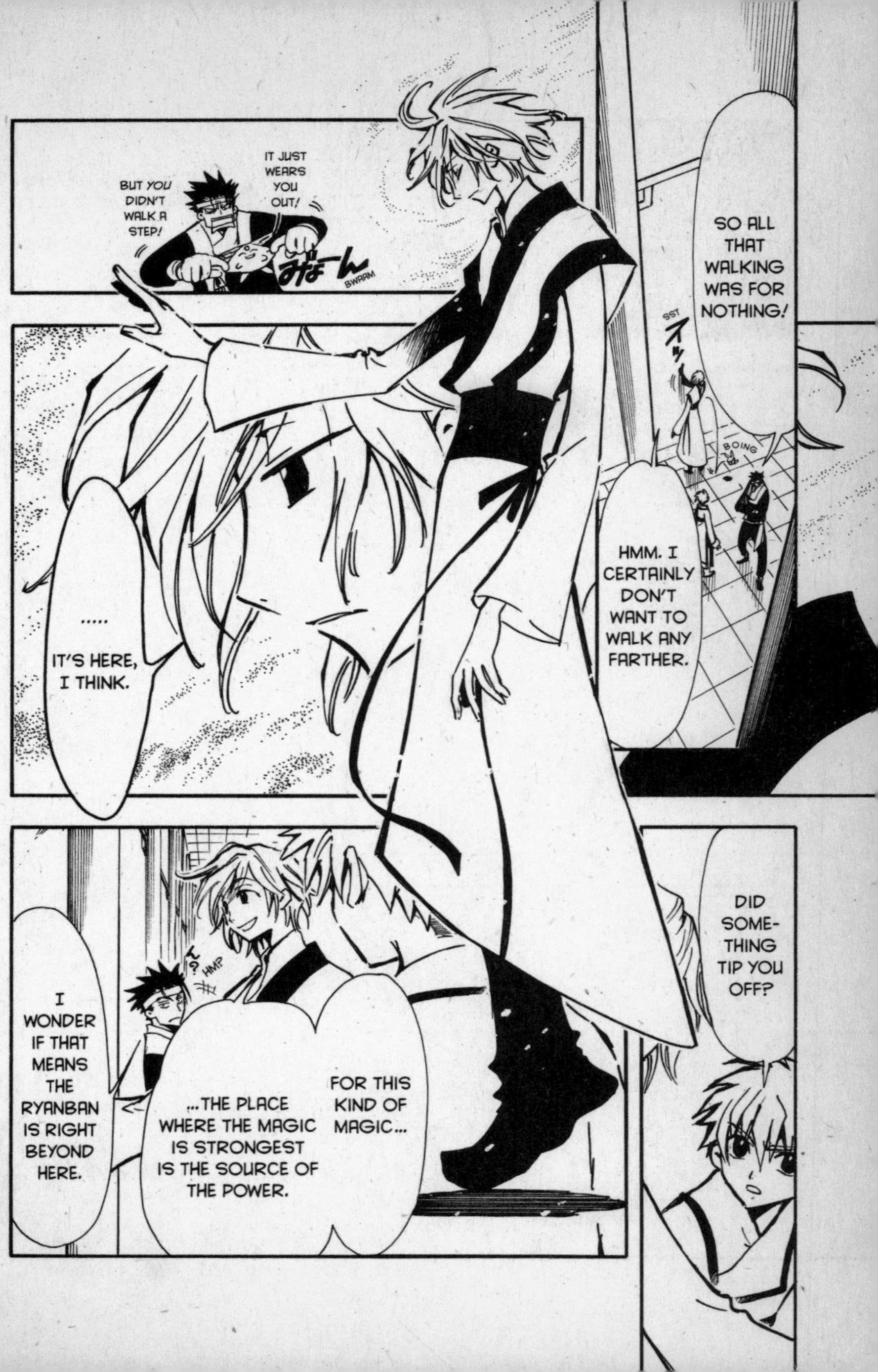
SO ALL THAT WALKING WAS FOR NOTHING!
SST
BOING
HMM. I CERTAINLY DON'T WANT TO WALK ANY FARTHER.
IT JUST WEARS YOU OUT!
BUT YOU DIDN'T WALK A STEP!
BWAAM
.....
IT'S HERE, I THINK.
DID SOMETHING TIP YOU OFF?
FOR THIS KIND OF MAGIC...
...THE PLACE WHERE THE MAGIC IS STRONGEST IS THE SOURCE OF THE POWER.
HM?
I WONDER IF THAT MEANS THE RYANBAN IS RIGHT BEYOND HERE.

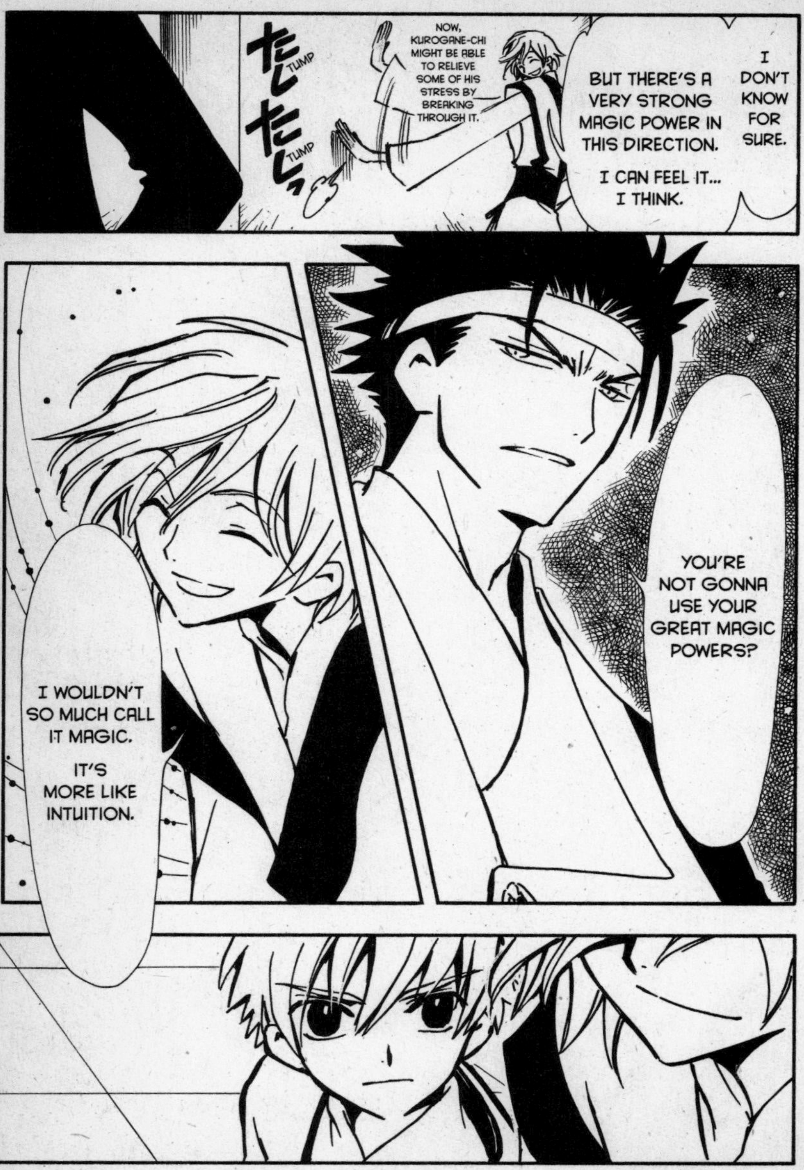
I DON'T KNOW FOR SURE.
BUT THERE'S A VERY STRONG MAGIC POWER IN THIS DIRECTION.
I CAN FEEL IT... I THINK.
NOW, KUROGANE-CHI MIGHT BE ABLE TO RELIEVE SOME OF HIS STRESS BY BREAKING THROUGH IT.
たし TUMP
たしっ TUMP
YOU'RE NOT GONNA USE YOUR GREAT MAGIC POWERS?
I WOULDN'T SO MUCH CALL IT MAGIC.
IT'S MORE LIKE INTUITION.

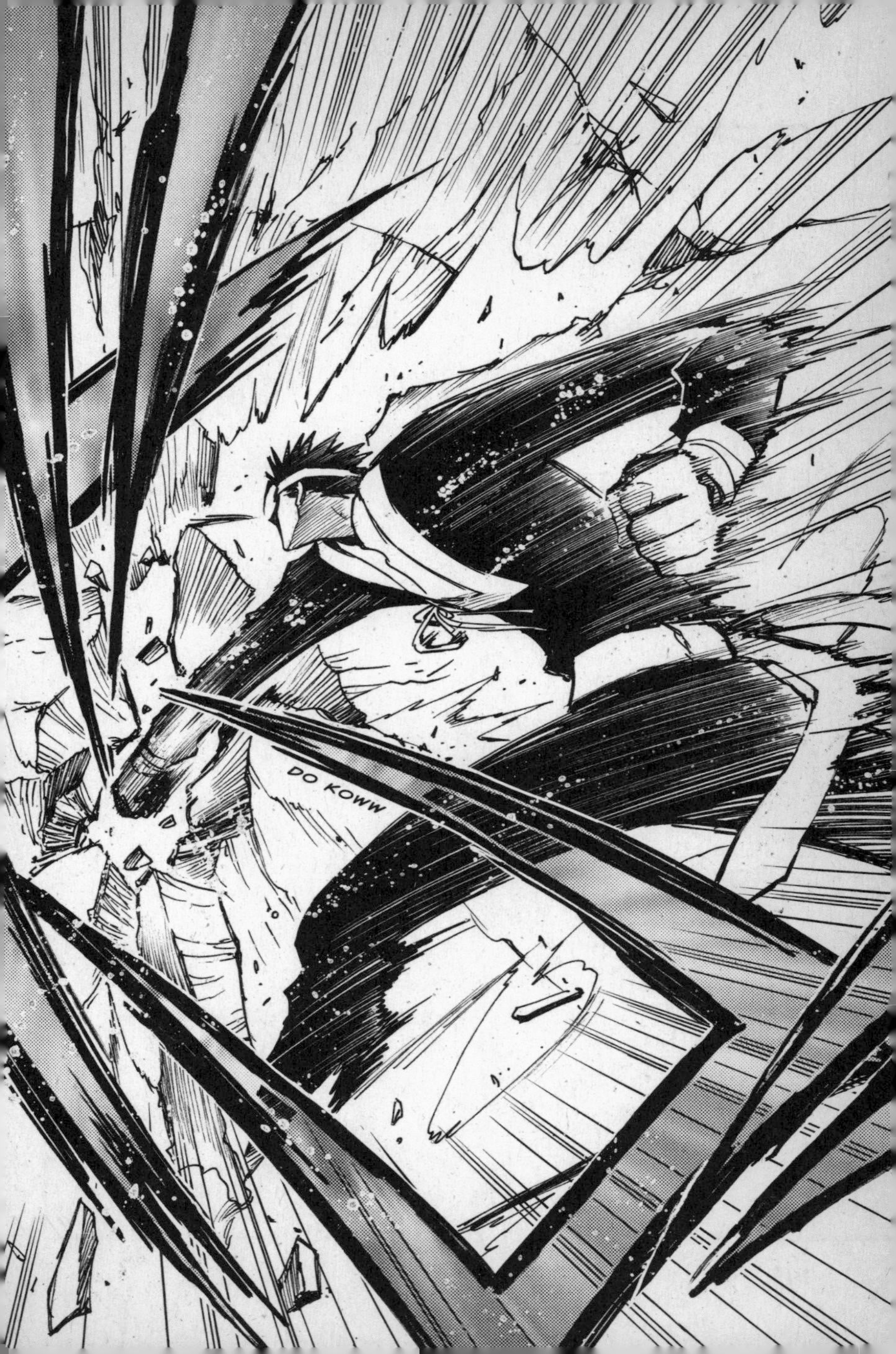
DO KOWW

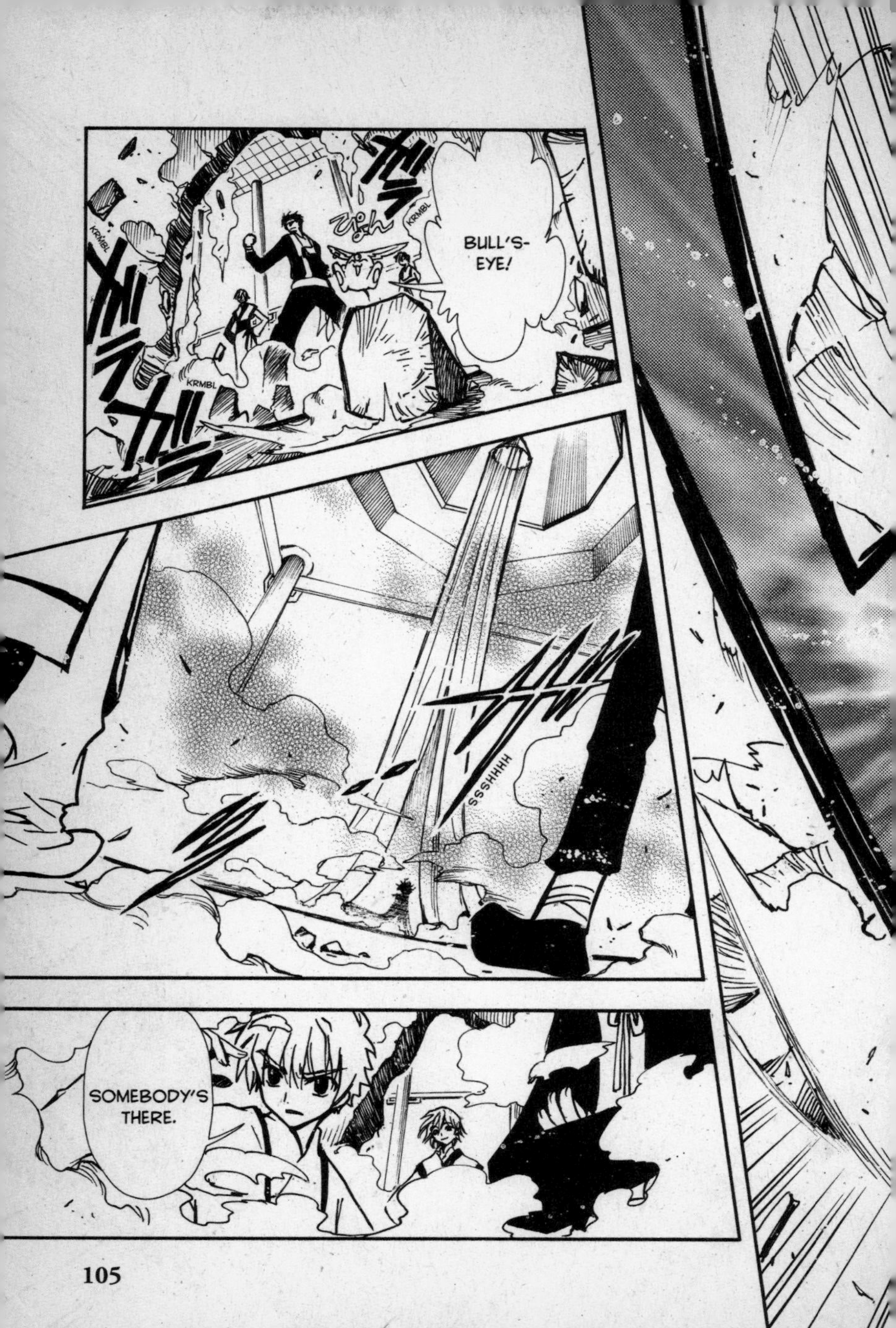
BULL'S-EYE!
KRMBL
ガラ
ぴょん
KRMBL
ガラガラ
KRMBL
SSSHHHH
SOMEBODY'S THERE.

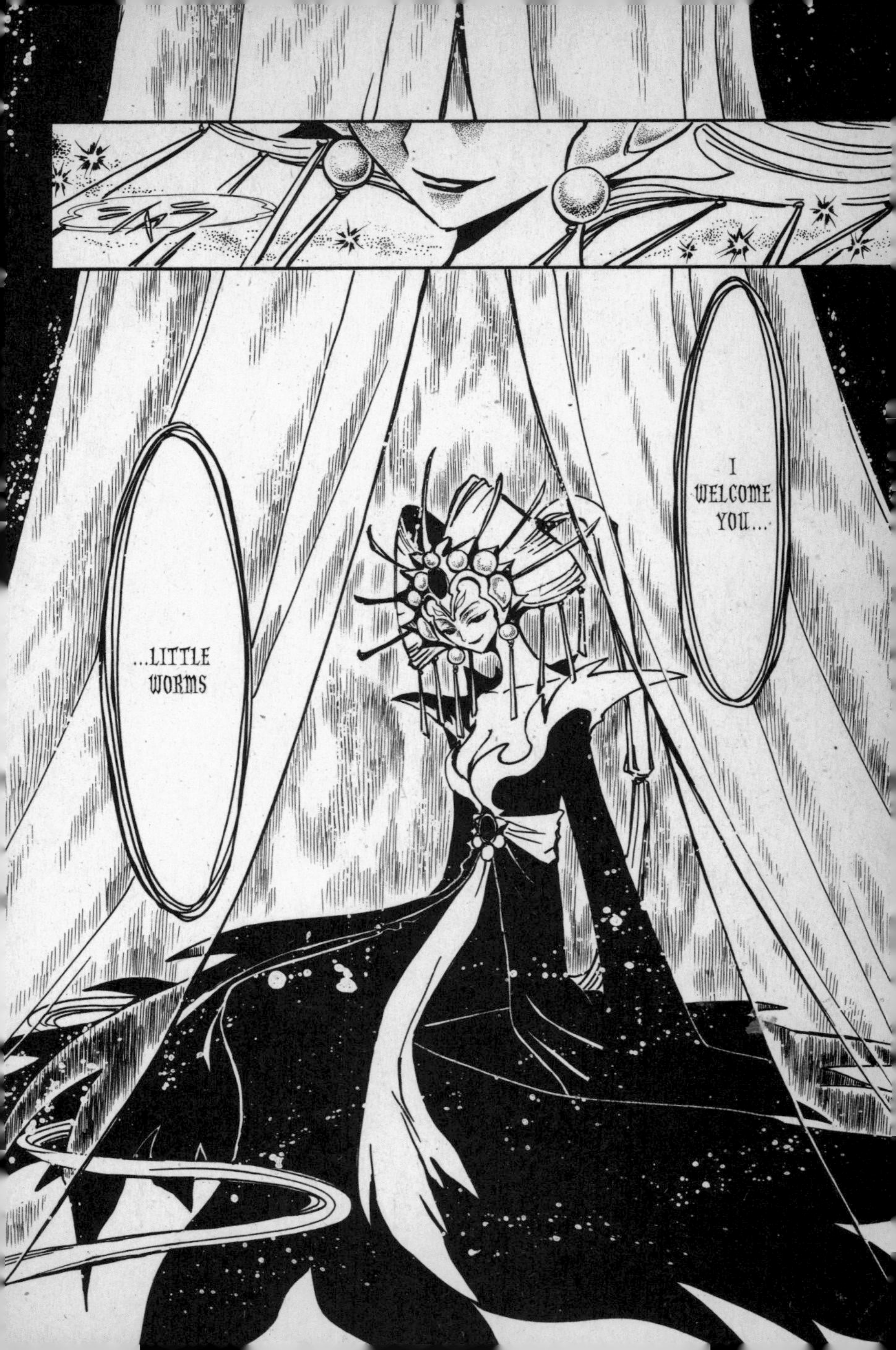
I WELCOME YOU...
...LITTLE WORMS

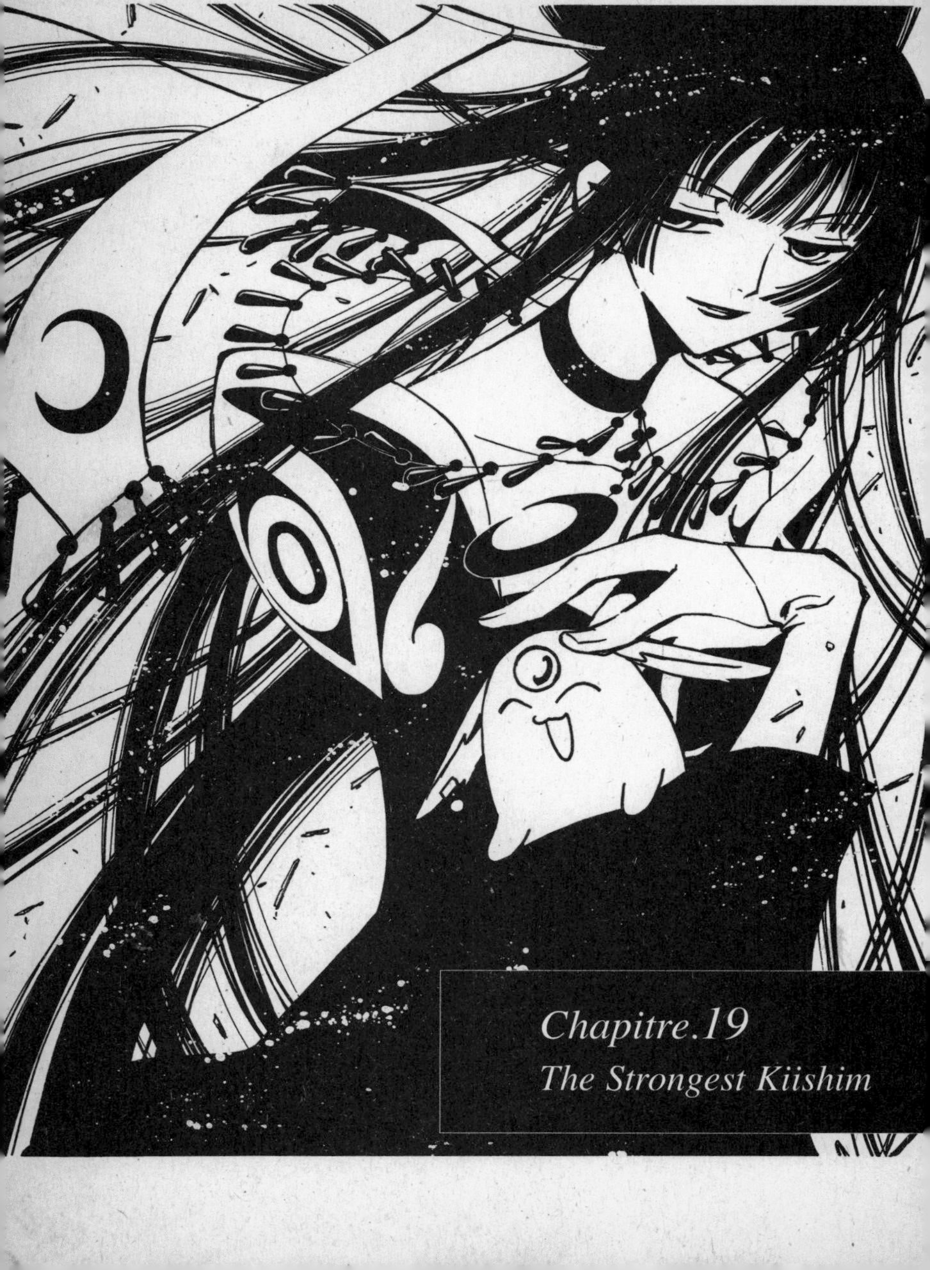

Chapitre.19
The Strongest Kiishim

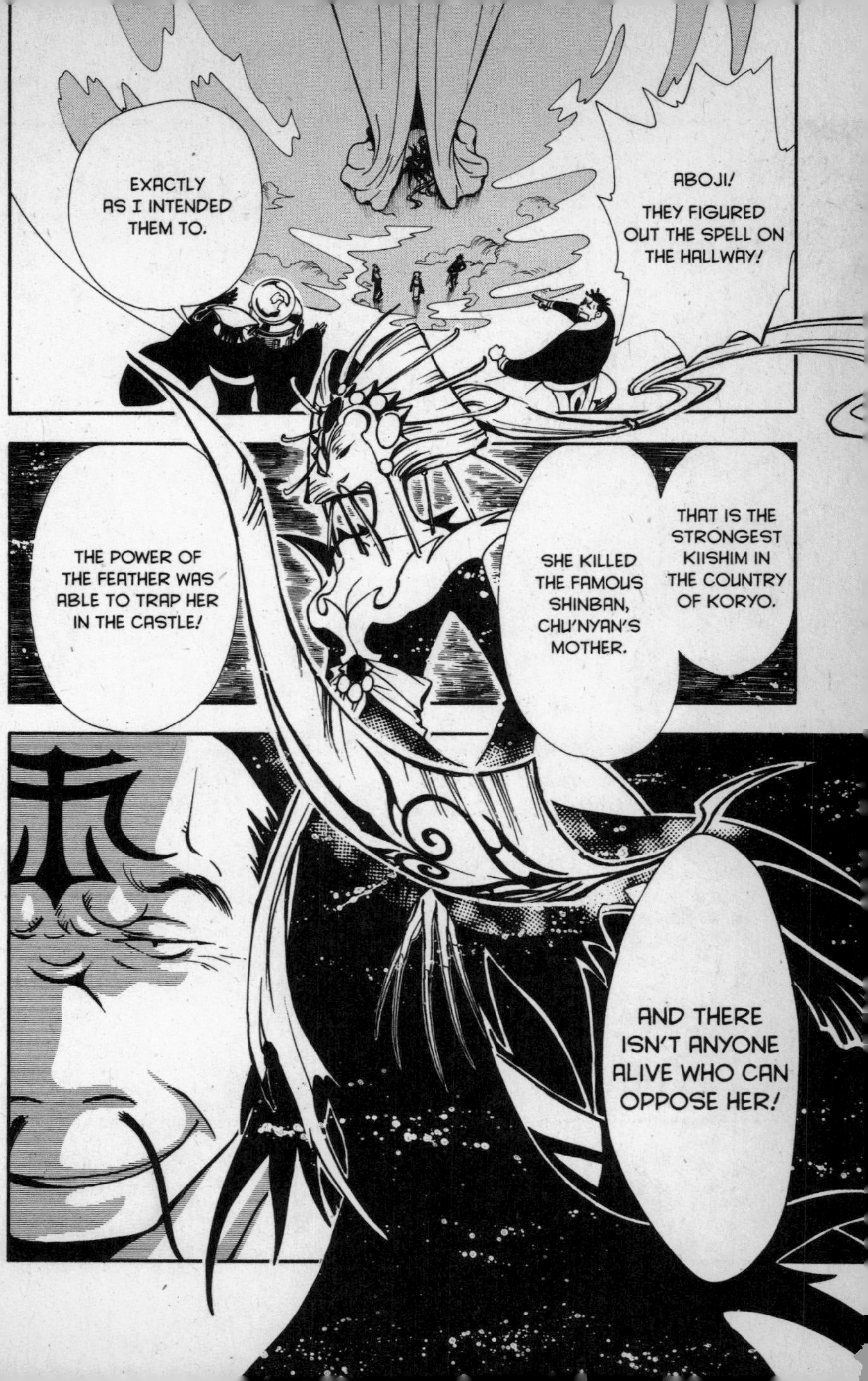
ABOJI! THEY FIGURED OUT THE SPELL ON THE HALLWAY!
EXACTLY AS I INTENDED THEM TO.
THAT IS THE STRONGEST KIISHIM IN THE COUNTRY OF KORYO.
SHE KILLED THE FAMOUS SHINBAN, CHU'NYAN'S MOTHER.
THE POWER OF THE FEATHER WAS ABLE TO TRAP HER IN THE CASTLE!
AND THERE ISN'T ANYONE ALIVE WHO CAN OPPOSE HER!

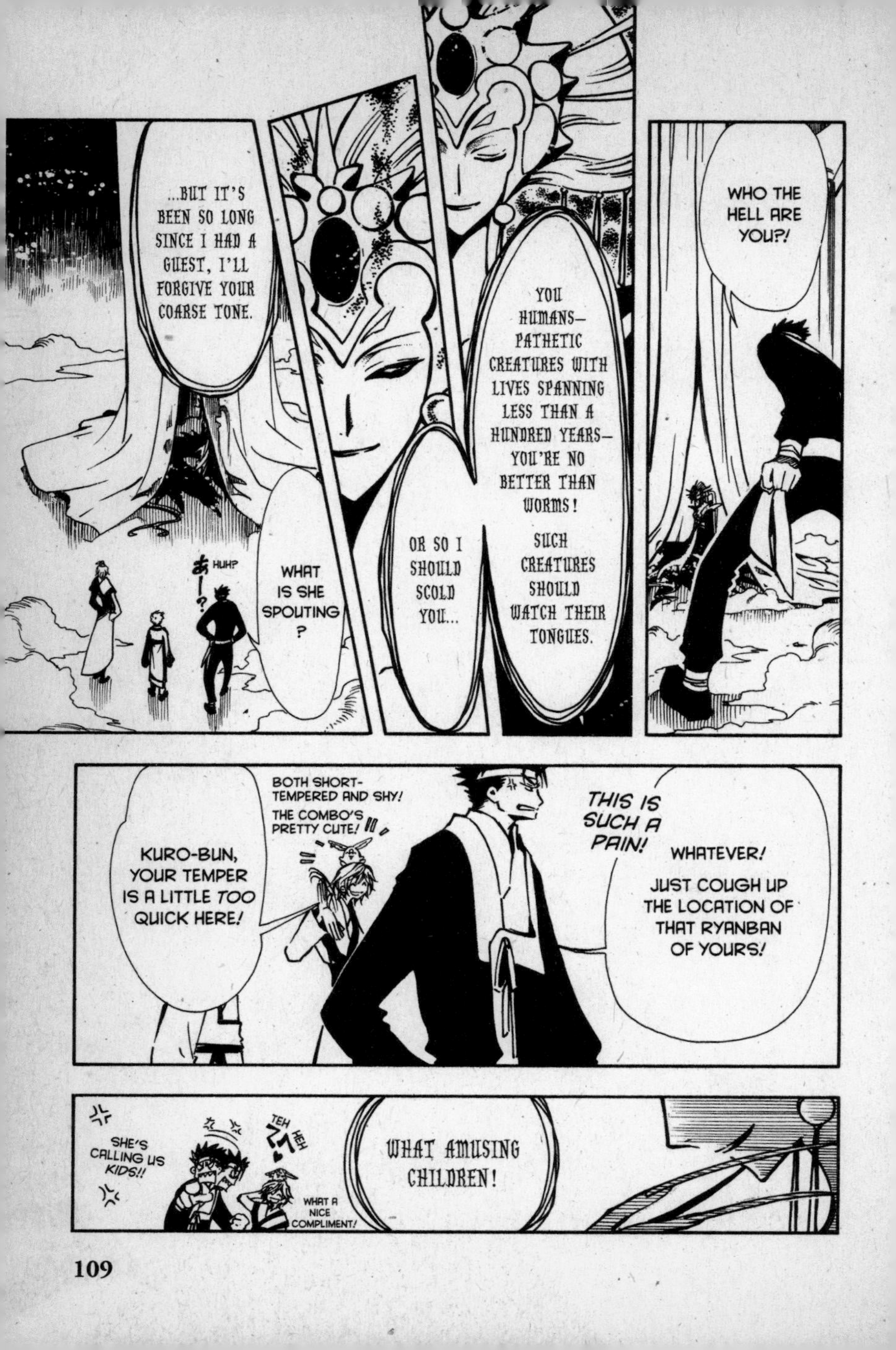
WHO THE HELL ARE YOU?!
YOU HUMANS—PATHETIC CREATURES WITH LIVES SPANNING LESS THAN A HUNDRED YEARS—YOU'RE NO BETTER THAN WORMS!
SUCH CREATURES SHOULD WATCH THEIR TONGUES.
OR SO I SHOULD SCOLD YOU...
...BUT IT'S BEEN SO LONG SINCE I HAD A GUEST, I'LL FORGIVE YOUR COARSE TONE.
WHAT IS SHE SPOUTING?
あー? HUH?
THIS IS SUCH A PAIN!
WHATEVER!
JUST COUGH UP THE LOCATION OF THAT RYANBAN OF YOURS!
BOTH SHORT-TEMPERED AND SHY! THE COMBO'S PRETTY CUTE!
KURO-BUN, YOUR TEMPER IS A LITTLE *TOO* QUICK HERE!
WHAT AMUSING CHILDREN!
TEH HEH
WHAT A NICE COMPLIMENT!
SHE'S CALLING US *KIDS!!*

I THINK THAT SOMETHING I'M SEARCHING FOR IS IN THIS CASTLE.

WILL YOU PLEASE TELL ME WHERE THE RYANBAN IS?

I LIKE THE LOOK IN YOUR EYES.

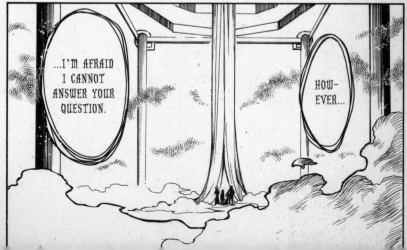

...I'M AFRAID I CANNOT ANSWER YOUR QUESTION.

HOW-EVER...

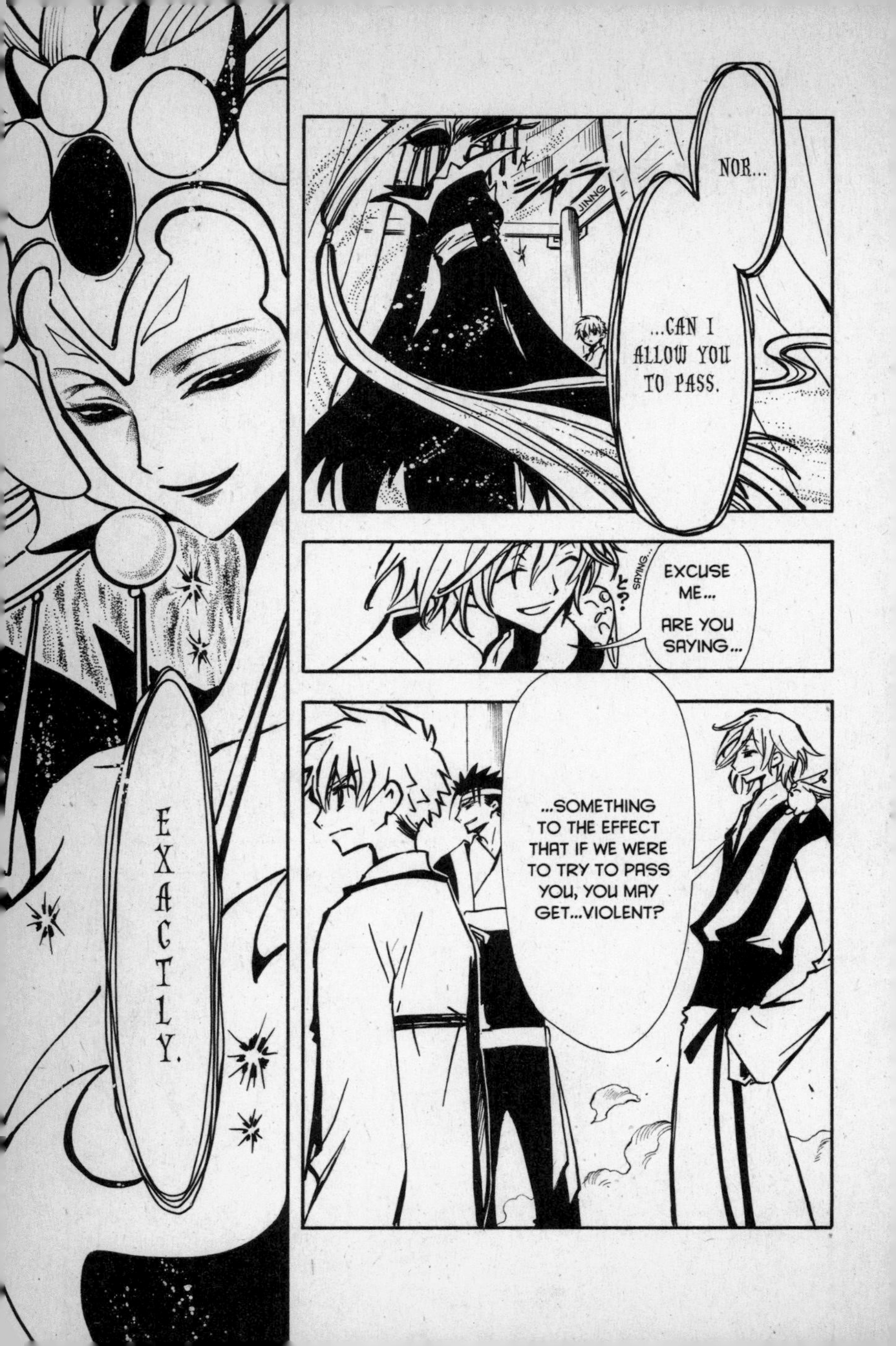
NOR...
JINNG
...CAN I ALLOW YOU TO PASS.
SAYING...
EXCUSE ME...
ARE YOU SAYING...
...SOMETHING TO THE EFFECT THAT IF WE WERE TO TRY TO PASS YOU, YOU MAY GET...VIOLENT?
EXACTLY.

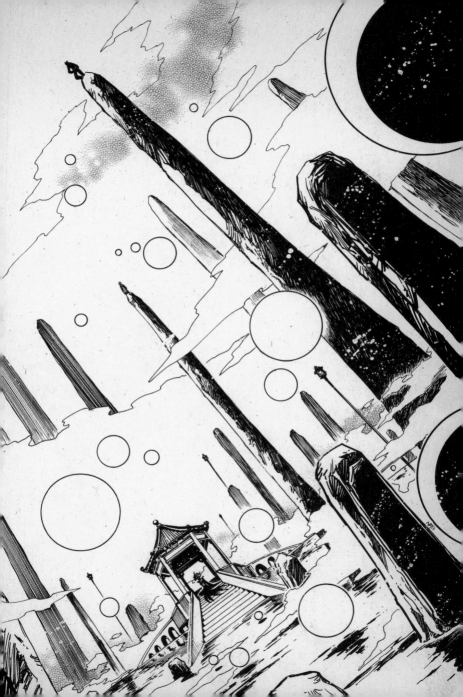

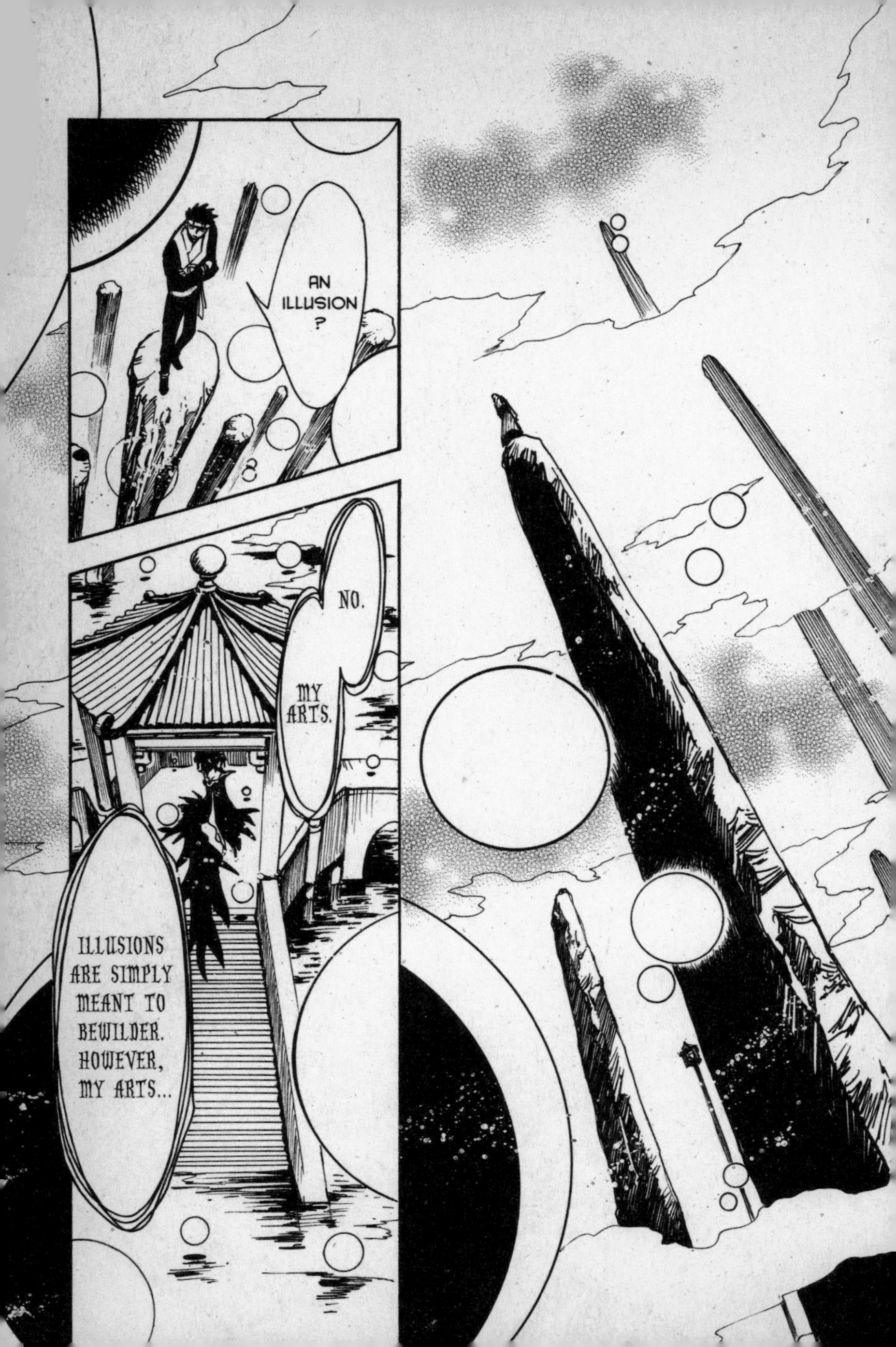
AN ILLUSION?
NO.
MY ARTS.
ILLUSIONS ARE SIMPLY MEANT TO BEWILDER. HOWEVER, MY ARTS...

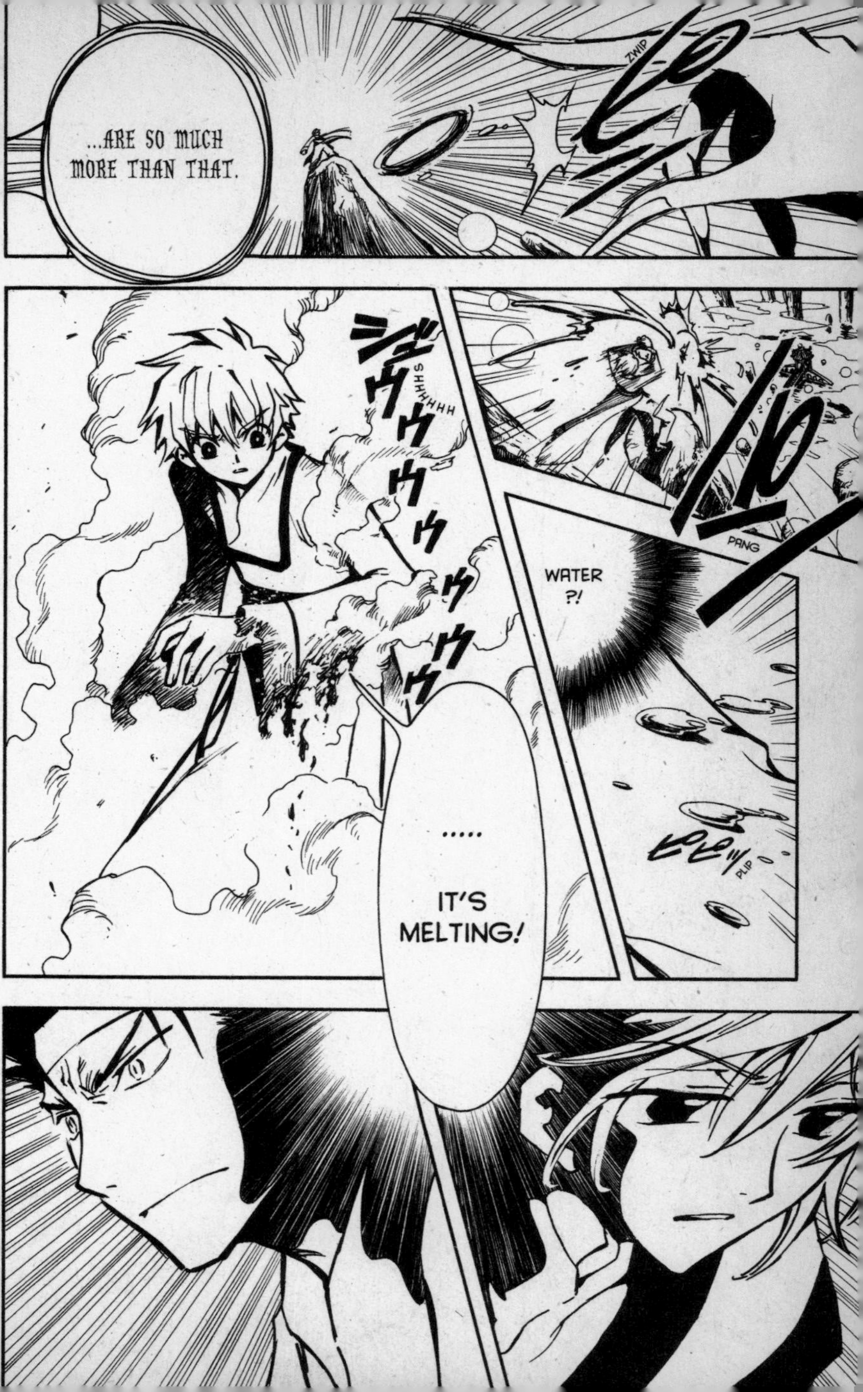
ZWIP
...ARE SO MUCH MORE THAN THAT.
PANG
WATER ?!
PLIP
SHHHHHH
.....
IT'S MELTING!

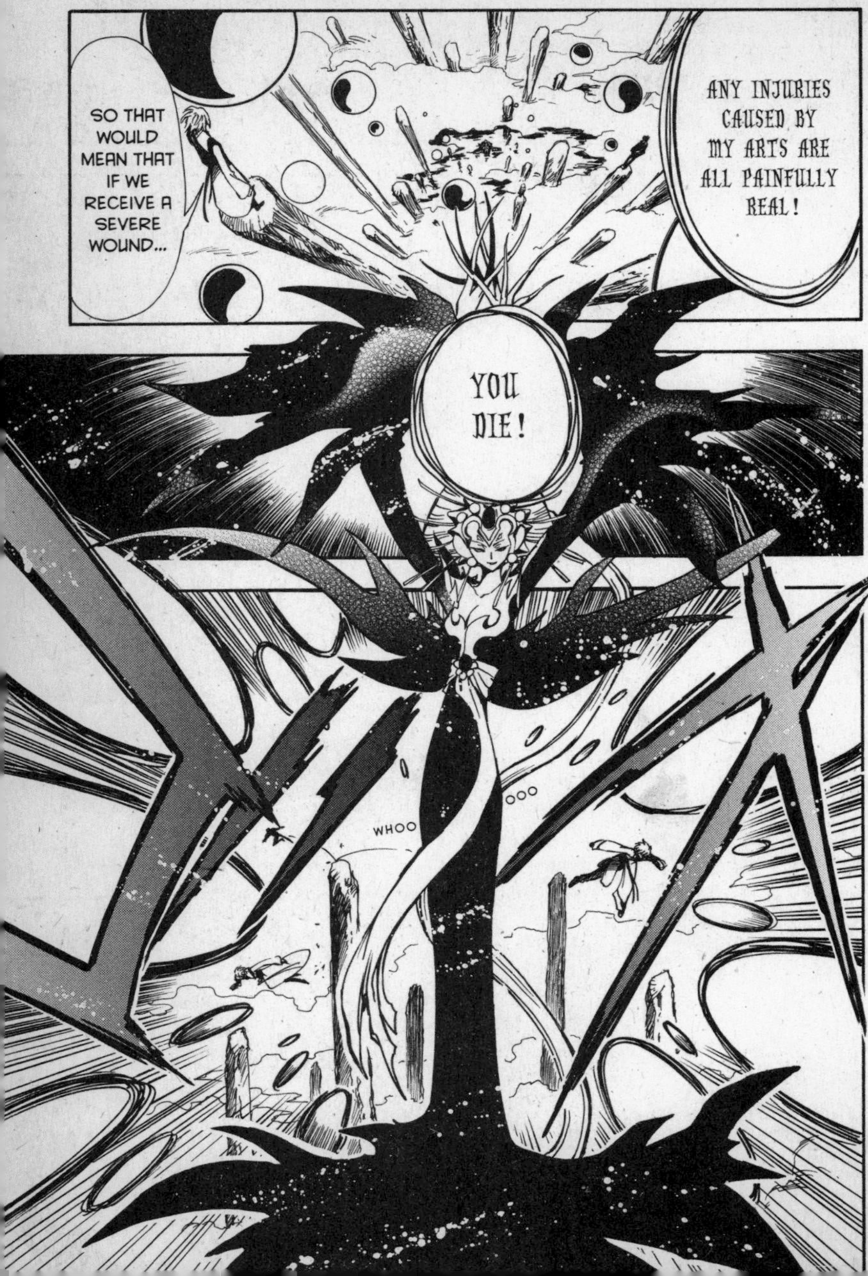
ANY INJURIES CAUSED BY MY ARTS ARE ALL PAINFULLY REAL!
SO THAT WOULD MEAN THAT IF WE RECEIVE A SEVERE WOUND...
YOU DIE!
WHOO
OOO

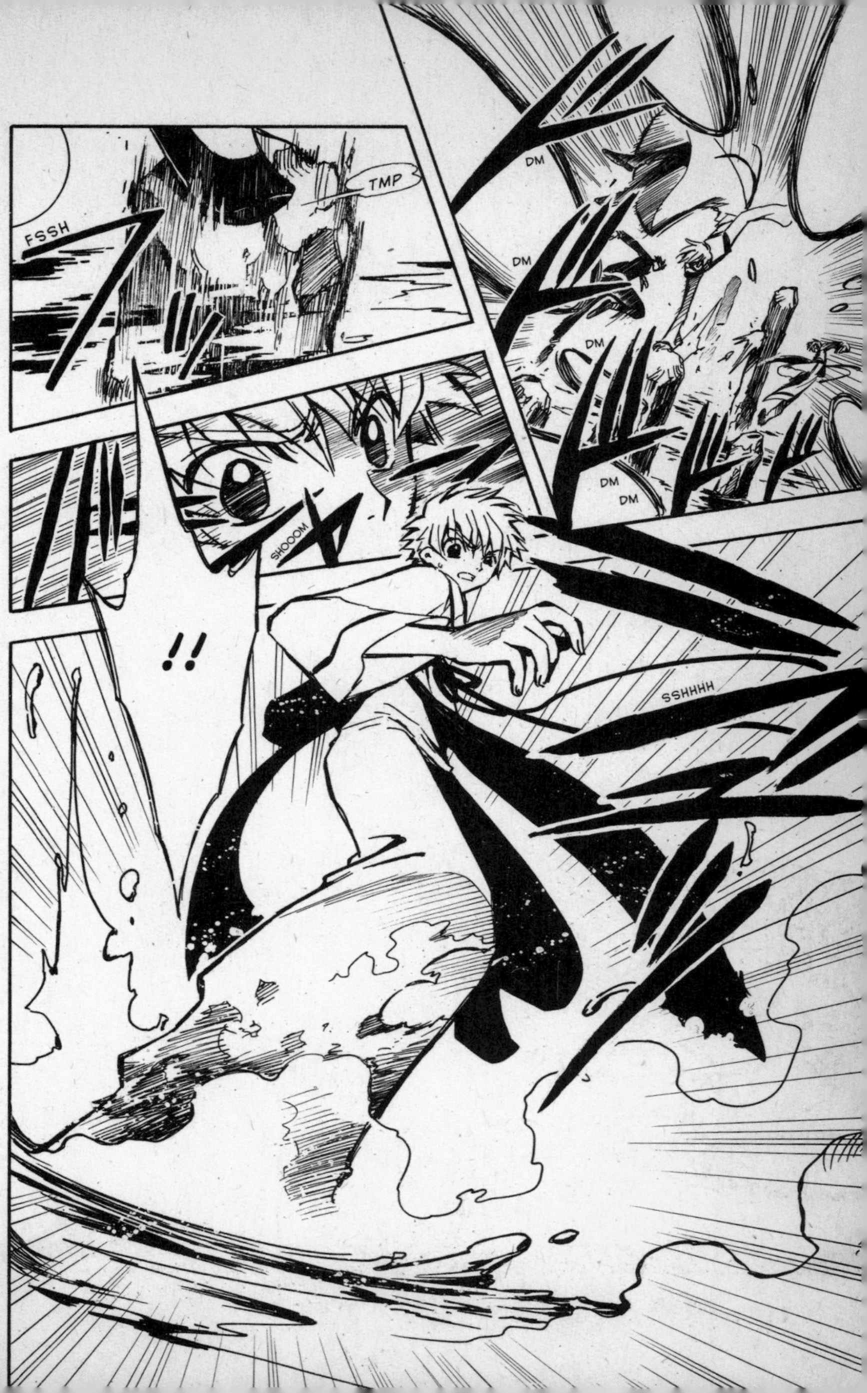
DM
DM
DM
DM
DM
TMP
FSSH
SHOOOM
!!
SSHHHH

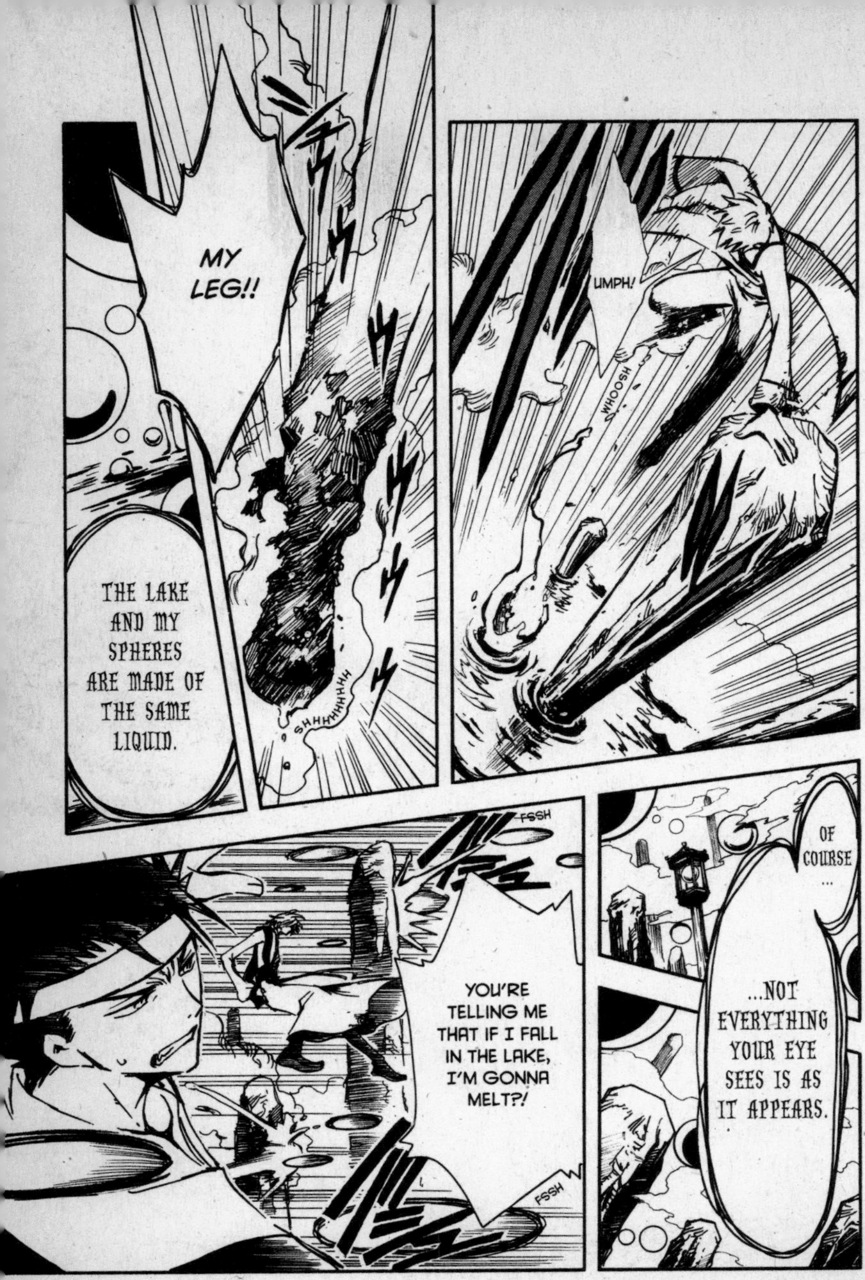
UMPH!
WHOOSH
MY LEG!!
SHHHHHHHH
THE LAKE AND MY SPHERES ARE MADE OF THE SAME LIQUID.
OF COURSE...
...NOT EVERYTHING YOUR EYE SEES IS AS IT APPEARS.
FSSH
YOU'RE TELLING ME THAT IF I FALL IN THE LAKE, I'M GONNA MELT?!
FSSH

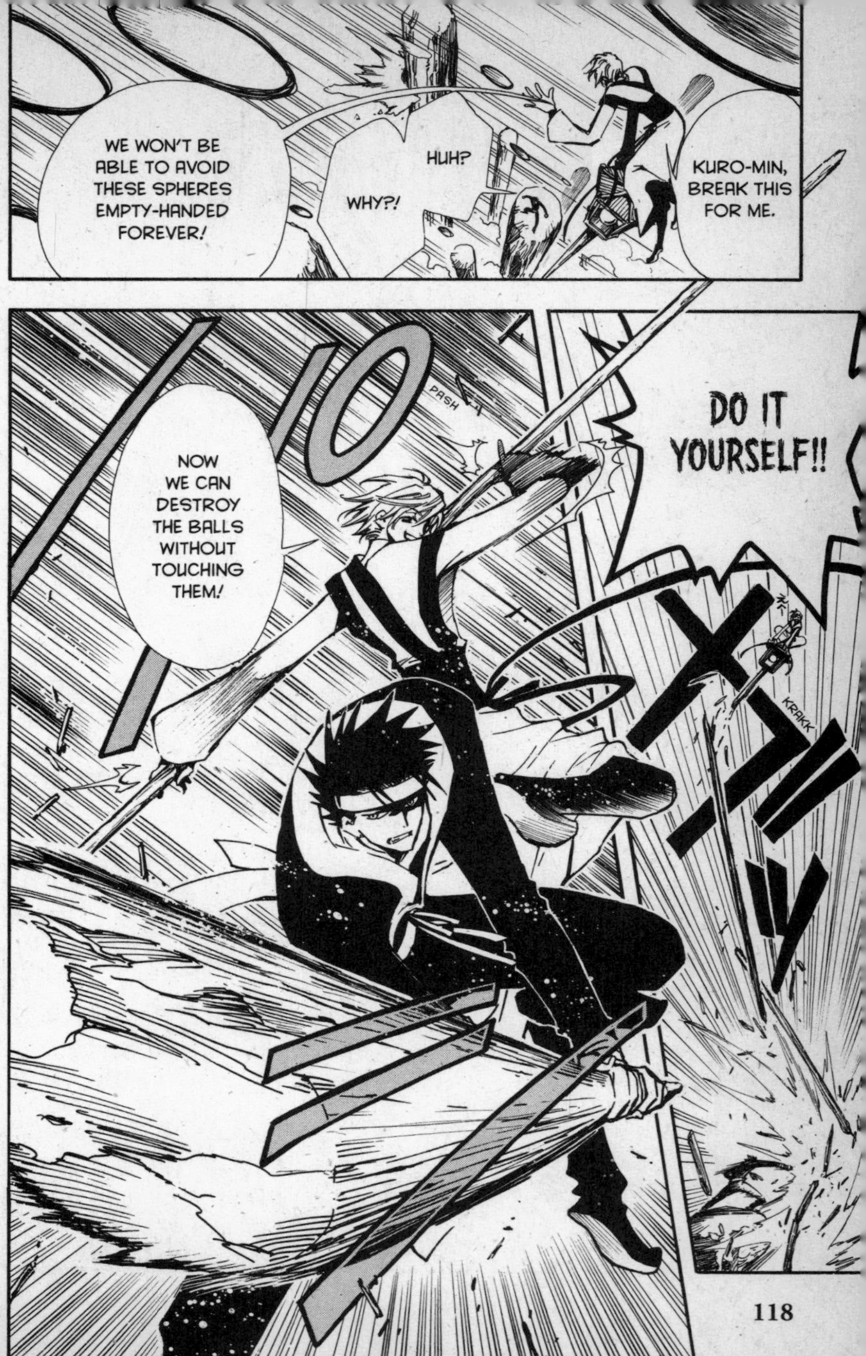
KURO-MIN, BREAK THIS FOR ME.
HUH?
WHY?!
WE WON'T BE ABLE TO AVOID THESE SPHERES EMPTY-HANDED FOREVER!
DO IT YOURSELF!!
PASH
NOW WE CAN DESTROY THE BALLS WITHOUT TOUCHING THEM!
KRAKK

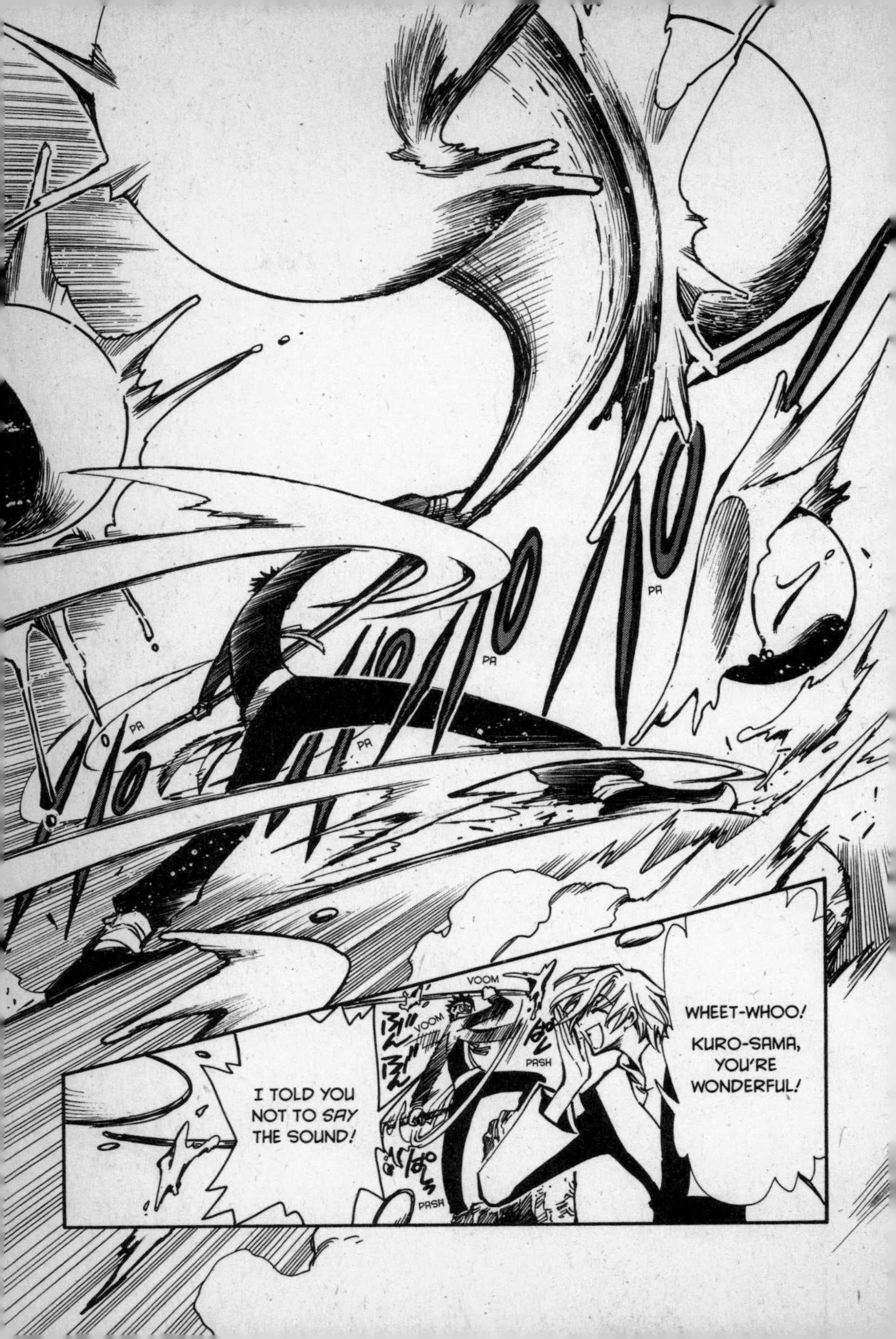
PA
PA
PA
PA
VOOM
VOOM
WHEET-WHOO!
KURO-SAMA, YOU'RE WONDERFUL!
PASH
I TOLD YOU NOT TO *SAY* THE SOUND!
PASH

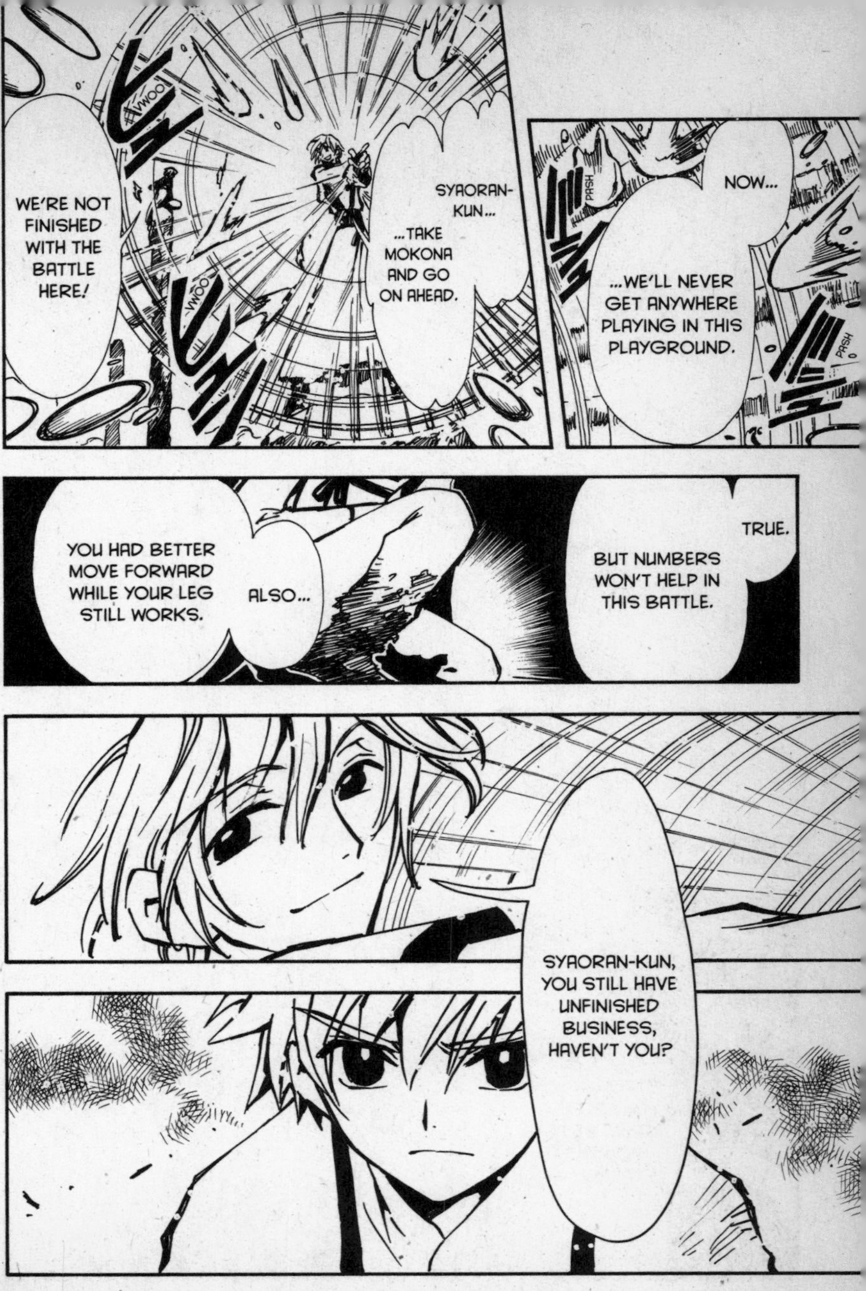
PASH
NOW...
...WE'LL NEVER GET ANYWHERE PLAYING IN THIS PLAYGROUND.
PASH
SYAORAN-KUN...
...TAKE MOKONA AND GO ON AHEAD.
VWOO
WE'RE NOT FINISHED WITH THE BATTLE HERE!
VWOO
TRUE.
BUT NUMBERS WON'T HELP IN THIS BATTLE.
ALSO...
YOU HAD BETTER MOVE FORWARD WHILE YOUR LEG STILL WORKS.
SYAORAN-KUN, YOU STILL HAVE UNFINISHED BUSINESS, HAVEN'T YOU?

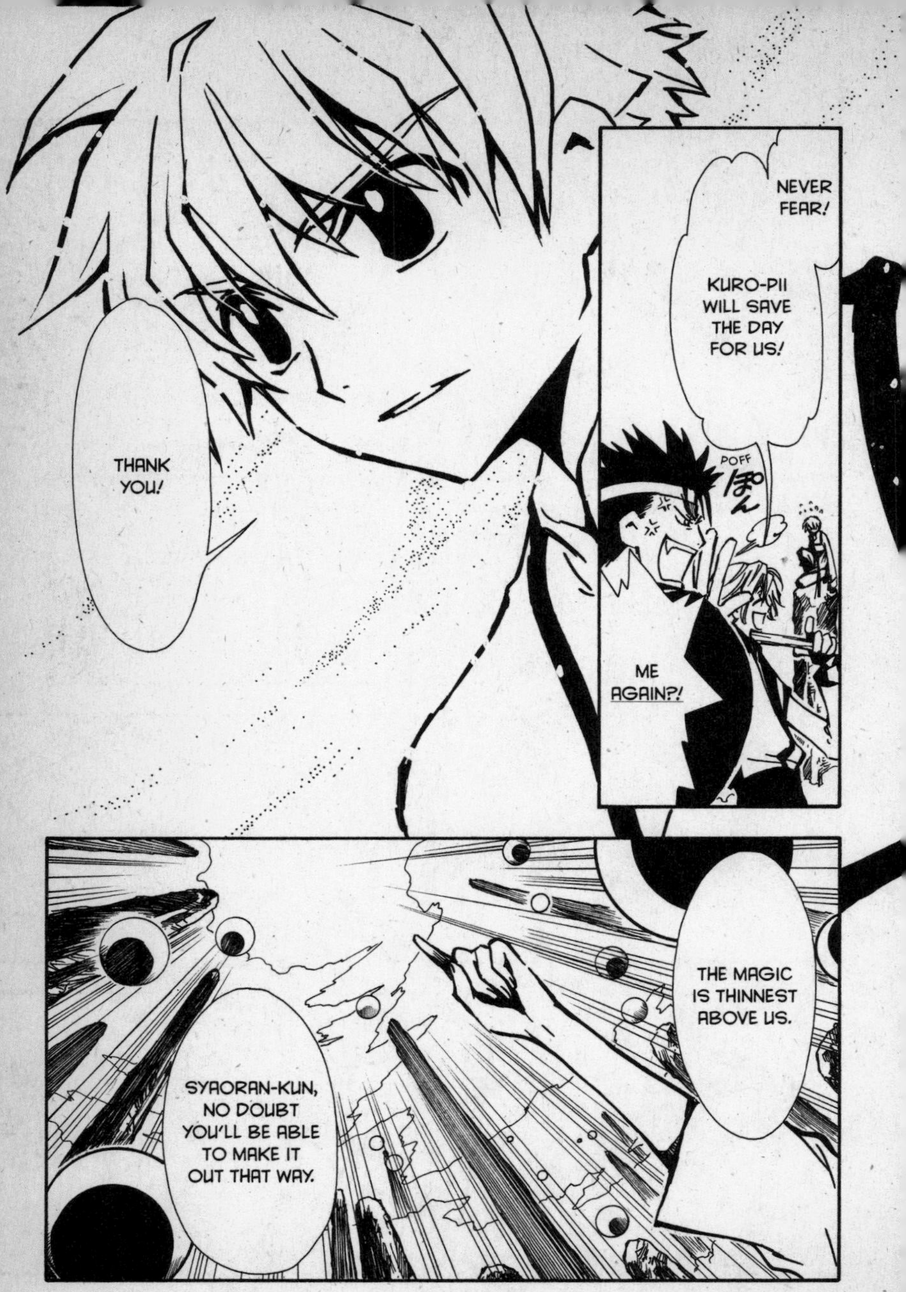
NEVER FEAR!
KURO-PII WILL SAVE THE DAY FOR US!
POFF
ぽん
ME AGAIN?!
THANK YOU!
THE MAGIC IS THINNEST ABOVE US.
SYAORAN-KUN, NO DOUBT YOU'LL BE ABLE TO MAKE IT OUT THAT WAY.

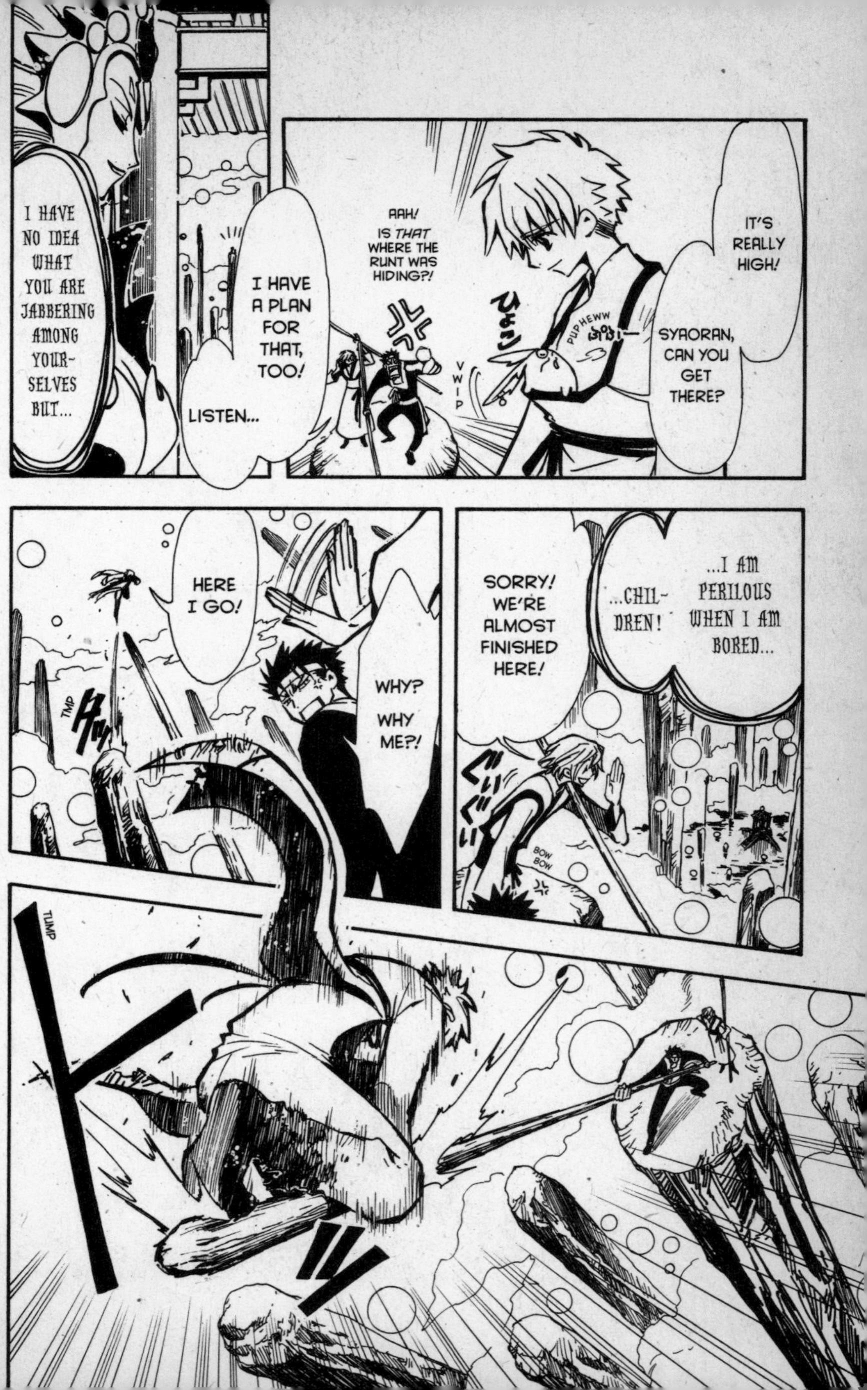
IT'S REALLY HIGH!
SYAORAN, CAN YOU GET THERE?
PUPHEWW
VWIP
AAH! IS THAT WHERE THE RUNT WAS HIDING?!
I HAVE A PLAN FOR THAT, TOO!
LISTEN...
I HAVE NO IDEA WHAT YOU ARE JABBERING AMONG YOURSELVES BUT...
...I AM PERILOUS WHEN I AM BORED...
...CHILDREN!
SORRY! WE'RE ALMOST FINISHED HERE!
BOW BOW
HERE I GO!
WHY? WHY ME?!
TMP
TUMP

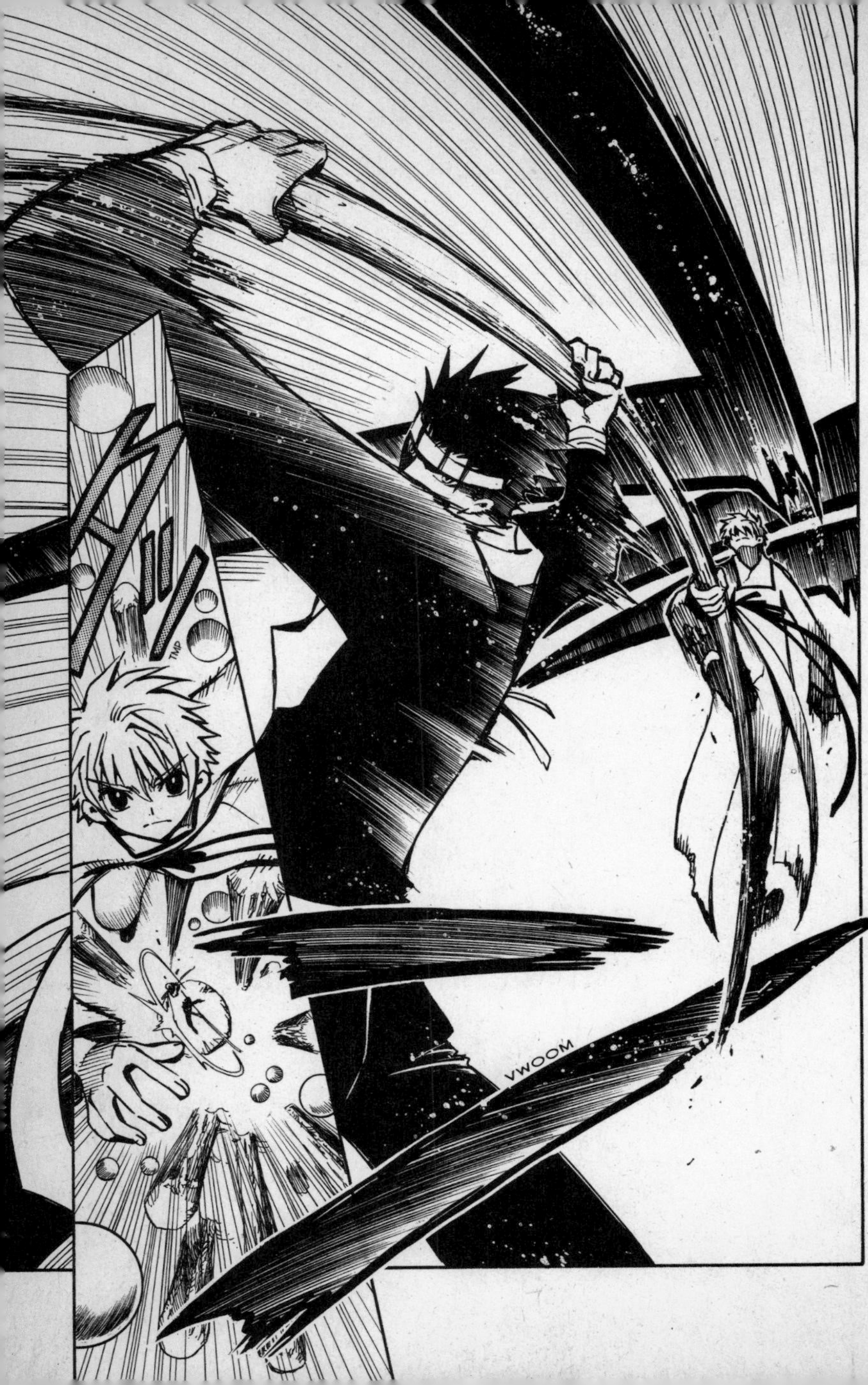
TMP
VWOOM

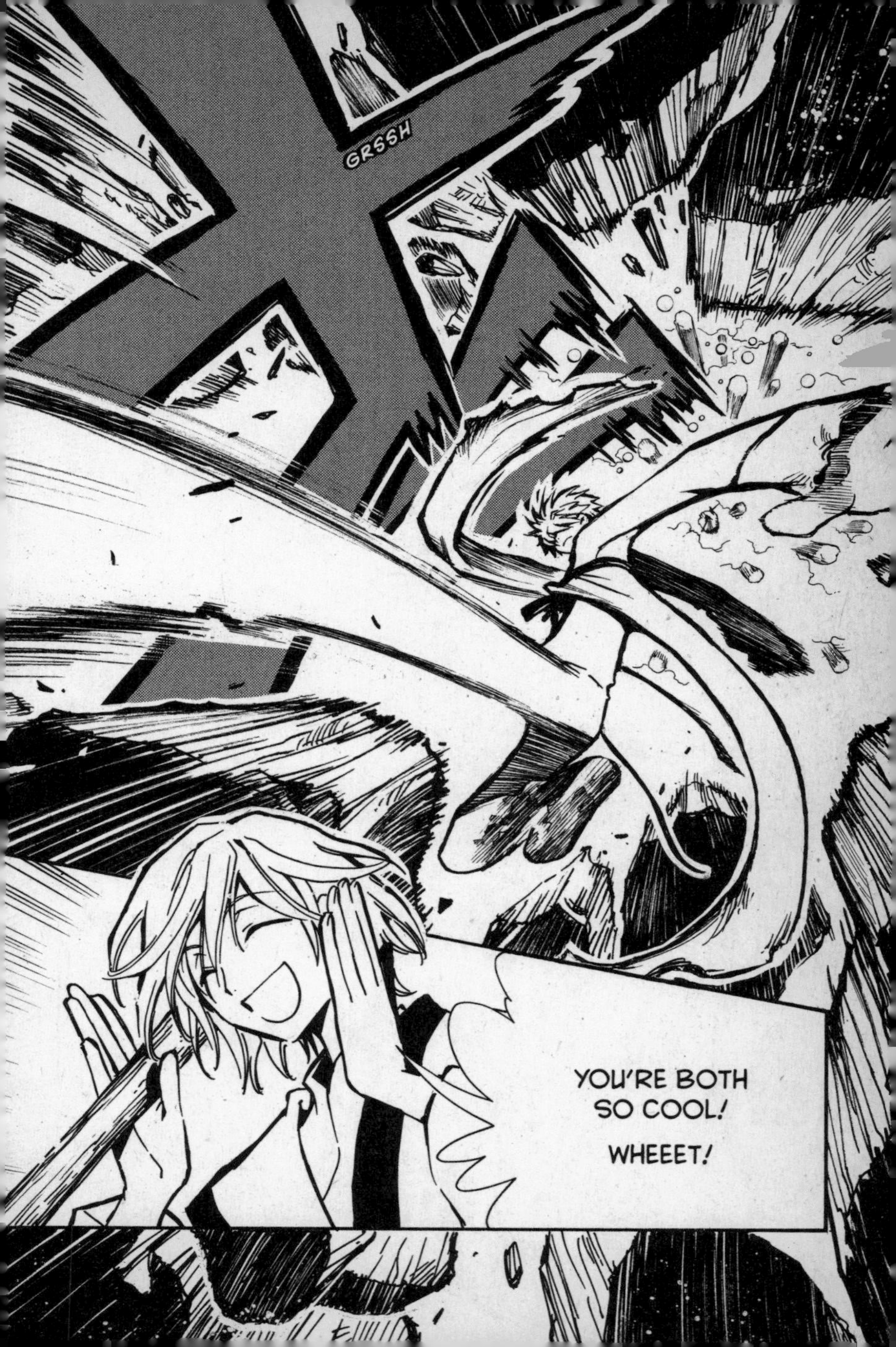
GRSSH
YOU'RE BOTH SO COOL!
WHEEET!

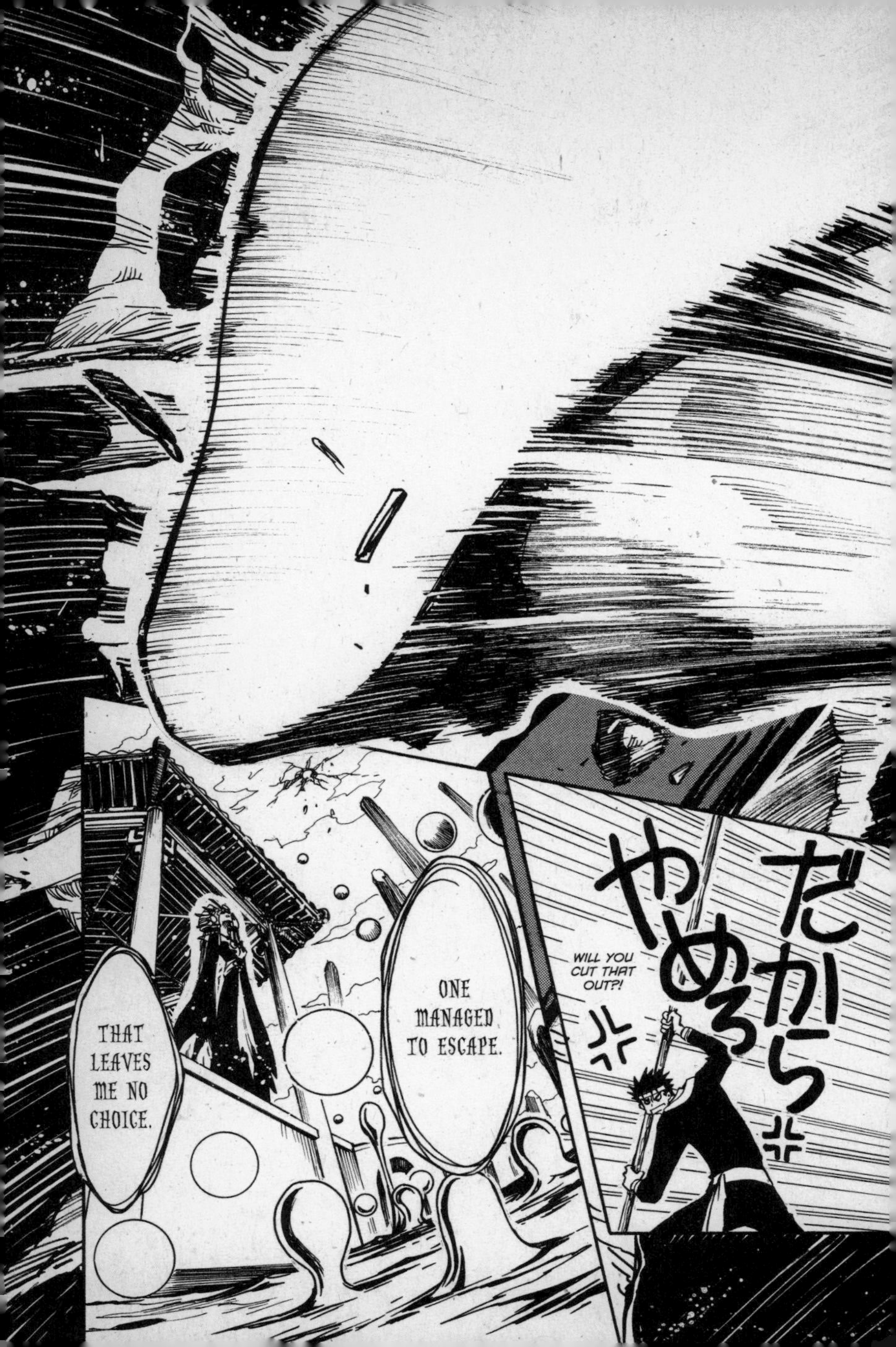
だからやめろ
WILL YOU CUT THAT OUT?!
ONE MANAGED TO ESCAPE.
THAT LEAVES ME NO CHOICE.

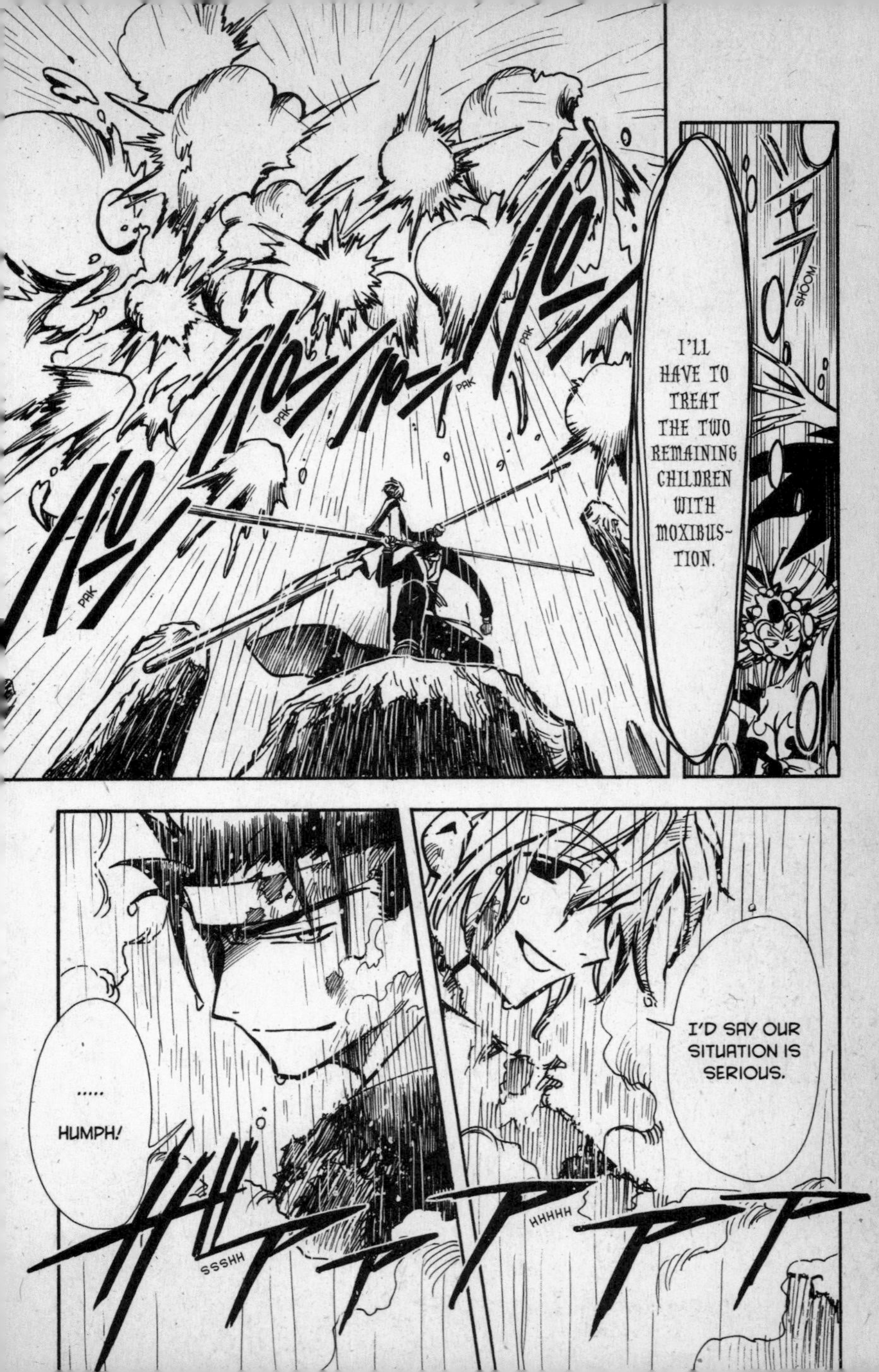
SHOOM
I'LL HAVE TO TREAT THE TWO REMAINING CHILDREN WITH MOXIBUSTION.
PAK
PAK
PAK
PAK
I'D SAY OUR SITUATION IS SERIOUS.
HHHHH
.....
HUMPH!
SSSHH

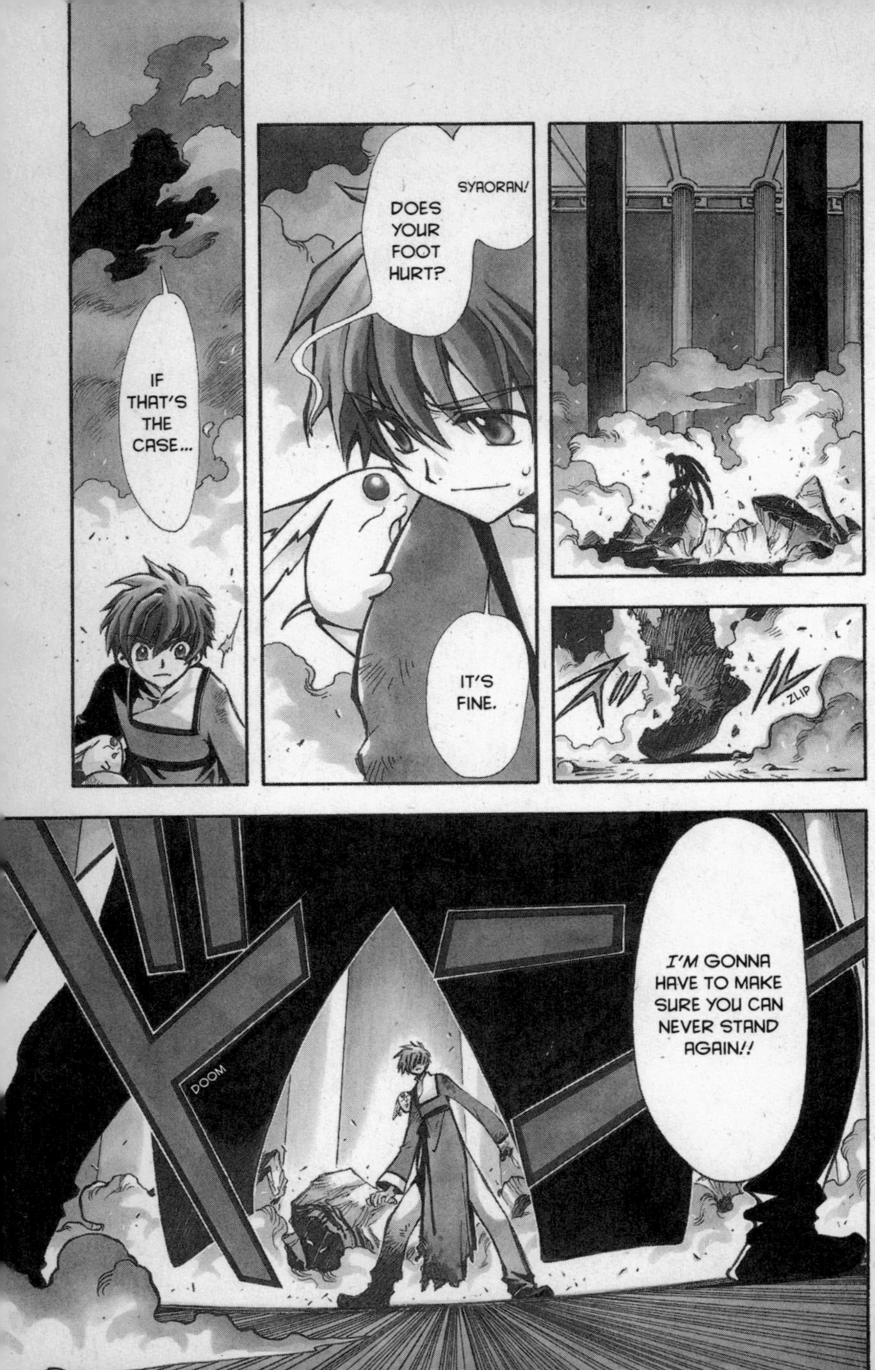
ZLIP
SYAORAN!
DOES YOUR FOOT HURT?
IT'S FINE.
IF THAT'S THE CASE...
I'M GONNA HAVE TO MAKE SURE YOU CAN NEVER STAND AGAIN!!
DOOM

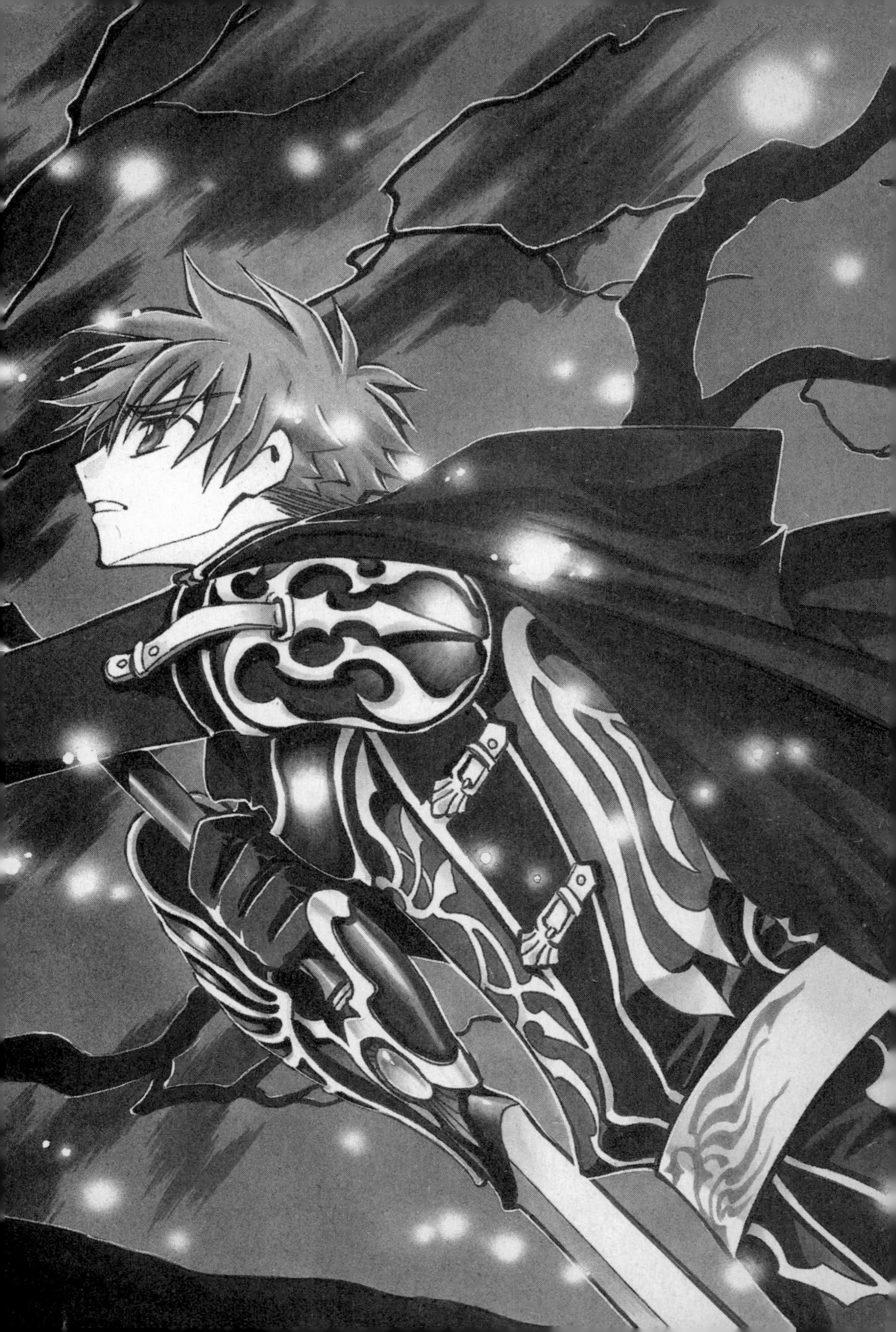

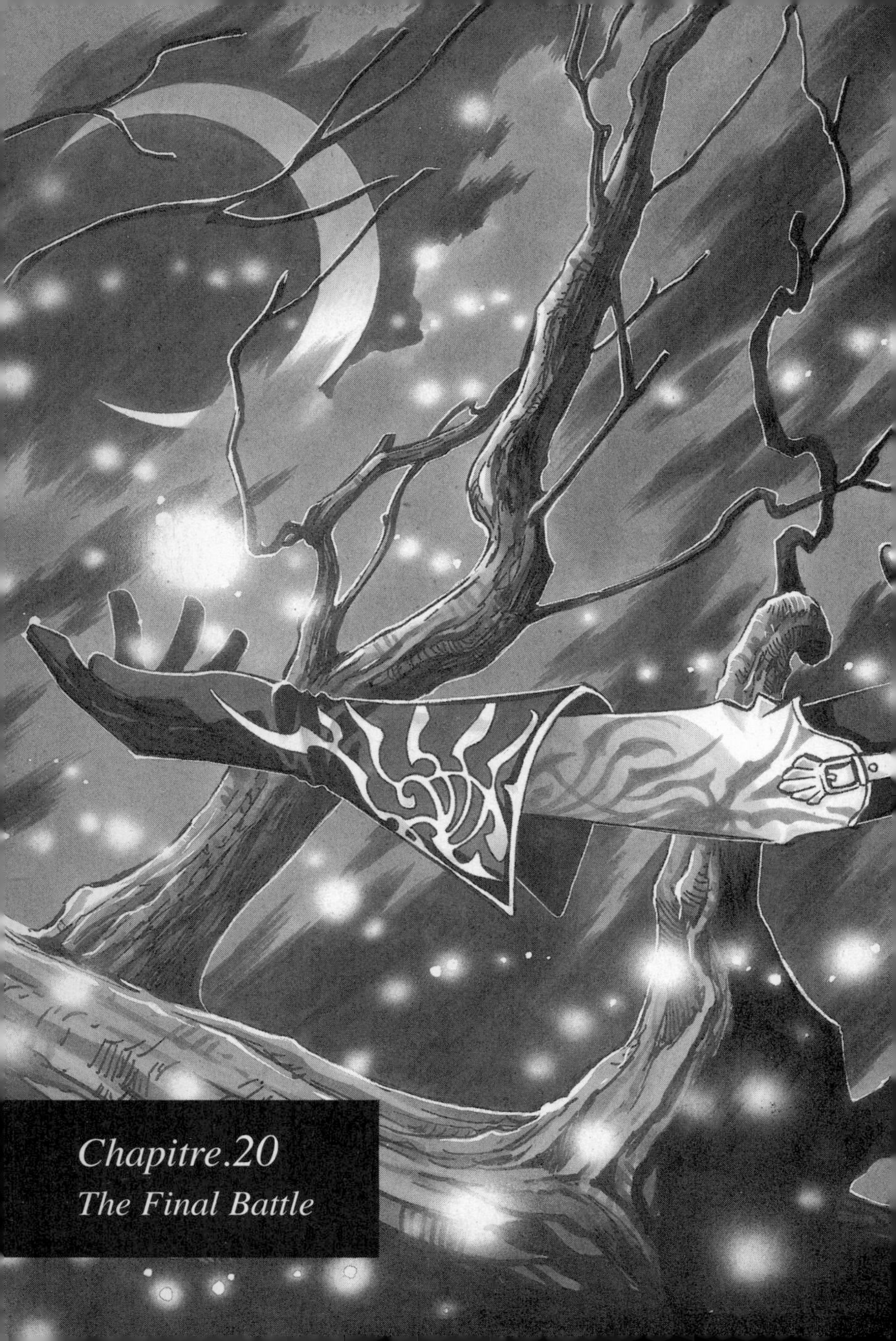

Chapitre.20
The Final Battle

ツバサ

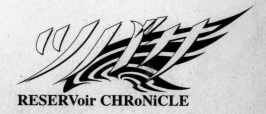

RESERVoir CHRoNiCLE

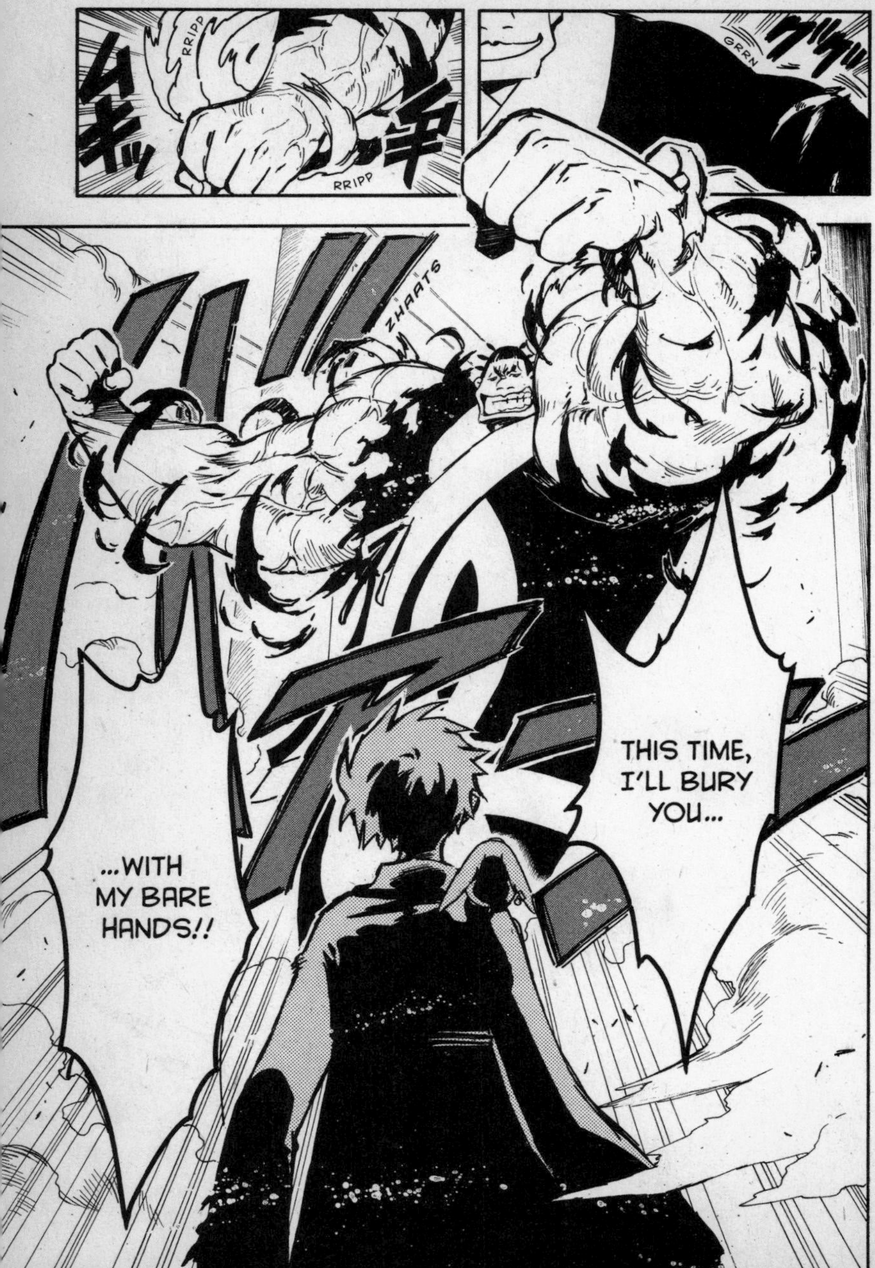
GRRN
RRIPP
RRIPP
ZHAATS
THIS TIME, I'LL BURY YOU...
...WITH MY BARE HANDS!!

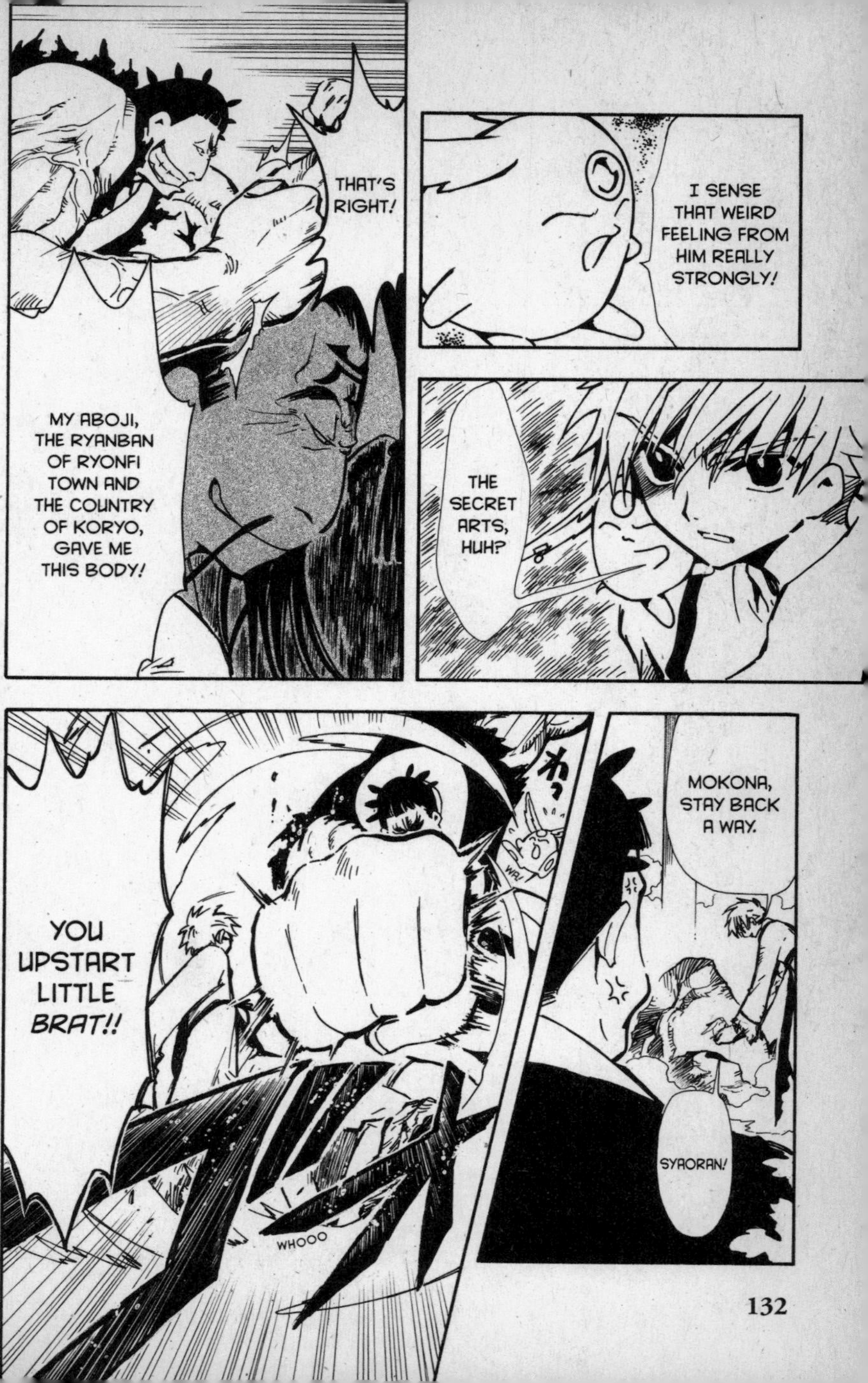
I SENSE THAT WEIRD FEELING FROM HIM REALLY STRONGLY!
THE SECRET ARTS, HUH?
THAT'S RIGHT!
MY ABOJI, THE RYANBAN OF RYONFI TOWN AND THE COUNTRY OF KORYO, GAVE ME THIS BODY!
MOKONA, STAY BACK A WAY.
SYAORAN!
WA!
YOU UPSTART LITTLE *BRAT!!*
WHOOO

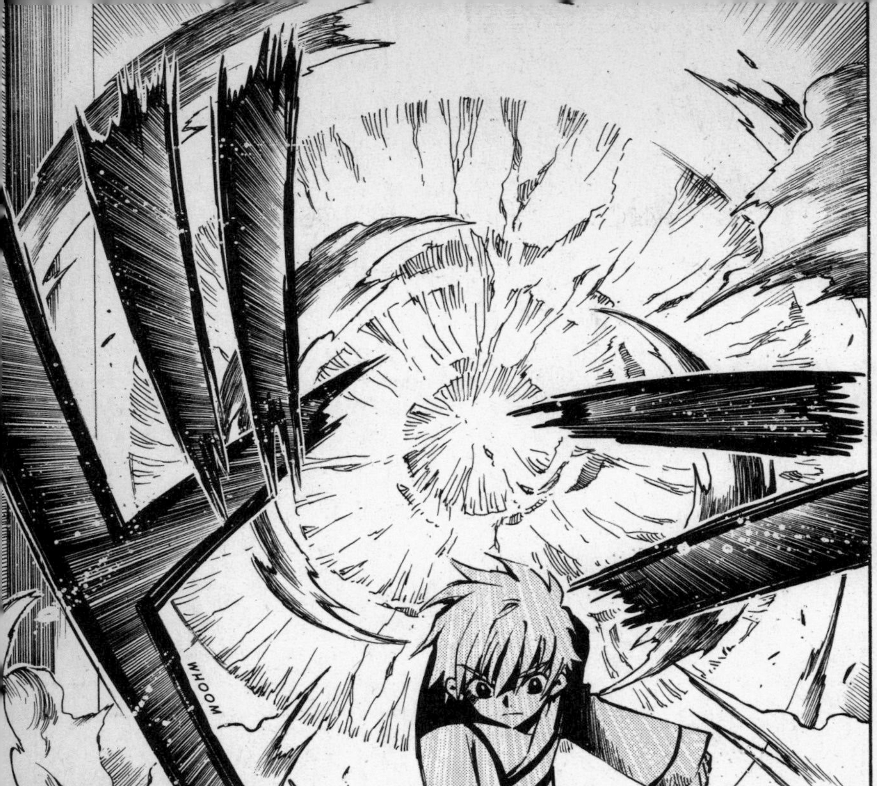
WHOOM

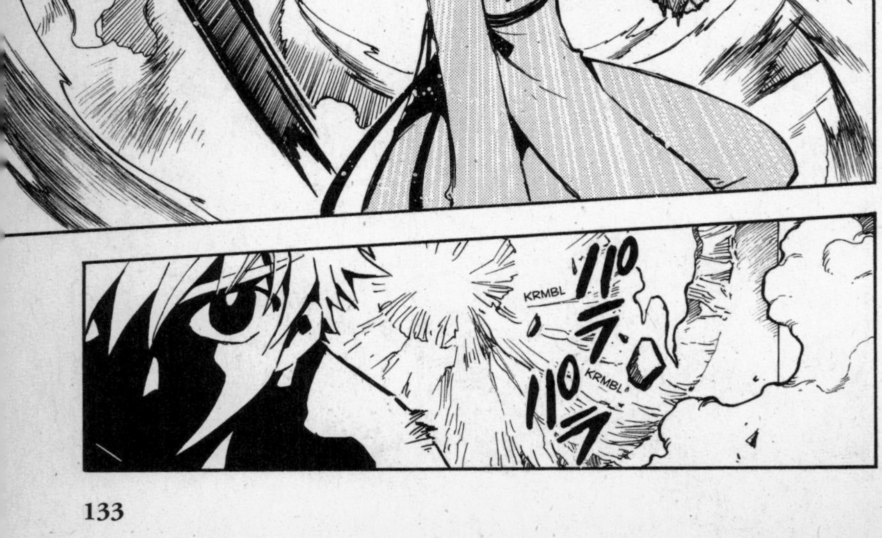
パラ
KRMBL
パラ
KRMBL

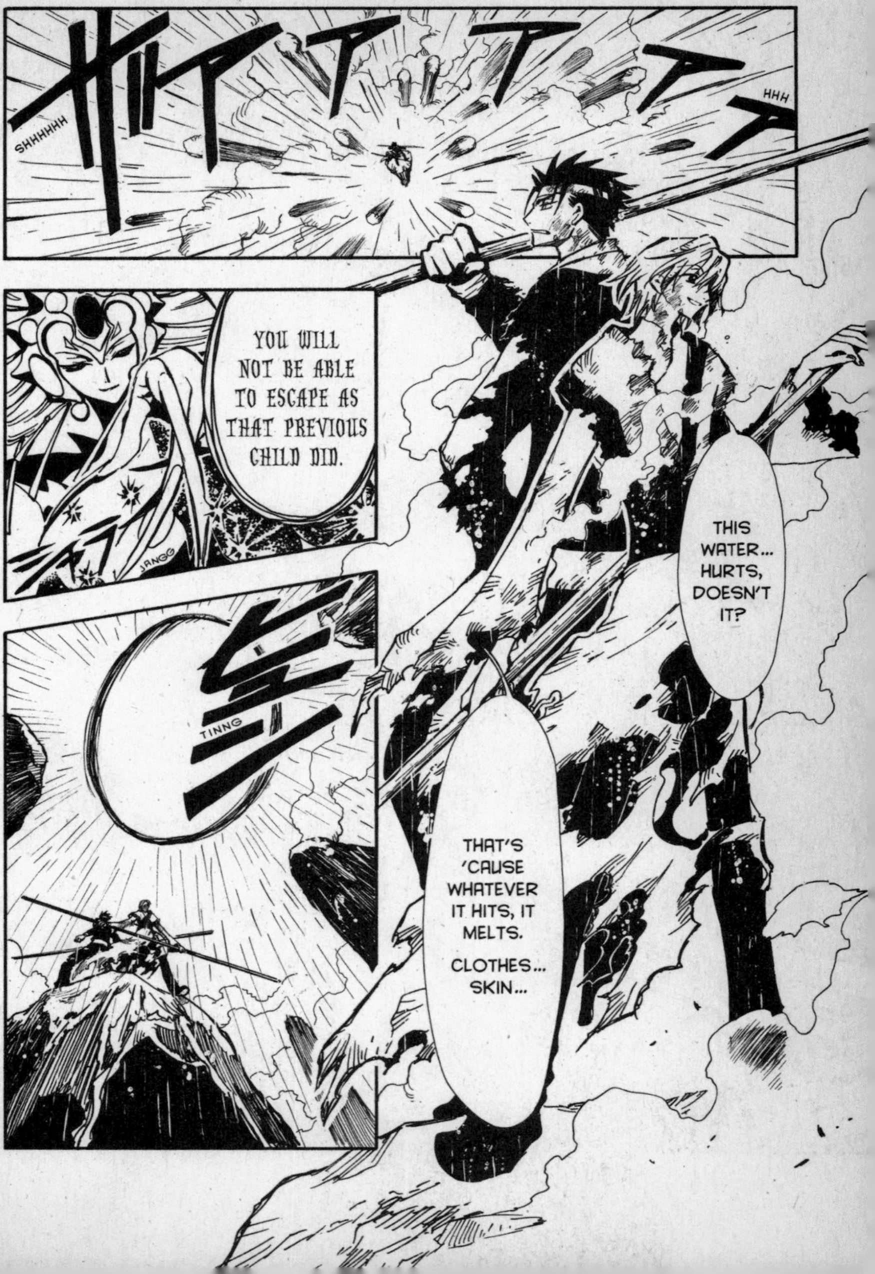
SHHHHHH
HHH
THIS WATER... HURTS, DOESN'T IT?
THAT'S 'CAUSE WHATEVER IT HITS, IT MELTS.
CLOTHES... SKIN...
YOU WILL NOT BE ABLE TO ESCAPE AS THAT PREVIOUS CHILD DID.
JANGG
TINNG

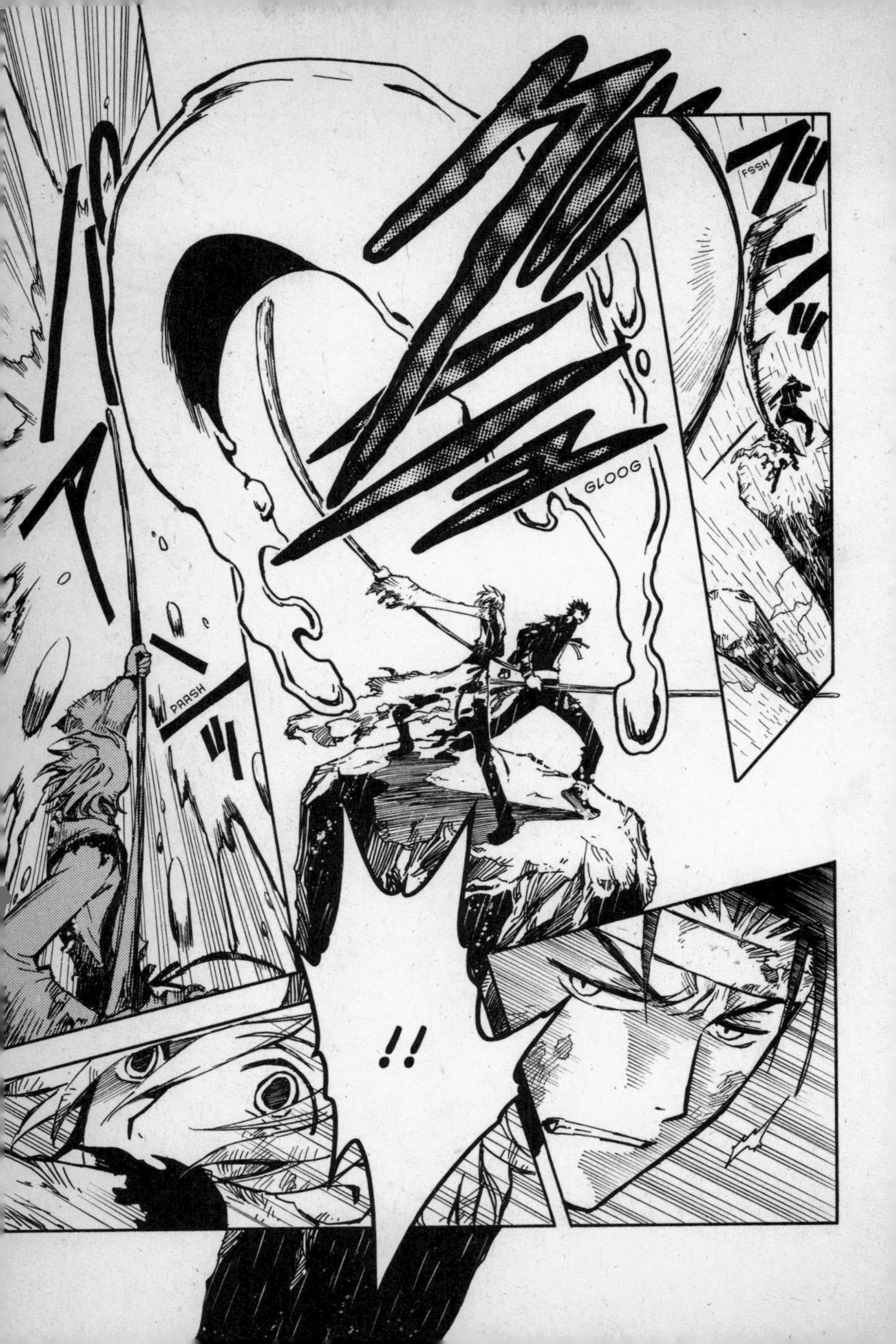
FSSH
GLOOG
PRASH
!!

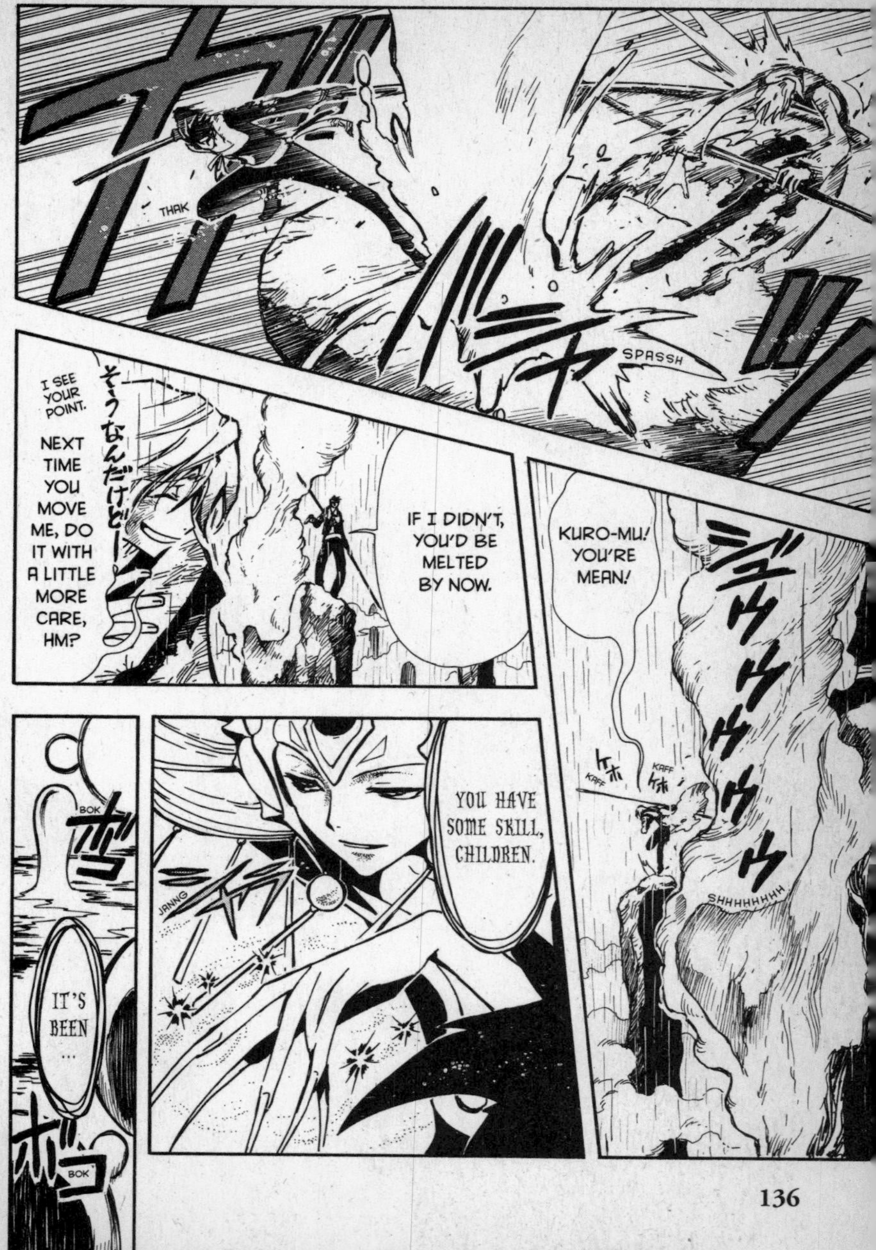
SPASSH
THAK
SHHHHHHHH
KURO-MU! YOU'RE MEAN!
KAFF
KAFF
IF I DIDN'T, YOU'D BE MELTED BY NOW.
I SEE YOUR POINT.
そうなんだけど
NEXT TIME YOU MOVE ME, DO IT WITH A LITTLE MORE CARE, HM?
YOU HAVE SOME SKILL, CHILDREN.
JANNG
BOK
IT'S BEEN ...
BOK

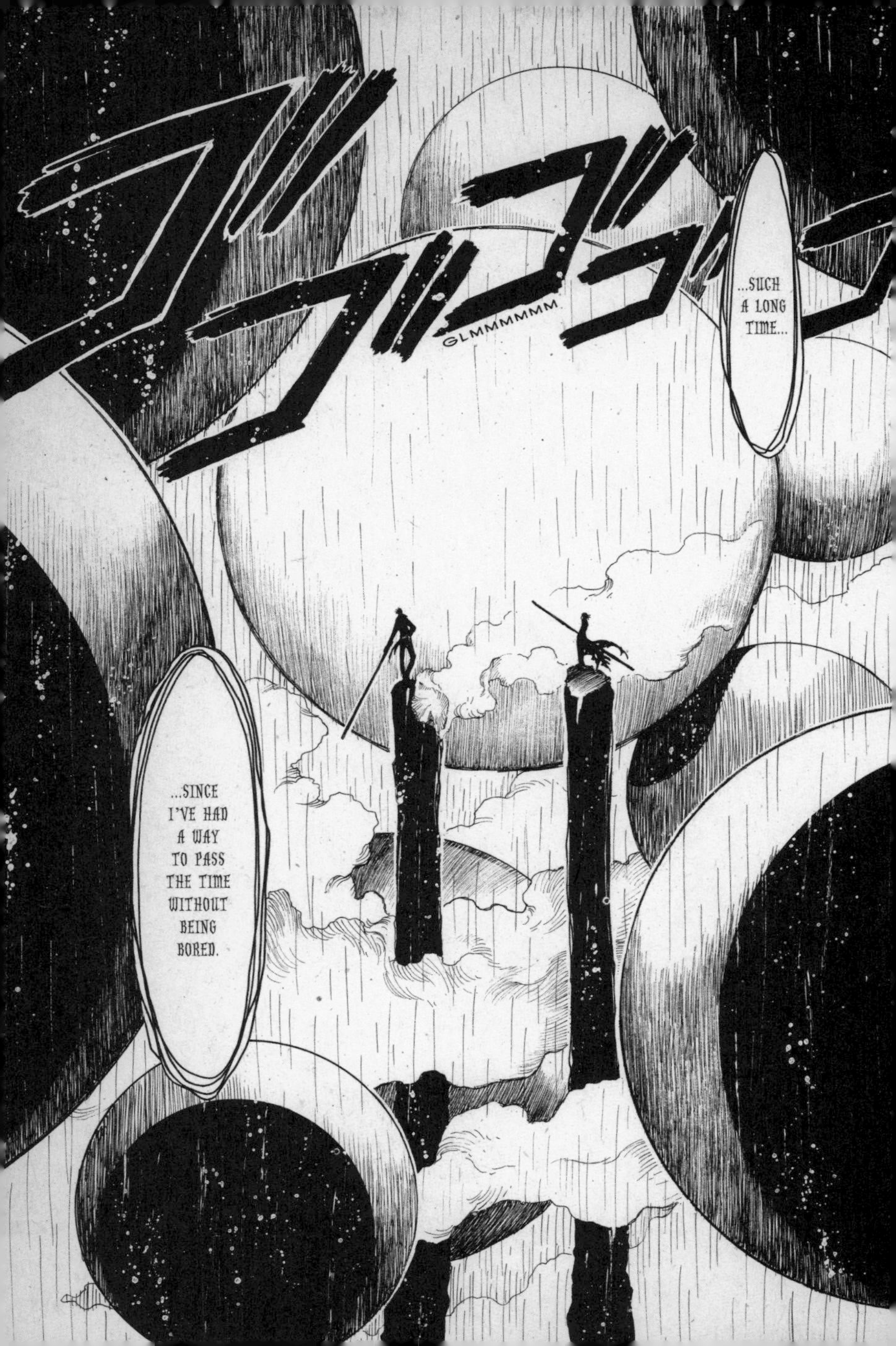
...SUCH A LONG TIME...
GLMMMMMM
...SINCE I'VE HAD A WAY TO PASS THE TIME WITHOUT BEING BORED.

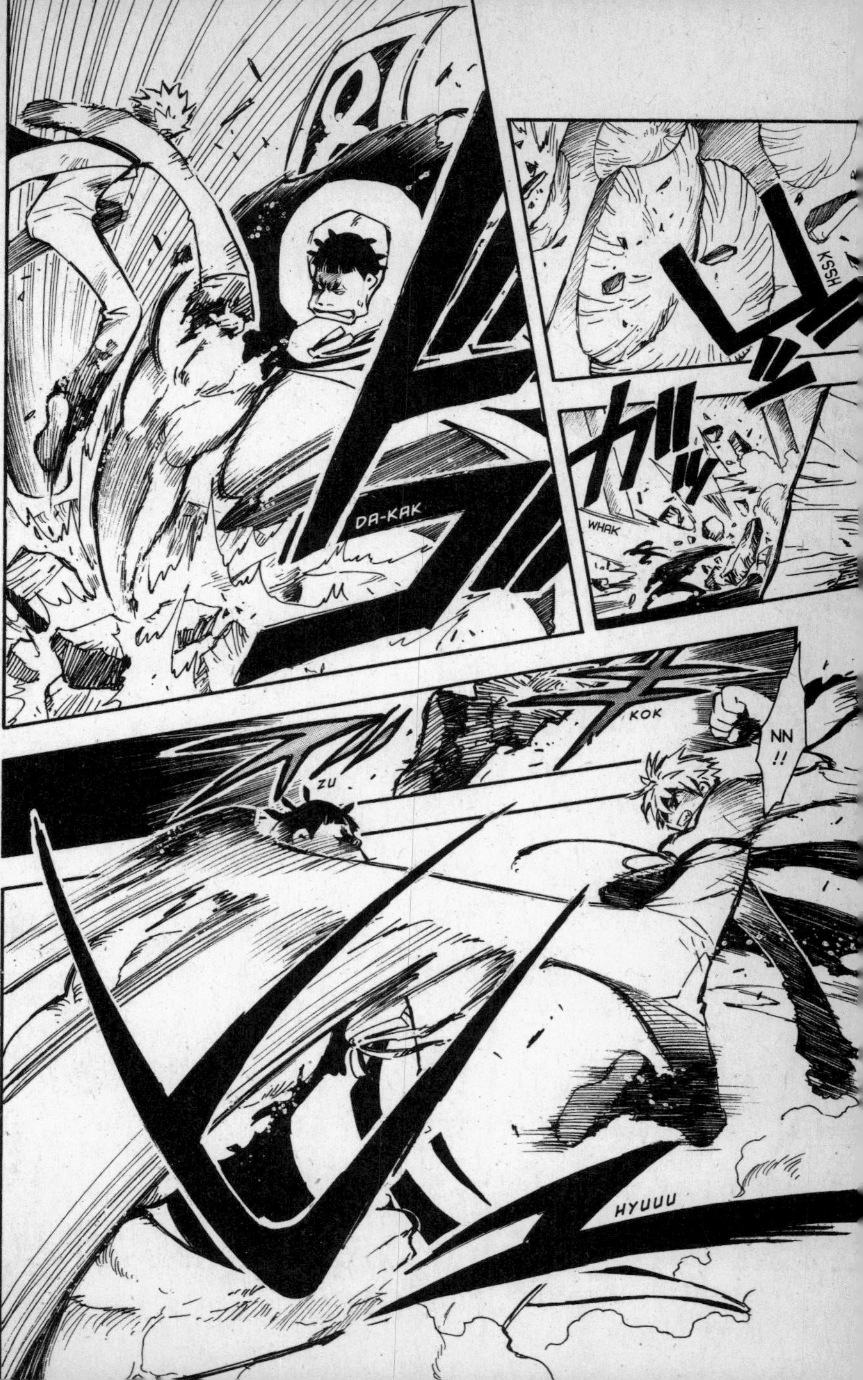
KSSH
WHAK
DA-KAK
NN!!
KOK
ZU
HYUUU

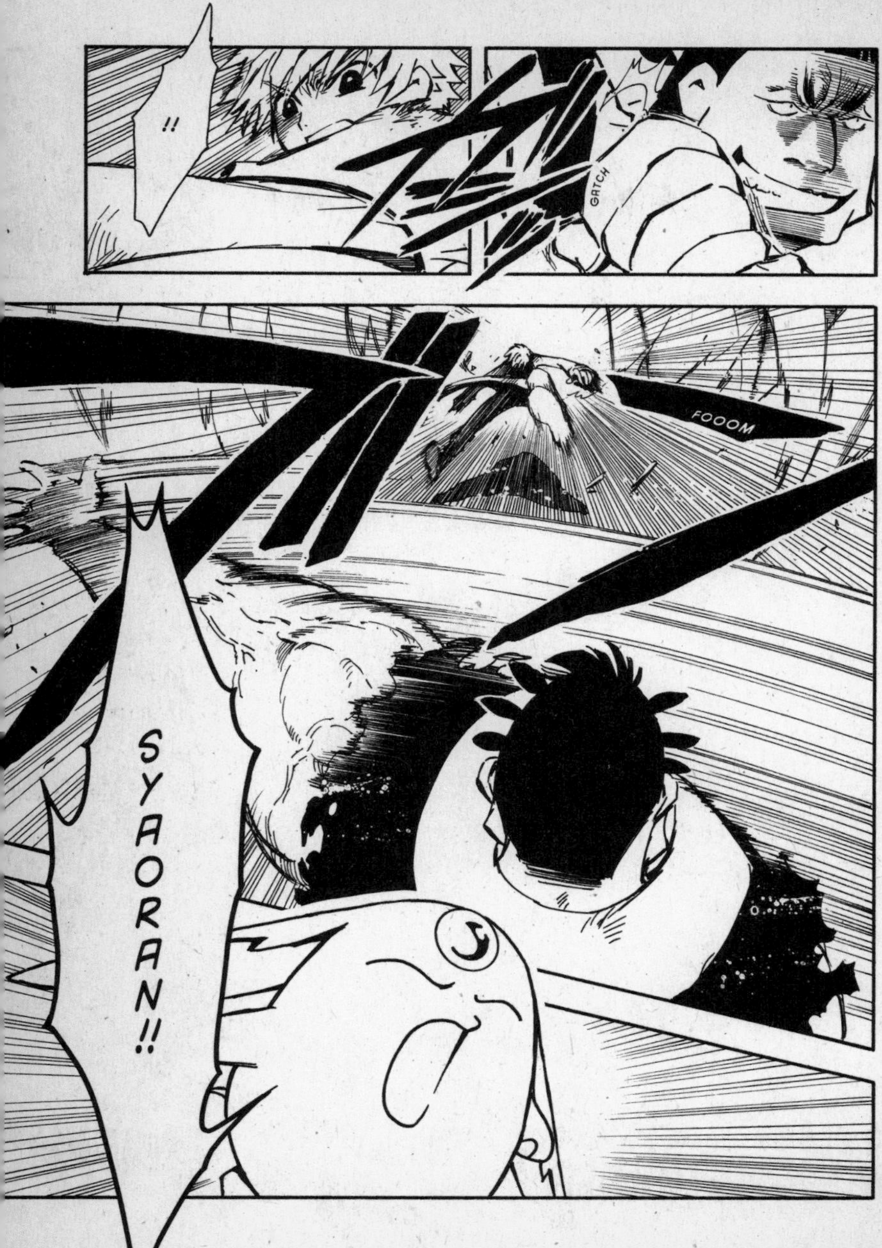
GATCH
!!
FOOOM
SYAORAN!!

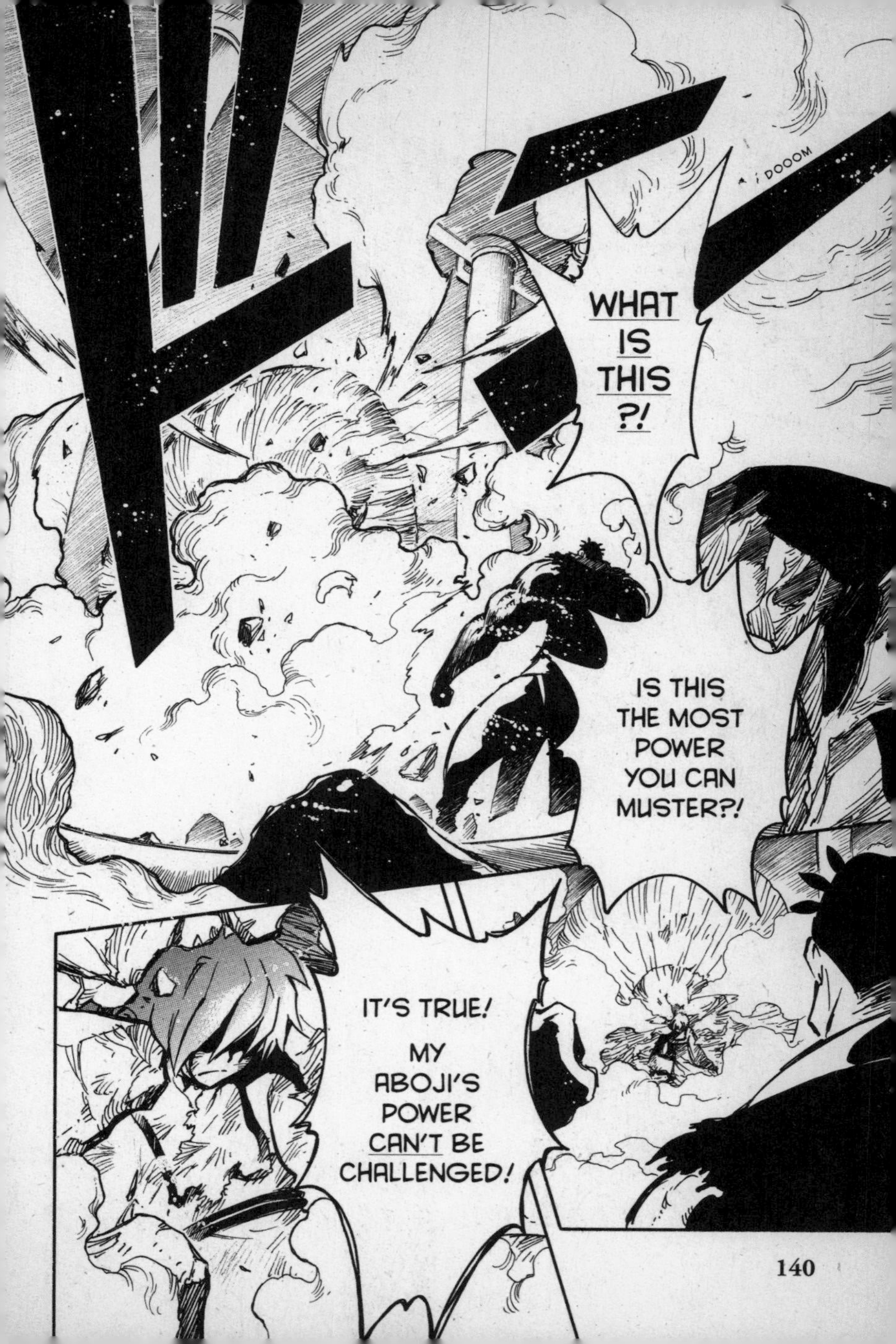
DOOOM
WHAT IS THIS ?!
IS THIS THE MOST POWER YOU CAN MUSTER?!
IT'S TRUE!
MY ABOJI'S POWER CAN'T BE CHALLENGED!

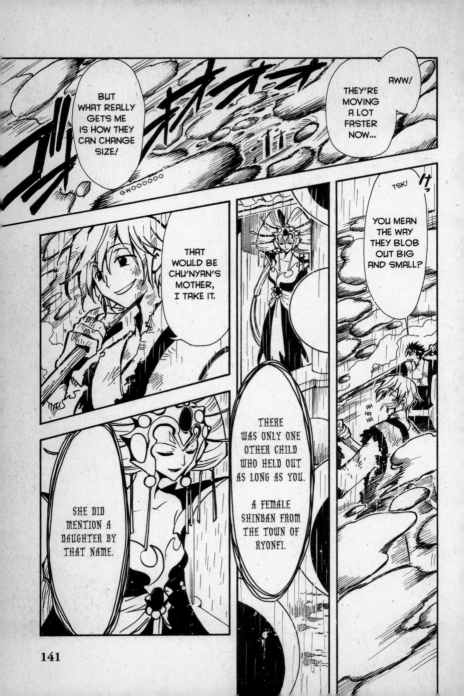

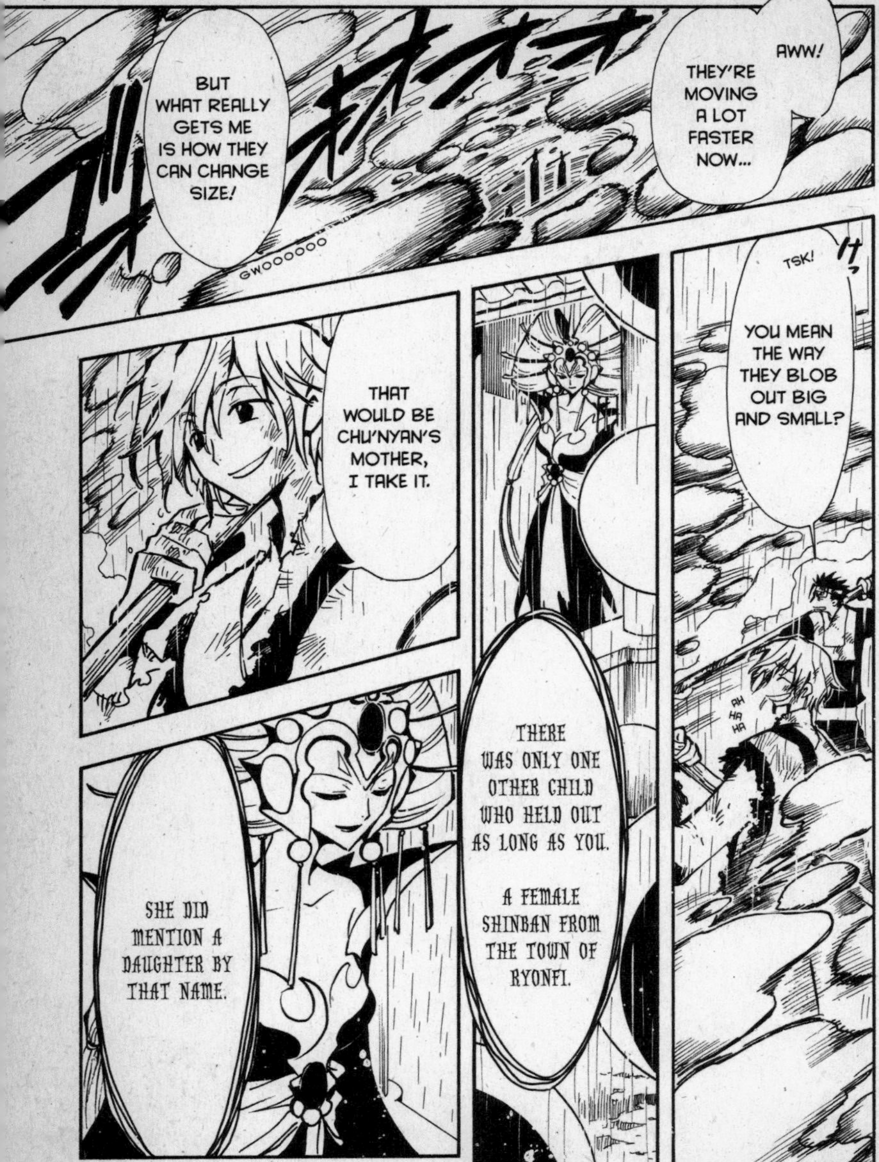
AWW!
THEY'RE MOVING A LOT FASTER NOW...
BUT WHAT REALLY GETS ME IS HOW THEY CAN CHANGE SIZE!
GWOOOOOOO
TSK!
YOU MEAN THE WAY THEY BLOB OUT BIG AND SMALL?
AH HA HA
THERE WAS ONLY ONE OTHER CHILD WHO HELD OUT AS LONG AS YOU.
A FEMALE SHINBAN FROM THE TOWN OF RYONFI.
THAT WOULD BE CHU'NYAN'S MOTHER, I TAKE IT.
SHE DID MENTION A DAUGHTER BY THAT NAME.

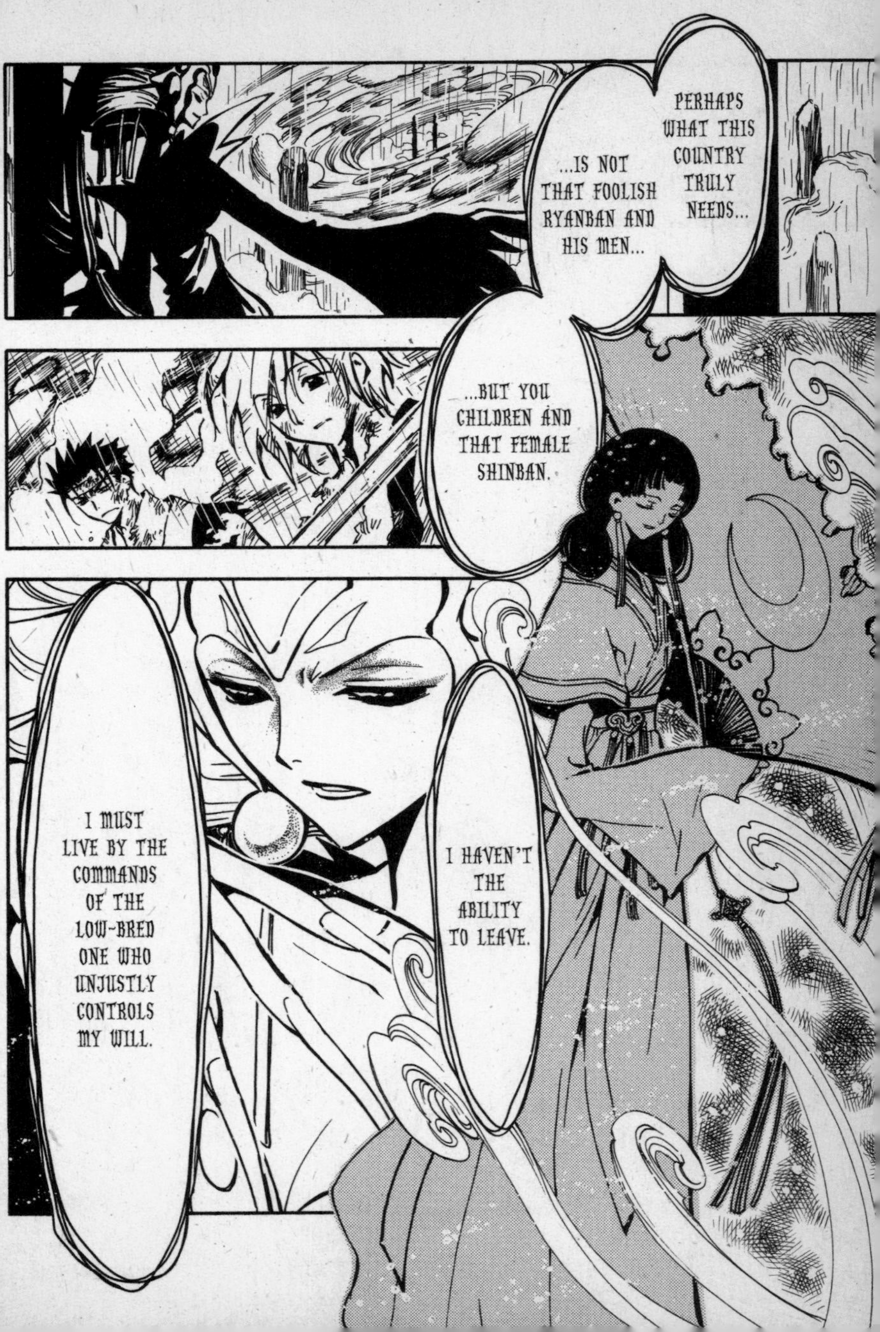
PERHAPS WHAT THIS COUNTRY TRULY NEEDS...
...IS NOT THAT FOOLISH RYANBAN AND HIS MEN...
...BUT YOU CHILDREN AND THAT FEMALE SHINBAN.
I HAVEN'T THE ABILITY TO LEAVE.
I MUST LIVE BY THE COMMANDS OF THE LOW-BRED ONE WHO UNJUSTLY CONTROLS MY WILL.

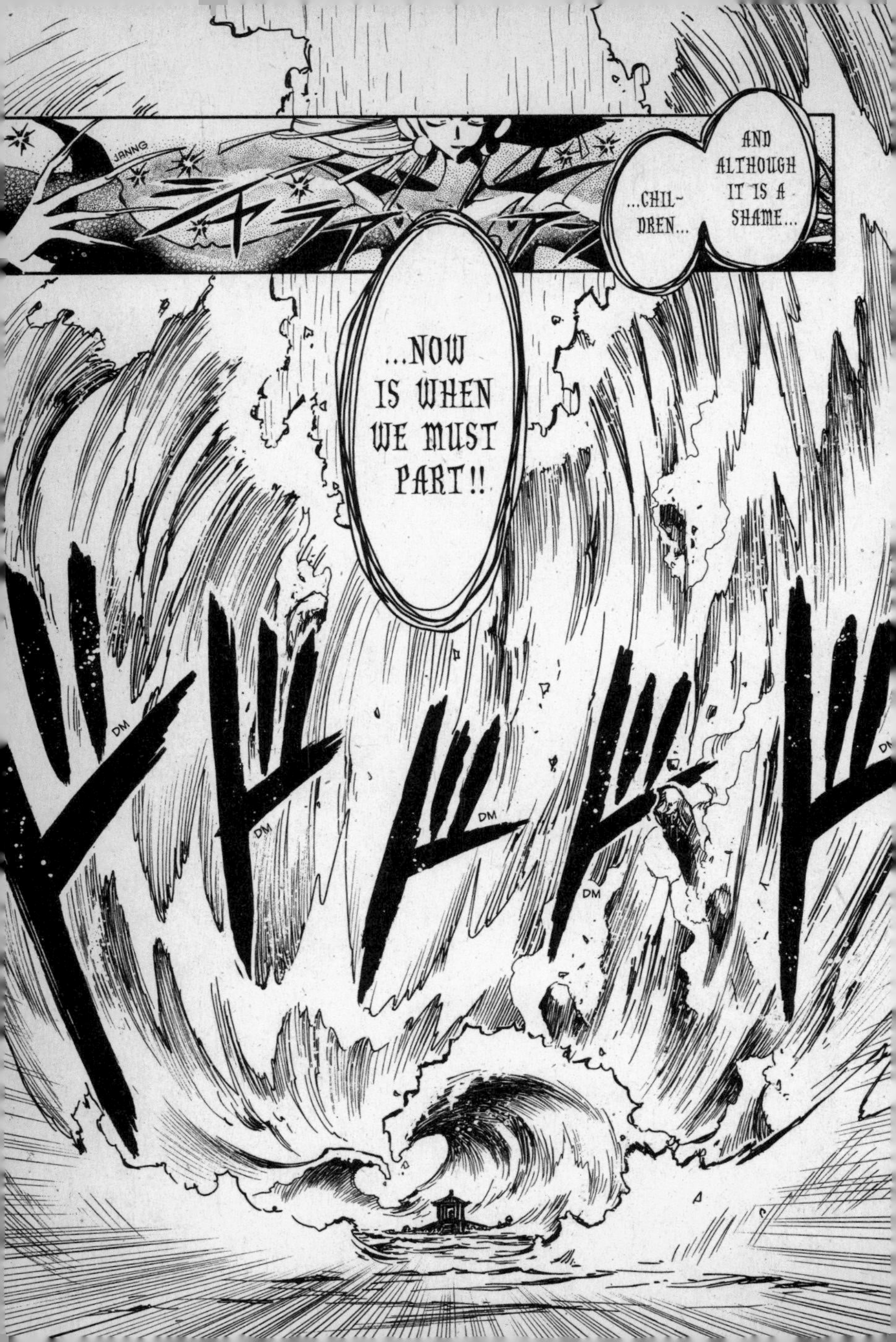
JANNG
AND ALTHOUGH IT IS A SHAME...
...CHIL-DREN...
...NOW IS WHEN WE MUST PART!!
DM
DM
DM
DM
DM
DM

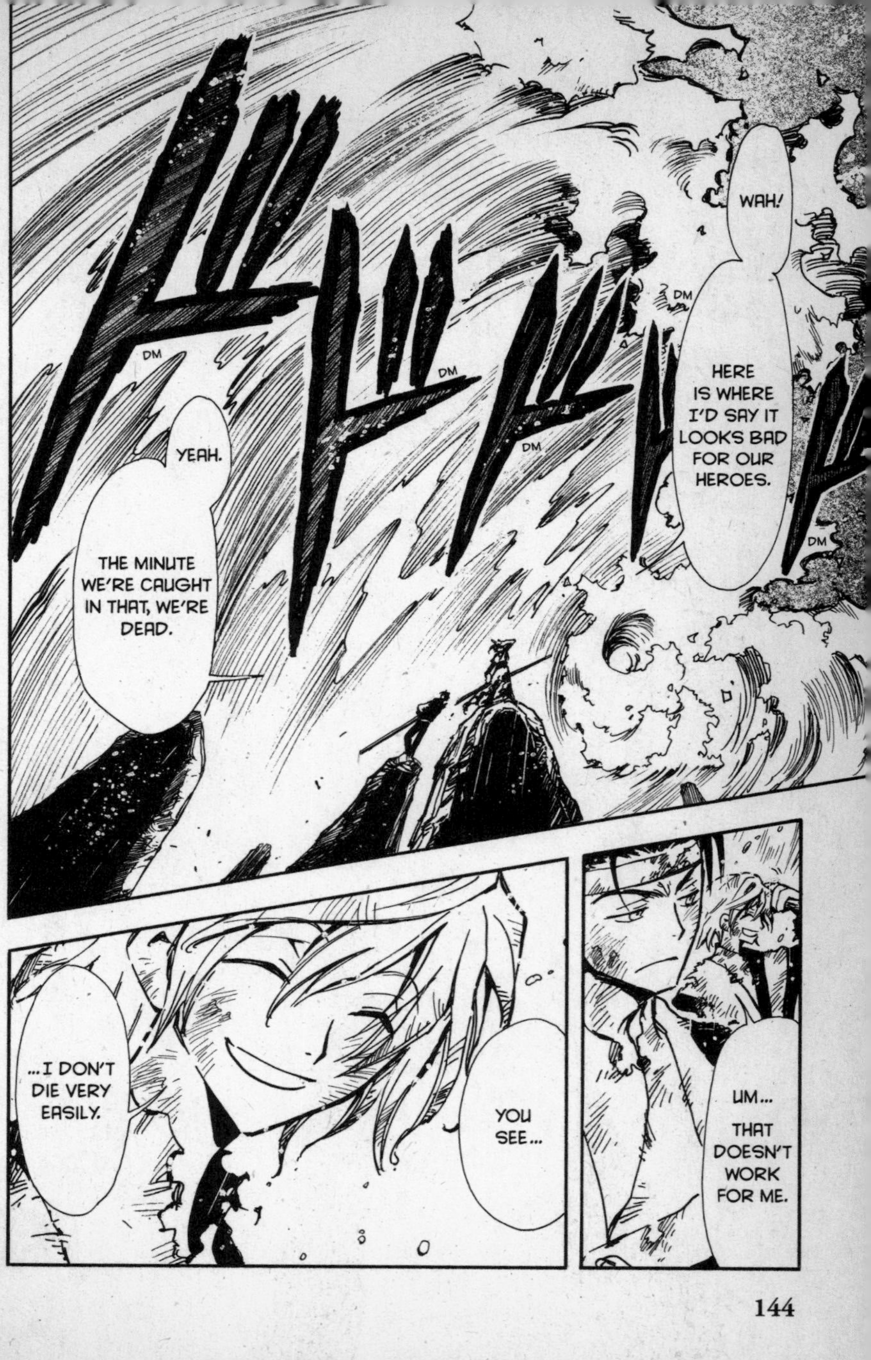
WAH!
HERE IS WHERE I'D SAY IT LOOKS BAD FOR OUR HEROES.
DM
DM
DM
DM
DM
YEAH.
THE MINUTE WE'RE CAUGHT IN THAT, WE'RE DEAD.
UM... THAT DOESN'T WORK FOR ME.
YOU SEE...
...I DON'T DIE VERY EASILY.

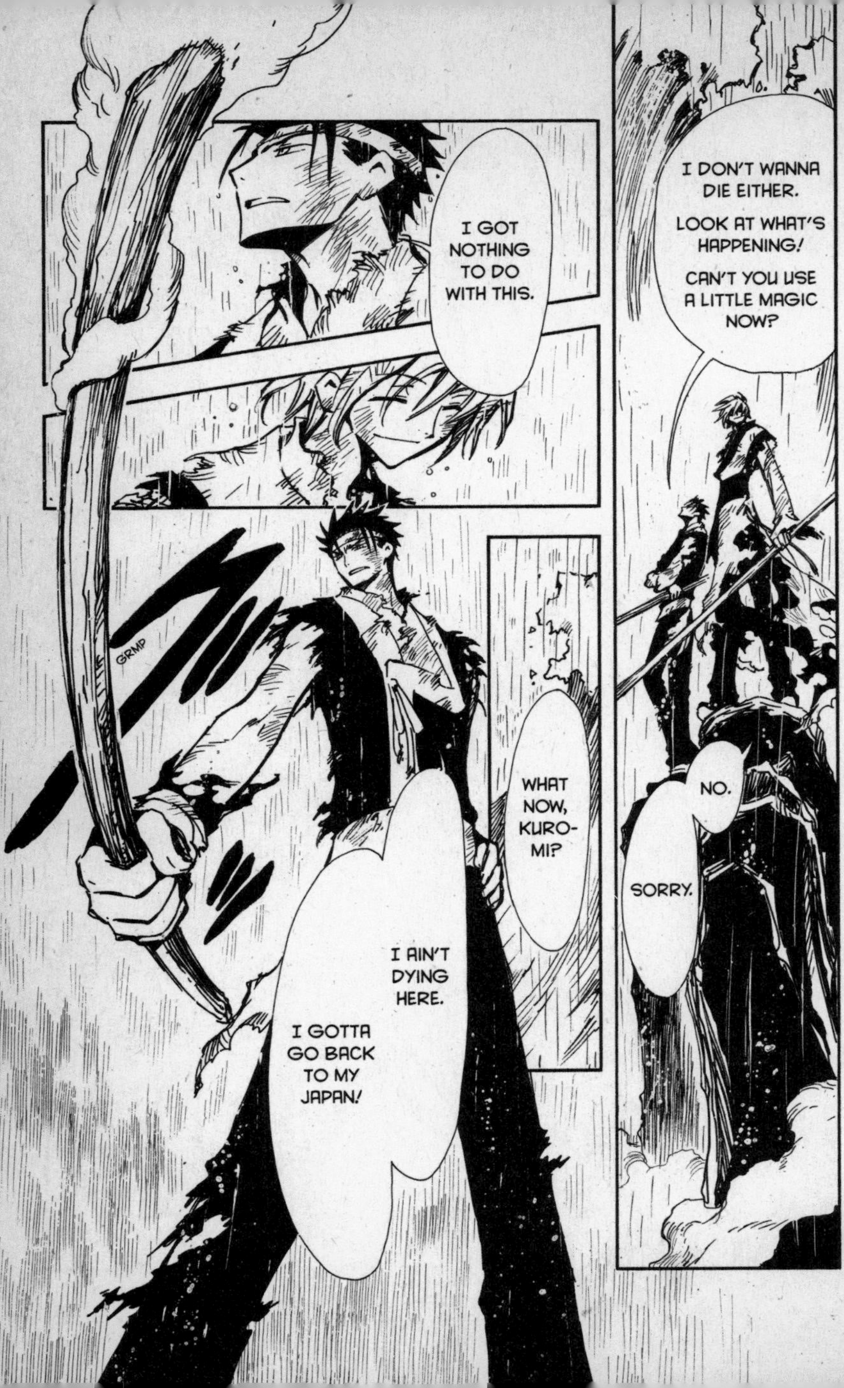
I DON'T WANNA DIE EITHER.
LOOK AT WHAT'S HAPPENING!
CAN'T YOU USE A LITTLE MAGIC NOW?
NO.
SORRY.
I GOT NOTHING TO DO WITH THIS.
WHAT NOW, KURO-MI?
GRMP
I AIN'T DYING HERE.
I GOTTA GO BACK TO MY JAPAN!

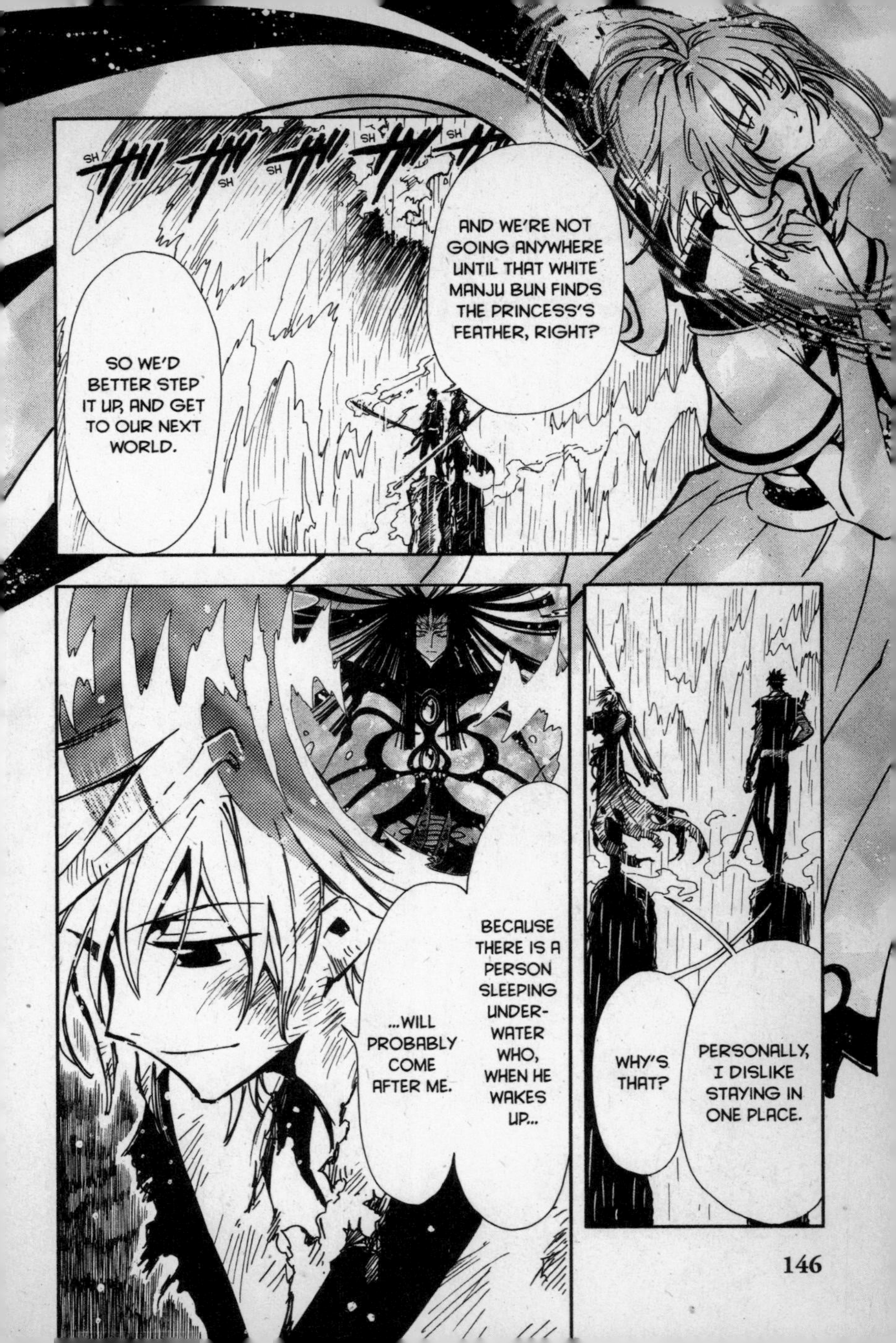
SH SH SH SH SH
AND WE'RE NOT GOING ANYWHERE UNTIL THAT WHITE MANJU BUN FINDS THE PRINCESS'S FEATHER, RIGHT?
SO WE'D BETTER STEP IT UP, AND GET TO OUR NEXT WORLD.
PERSONALLY, I DISLIKE STAYING IN ONE PLACE.
WHY'S THAT?
BECAUSE THERE IS A PERSON SLEEPING UNDER-WATER WHO, WHEN HE WAKES UP...
...WILL PROBABLY COME AFTER ME.

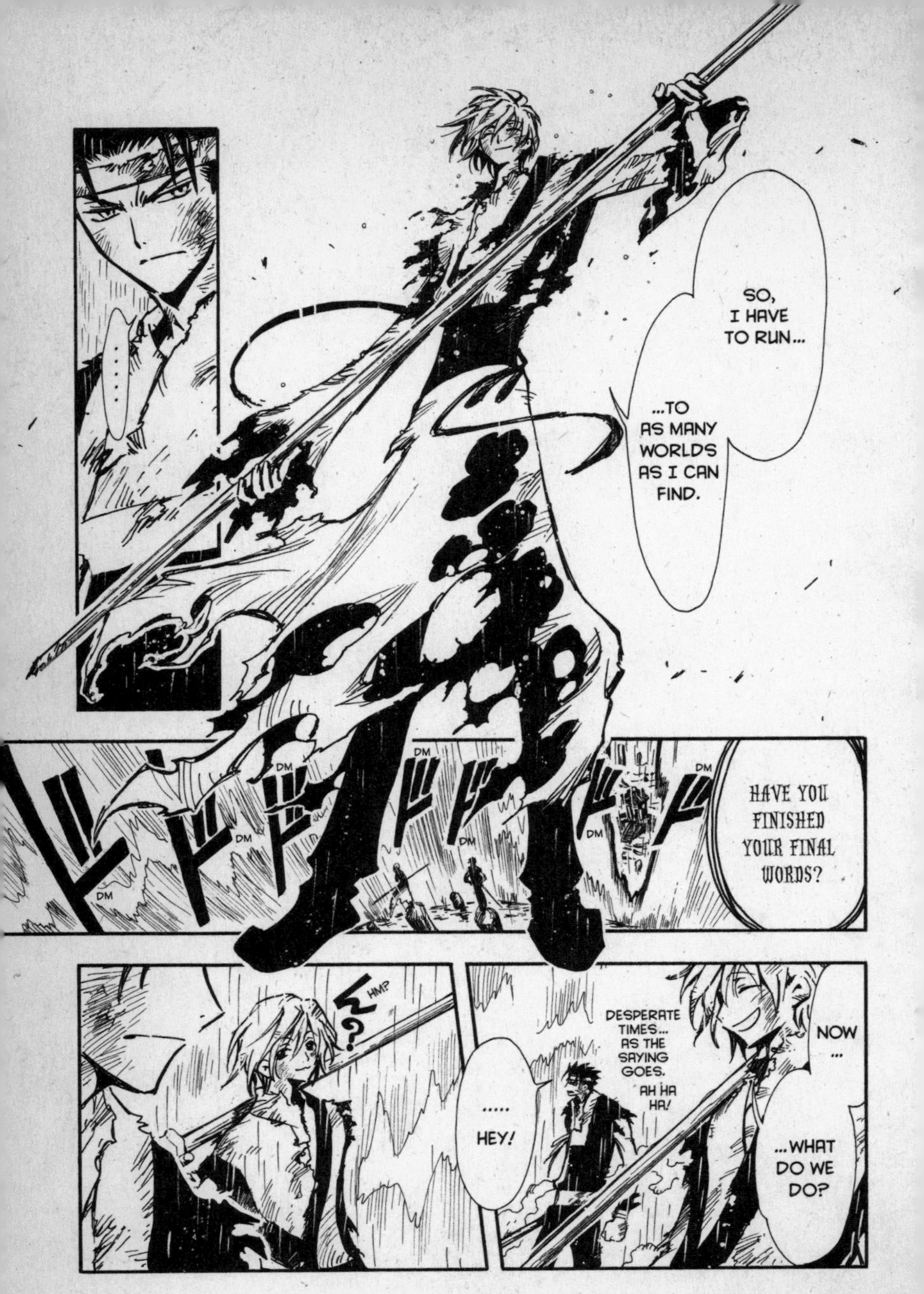

SO, I HAVE TO RUN...
...TO AS MANY WORLDS AS I CAN FIND.
......
HAVE YOU FINISHED YOUR FINAL WORDS?
DM
DM
DM
DM
DM
DM
DM
NOW ...
...WHAT DO WE DO?
DESPERATE TIMES... AS THE SAYING GOES.
AH HA HA!
..... HEY!
HMP?

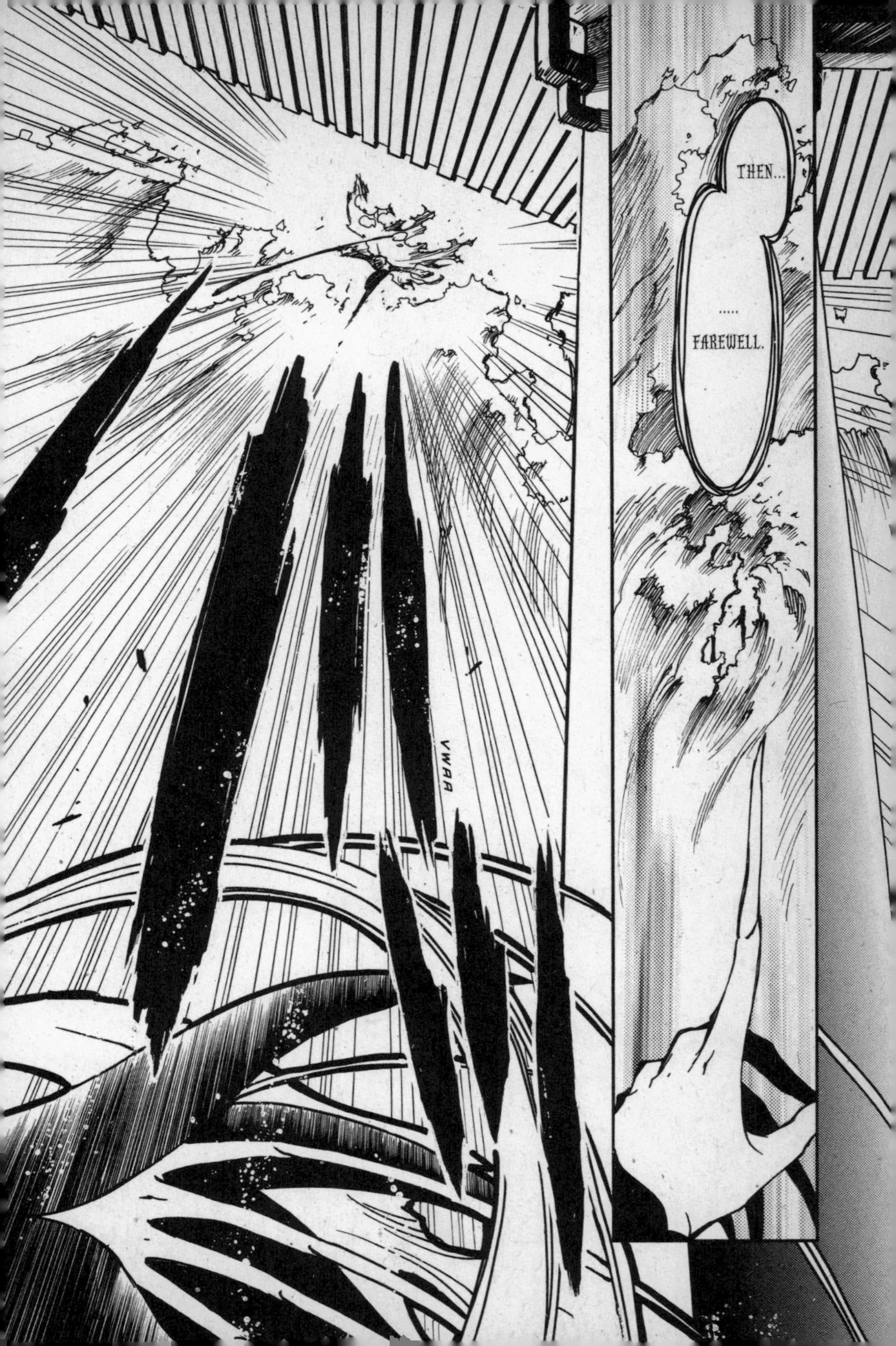
THEN...
..... FAREWELL.
VWAA

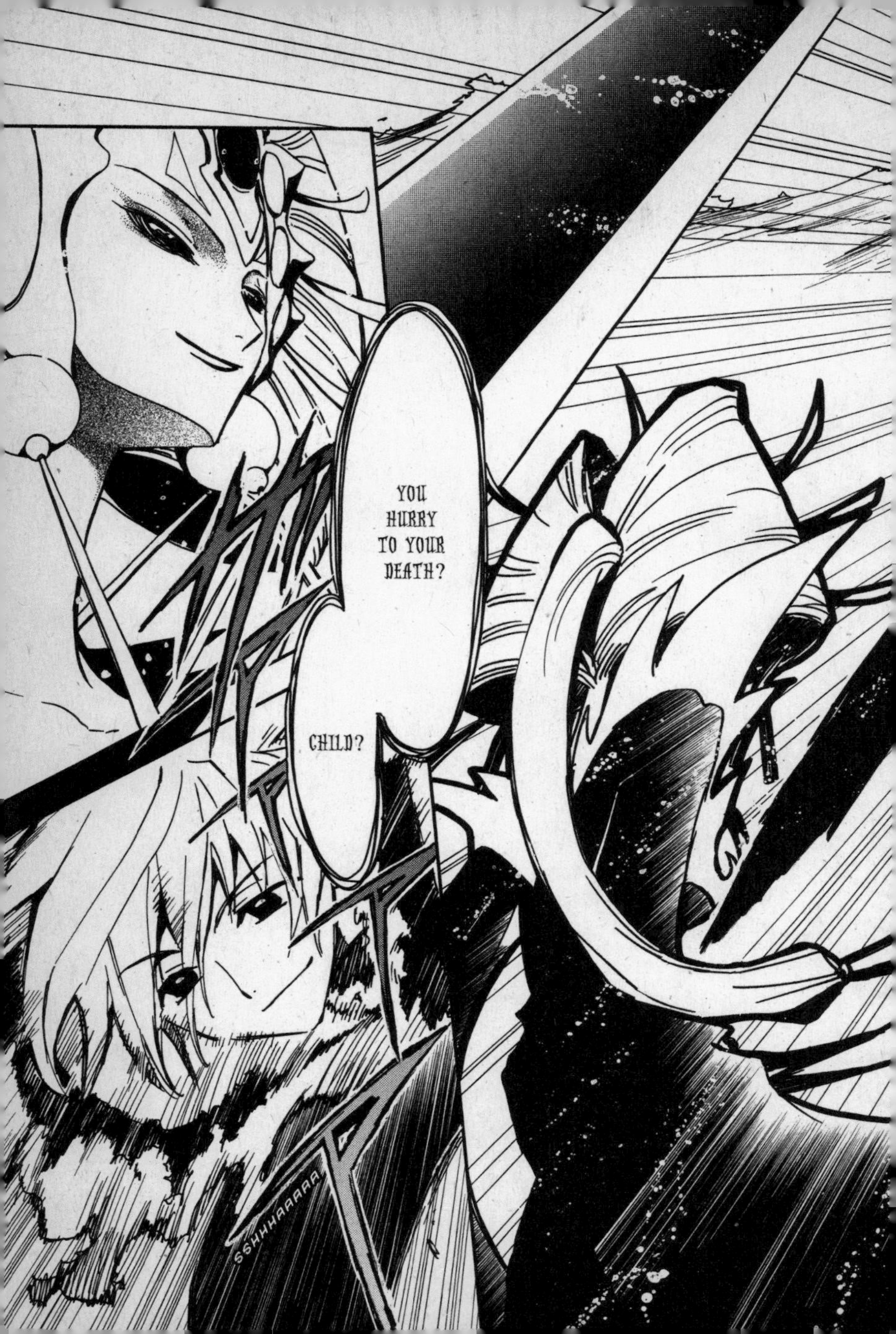
YOU HURRY TO YOUR DEATH?
CHILD?
SSHHAAAAAA

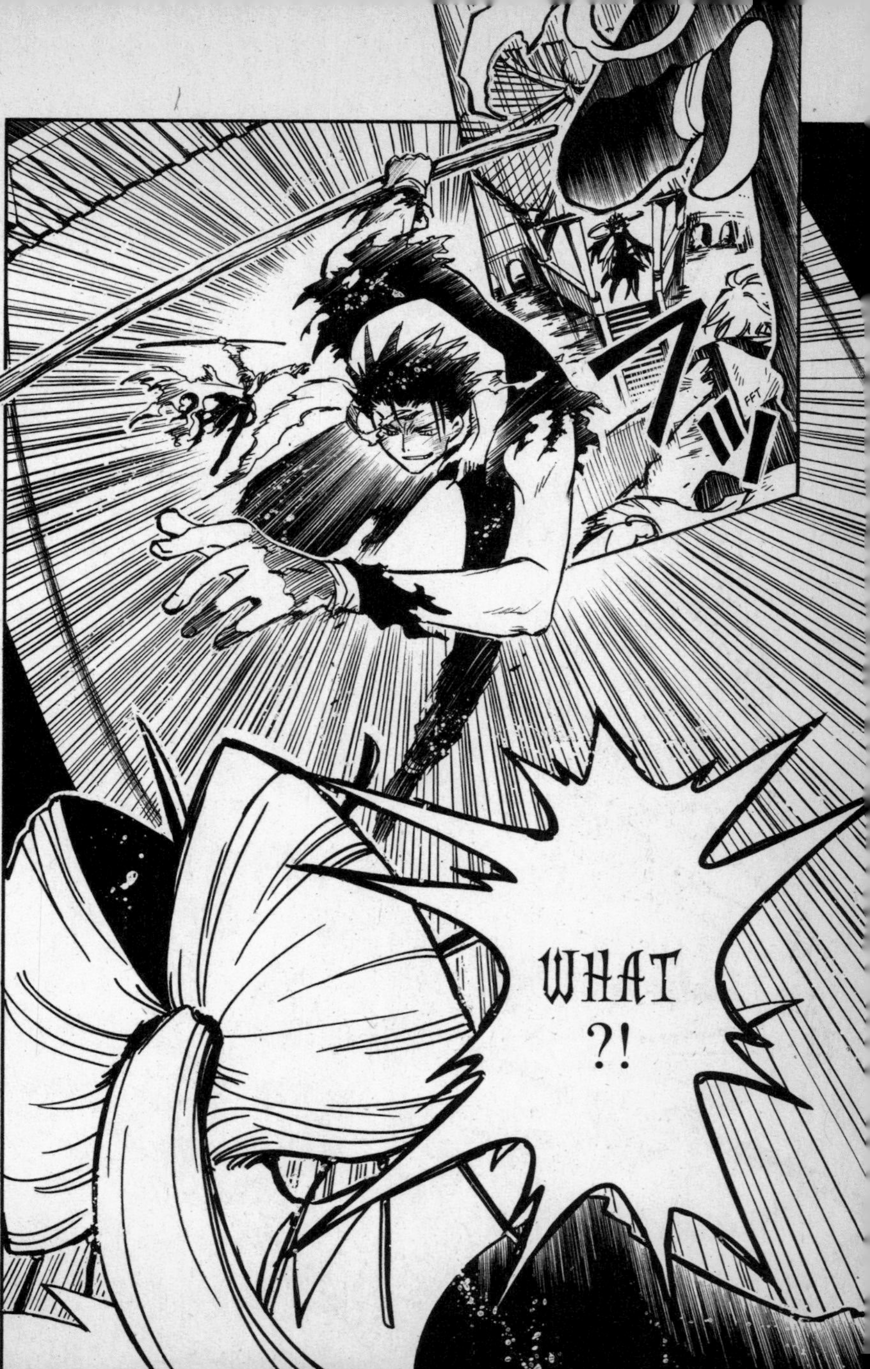
FFT
WHAT ?!

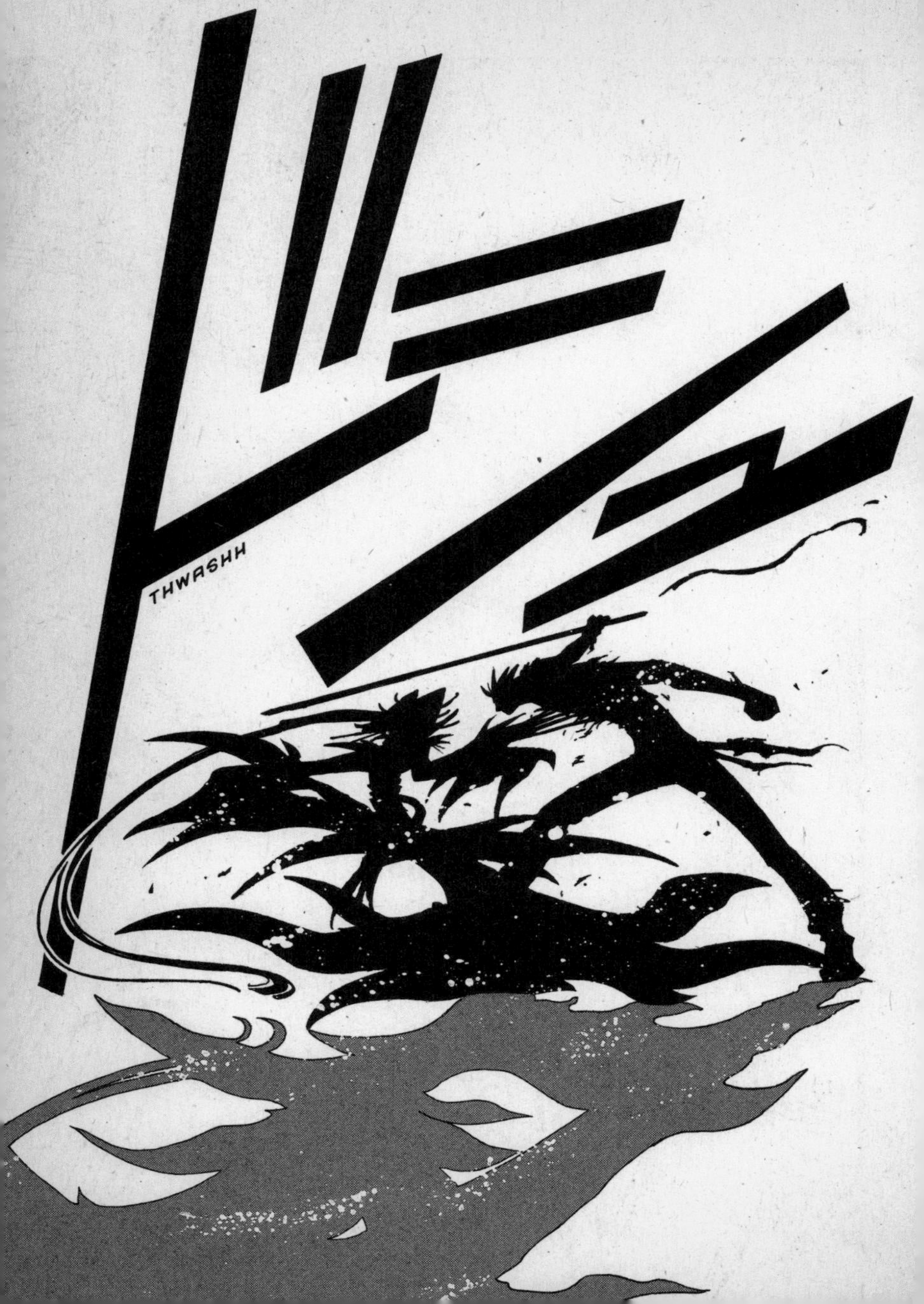
THWASHH

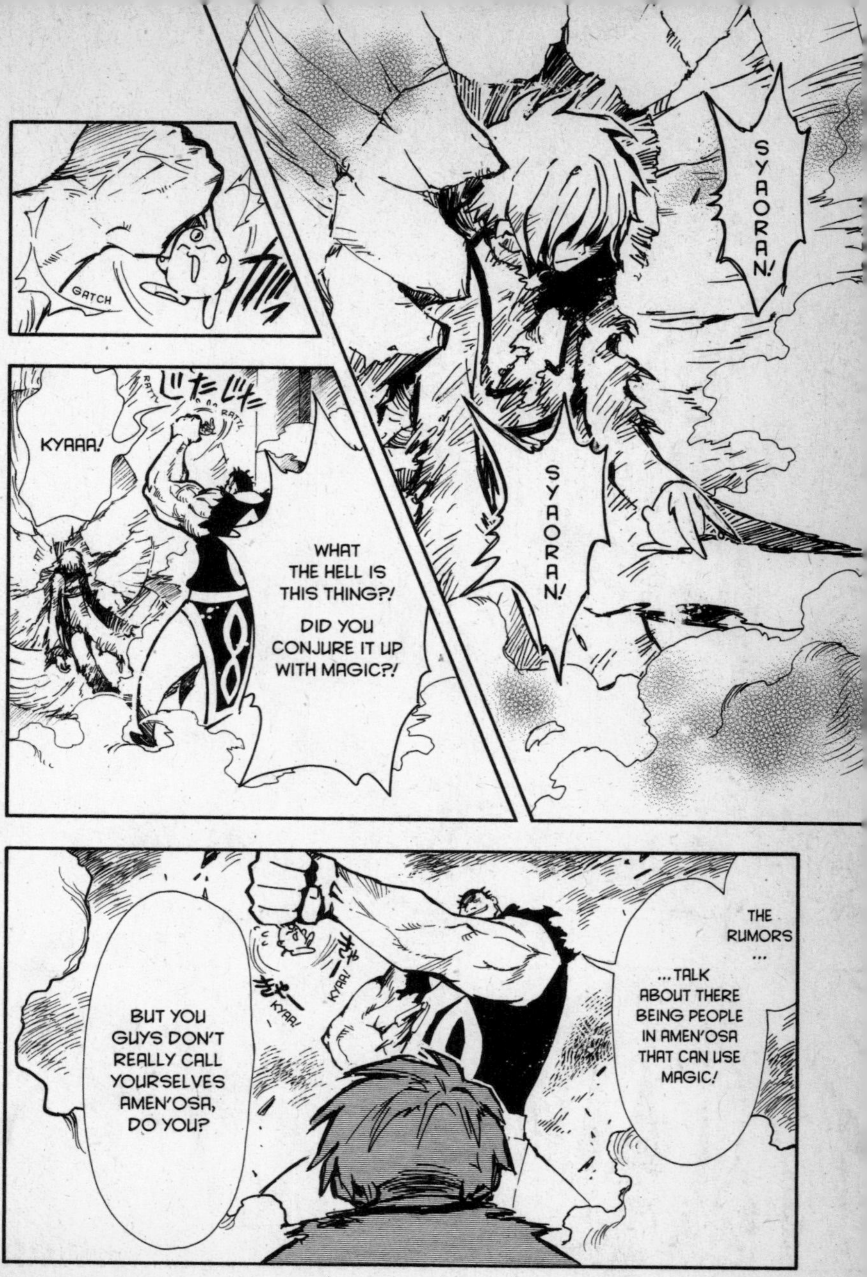
SYAORAN!
SYAORAN!
GATCH
KYAAA!
RATTL RATTL
WHAT THE HELL IS THIS THING?!
DID YOU CONJURE IT UP WITH MAGIC?!
THE RUMORS...
...TALK ABOUT THERE BEING PEOPLE IN AMEN'OSA THAT CAN USE MAGIC!
KYAA!
KYAA!
BUT YOU GUYS DON'T REALLY CALL YOURSELVES AMEN'OSA, DO YOU?

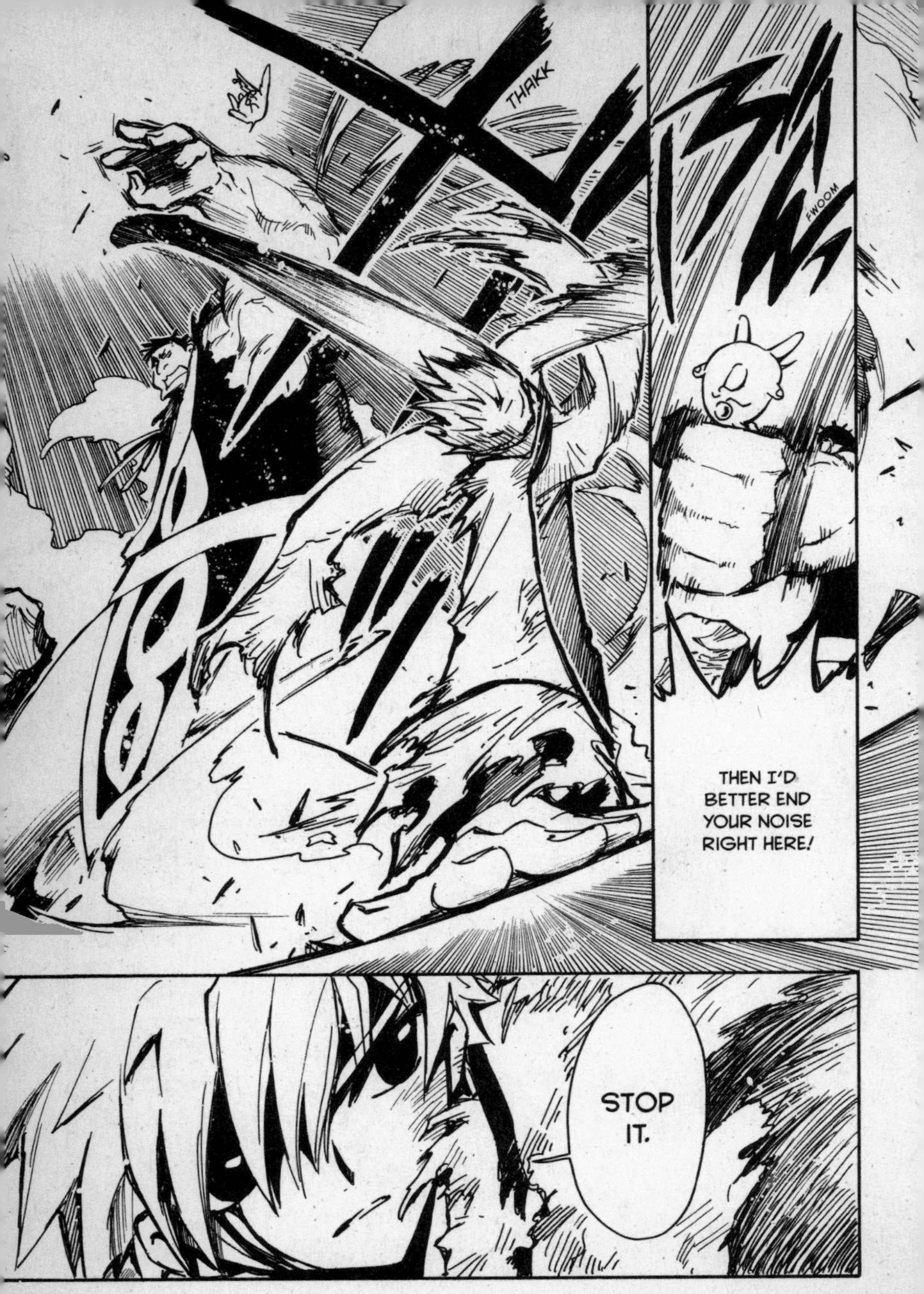
FWOOM
THEN I'D BETTER END YOUR NOISE RIGHT HERE!
THAKK
STOP IT.

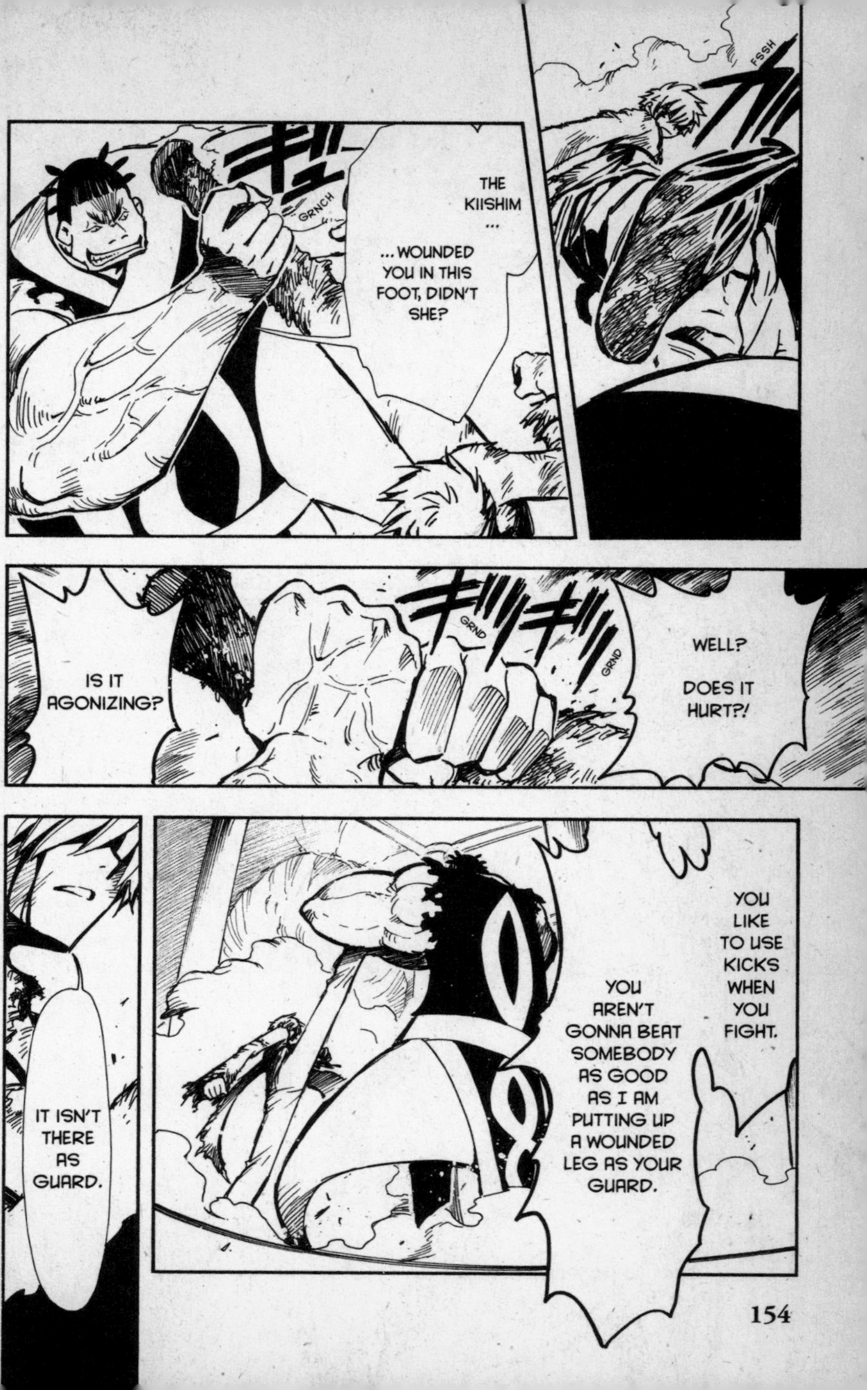
FSSH
GRNCH
THE KIISHIM ...
...WOUNDED YOU IN THIS FOOT, DIDN'T SHE?
GRND
GRND
WELL?
DOES IT HURT?!
IS IT AGONIZING?
YOU LIKE TO USE KICKS WHEN YOU FIGHT.
YOU AREN'T GONNA BEAT SOMEBODY AS GOOD AS I AM PUTTING UP A WOUNDED LEG AS YOUR GUARD.
IT ISN'T THERE AS GUARD.

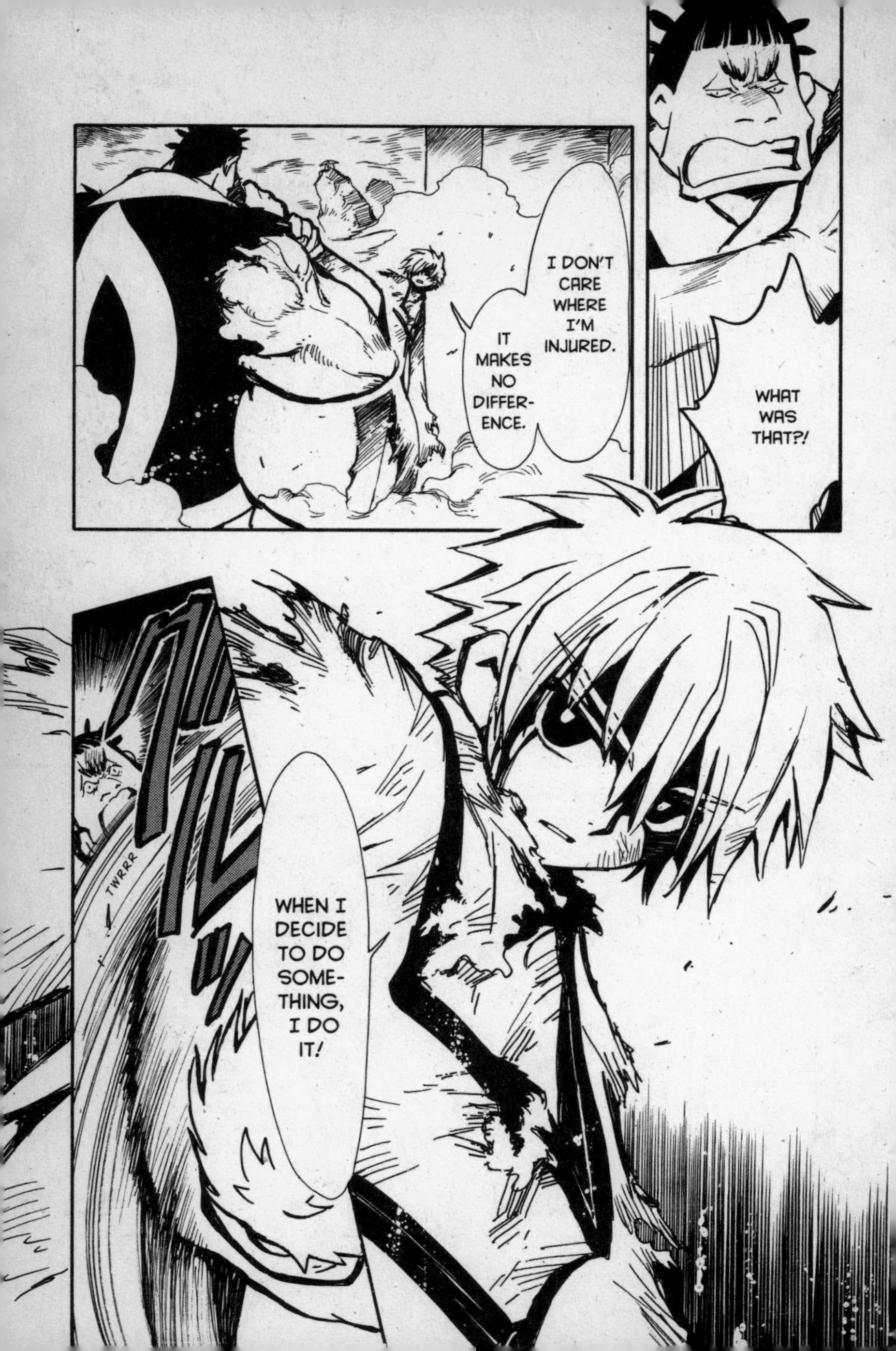
WHAT WAS THAT?!
I DON'T CARE WHERE I'M INJURED.
IT MAKES NO DIFFERENCE.
WHEN I DECIDE TO DO SOMETHING, I DO IT!
TWRRR

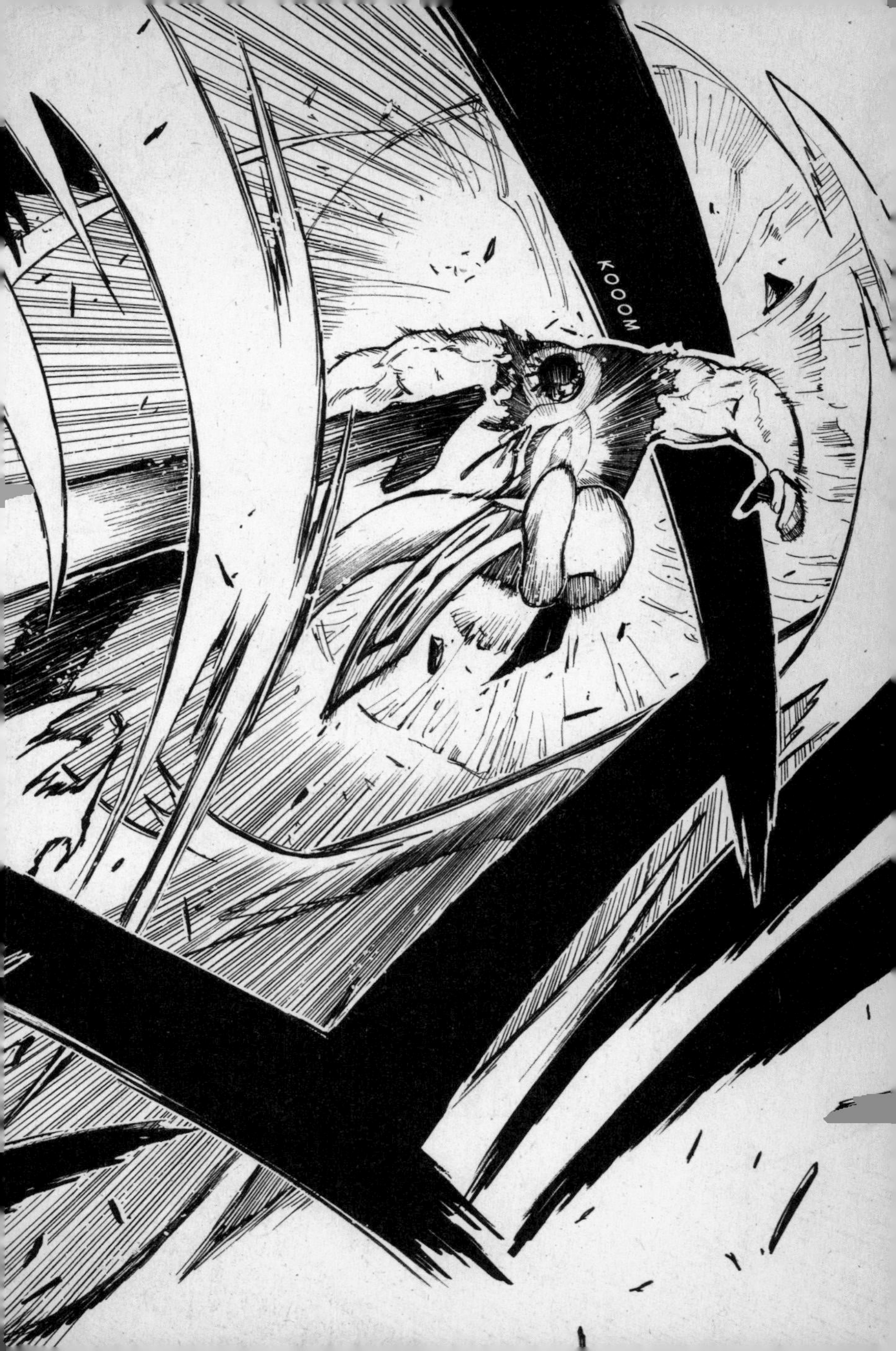
KOOOM

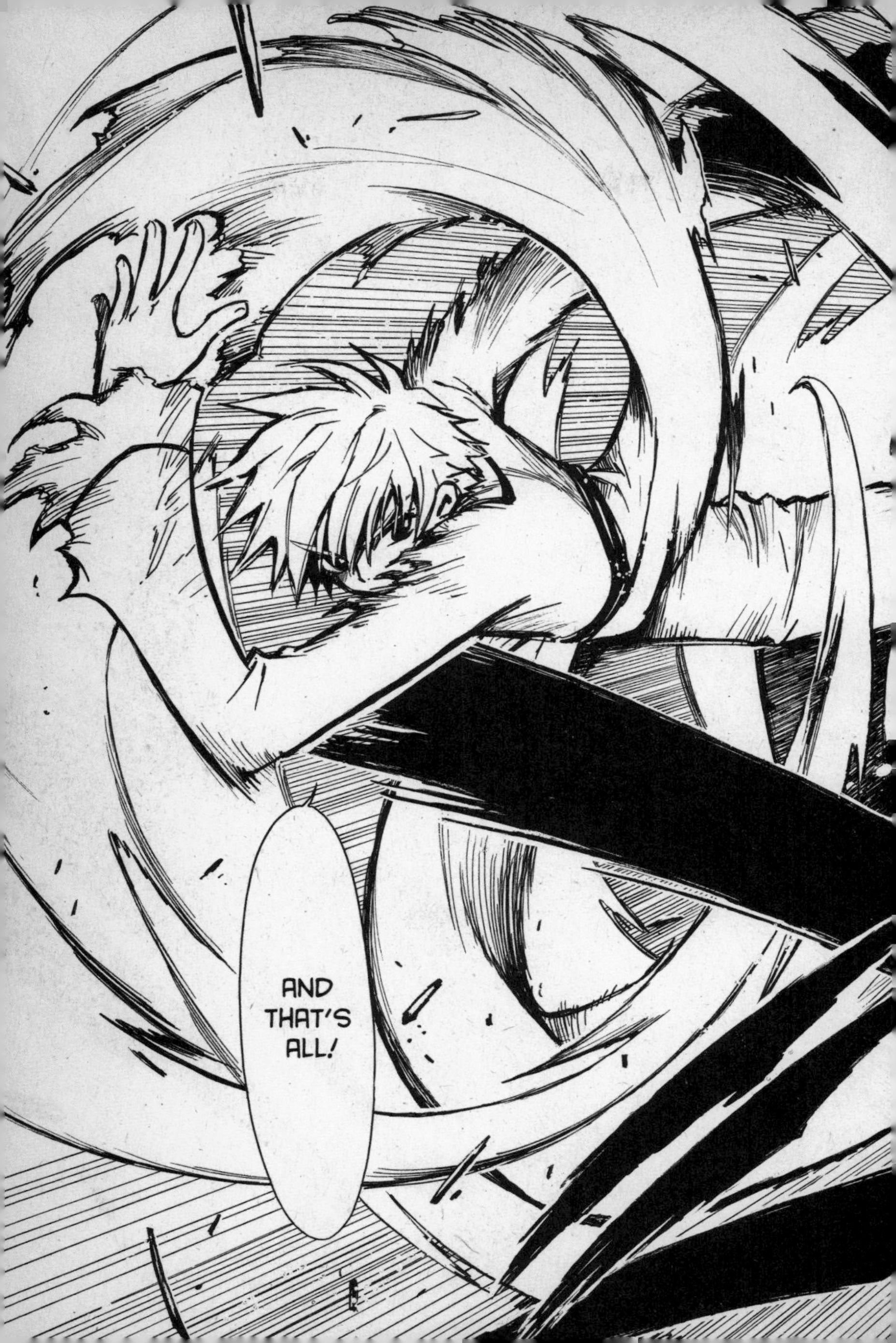
AND THAT'S ALL!

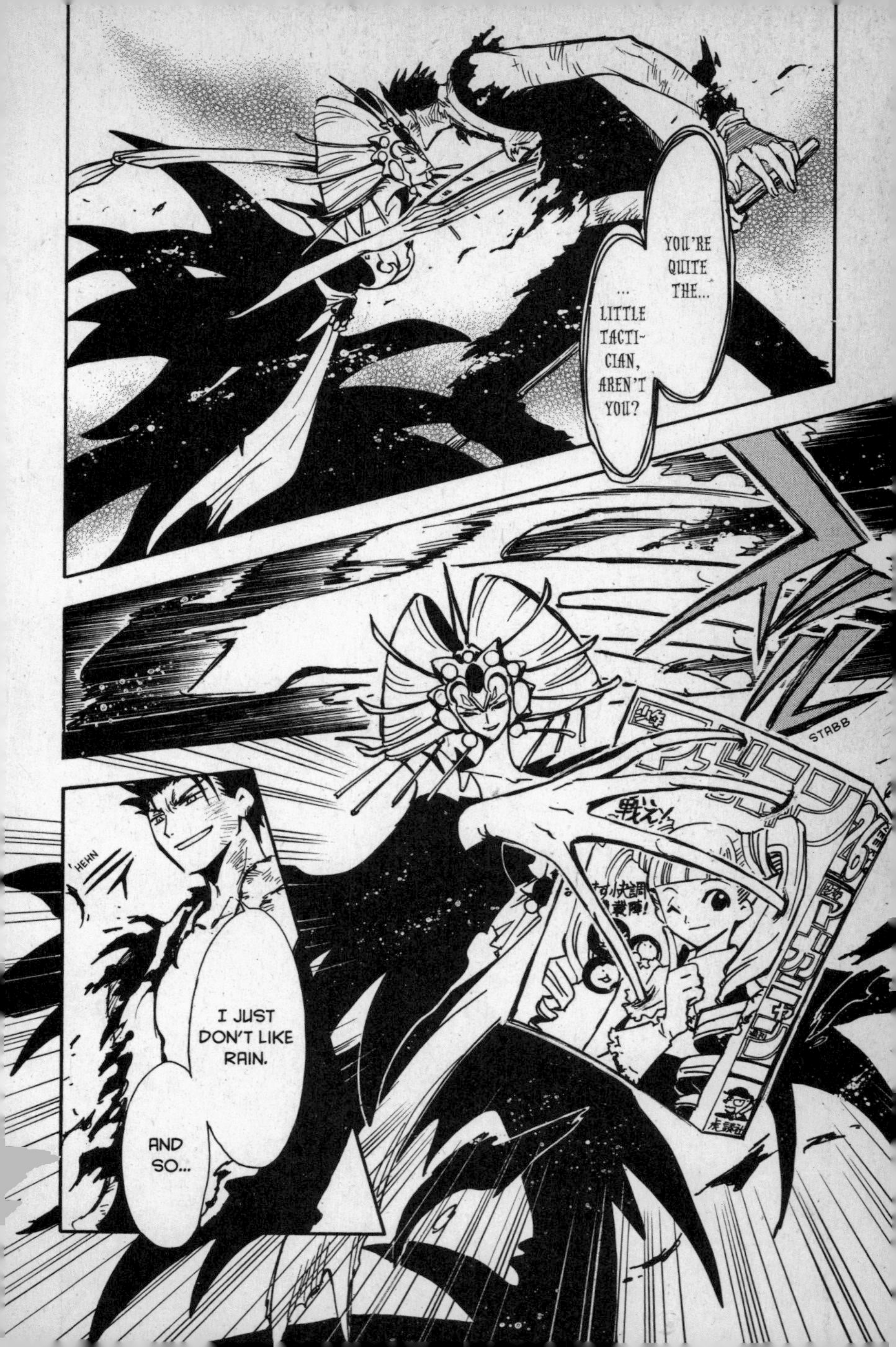
YOU'RE QUITE THE...
...LITTLE TACTI-CIAN, AREN'T YOU?
STABB
HEHN
I JUST DON'T LIKE RAIN.
AND SO...

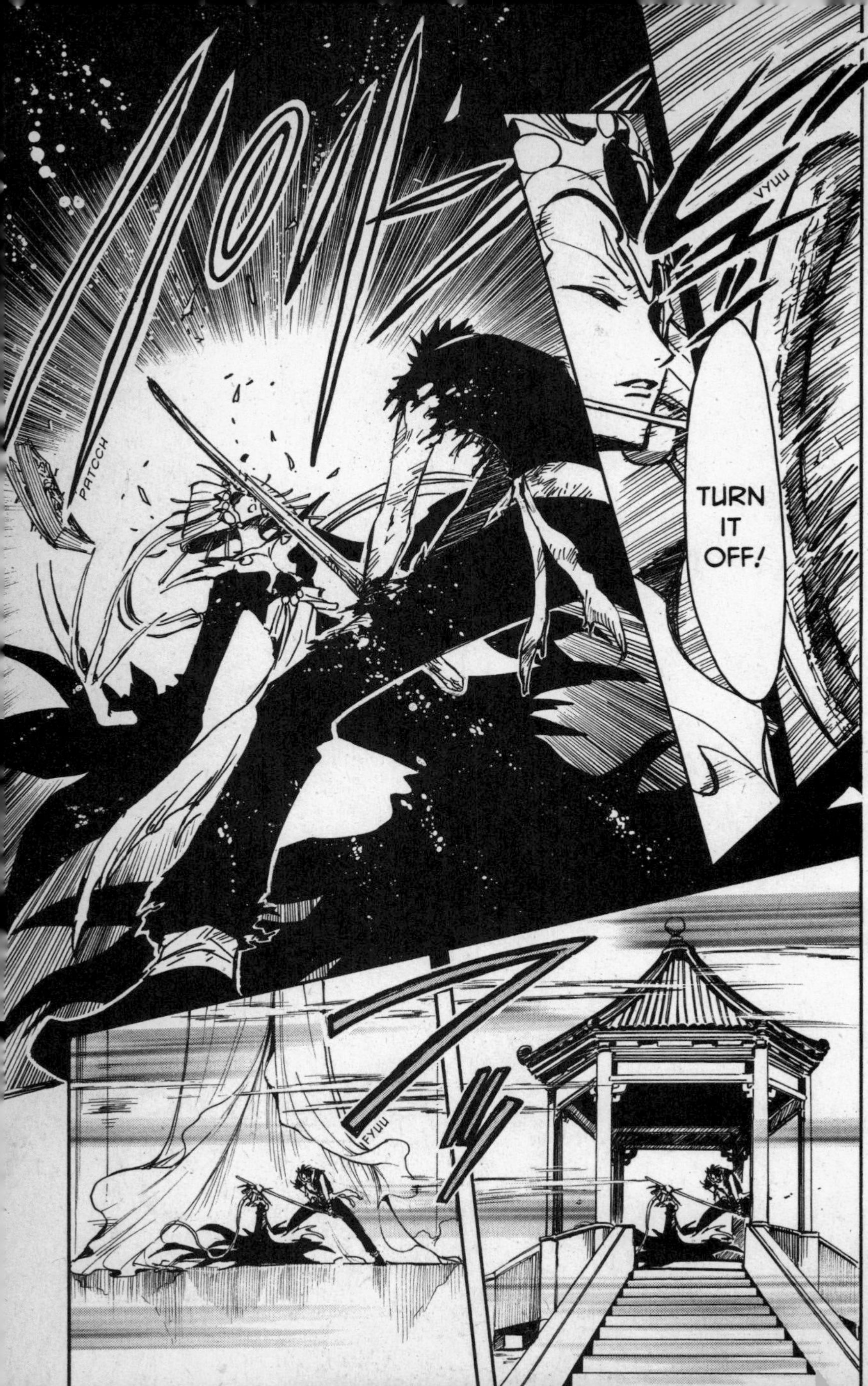
VYUU
TURN IT OFF!
PATCCH
FYUU

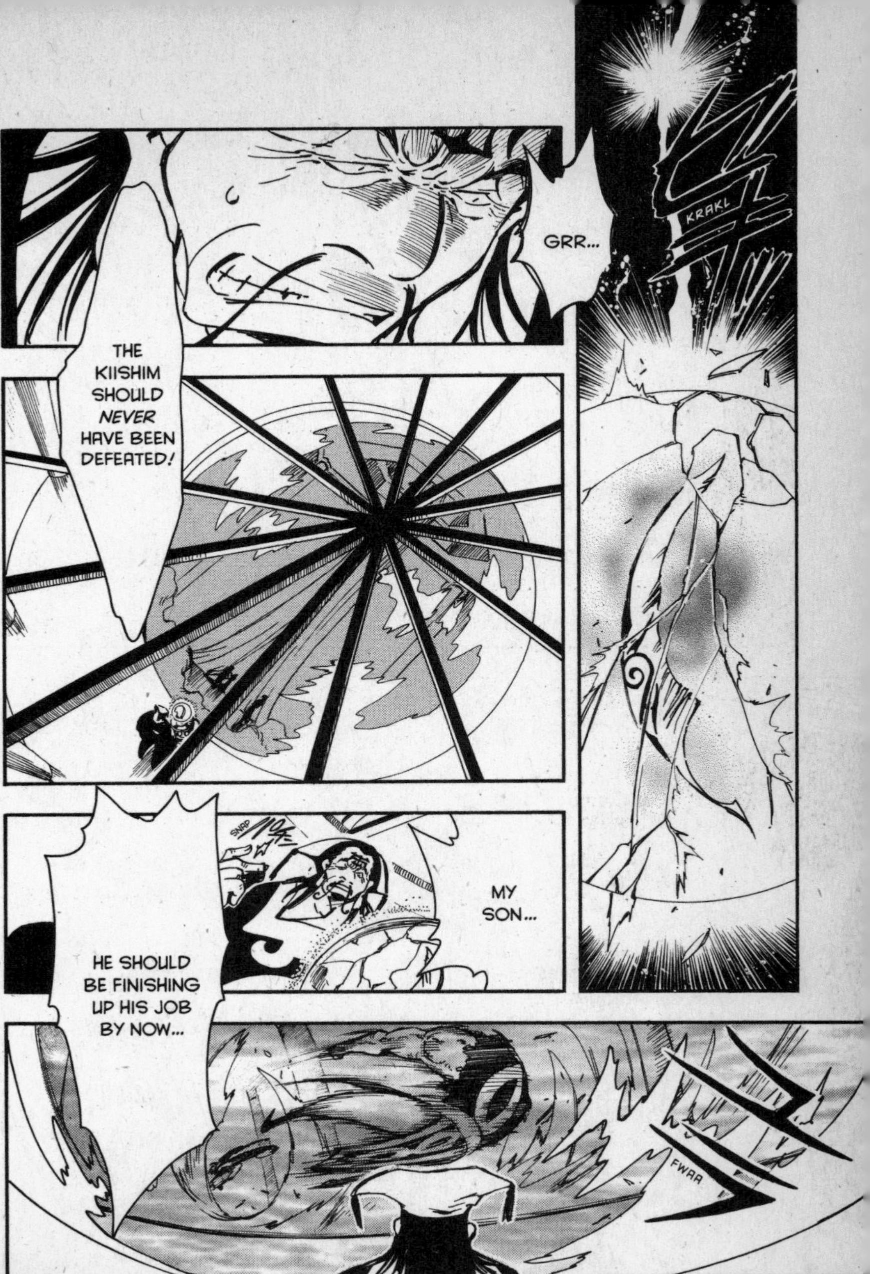
KRAKL
GRR...
THE KIISHIM SHOULD *NEVER* HAVE BEEN DEFEATED!
SNAP
MY SON...
HE SHOULD BE FINISHING UP HIS JOB BY NOW...
FWAA

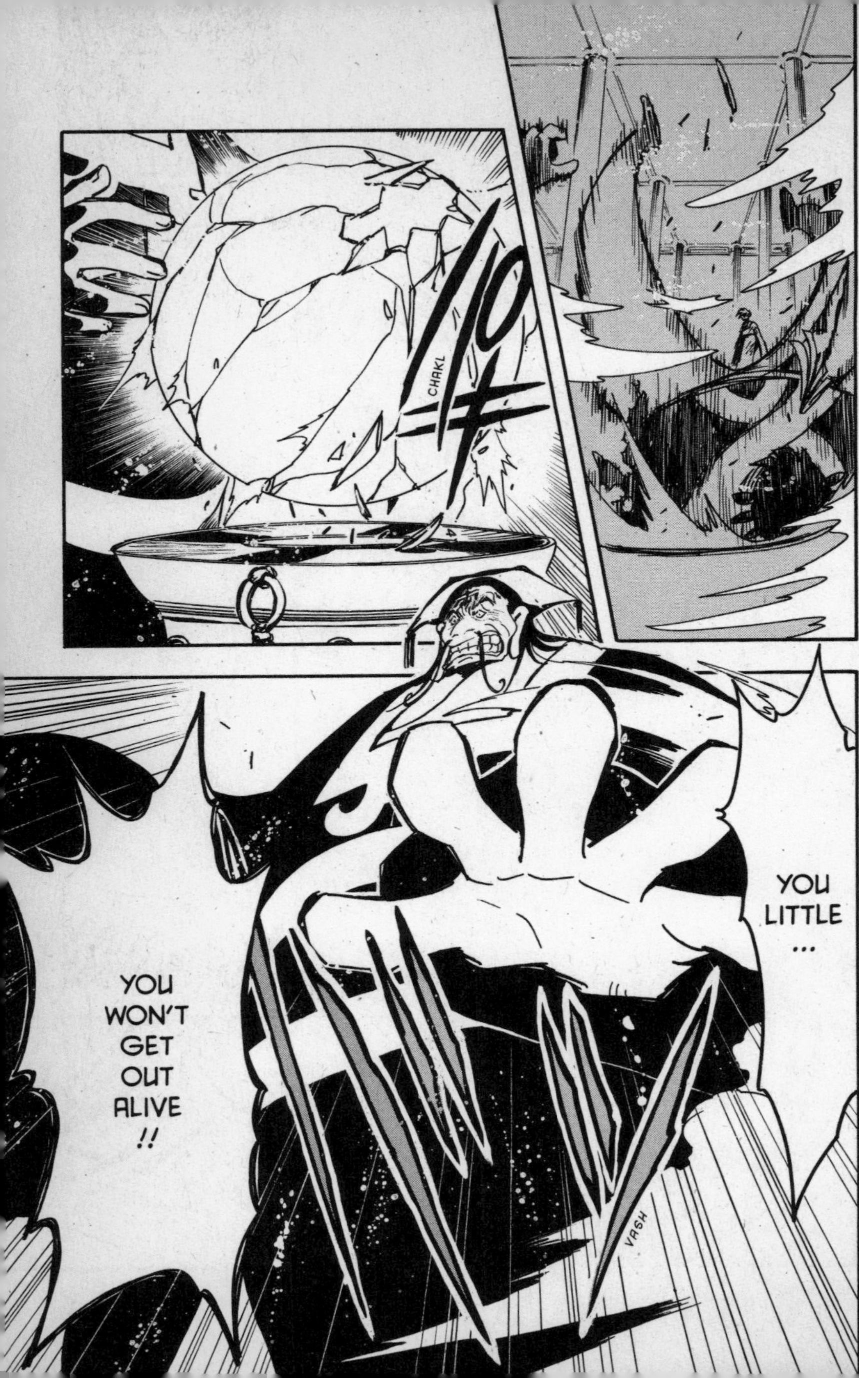
CHAKL
YOU LITTLE ...
YOU WON'T GET OUT ALIVE !!
VASH

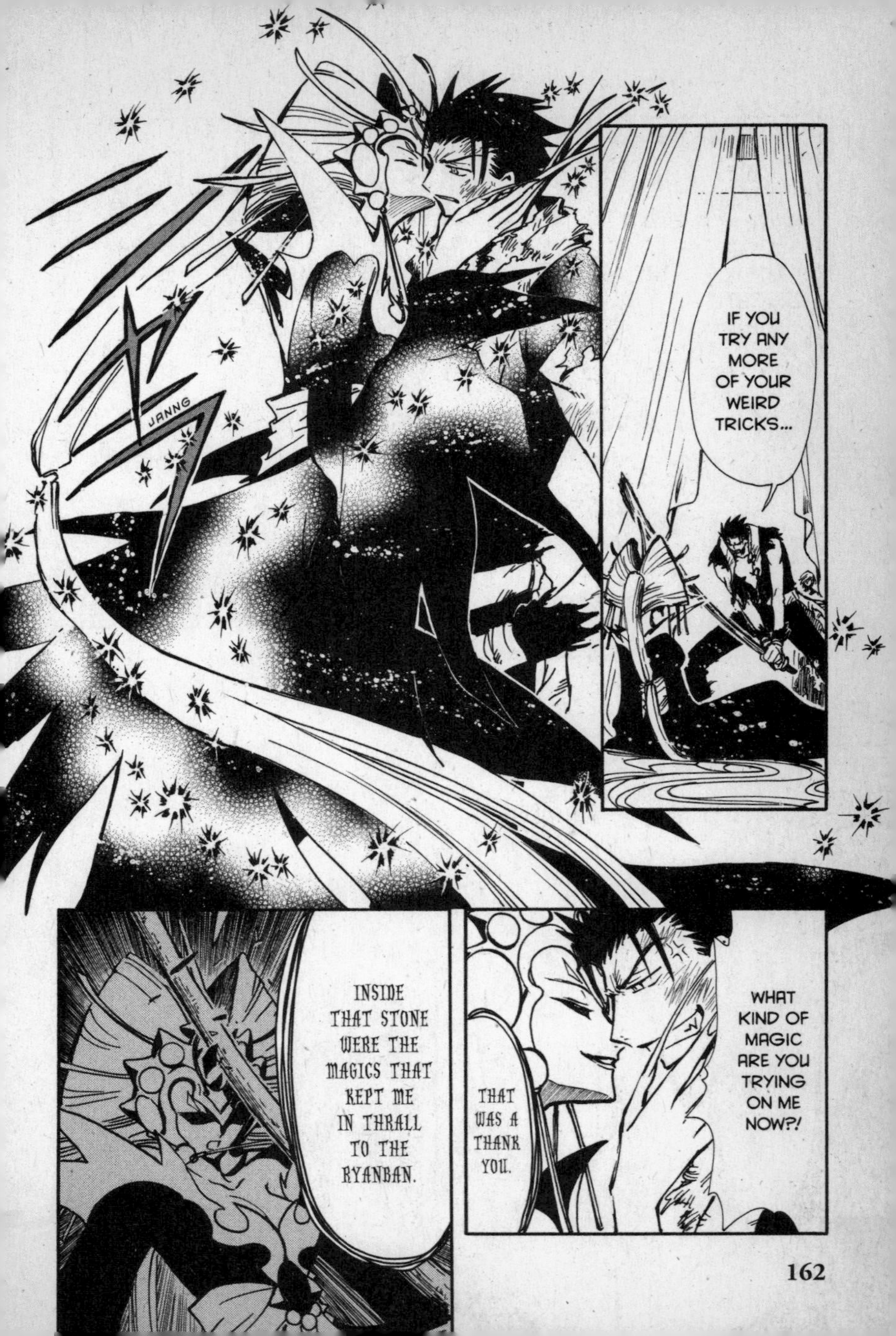
IF YOU TRY ANY MORE OF YOUR WEIRD TRICKS...
JANNG
WHAT KIND OF MAGIC ARE YOU TRYING ON ME NOW?!
THAT WAS A THANK YOU.
INSIDE THAT STONE WERE THE MAGICS THAT KEPT ME IN THRALL TO THE RYANBAN.

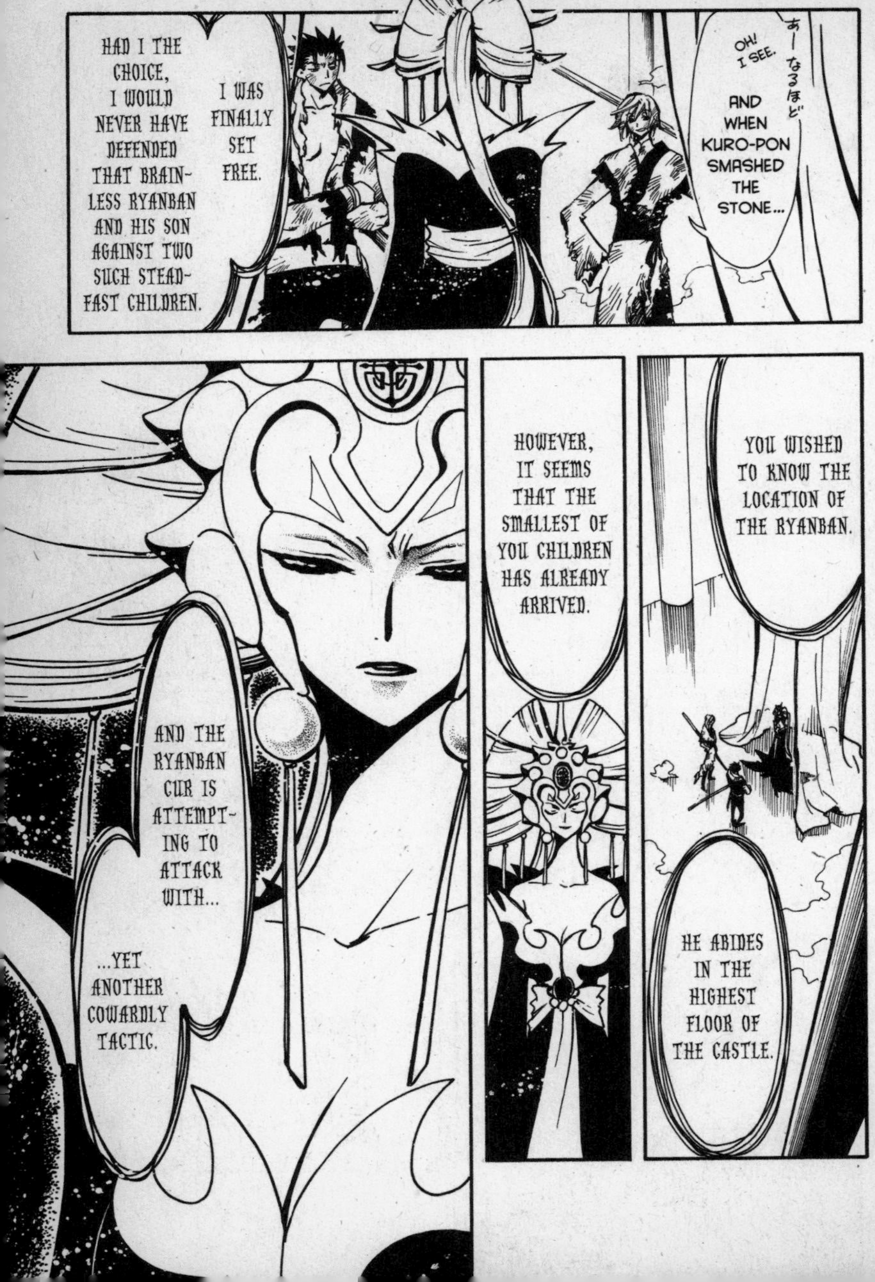
あー なるほど
OH! I SEE.
AND WHEN KURO-PON SMASHED THE STONE...
I WAS FINALLY SET FREE.
HAD I THE CHOICE, I WOULD NEVER HAVE DEFENDED THAT BRAIN-LESS RYANBAN AND HIS SON AGAINST TWO SUCH STEAD-FAST CHILDREN.
YOU WISHED TO KNOW THE LOCATION OF THE RYANBAN.
HE ABIDES IN THE HIGHEST FLOOR OF THE CASTLE.
HOWEVER, IT SEEMS THAT THE SMALLEST OF YOU CHILDREN HAS ALREADY ARRIVED.
AND THE RYANBAN CUR IS ATTEMPT-ING TO ATTACK WITH...
...YET ANOTHER COWARDLY TACTIC.

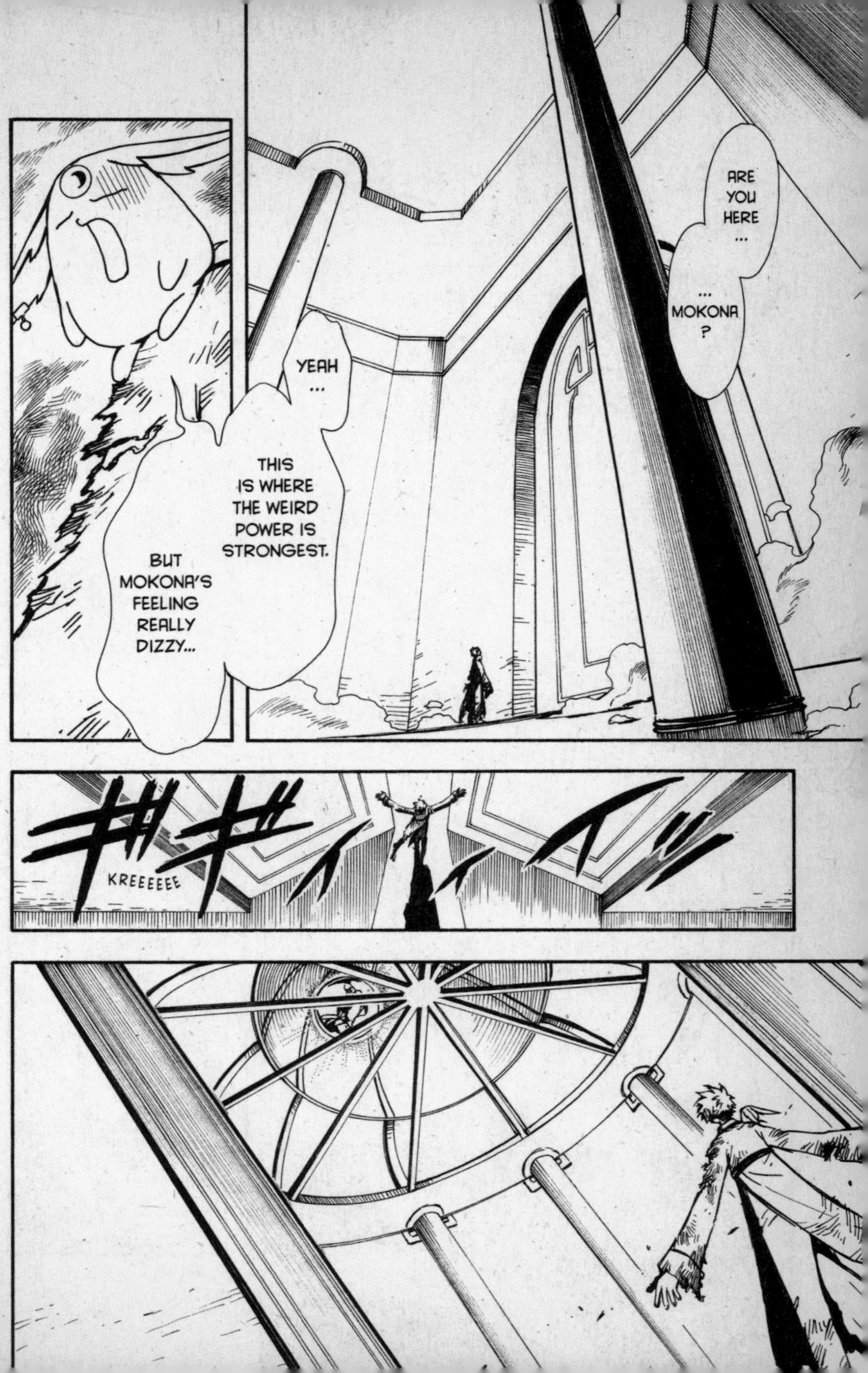
ARE YOU HERE ...
... MOKONA ?
YEAH ...
THIS IS WHERE THE WEIRD POWER IS STRONGEST.
BUT MOKONA'S FEELING REALLY DIZZY...
KREEEEEEE

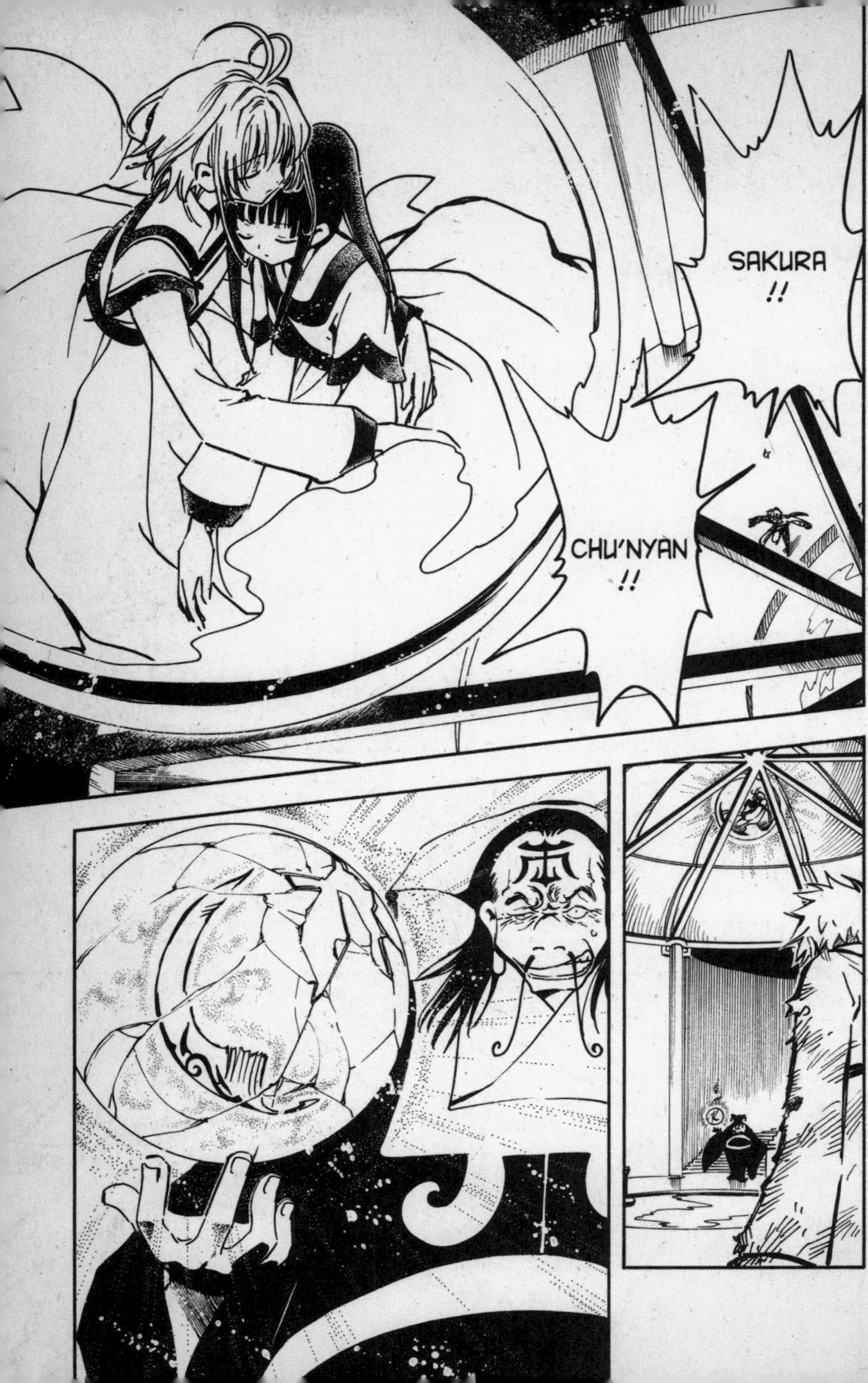
SAKURA !!
CHU'NYAN !!

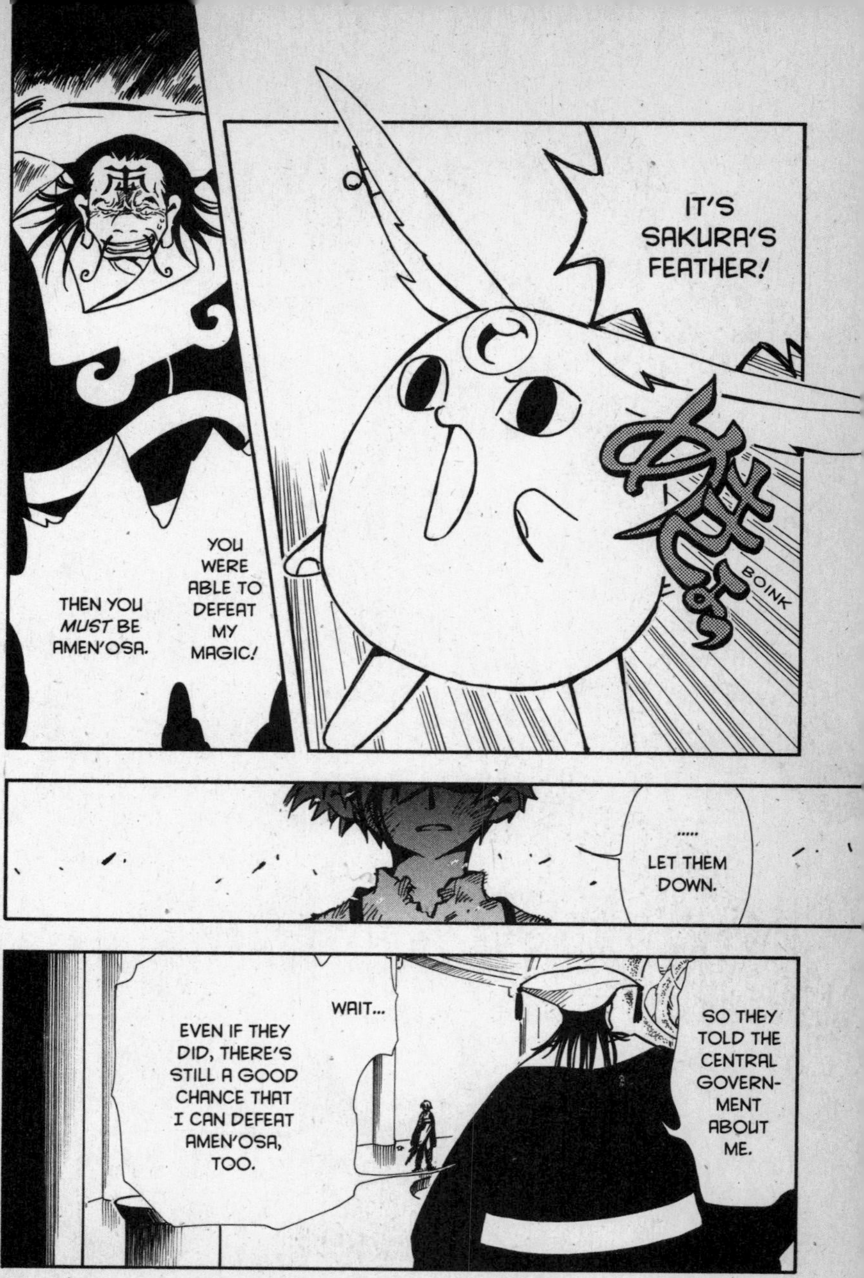
IT'S SAKURA'S FEATHER!
BOINK
YOU WERE ABLE TO DEFEAT MY MAGIC!
THEN YOU *MUST* BE AMEN'OSA.
..... LET THEM DOWN.
SO THEY TOLD THE CENTRAL GOVERN-MENT ABOUT ME.
WAIT...
EVEN IF THEY DID, THERE'S STILL A GOOD CHANCE THAT I CAN DEFEAT AMEN'OSA, TOO.

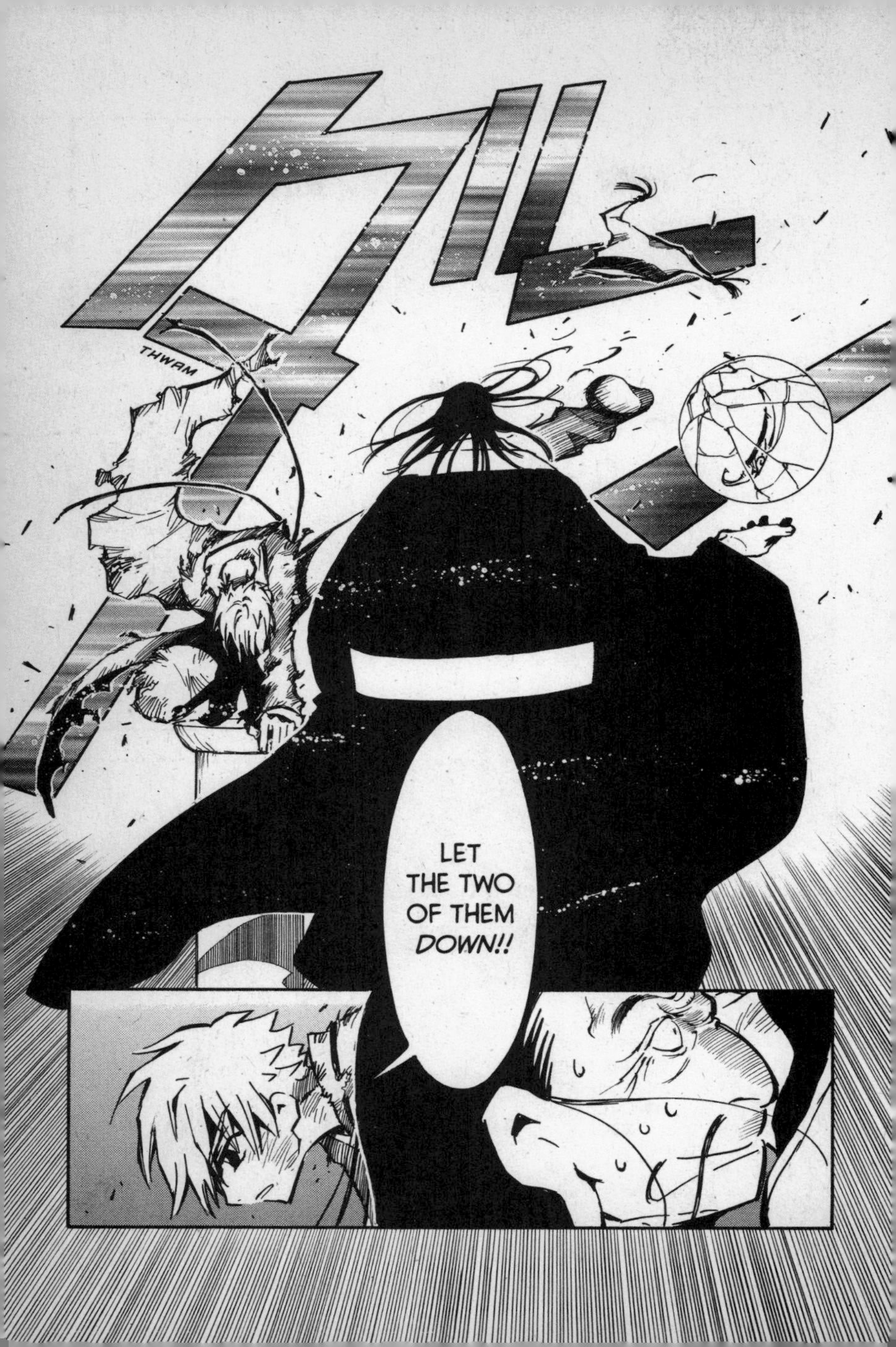
THWAM
LET THE TWO OF THEM DOWN!!

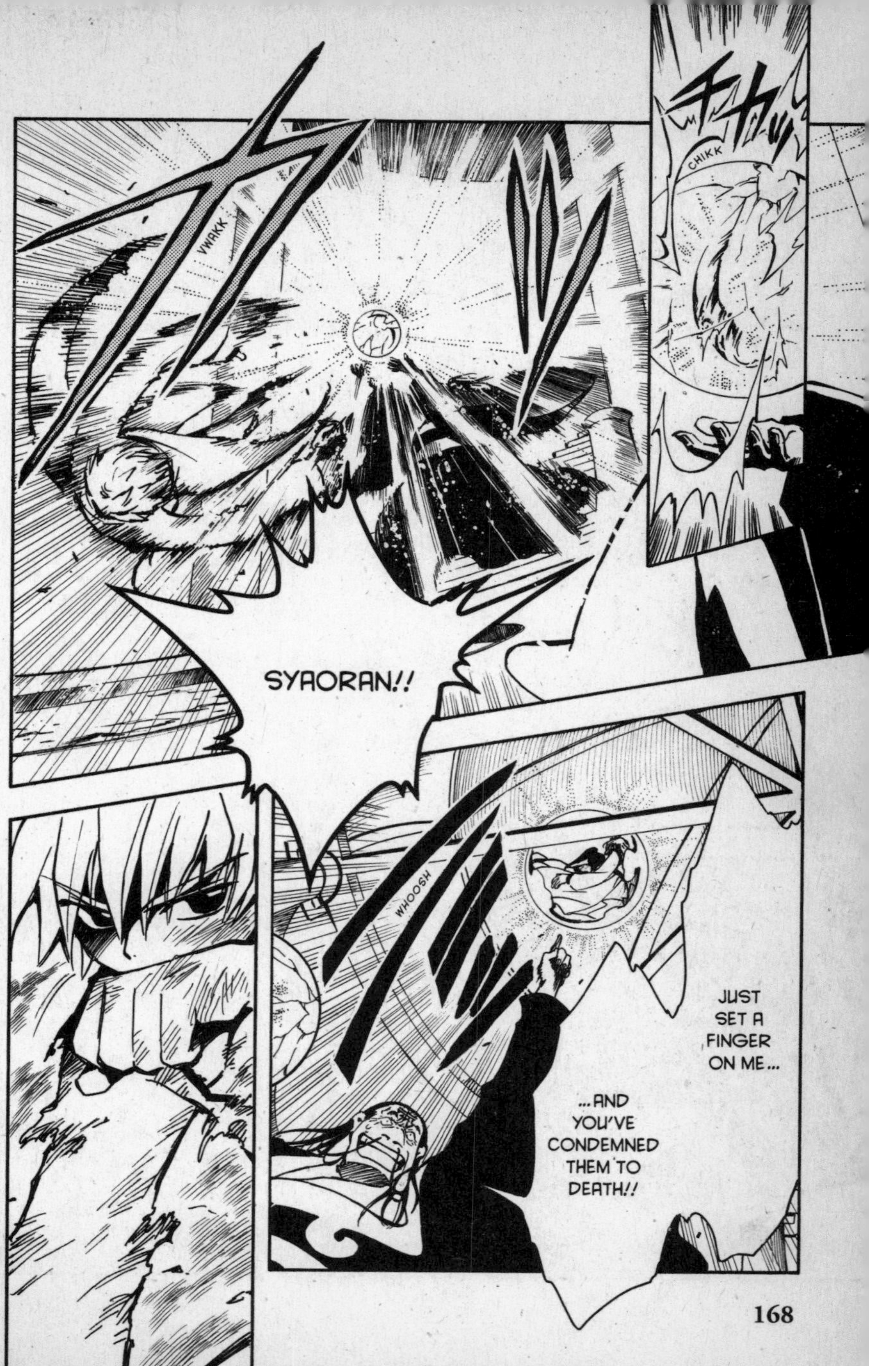
チカッ
CHIKK
VWAKK
SYAORAN!!
WHOOSH
JUST SET A FINGER ON ME...
...AND YOU'VE CONDEMNED THEM TO DEATH!!

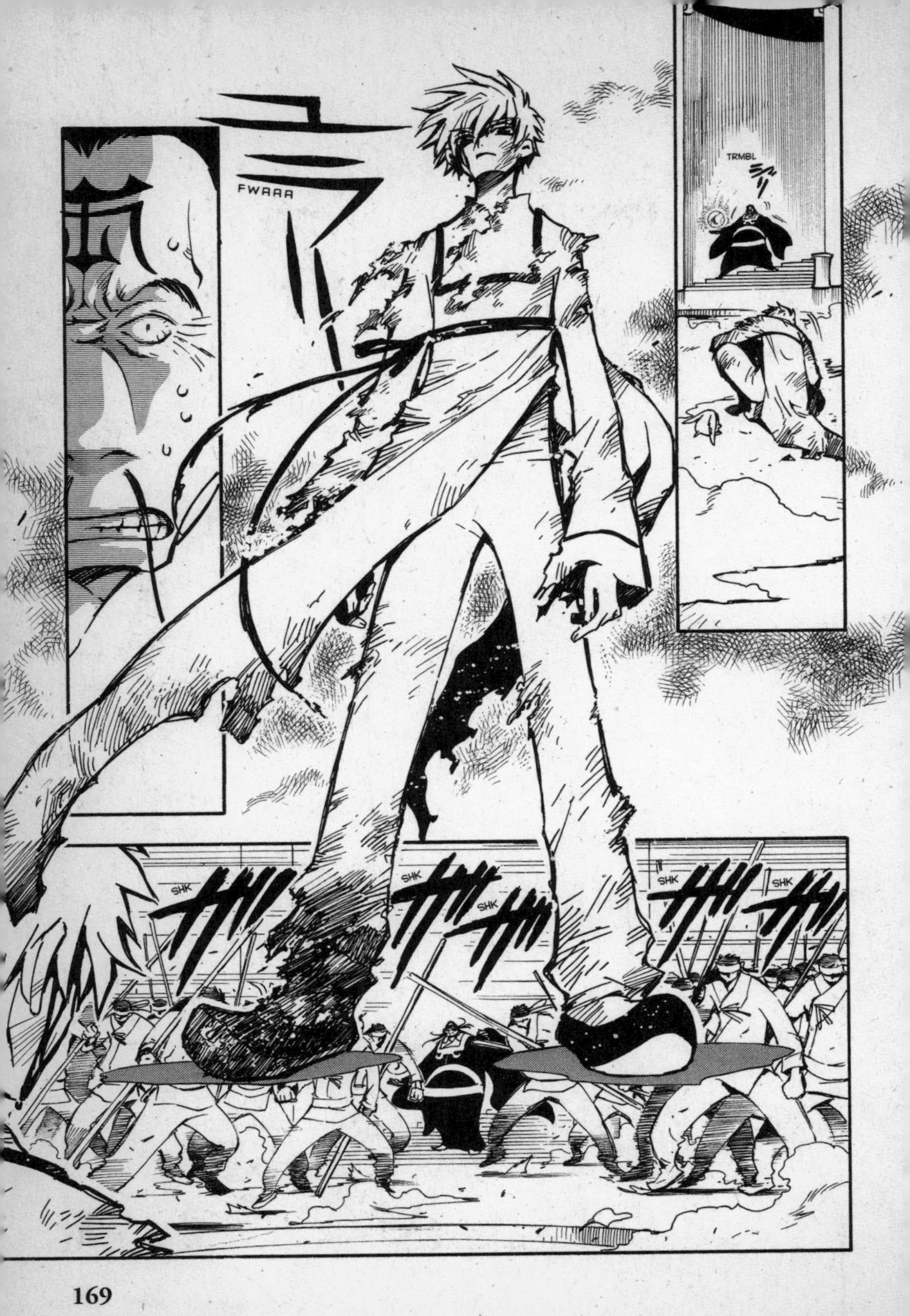
TRMBL
FWAAA
SHK
SHK
SHK
SHK

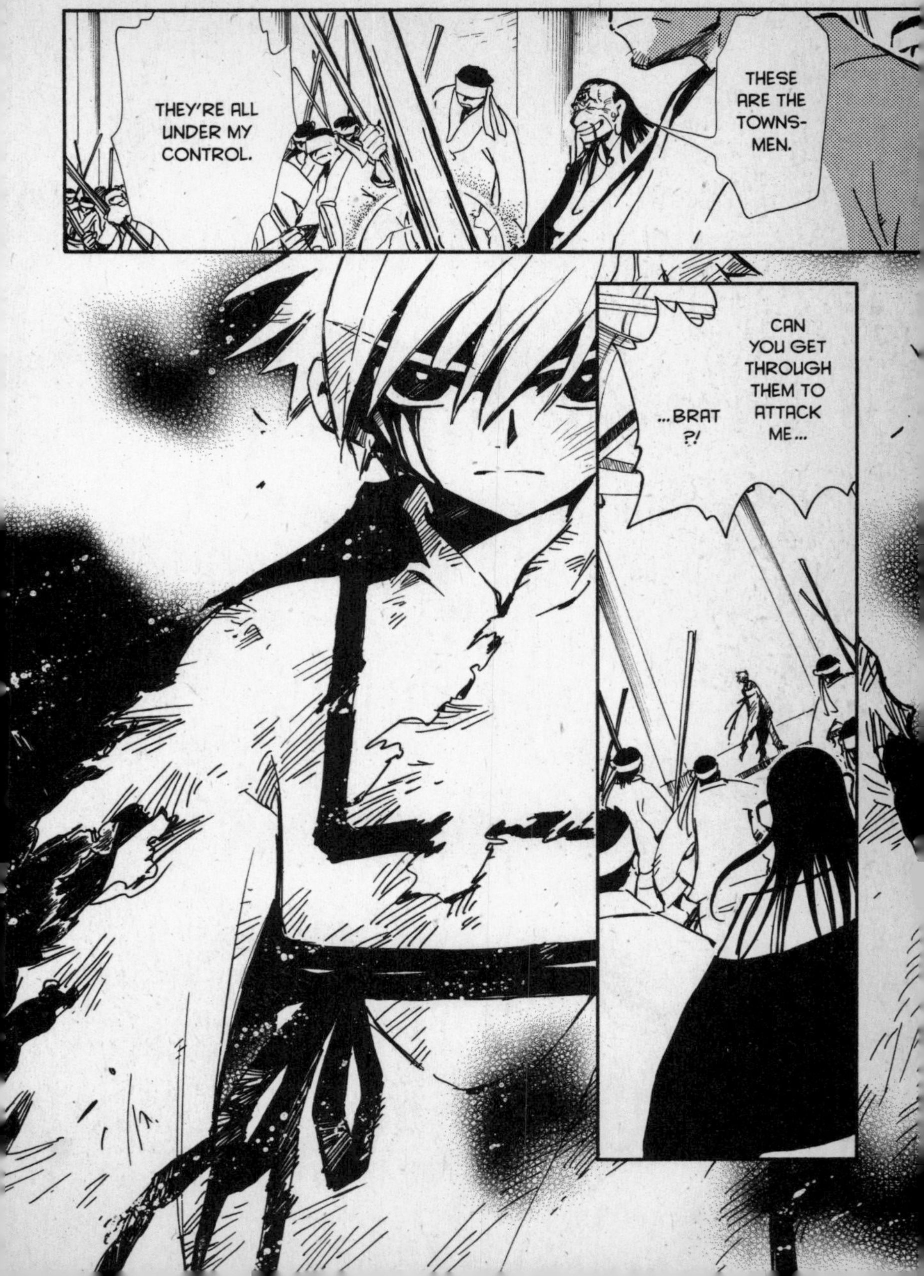
THESE ARE THE TOWNS-MEN.
THEY'RE ALL UNDER MY CONTROL.
CAN YOU GET THROUGH THEM TO ATTACK ME...
...BRAT?!

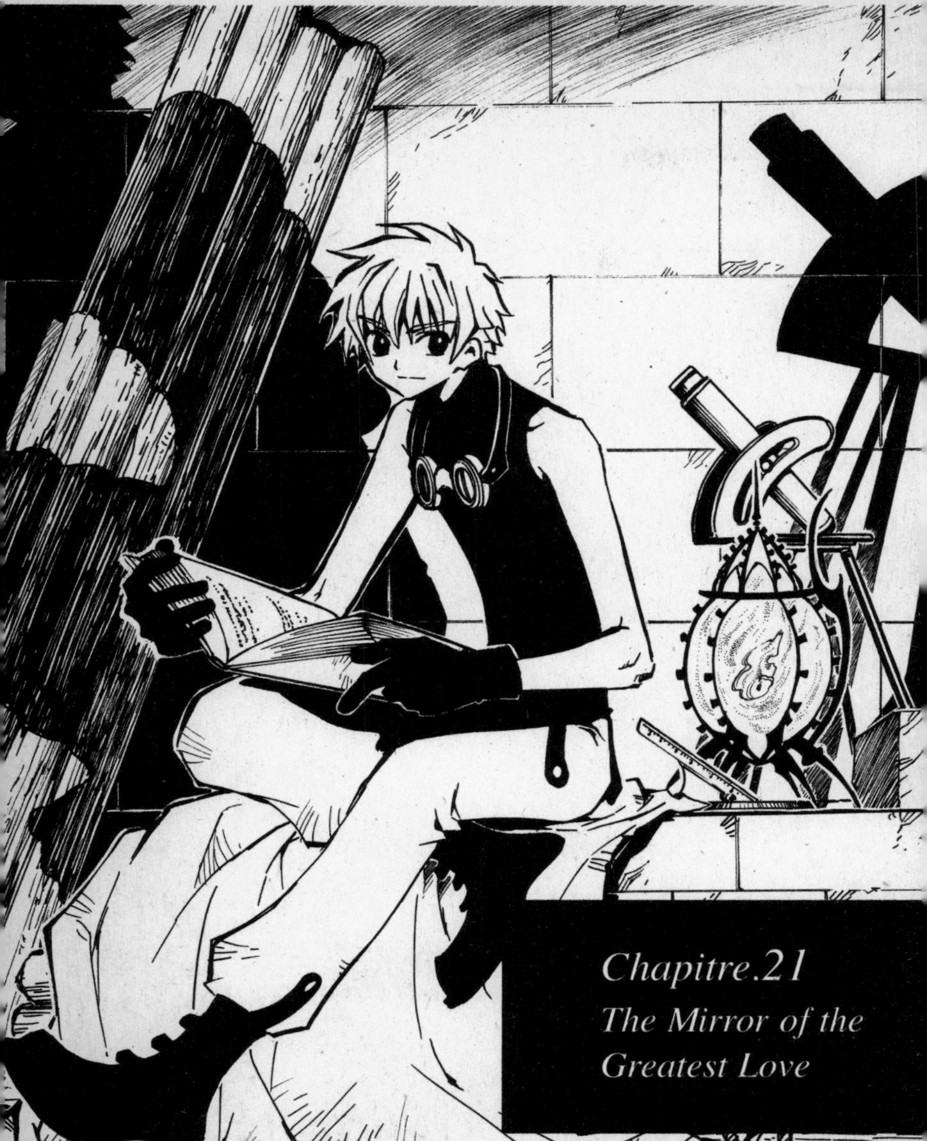
Chapitre.21
The Mirror of the Greatest Love

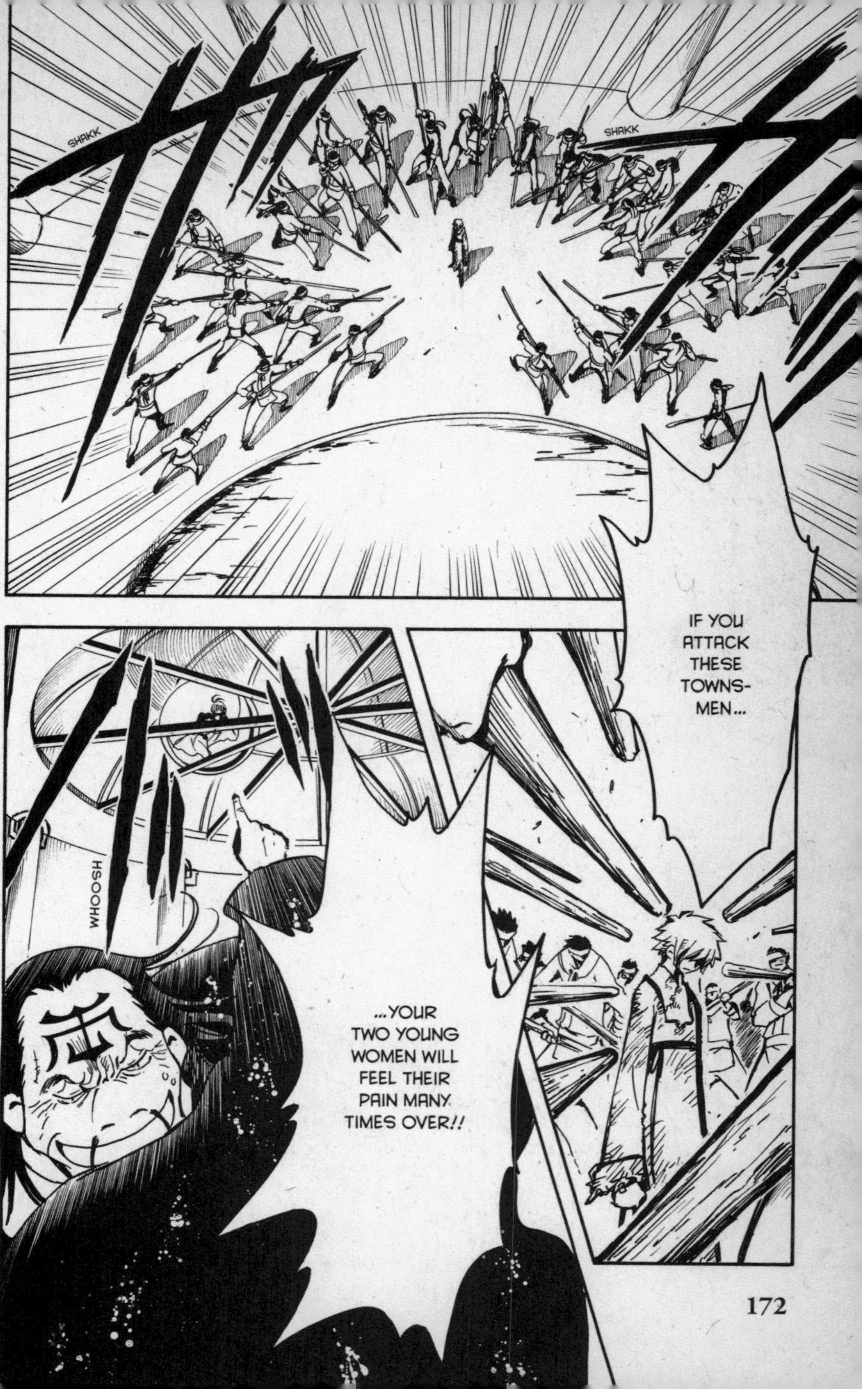
SHAKK
SHAKK
IF YOU ATTACK THESE TOWNS-MEN...
...YOUR TWO YOUNG WOMEN WILL FEEL THEIR PAIN MANY TIMES OVER!!
WHOOSH

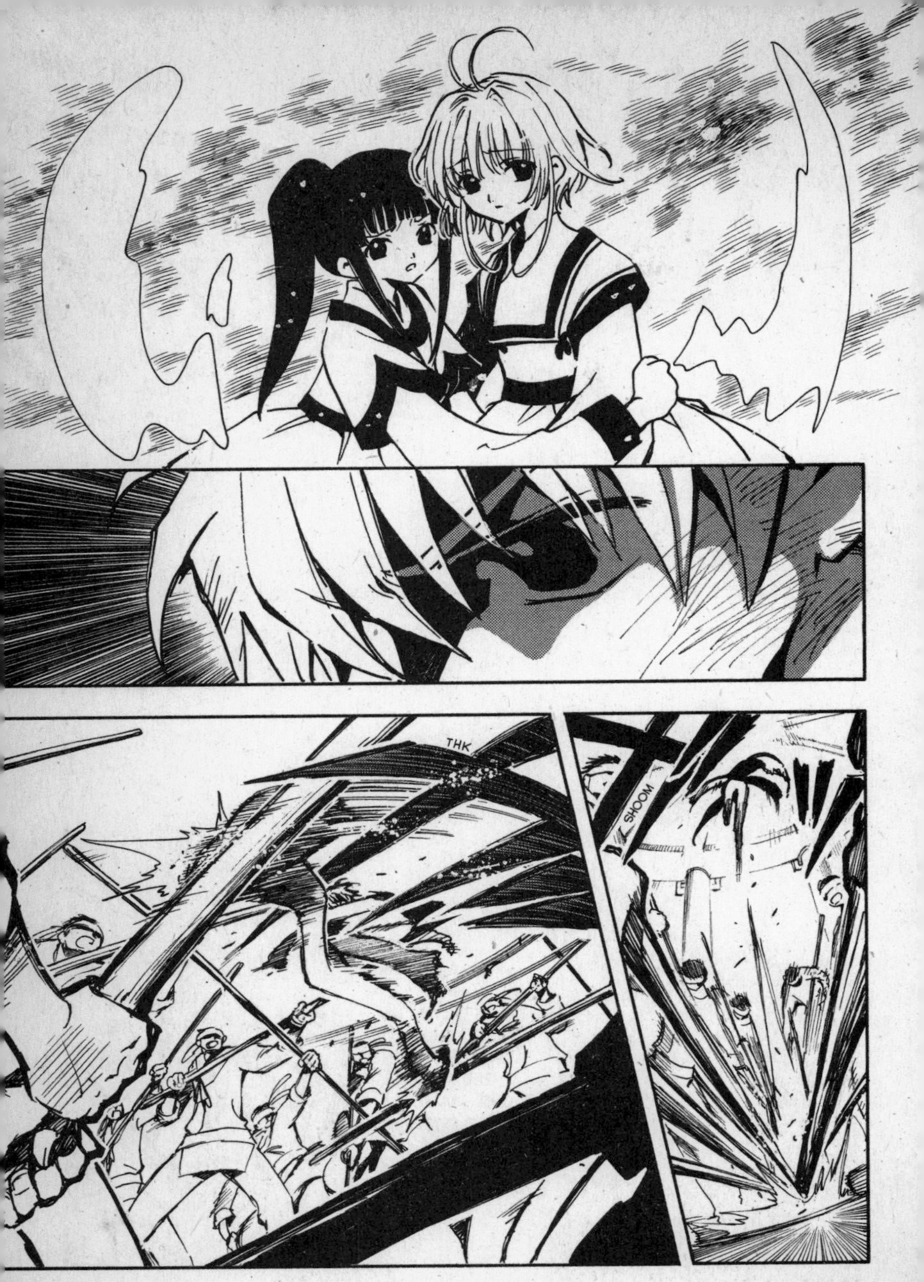
SHOOM
THK

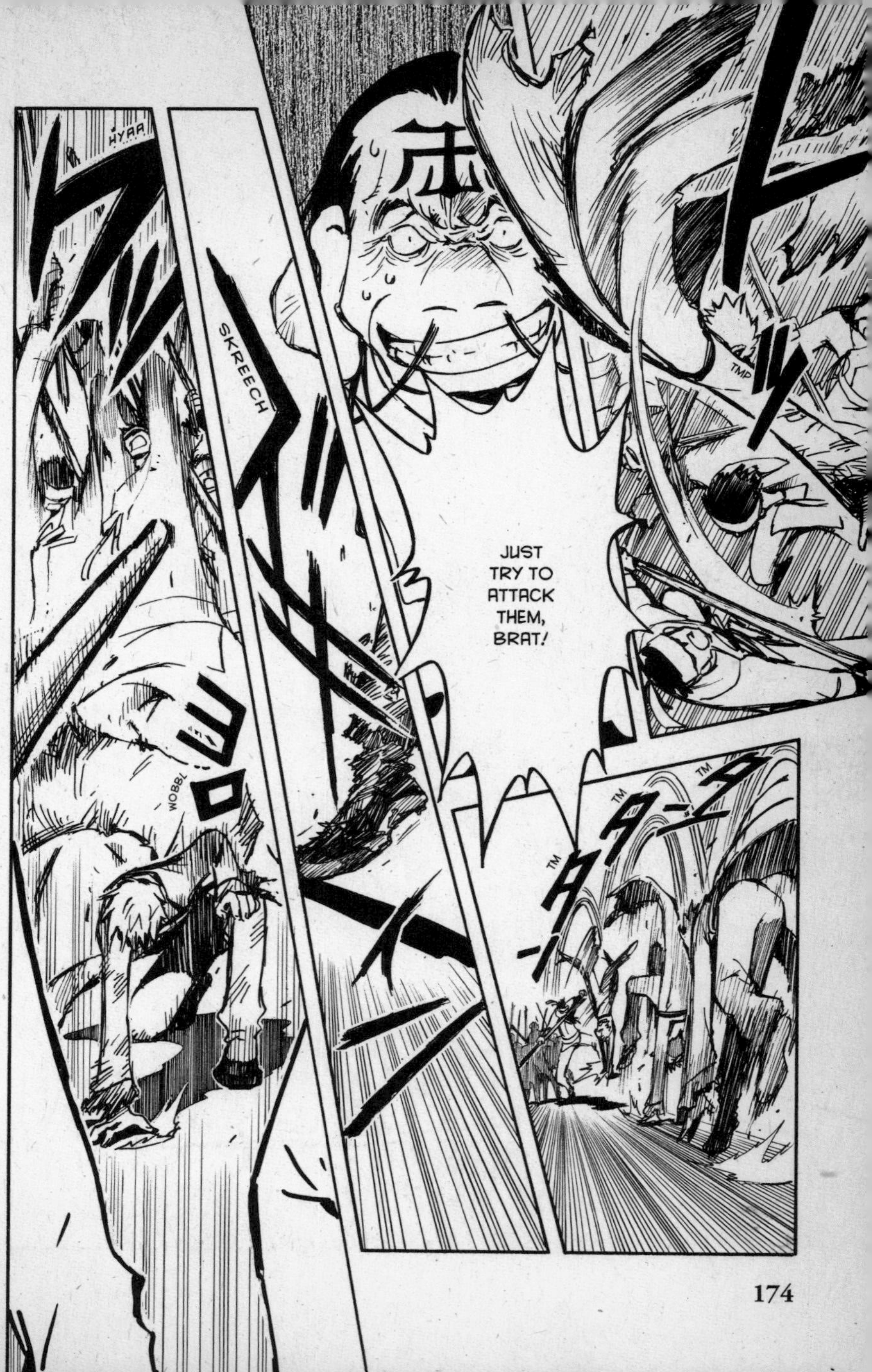
TMP
JUST TRY TO ATTACK THEM, BRAT!
TM
TM
TM
SKREECH
HYAA
WOBBL

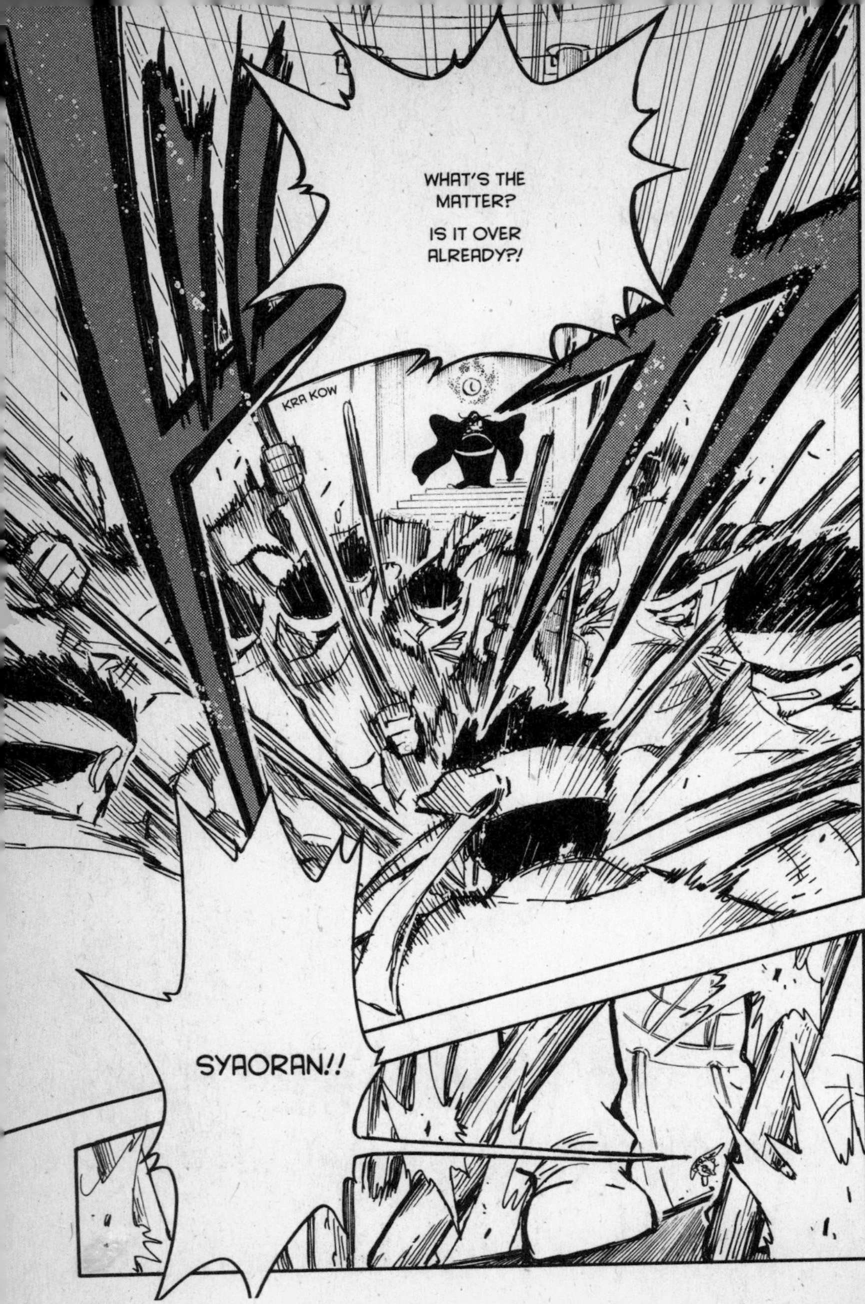
WHAT'S THE MATTER?
IS IT OVER ALREADY?!
KRA KOW
SYAORAN!!

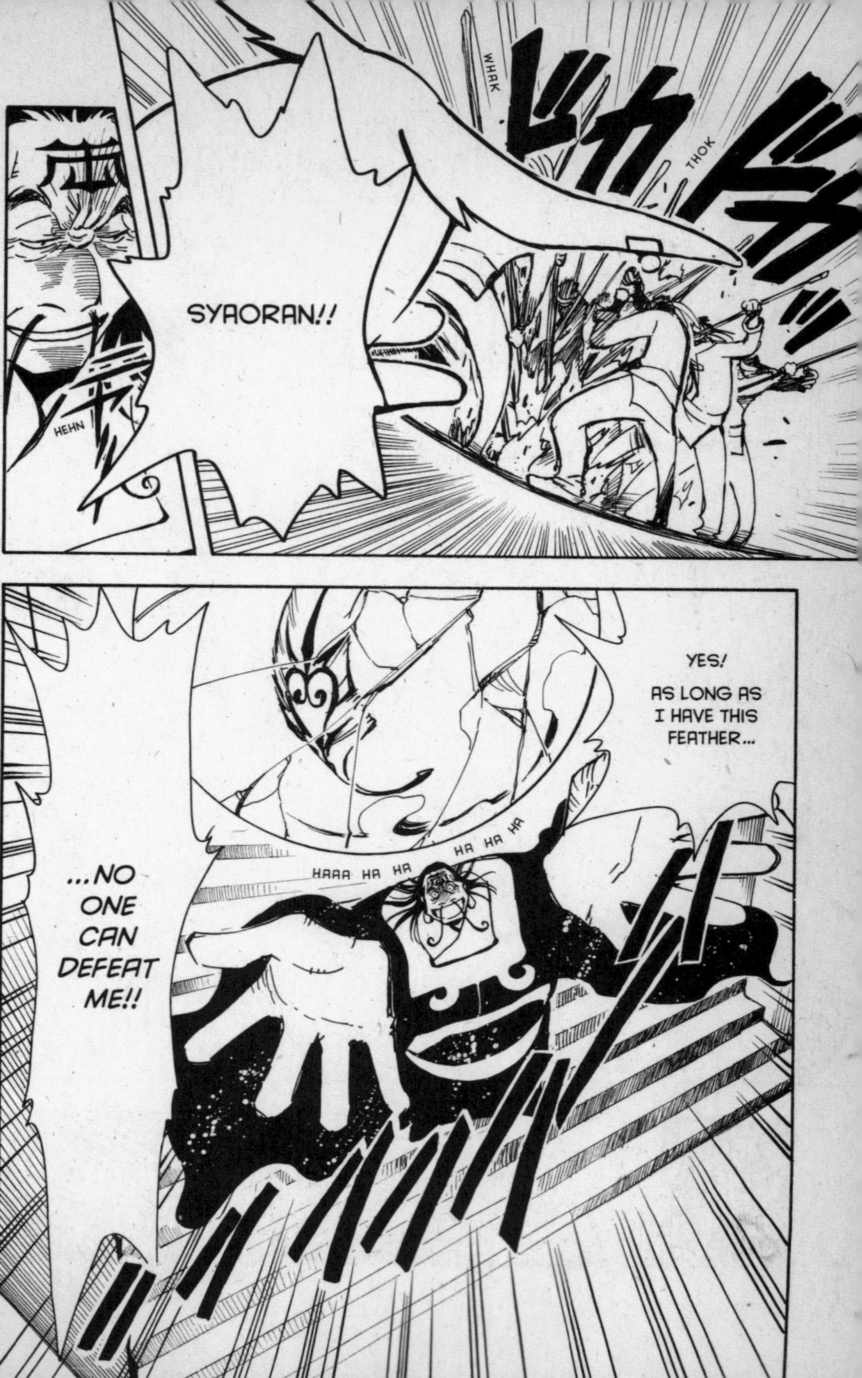
WHAK
THOK
SYAORAN!!
HEHN
YES!
AS LONG AS I HAVE THIS FEATHER...
HAAA HA HA HA HA HA
...NO ONE CAN DEFEAT ME!!

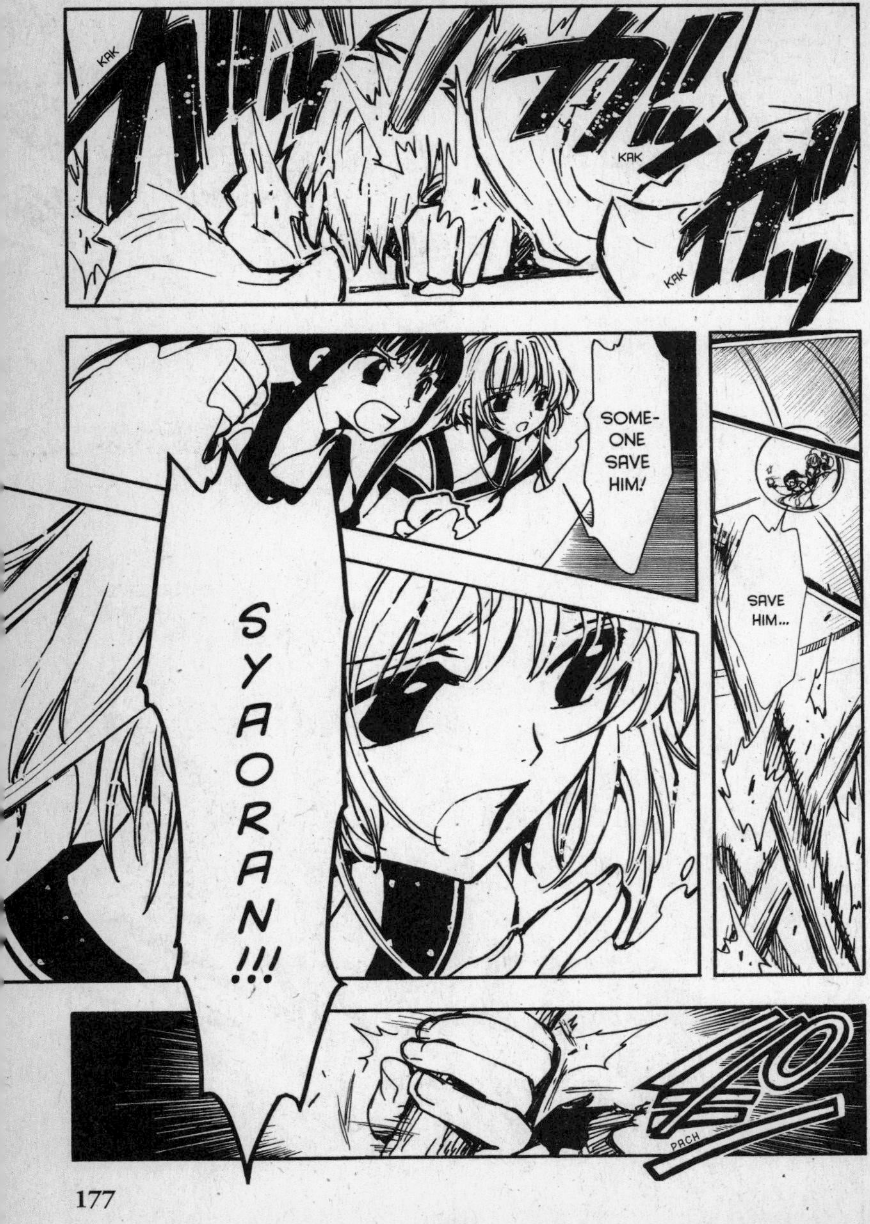
KAK
KAK
KAK
SAVE HIM...
SOME-ONE SAVE HIM!
SYAORAN!!!
PACH

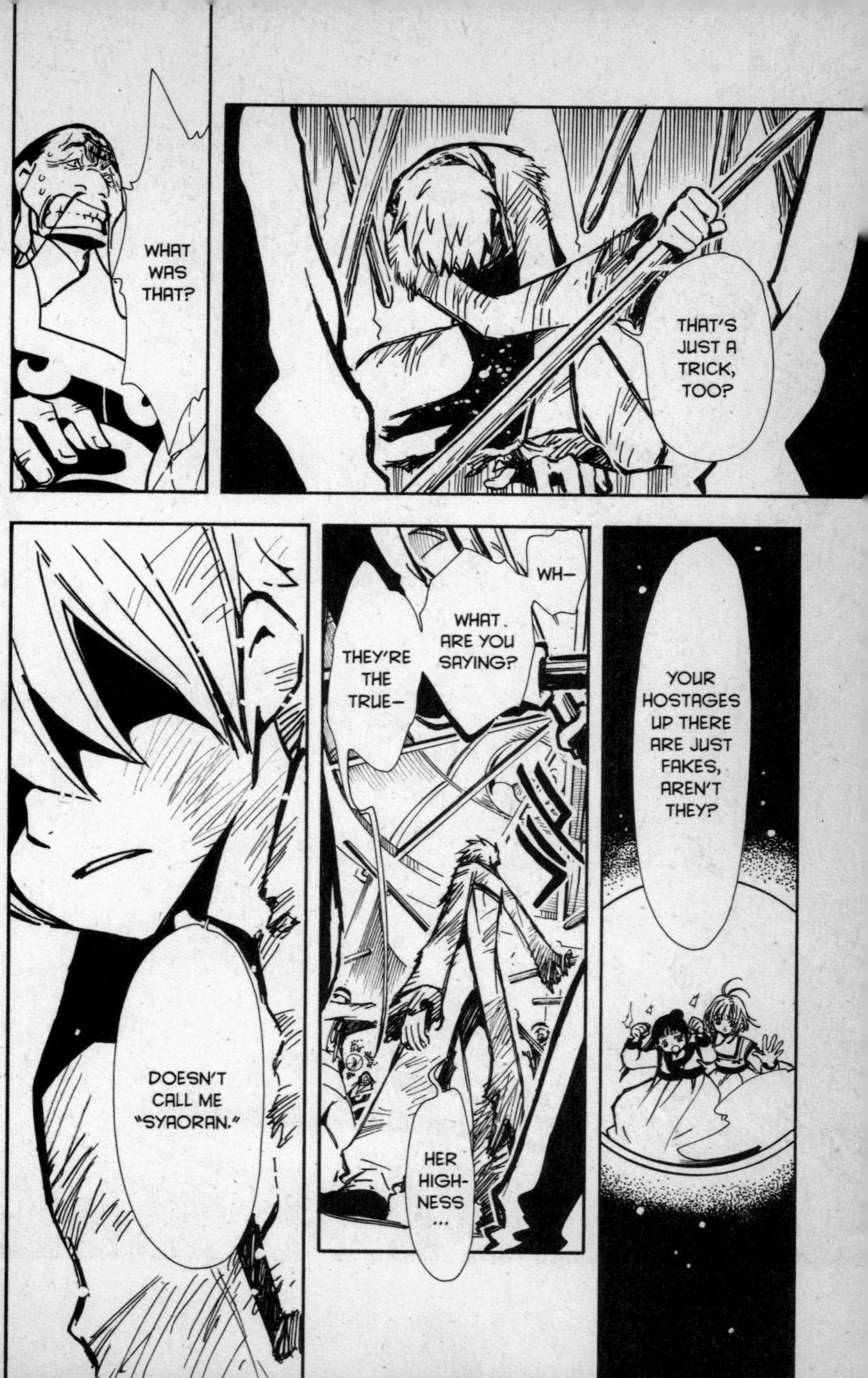
THAT'S JUST A TRICK, TOO?
WHAT WAS THAT?
YOUR HOSTAGES UP THERE ARE JUST FAKES, AREN'T THEY?
WH-
WHAT ARE YOU SAYING?
THEY'RE THE TRUE-
HER HIGH-NESS ...
DOESN'T CALL ME "SYAORAN."

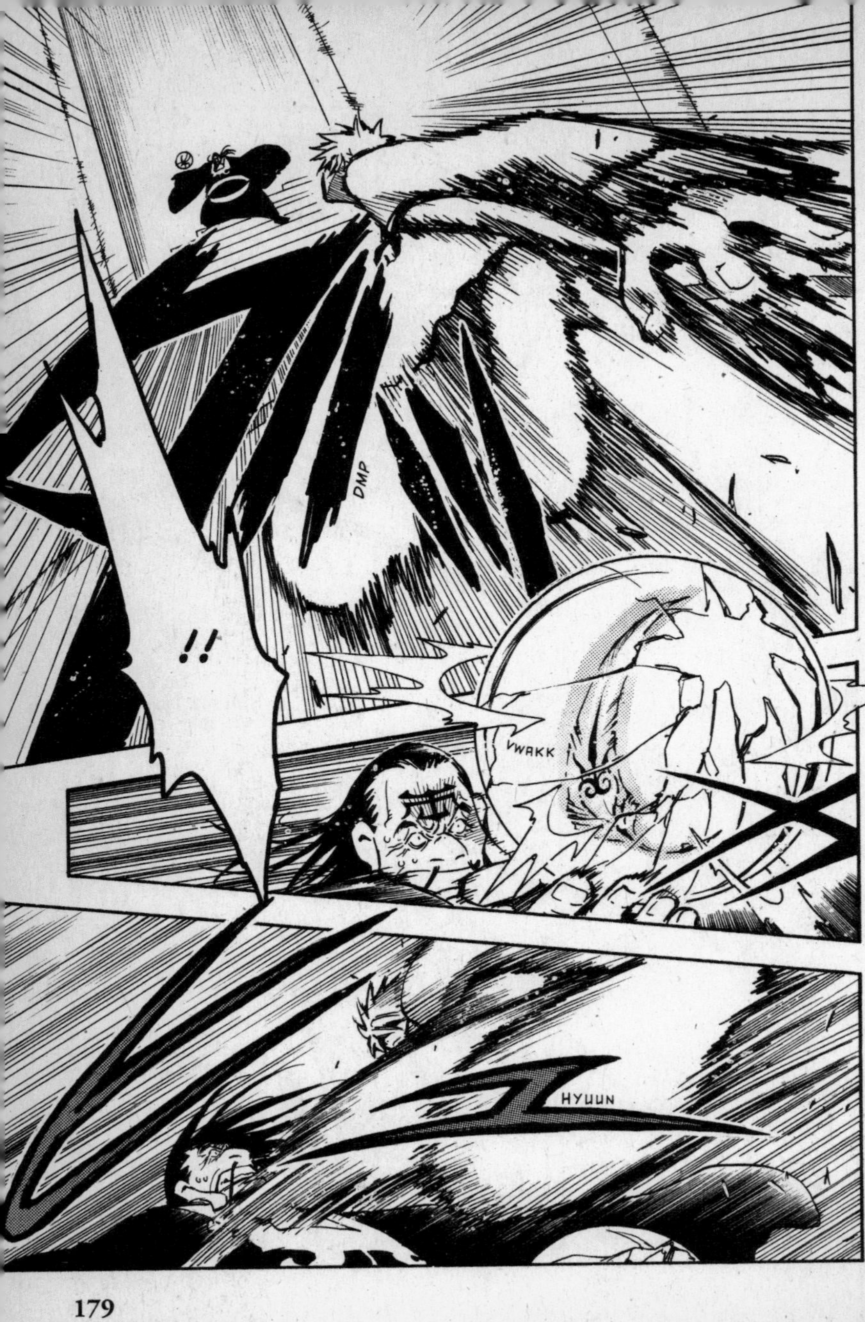
DMP
!!
VWAKK
HYUUN

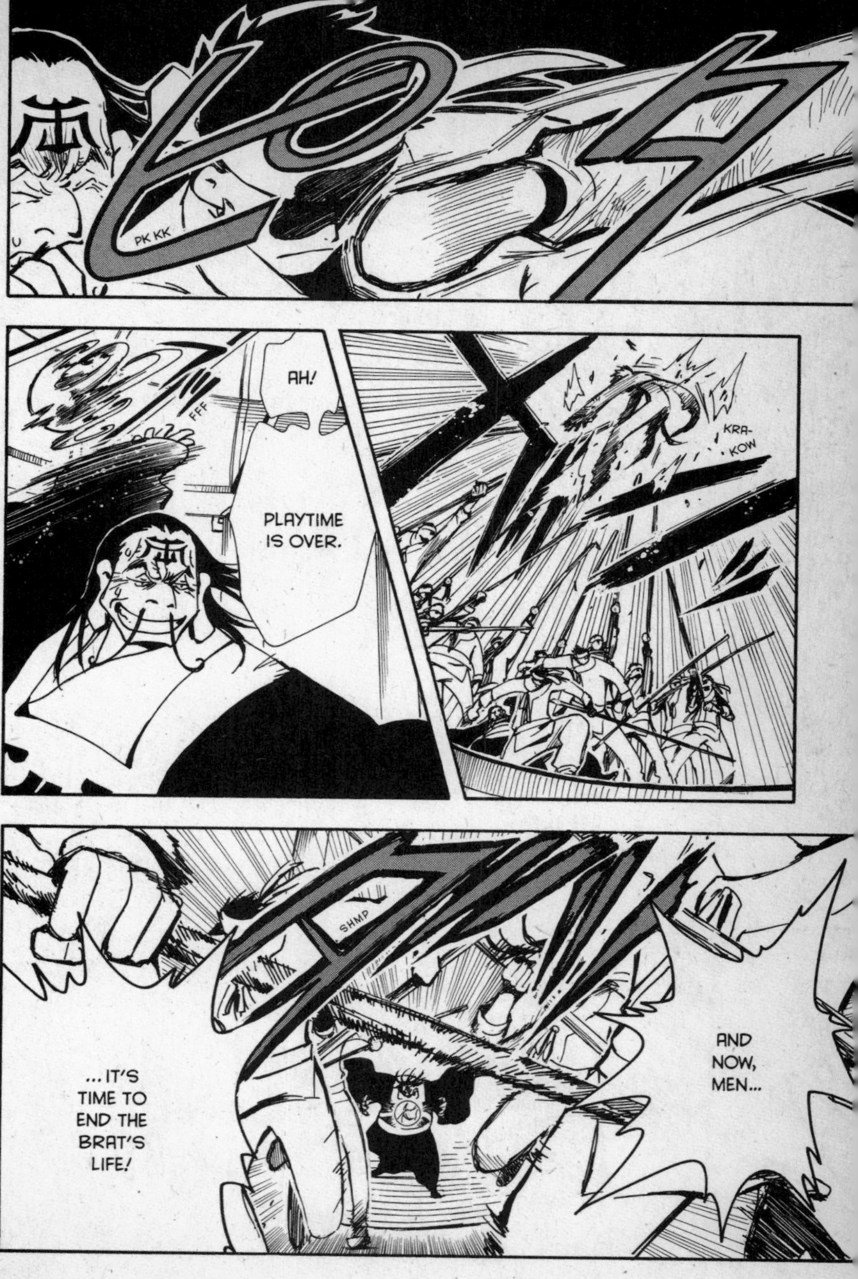
PK KK
KRA-KOW
AH!
FFF
PLAYTIME IS OVER.
SHMP
AND NOW, MEN...
...IT'S TIME TO END THE BRAT'S LIFE!

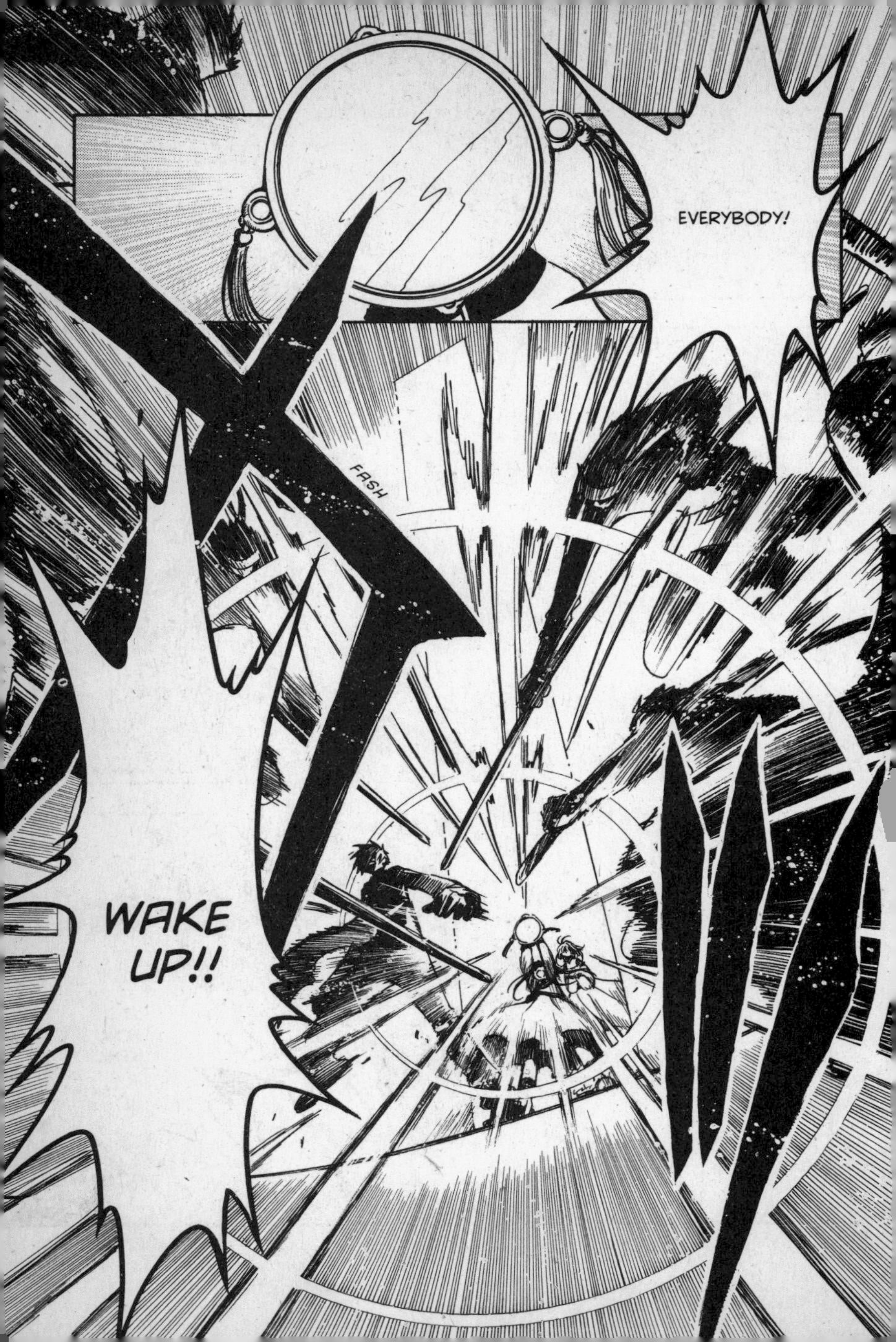
EVERYBODY!
FASH
WAKE UP!!

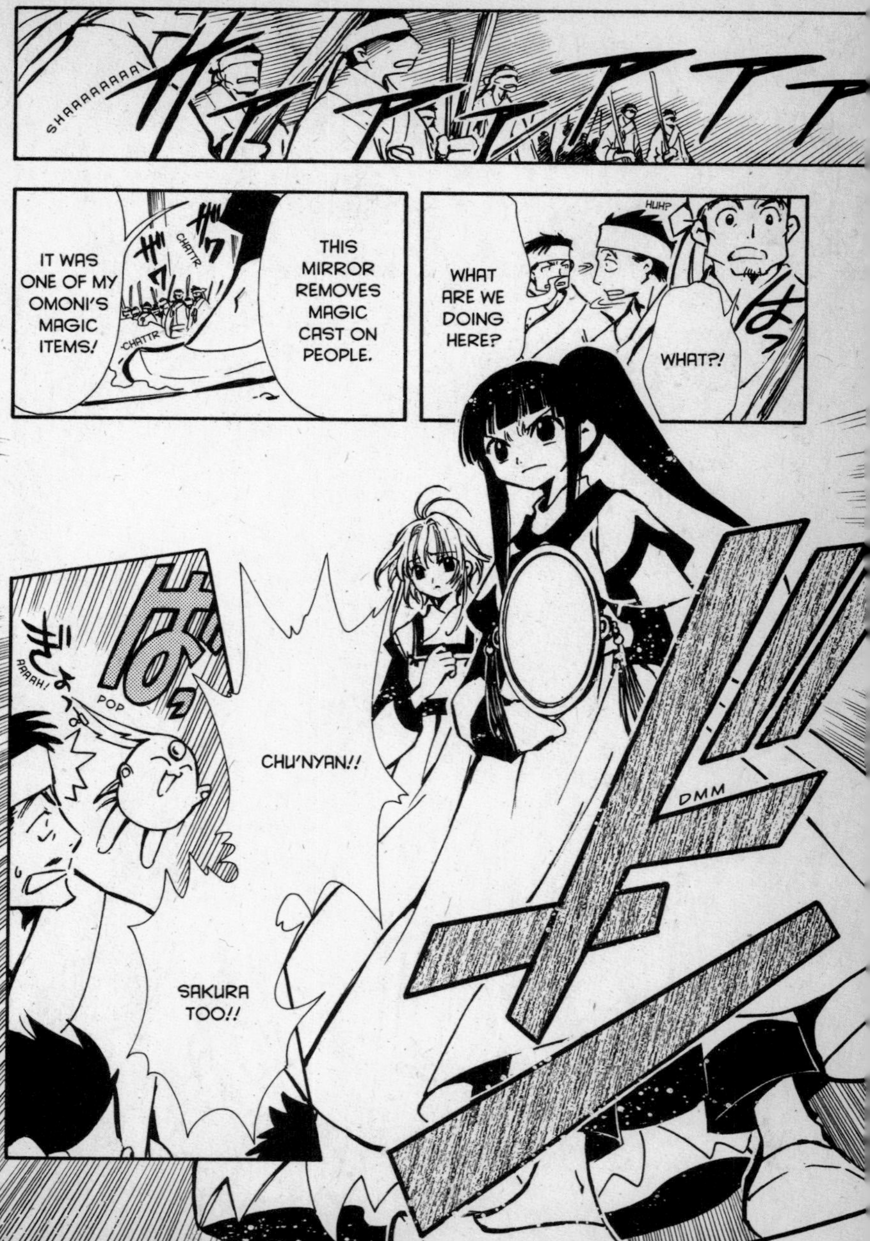
SHAAAAAAAA
HUH?
WHAT ARE WE DOING HERE?
WHAT?!
THIS MIRROR REMOVES MAGIC CAST ON PEOPLE.
IT WAS ONE OF MY OMONI'S MAGIC ITEMS!
CHATTR
CHATTR
DMM
CHU'NYAN!!
SAKURA TOO!!
POP
AAAAH!

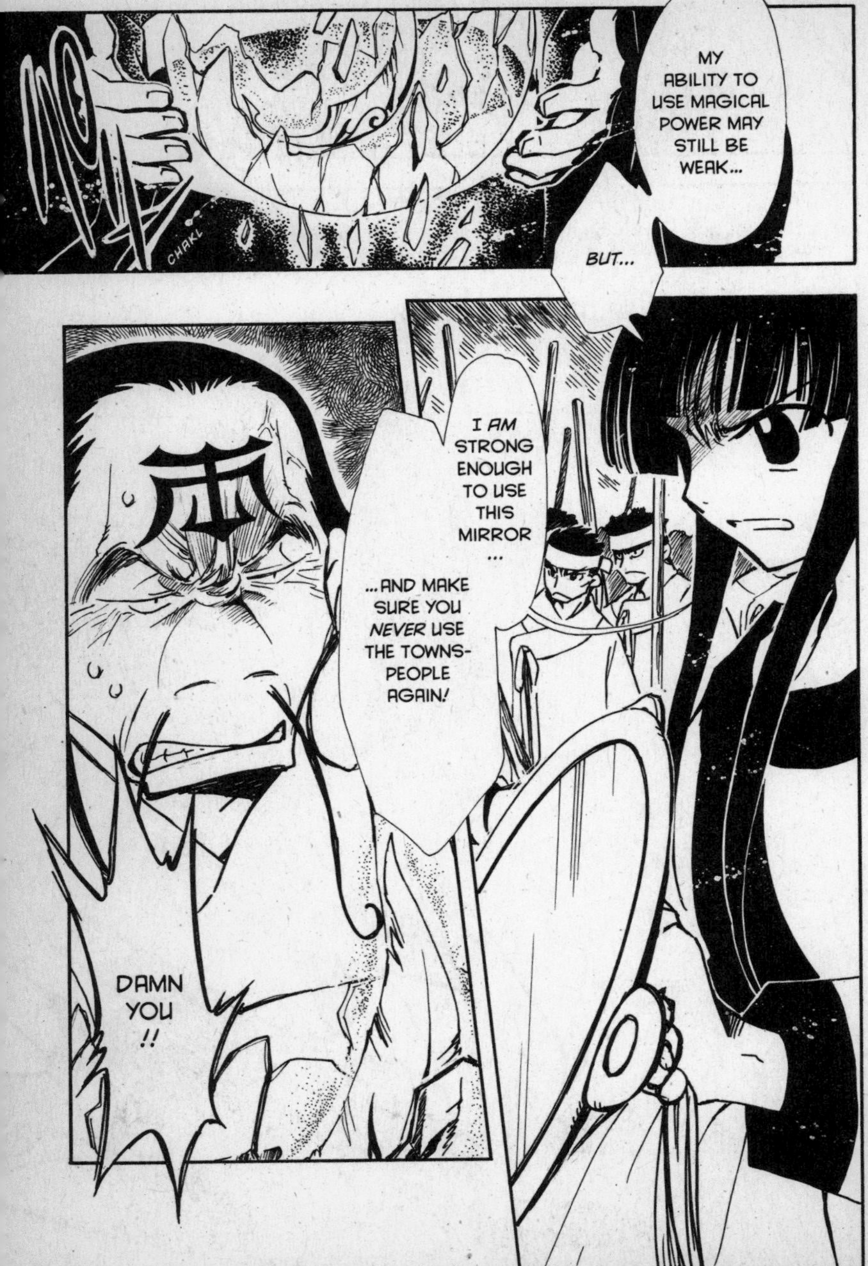
MY ABILITY TO USE MAGICAL POWER MAY STILL BE WEAK...
BUT...
CHAKI
I AM STRONG ENOUGH TO USE THIS MIRROR ...
...AND MAKE SURE YOU *NEVER* USE THE TOWNS-PEOPLE AGAIN!
DAMN YOU !!

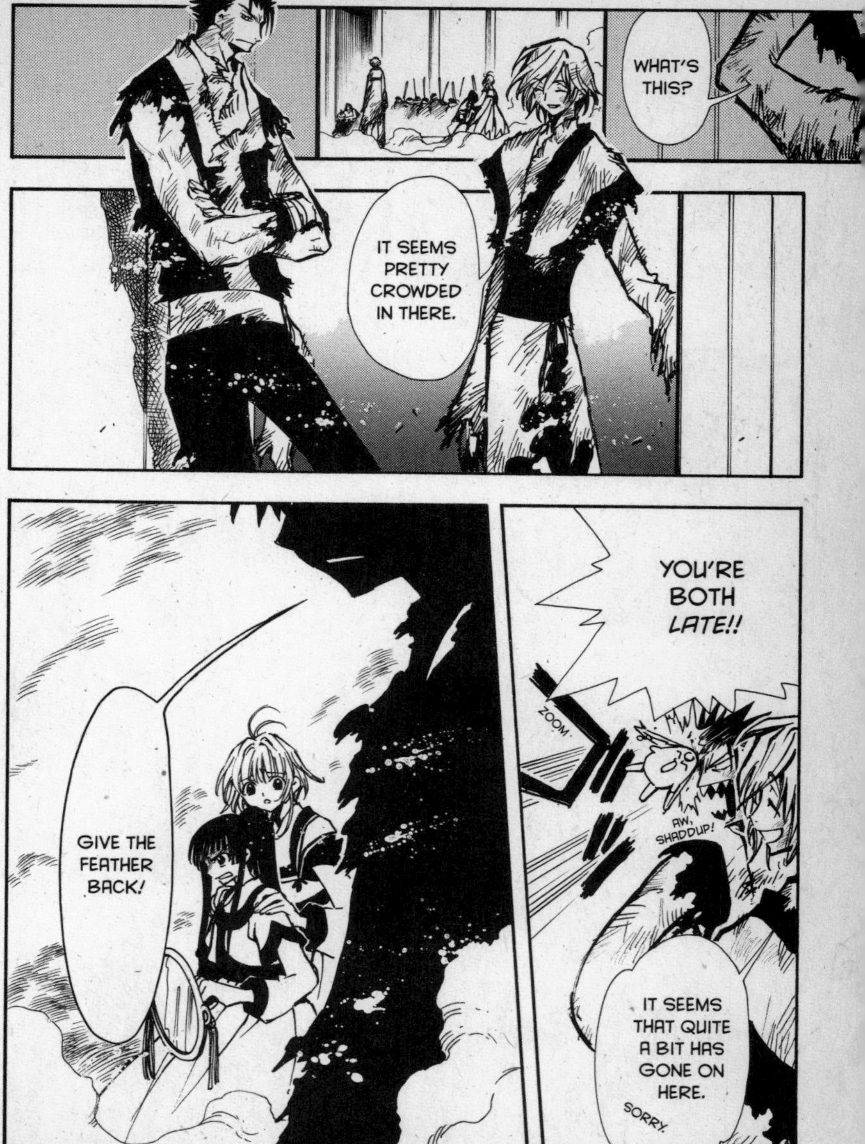
WHAT'S THIS?
IT SEEMS PRETTY CROWDED IN THERE.
YOU'RE BOTH *LATE!!*
ZOOM
AW, SHADDUP!
IT SEEMS THAT QUITE A BIT HAS GONE ON HERE.
SORRY.
GIVE THE FEATHER BACK!

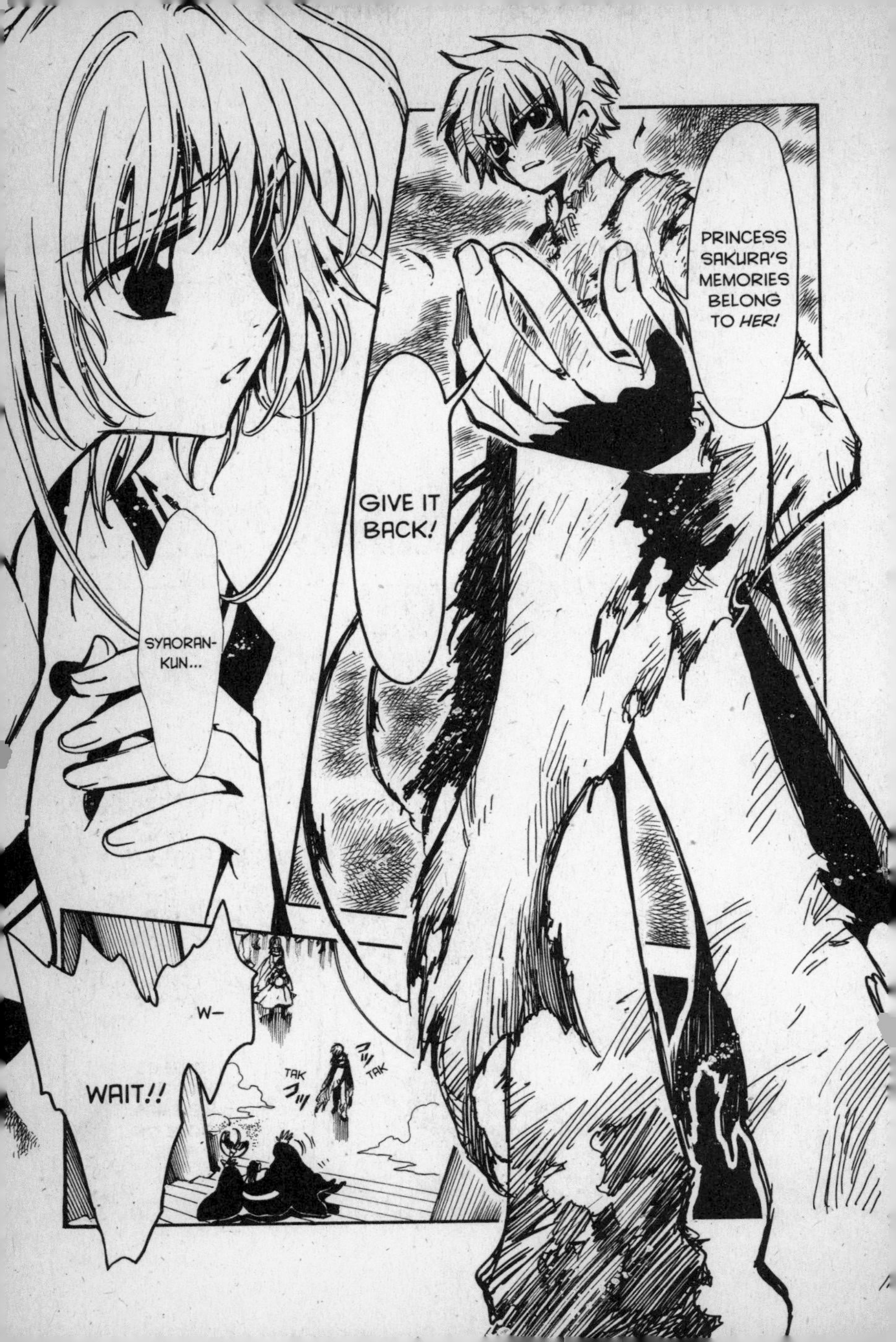
PRINCESS SAKURA'S MEMORIES BELONG TO HER!
GIVE IT BACK!
SYAORAN-KUN...
TAK
TAK
W–
WAIT!!

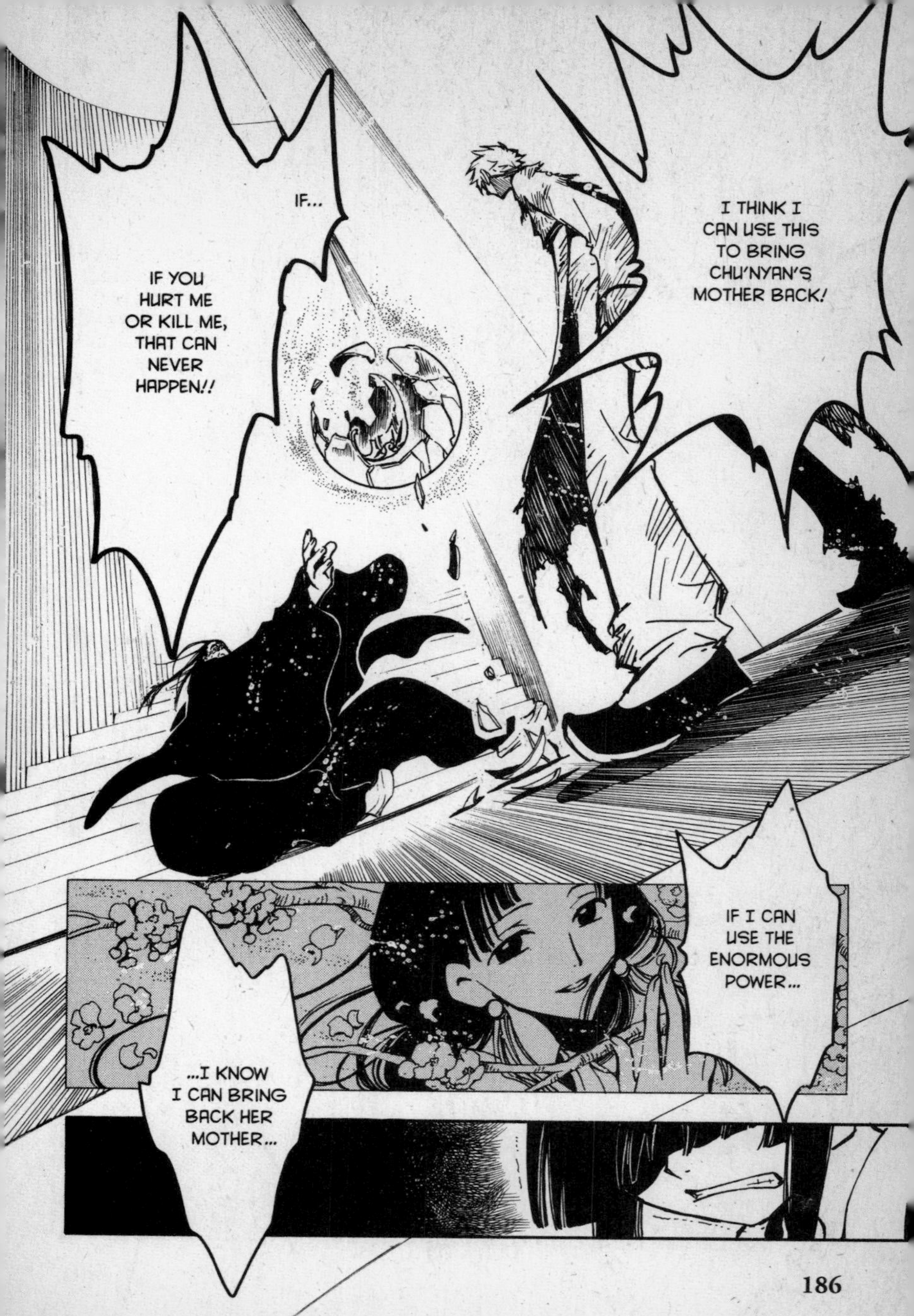
I THINK I CAN USE THIS TO BRING CHU'NYAN'S MOTHER BACK!
IF...
IF YOU HURT ME OR KILL ME, THAT CAN NEVER HAPPEN!!
IF I CAN USE THE ENORMOUS POWER...
...I KNOW I CAN BRING BACK HER MOTHER...

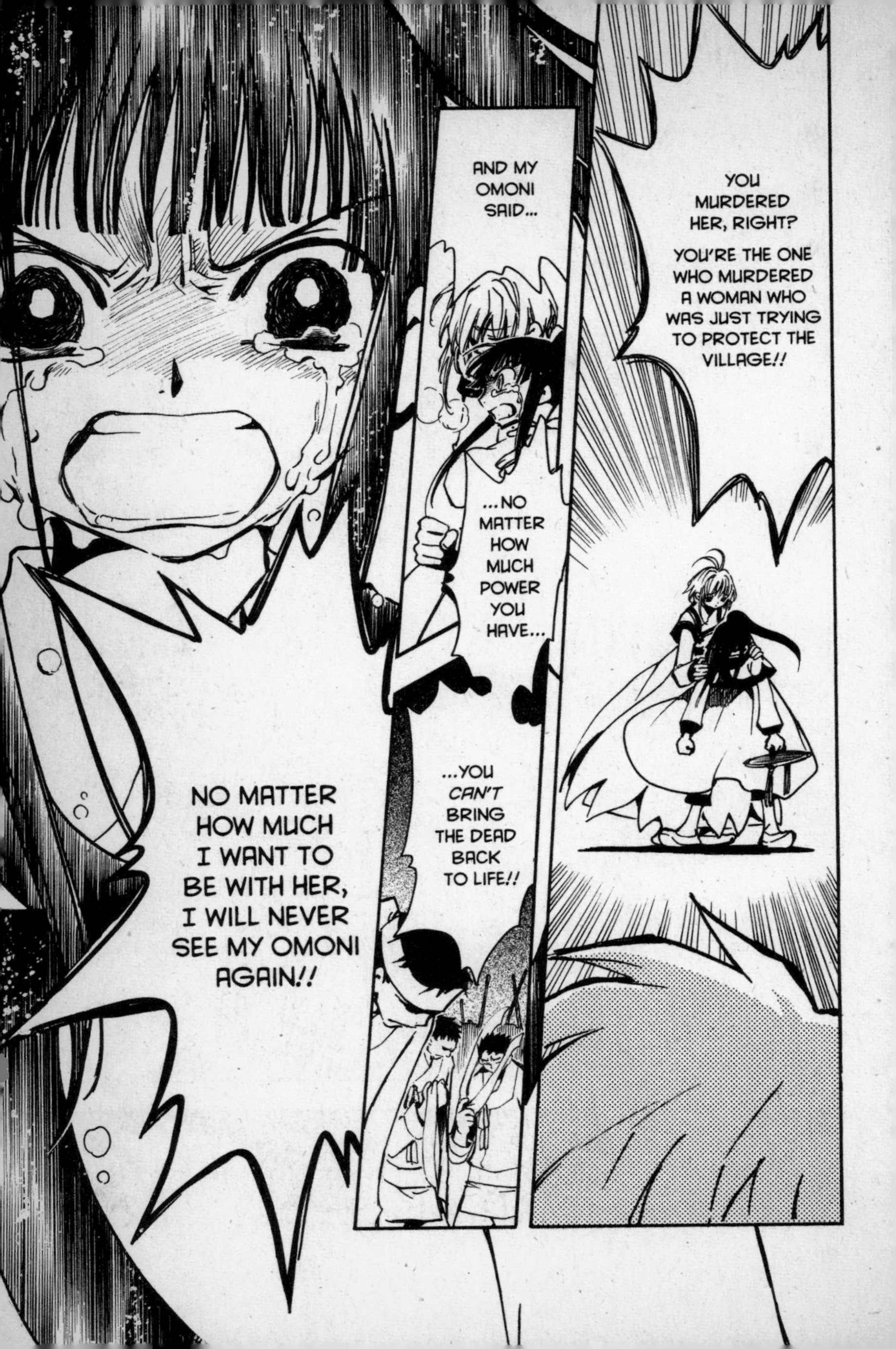
YOU MURDERED HER, RIGHT?
YOU'RE THE ONE WHO MURDERED A WOMAN WHO WAS JUST TRYING TO PROTECT THE VILLAGE!!
AND MY OMONI SAID...
...NO MATTER HOW MUCH POWER YOU HAVE...
...YOU *CAN'T* BRING THE DEAD BACK TO LIFE!!
NO MATTER HOW MUCH I WANT TO BE WITH HER, I WILL NEVER SEE MY OMONI AGAIN!!

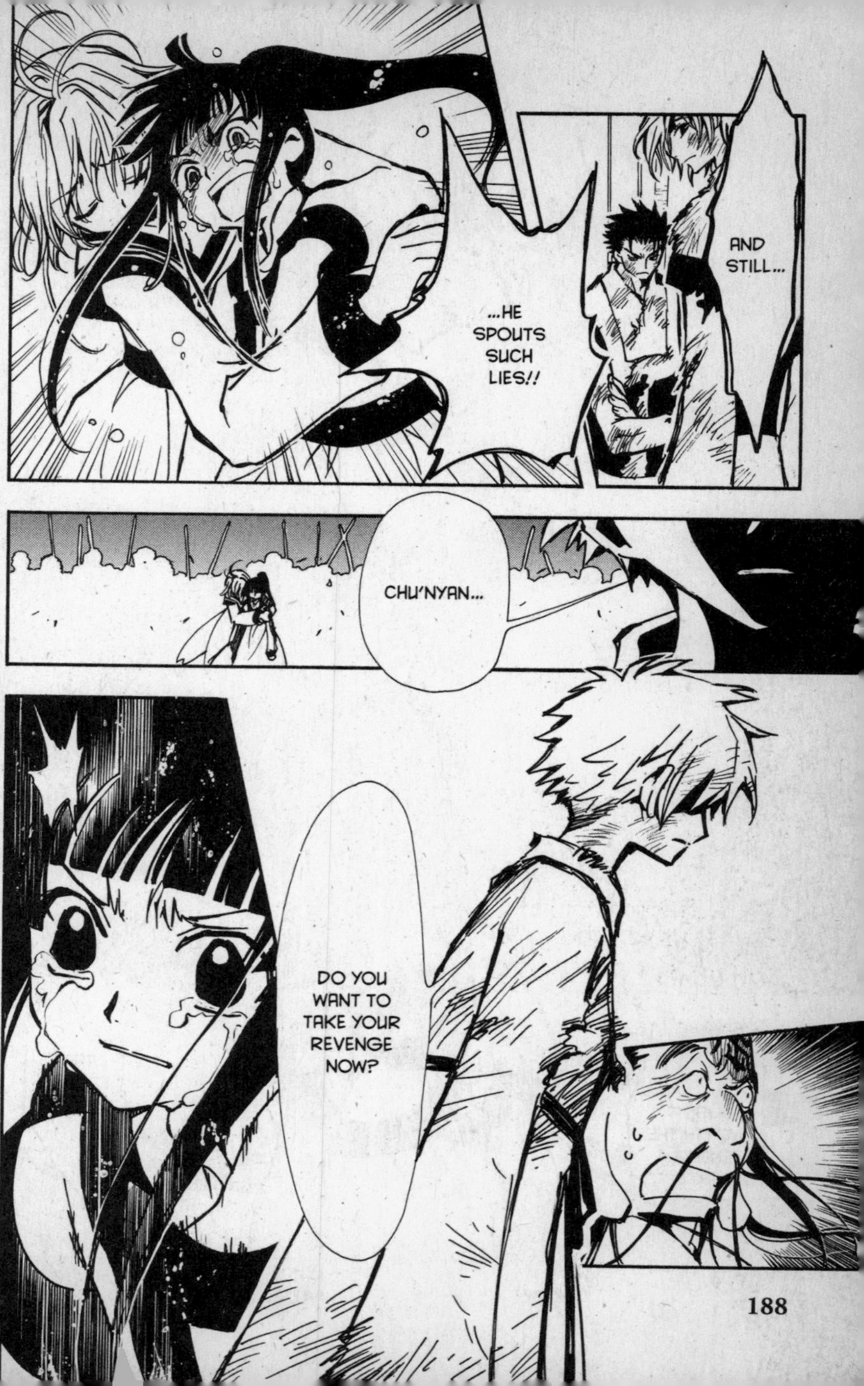
AND STILL...
...HE SPOUTS SUCH LIES!!
CHU'NYAN...
DO YOU WANT TO TAKE YOUR REVENGE NOW?

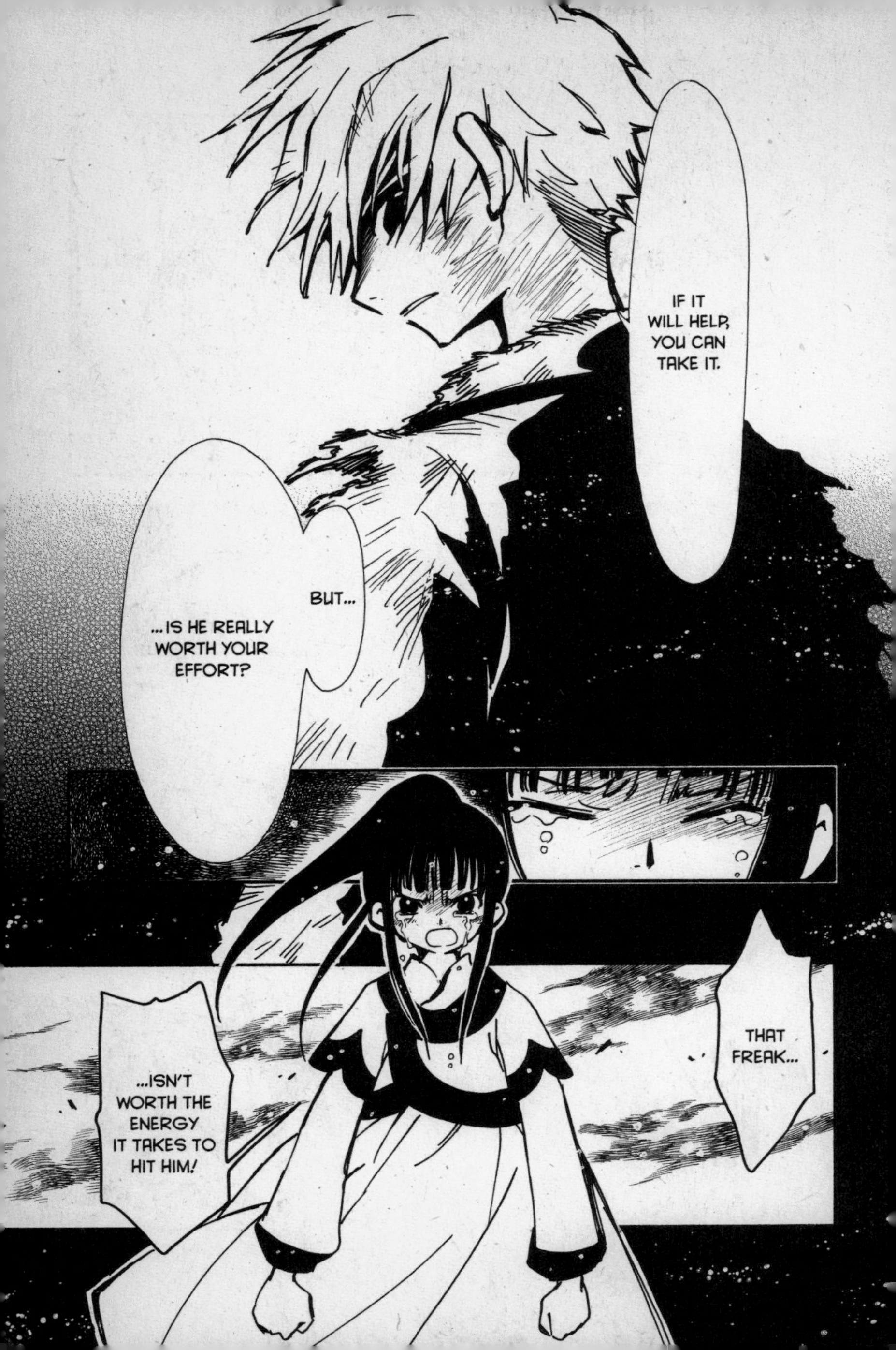
IF IT WILL HELP, YOU CAN TAKE IT.
BUT...
...IS HE REALLY WORTH YOUR EFFORT?
THAT FREAK...
...ISN'T WORTH THE ENERGY IT TAKES TO HIT HIM!

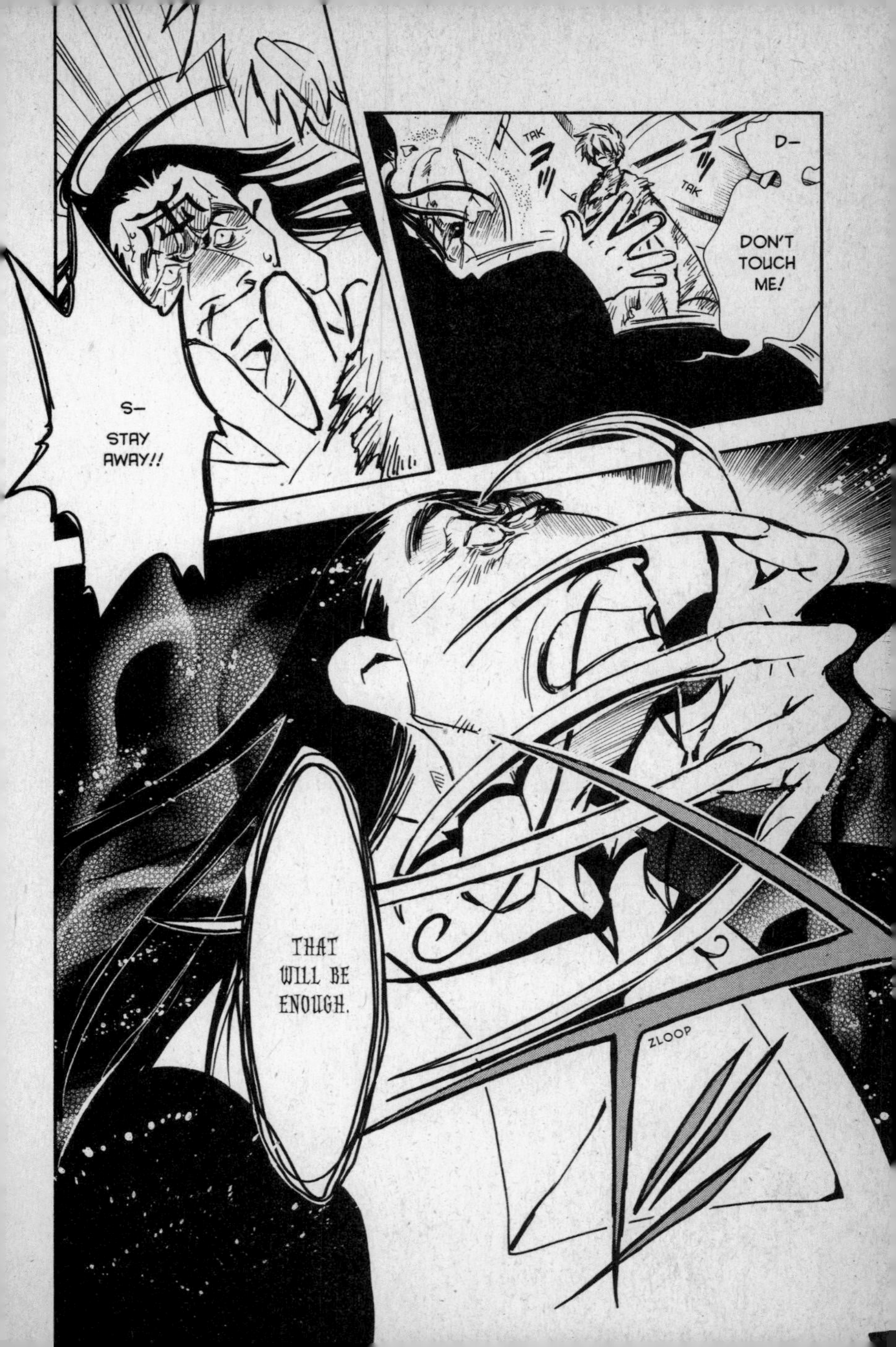
D—
TAK
TAK
DON'T TOUCH ME!
S— STAY AWAY!!
THAT WILL BE ENOUGH.
ZLOOP

To Be Continued

About the Creators

CLAMP is a group of four women who have become the most popular manga artists in America—Ageha Ohkawa, Mokona, Satsuki Igarashi, and Tsubaki Nekoi. They started out as doujinshi (fan comics) creators, but their skill and craft brought them to the attention of publishers very quickly. Their first work from a major publisher was *RG Veda*, but their first mass success was with *Magic Knight Rayearth*. From there, they went on to write many series, including *Cardcaptor Sakura* and *Chobits*, two of the most popular manga in the United States. Like many Japanese manga artists, they prefer to avoid the spotlight, and little is known about them personally.

CLAMP is currently publishing three series in Japan: *Tsubasa* and *xxxHOLiC* with Kodansha and *Gohou Drug* with Kadokawa.

Translation Notes

Japanese is a tricky language for most Westerners, and translation is often more art than science. For your edification and reading pleasure, here are notes on some of the places where we could have gone in a different direction in our translation of the work, or where a Japanese cultural reference is used.

Tora-Cola

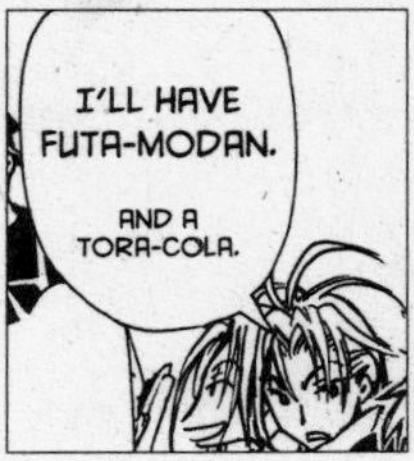
I'LL HAVE FUTA-MODAN.
AND A TORA-COLA.

If you will remember from the previous volume, "Tora" means Tiger—the mascot of Osaka's baseball team, the Hanshin Tigers, and the symbol of the entire Hanshin Republic. History buffs might also recognize "Tora" as the Japanese Navy's signal to start the attack on Pearl Harbor: "Tora Tora Tora."

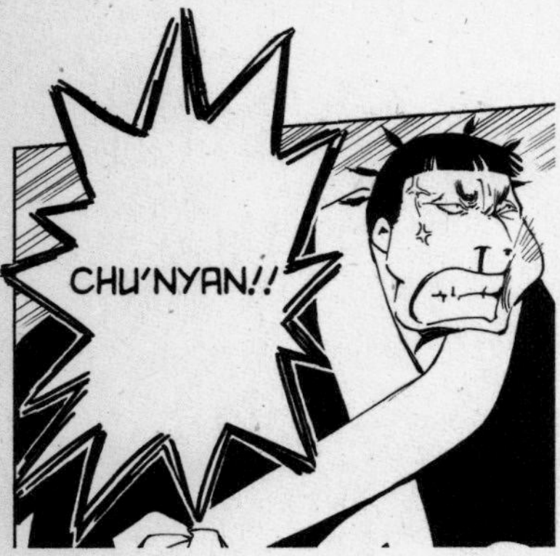
CHU'NYAN!!

Chu'nyan

What's with the apostrophe? It's just to note that the *n* belongs with "nyan" rather than with "Chu." By the way, "chu" uses the kanji (the Japanese system of writing) for "spring," and "nyan" uses the kanji for "scent."

Ryanban

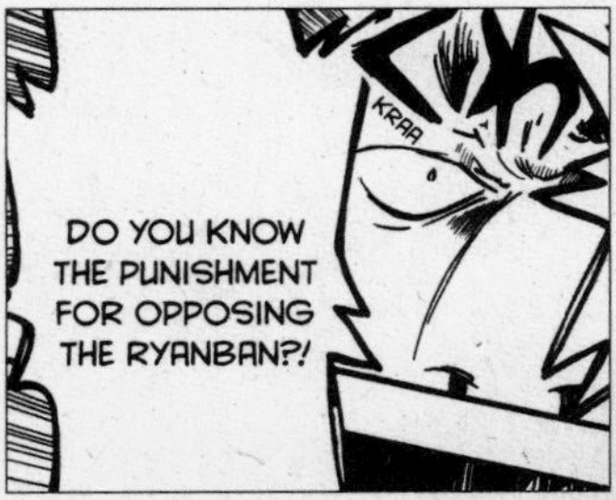
KRAA
DO YOU KNOW THE PUNISHMENT FOR OPPOSING THE RYANBAN?!

The "Ry" combination is one of the most difficult combination of sounds for native, monolingual English speakers to wrap their lips around. Many would pronounce "Ryan" as if they were saying the first name of Ryan O'Neal. Not quite. First, remember that the "r"

sound in Japanese sounds like a very light "d" sound—similar to the "r" sound that an upper-class British person would use to pronounce the word "very." Add that to a "ya" sound, and you get a single syllable that sounds a little like "dya." Remember, it's not "di-ya" or "ri-ya," but "rya."

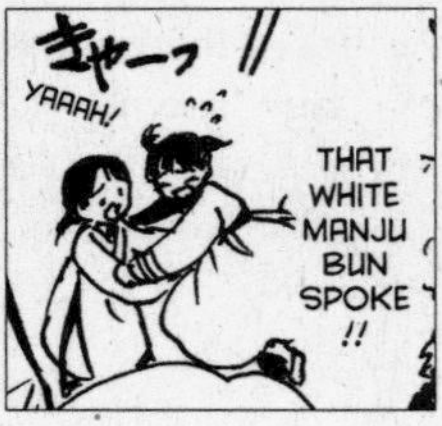
きゃーっ
YAAAH!
THAT WHITE MANJU BUN SPOKE !!

Manju

The same type of big, white, wheat-dough bun as Siu Bao found in dim sum restaurants, and sometimes sold steaming hot on a chilly autumn day by street vendors in Yokohama's Chinatown. Mmmm.

Mito Kômon

One of Japan's most popular hour-long TV dramas, "Mito Kômon" began its run in 1970 and continues today. The main character is an elderly aristocrat who travels Japan with his three retainers, finding injustice and doing what he can to correct it. In the last act of every show, just when the bad guys seem to have the upper hand (reportedly at exactly the same minute mark of every program), Mito-sama pulls out the emblem of his nephew, the Shogun! The bad guys realize that Mito-sama's influence trumps any power they might have, and they capitulate. Like James Bond, the title character has been played by a number of different actors.

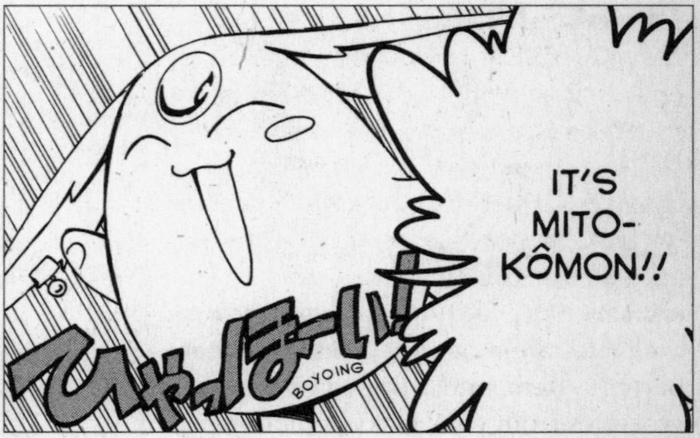
IT'S MITO-KÔMON!!
ひゃっほーい!
BOYOING

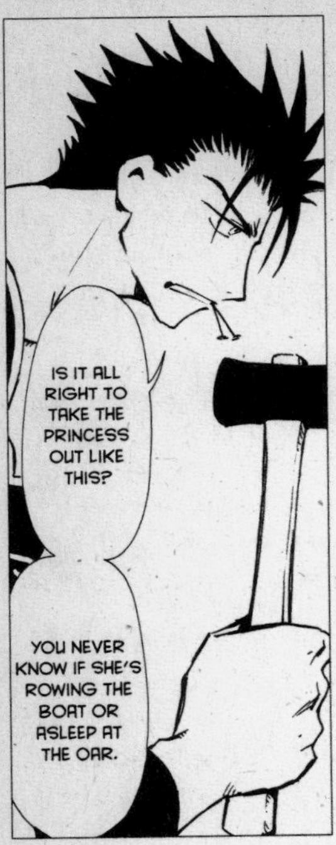
IS IT ALL RIGHT TO TAKE THE PRINCESS OUT LIKE THIS?
YOU NEVER KNOW IF SHE'S ROWING THE BOAT OR ASLEEP AT THE OAR.

Rowing the Boat or Asleep at the Oar

Actually, both of these phrases mean the same thing . . . that Sakura is basically asleep. "Asleep at the oar" is obvious, but "rowing the boat" also means that she's a little brain-numb—probably because of the less-than-towering amount of brain work it takes to row.

Gambling Prizes

Cash payoffs for gambling are illegal in Japan, so you will find that gambling for prizes is a very normal occurrence. Unlike skeeball-style amusement centers in the U.S., the prize counters at pachinko parlors are more like mini convenience stores with food, cigarettes, and household items. In Chu'nyan's country the prizes are a natural product of the barter system, and bringing home groceries from your lucky gambling trip is very common to Japanese readers.

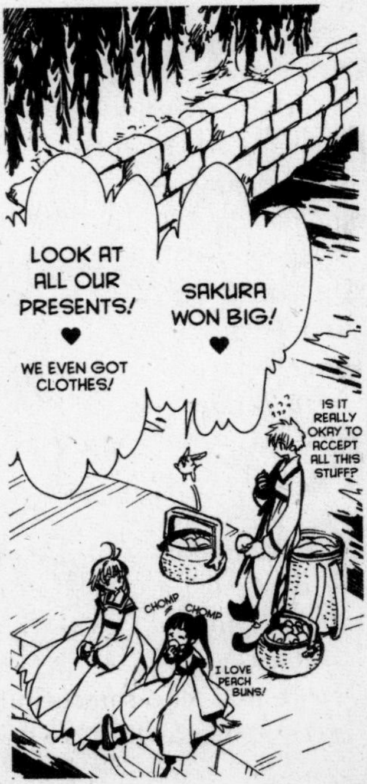
SAKURA WON BIG! ♥
LOOK AT ALL OUR PRESENTS! ♥
WE EVEN GOT CLOTHES!
IS IT REALLY OKAY TO ACCEPT ALL THIS STUFF?
CHOMP
CHOMP
I LOVE PEACH BUNS!

Moxibustion

An ancient Chinese remedy, possibly even the precursor to acupuncture, since the Chinese word for acupuncture literally means "acupuncture-moxibustion." A lit and smoldering stick of mugwort is placed on or over an acupuncture point (sometimes to the point of scarring the skin). When combined with acupuncture, the lit mugwort is attached to heat the needle. Like most Chinese medicine, the purpose of moxibustion is to enhance the blood flow and elevate the chi. The Kiishim intends to treat Kurogane and Fai with a full-body acid-based moxibustion, which would almost assuredly be . . . unpleasant.

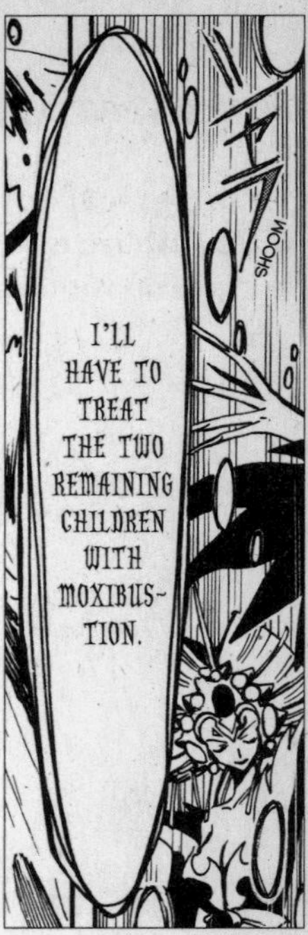
SHOOM
I'LL HAVE TO TREAT THE TWO REMAINING CHILDREN WITH MOXIBUS-TION.

Mirrors

Mirrors are a traditional mystic element of the earliest parts of Japanese culture. According to the Kojiki (the book of Japanese myths), the Sun Goddess Amaterasu ordered her son, Ninigi-no-Mikoto, to go to Earth, and with him she sent three sacred objects: a magatama (a beadlike jewel accessory), a sword, and a mirror. Those three objects have been passed down in the Japanese imperial family. Mystical mirrors have also crept into Japan's fox-spirit tales and other traditional stories.

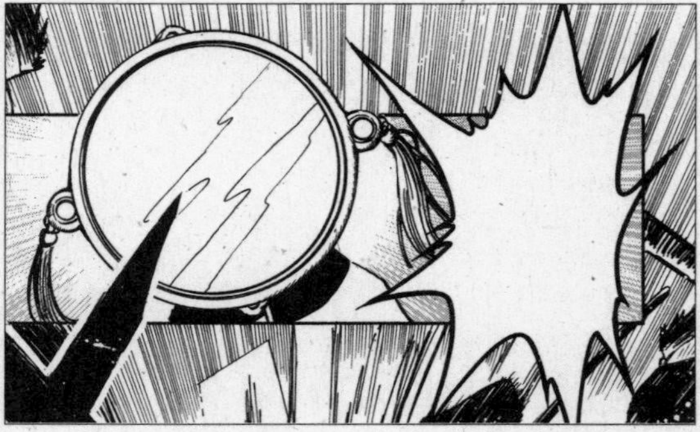

Preview of Volume 4

We're pleased to present you a preview from Volume 4. This volume will be available in English in February 2005, but for now you'll have to make do with Japanese!

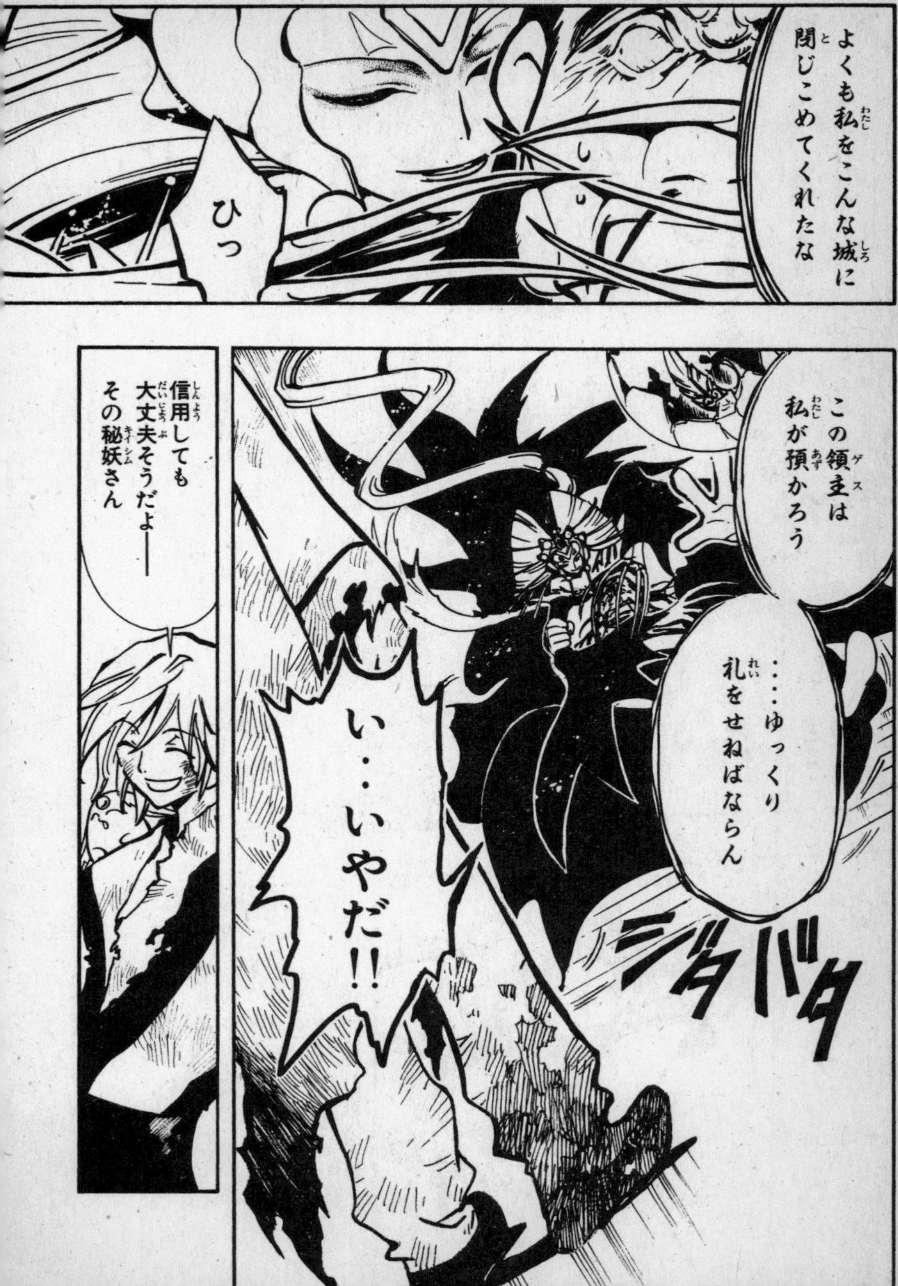
よくも私をこんな城に閉じこめてくれたな
ひっ
この領主は私が預かろう
……ゆっくり礼をせねばならん
ジタバタ
い……いやだ!!
信用しても大丈夫そうだよ――
その秘妖さん

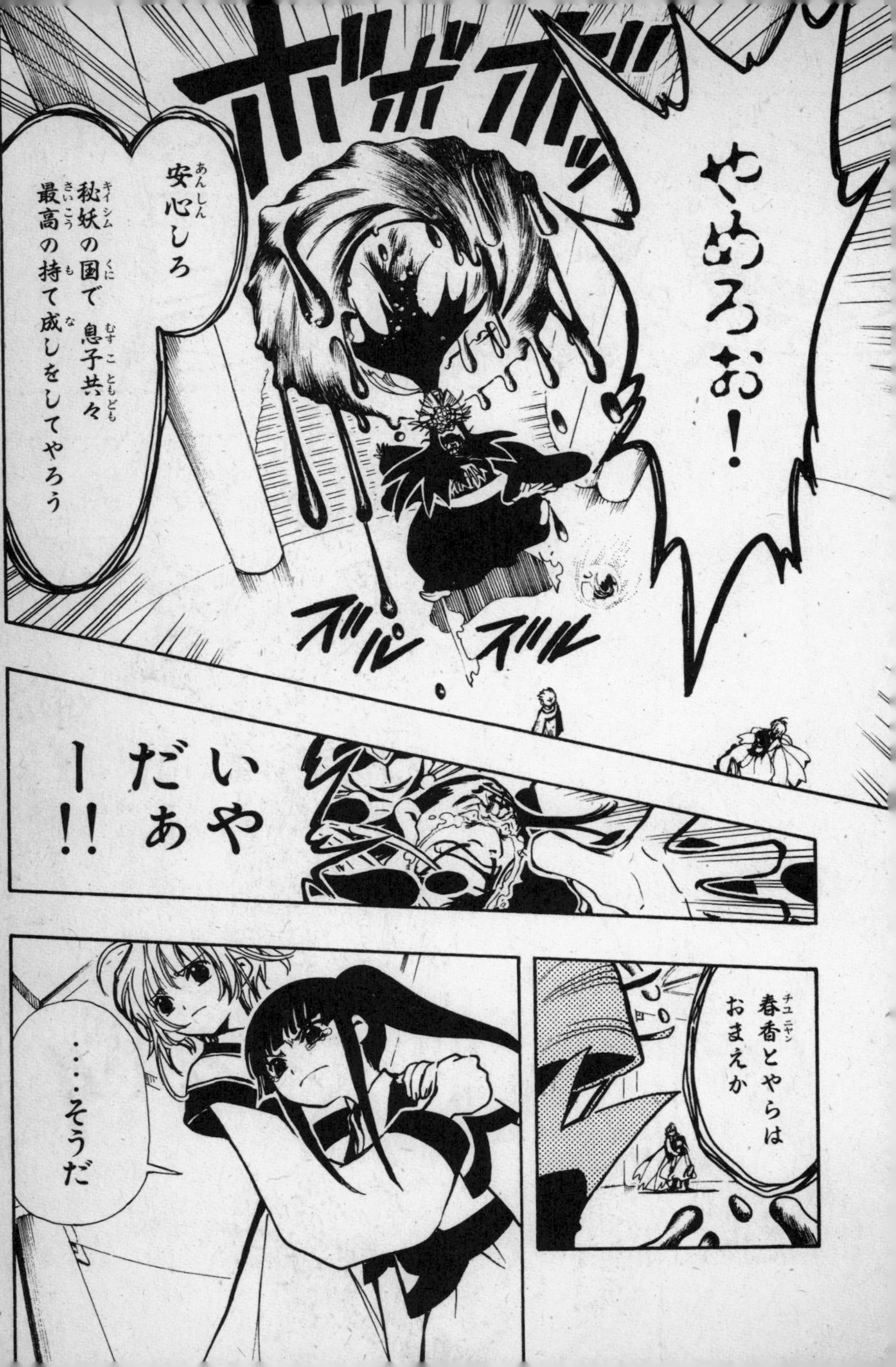
やめろぉ！
ボボボッ
安心しろ
秘妖の国で　息子共々
最高の持て成しをしてやろう
ズル
ズル
いやだぁー!!
春香とやらはおまえか
……そうだ

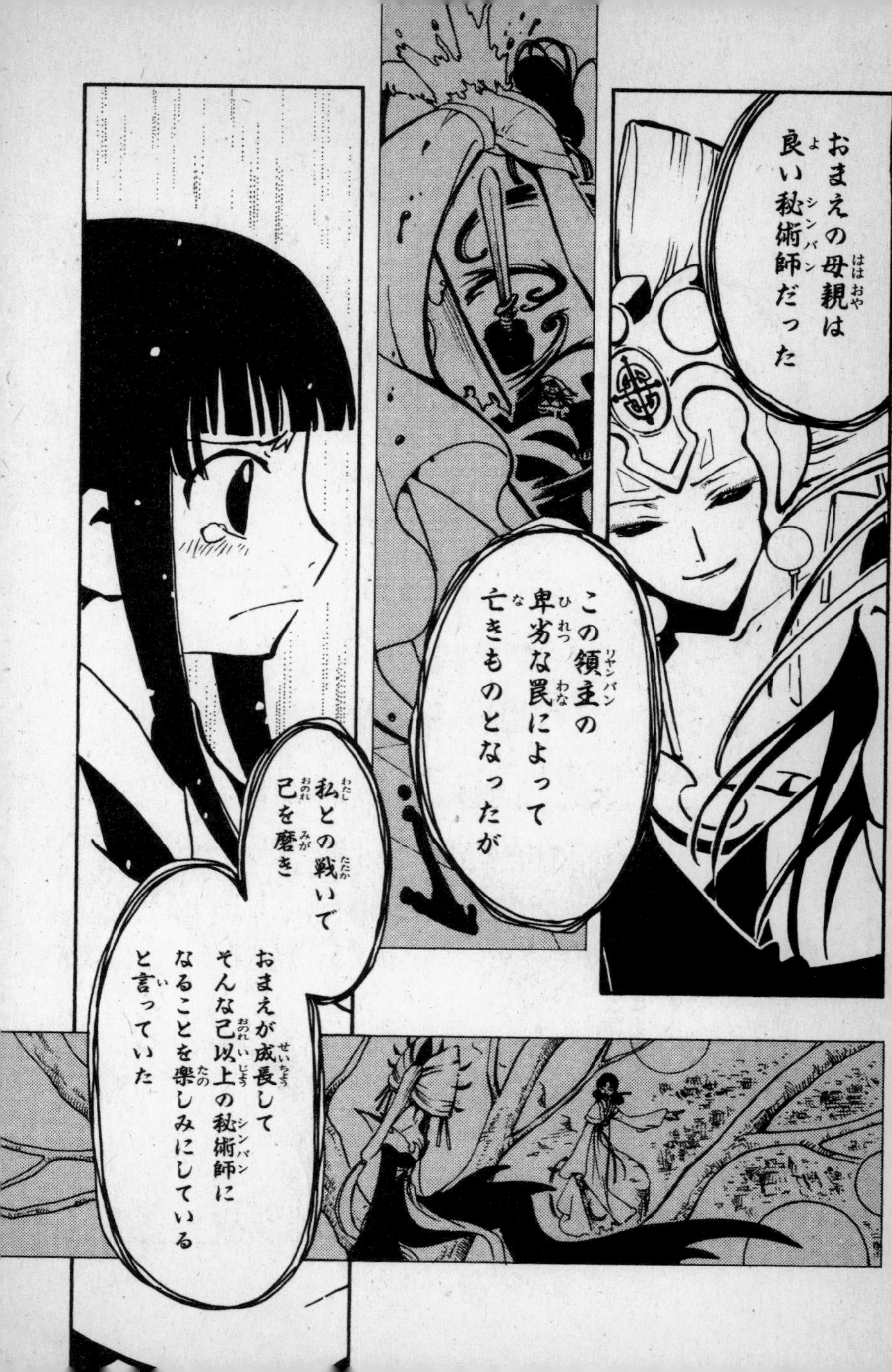
おまえの母親は良い秘術師だった
この領主の卑劣な罠によって亡きものとなったが
私との戦いで己を磨き
おまえが成長してそんな己以上の秘術師になることを楽しみにしていると言っていた

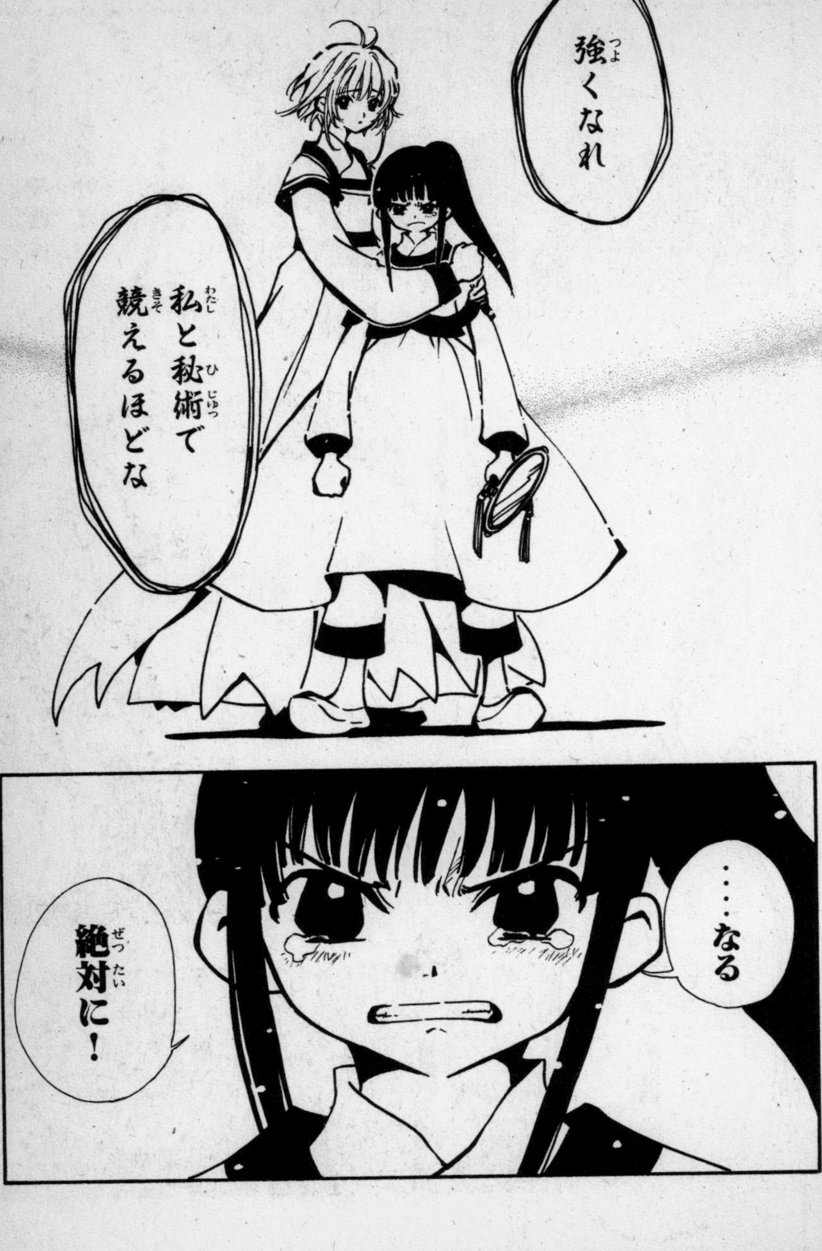
強くなれ
私と秘術で競えるほどな
……なる
絶対に！

TOMARE!

[STOP!]

You're going the wrong way!

Manga is a completely different type of reading experience.

To start at the *beginning*, go to the *end*!

That's right! Authentic manga is read the traditional Japanese way—from right to left. Exactly the *opposite* of how American books are read. It's easy to follow: Just go to the other end of the book, and read each page—and each panel—from right side to left side, starting at the top right. Now you're experiencing manga as it was meant to be.